KENDRINH, the Starlit Land, lay glimmering in the shadow of the Powers of Darkness: for Fendarl, fallen Enchanter of the Star magic and banished Lord of Black Mountain, had in his long exile grown strong—strong enough to challenge the rule of the Starborn.

Fendarl's power waxed with the rising of the Red Moon, and nowhere in all the stricken land was there a champion who could stand against him.

Oliver, Nicholas and Penelope Powell seemed to be mere pawns in the savage conflict developing between the frozen horror of Fendarl's power and the waning strength of the White Moon. But Oliver was called Tuvoi—Chosen One—and as the Night of the Red Moon drew close he learned that victory and safety for his beloved Starlit Land depended on him. But even that was not the end, for conquest does not mean victory. Much more was needed from Tuvoi—Chosen One—before the old prophecies could be fulfilled.

Red Moon
and
Black Mountain
THE END OF THE HOUSE OF KENDRETH

by Joy Chant

Introduction by Lin Carter

BALLANTINE BOOKS • NEW YORK

BALLANTINE BOOKS, INC.
201 East 50th Street, New York, N.Y. 10022

For Julian and Cheryl

ACKNOWLEDGEMENT

I would like to thank my friend Ann Walland for all her help during the writing of this book, and for allowing me to mention her half of Khendiol.

I am also very grateful to Mr Morlais Hughes of the University of Wales, Aberystwyth, for his advice on the geography of Vandarei.

About
RED MOON AND BLACK MOUNTAIN,
and *Joy Chant:*

Lords of the Star Magic

That morning it was cold and grey and drizzly, as February usually is in Manhattan, but I made the long trip in from my home on Long Island to the Fifth Avenue office of Ballantine Books where we were to discuss the tentative schedule for Adult Fantasy in the coming year.

Among other things, Mrs. Ballantine handed me two fat volumes of manuscript carbons bound in rose leatherette, with the comment, "I think we have a jewel here."

"*Red Moon and Black Mountain,* by Joy Chant," I read. "What is it—and who's Joy Chant?"

She shook her head. "I've no idea. This is evidently her first book, but Rayner Unwin thinks highly enough of it to be reminded of Tolkien, and there's certainly no doubt that the lady is a very considerable talent."

It was an exciting thought. But ever since the success of *The Lord of The Rings,* publishers' ads for various fantasies have been headlined, "Not since Tolkien . . .", and I had been disappointed too often to feel much optimism at yet another such discovery. Still . . . Mr. Unwin was of George Allen and Unwin, the original British publishers of the Professor's great fantasy epic. They had actually *discovered* Tolkien, and if anyone should be able to detect another new author of comparable talent, it should be Rayner Unwin.

After delivering the copies of Clark Ashton Smith's *Hyperborea* and James Branch Cabell's *The Cream of the Jest* to Mrs. Ballantine, I tucked the two fat manuscript volumes into my attaché case, and caught the Queens Express for home. The trip takes over an hour, and I was curious to see what Joy Chant had written, so I leaned back and took out the volume marked "*Red Moon and Black Mountain,* Chapters I—XV," and began reading.

At first I thought the book was going to be a children's fantasy, and my heart sank. After all, on the first few pages we are introduced to two little children, Nicholas and Penelope, and their older brother Oliver, bicycling down an English country lane, heading straight into a magical adventure. But I kept reading, and before the train was very deep into Long Island I had reached Chapter Three and knew that this was not only not going to be a children's book, as we usually mean the term, but also that it was going to be a masterpiece.

"Masterpiece," is not a word that I use lightly. But that third chapter, the battle between the Black Eagles and the White Eagles, is, in its eerie power and tension and mood, quite the equal of anything I have found in *The Lord of the Rings.*

This book is a splendid example of heroic fantasy on a world-wide scale. Since the Adult Fantasy imprint was inaugurated in May, 1969, with the first printing of Fletcher Pratt's *The Blue Star,* Mrs. Ballantine and I have been on the alert for new novels of publishable quality, but virtually everything the various literary agents have submitted for our attention has been mere Sword & Sorcery: good enough in its way, but hardly comparable to Cabell and Dunsany and the other major authors we have been busily reviving.

Red Moon and Black Mountain came as a revelation. Joy Chant may not be "another Tolkien"—in all honesty, I shall have to see more of her work before I can form an accurate estimate of her full powers—but *Red Moon* is a strong and beautiful and perfect book. And one well worthy of a place among the Old Masters under the Sign of the Unicorn's Head.

In my *Tolkien,* a book-length study of *The Lord of the Rings* and its author, which Ballantine published in March 1969, a few months before we began the Adult Fantasy Series, I predicted that major new fantasy from now on would most likely bear the marks of Tolkien's influence. This is quite true of *Red Moon.* Merekarl, the King of the White Eagles, reminds me of Gwaihir, the Windlord in *LOTR*; and, of course, the evil arch-sorcerer, Fendarl, is of a tradition that includes both Saruman and Sauron himself. As well, the Princess In'serinna, Daughter of the Stars, Princess of Rennath and Enchantress of the Star Magic, will remind many readers of the Elf Queen Galadriel, in Tolkien.

There is no question that Joy Chant has read Tolkien carefully; but she has also read other fantasy novelists as well, and her work derives from the full heroic fantasy tradition, rather than from its most important contemporary master only. The whole opening sequence of the book, where the three children are brought into the magic world, suggests to me the possibility that Miss Chant is familiar with the Narnia books of Professor Tolkien's old friend and fellow Oxford don, C. S. Lewis. And, at various places in her story, I thought I detected signs of George MacDonald also. The sequence of Oliver living among the Hurnei nomads makes me wonder if it is at all possible Joy Chant has read some of Andre Norton's splendid books for teenagers . . . .

But I do not mean to say, or even imply, that *Red Moon and Black Mountain* is to be considered merely a patchwork pastiche of other authors. Quite the opposite: Miss Chant has read deeply in the literature, and she has been subjected to the influences of various writers, but her novel is a glorious original with a strength and passion and beauty all its own.

Her world, which is named Khendiol, is most fascinating. The gods play an active role in its history, in its conflicts against the Forces of Darkness—Irananni in particular. Only Kuvorei Naracan, "the God who is above the gods," seems to play no visible role in this unfolding drama.

Hers is a world of peculiarly fluid time; time moves differently for Oliver, who grows to manhood among the Hurnei, than it does for his younger brother and sister, for whom only days pass, whereas he seems to experience years. A strange and magical place, indeed, this Khendiol—newest of the enchanted worlds of heroic fantasy.

I admire her insight into her characters. She seems never to falter, whether depicting the way in which the young children, Penelope and Nicholas, react to their adventures ("I've got *seven* skirts on!" Penelope says excitedly to Nicholas, when they meet on the morning after the Battle of the Eagles), or describing the dread the older boy, Oliver, feels just before his first battle . . . a dread of finding out that he is a coward, not just fear of being injured in the conflict. In all ways, her people are real and believable.

Miss Joy Chant is an Englishwoman. She lives in Leigh-on-Sea, Essex, and this is her first published book. She is not a professional novelist at all—but then, neither was Tolkien!—and obviously this book has been slowly and carefully built, with loving attention to detail, over years of patient work. It shows. And it makes me eagerly await the books she may go on to write in the years ahead.

—LIN CARTER
Editorial Consultant
The Ballantine Adult Fantasy Series

Hollis, Long Island, New York.

Contents

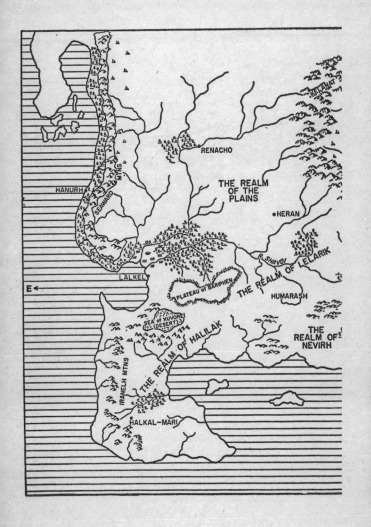

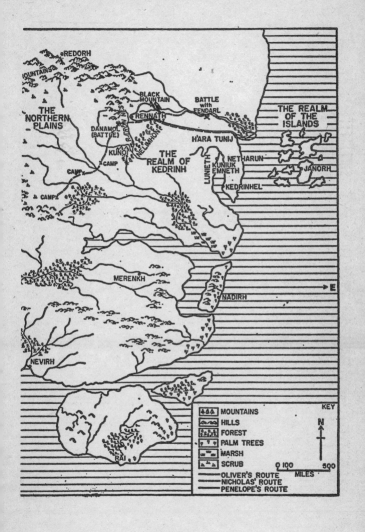

REDORH

MOUNTAINS

THE NORTHERN PLAINS

BLACK MOUNTAIN

RENNATH

BATTLE with FENDARL

THE REALM OF THE ISLANDS

DANAMOL (BATTLE)

NELAMHOH

KUNO

CAMP

H'ARA TUNIJ

THE REALM OF KEDRINH

LUNETH

NETHARUN

KUNIUK EMNETH

JANORH

CAMP

CAMP

KEDRINHEL

CAMP

MERENKH

NADIRH

E

NEVIRH

RAI

KEY

MOUNTAINS

HILLS

FOREST

PALM TREES

MARSH

SCRUB

N

0   100   500
MILES

—— OLIVER'S ROUTE
—— NICHOLAS' ROUTE
—— PENELOPE'S ROUTE

Red Moon
and
Black Mountain

Chapter One

The Trembling Air

Easter was early that year. It fell in blackthorn winter, when the blossom on the sloe could have been taken for frost, and the hawthorn had barely sprouted its buds of green and copper. Every morning the grass was patched with white, and there was iron in the air.

But spring had come with a rush, that day, and the clamour of life renewed was all about the boy who waited in the tree by the gate. Birds gossiped and squabbled over their nesting, voles rustled in the ditch, and dormice stirred in the hedge. The boy's indigo eyes sparkled, and his smile was almost a laugh of pleasure. He felt life surging up the tree behind him, out along the twisting boughs and overflowing into the soft new-born leaves, still crumpled from the bud. Beside him, a blackbird's excitement erupted into song, and a squirrel, smoothing his whiskers with fragile hands, leapt suddenly with a high chatter from the tree to the verge of the road, bounded across in a series of small russet curves, and vanished into the wood opposite. A small eager breeze flowed through the boy's dark hair, and the sun glowed in his brown cheek; he laughed aloud in delight, and the blackbird whistled.

But he had come on a different errand, more important to others if not to him; and the sound of voices on the road recalled him. He stood up among the branches, and looked down on them.

There was a flash of colour through the hedge; the elder of the boys was wearing a scarlet sweater. That alone would have told him that these were the three he awaited. Two boys and a girl. He watched them cycling slowly along the main road, and shook his head, almost regretfully. The girl

1

looked so young, wavering along behind her brothers: and they came so unsuspecting.

Yet necessity has no heart, and his errand was dictated by black necessity. They were approaching the crossroads. He sat back, and set the pipe to his lips that until now had idled in his fingers.

So sweet was the music it seemed the world must pause to listen; and yet the musician played so softly, surely only he himself could hear. So soft, so soft, not even the watchful thrush turned her head; but he saw the boy hesitate, stop, and look about, and laughed even while he pitied him.

Oliver stopped and looked back. They had fallen behind again, and he span his pedal impatiently. Penny was up on the verge again, wobbling along with the grass tangling her wheels. Nicholas had stopped, and straddling his bicycle was bending over his compass.

'Penny, get back on the road! You'll land in the ditch that way. Oh, come on now, Nick! Nick!'

Penelope bumped and bounced back on to the road, twisting her front wheel to make the grit crunch, and laughing at him. He gave her a speaking look, and called Nicholas again. His brother came on, slowly and rather unsteadily, still holding his compass in one hand.

'We're going almost north-east,' he announced, as he drew level with Oliver. 'It keeps joggling about because the bike is wobbling, but when I stand still . . .'

'Oh no you don't! You've stood still quite enough already. Honestly, Nick, what with your knife and now the compass, you only need a pith helmet to be on safari.'

'Well, we're sort of exploring. We haven't been this way before. We might get lost. Dad did say watch out that we didn't.'

'Are you kidding? He told me to do my best, and with luck I'd get rid of one of you at least.'

'Oh, Oliver, he didn't really! Did he? He would tell the police, wouldn't he, if we were really lost?'

'Of course. Dangerous Lunatic at Large: Penelope Powell Escapes Custodian.' She laughed and stuck out her tongue, and he grinned; then groaned. 'Nicholas, if you look at that thing once more I'll take it and jump on it, I swear I will.'

Nicholas hastily put the compass in his pocket and tried to look as if he had never stopped pedalling.

'Which way now?' he asked.

'Straight on,' replied Oliver, cycling ahead to the cross-roads. Then he wavered suddenly. 'At least, I think—no—hang on a minute.'

His cycle tilted, and he put a foot on the bank. He looked about him, perplexed.

He had been sure that they had said straight on; but just then he had felt a check so sharp it was almost physical, as if he had ridden into a cord stretched across the road. All at once he had a feeling that he had nearly taken the wrong way, that he should turn—turn. . . .

'Left,' he said at last, slowly. 'We turn left here.'

Nicholas watched disbelievingly. 'Oliver! Hey, Oliver! You said straight on! Where are you going? Straight on!'

'Left!' he called back with conviction. 'This is the right way.'

Nicholas protested until he reached the corner, then forgot his doubts and followed. Penelope made no remark until she caught up with Oliver; then she puffed, 'Oliver, I thought you said there wouldn't be any hills in Essex.'

'I didn't say there were none, I said everyone thought that.' He rode slowly, standing on his pedals. About a hundred yards ahead a gate was set into the hedge. There was an oak tree just inside the field, and a green signpost by the gate. 'Let's see what the sign says.'

The boy in the tree played them on up the hill, watching them. The younger boy suddenly passed his brother, and racing on to the gate looked up at the signpost. 'It says public footpath,' he called back, 'but it doesn't say where to.' The music quivered with the piper's laughter.

The other two reached the gate, and dismounted. The younger ones were very alike, tall children, with curly brown-gold hair: though Nicholas' eyes were brown instead of blue, and his hair was very slightly touched with red. Oliver could not have looked less like them. He was five or six years older than his brother, not as tall as most boys of his age, but very strong. His rough dark hair was almost straight, and his thick-browed eyes flint grey. He put his hand on the gate, and looked uncertainly up at the signpost. It was the last moment for decision; and the music filled the air with aching power.

'Boys and girls come out to play,' sang Penelope softly, 'The moon doth shine as bright as day . . .'

'Shush,' said Oliver, not knowing why: only that it was very quiet there—silent, in fact, save for Penelope and the warning 'pink-pink' of the blackbird in the tree, and yet there was something in the silence that he wanted to hear. He looked at the faint track of the footpath across the meadow, and made his choice.

'We'll go through here.'

'There's cows in there,' objected Penelope.

'Oh, don't be such an idiot! You've seen cows before! Oliver, what shall we do with our bikes?'

'Leave them inside the gate. No one will see them there, and the farmer won't mind—I hope. Oh, I can't open this gate. Stand back and watch a display of superhuman strength.' He hoisted their bicycles over the gate, then jumped over and leant them against the hedge. The children climbed to the top of the gate.

'Suppose it's locked to keep us out?' said Nicholas suddenly.

'If there's a public footpath it shouldn't be. Maybe I'd better go and look, though, in case there's a bottomless bog ahead. You wait here a minute.'

He walked away from them. Nicholas took out his sheathknife and began trying to whet it on the concrete gatepost, but it did not seem to work very well; and anyway, his father would be angry if he did succeed, having forbidden him to sharpen it. Only it was such a very good knife, it seemed a waste. He sheathed it, and took out his compass, glancing at Penelope. She was gazing wide-eyed into the oak tree.

'What are you looking at?'

'Nothing. I thought I might see a squirrel.'

'They might not be about yet. Hey! Hey, Pen, look at this!'

He held out his compass. The needle whirled giddily, vainly seeking north. It slowed, but did not settle, swaying uncertainly around the face.

'It's broken!'

'But I didn't think compasses *could* break.' He turned, and as his hand passed the line of the gate the needle found north. He stared, and shook it, and turned it, but it was certain now.

'Well, that's funny ...' but as he turned back the needle ran wild again, racing in circles. Penny looked at him perplexed. Frowning, he put his hand first on one side of the gatepost and then on the other, but it was always the same. Outside, the needle knew where to find north. Inside, it knew nothing.

'Oliver!' called Penelope. 'Oliver! Come and see!'

He turned; and Penny forgetting where she sat, sprang to her feet. Nicholas saw her falling, caught hold of her with a warning cry, and toppled forward himself.

There is in every fall a split second when one is entirely airborne. Nicholas wondered why he had never noticed it before. Then he tasted something bitter at the back of his throat, and would have cried out, but he could find no voice. For that second did not end.

They were soaring. Field, gate and tree had vanished, and they were tumbled over and over in a silver-grey haze. All Nicholas could feel was Penelope's wrist in his hand; he could see nothing. The big dipper feeling of having lost his stomach grew worse, until it seemed that his body was hollow, save for his drumming heart. Then at last his mind too whirled away, and his head filled with darkness.

Oliver had gone some way before he noticed something disquieting about the field. The day was only mildly warm, but the air over the grass danced and quivered as if in burning heat. The faint path rippled in the haze, and the cattle looked distorted and unreal.

'That's odd,' he said aloud, and paused. It was very quiet; the air tingled with stillness. Suddenly a strange chill excitement surged through him; he felt a prickling, and a tightness in his throat; then he shuddered. All at once a small voice in him insisted that he should turn back now—now! But the stronger voice of reason demanded, why? Because it was quiet, and there was a heat haze over the fields? The silence was to be expected; and he was no scientist, so for all he knew the haze too was perfectly reasonable. He looked back at Nicholas and Penelope. They were bending over something, doubtless the compass again. He grinned and shook himself, and went on.

Yet there was no denying his nervousness. Something within him was wakened and quivering, but whether the feeling filling him was fear or excitement, horror or longing, he could not have said. Maybe it was imagination, but the rippling air seemed to pulse more urgently. He glanced back once more, and saw that now everything left behind him trembled as if beneath a pitiless noon-day sun. The silence grew deeper, and the song in it yet sweeter.

He drew a deep breath and marched determinedly forward. The path sloped slightly down; the grass grew taller, and was a less vivid green. The cows had moved; he could no longer see them. The air steadied and seemed to grow cooler. Then he heard the children call him, and he turned.

His skin faded to dead white, and stone cold. He shook all over and gave a hoarse cry.

Before his eyes hung the road which he had just left. He could see his brother and sister and their bicycles, but they were faint and wavered as if painted on fine gauze. Then the picture trembled, and began to break up and scatter, and as he watched they drifted away like smoke shivered by the wind. Then there was only a faint blur, dusty pale; then nothing. The tree alone remained.

He gave another cry and ran desperately back, unable to believe, sure of finding them somehow still there. The grass was certainly much taller, scattered with unfamiliar flowers. The wind carried a scent strange to him, bitter-sweet, cold and wild. The tree whose wrinkled bark and gnarled boughs had deceived him into thinking it an oak, had feathery leaves like ash. He leaned a hand on its trunk and looked wildly about.

They were gone. Gone. He was alone. He could see nothing but grass in every direction, and the clear pale blue of a sky so wide it almost frightened him. And instead of the singing silence there was the flutter of leaves, the rustle of grasses, and the song of birds.

The shock was worse than a physical one; it was deeper more fundamental, more shattering. But physically he felt winded, shaken, sick. Cold serpents writhed and piled and heaved in his stomach. He sobbed, and felt the tears running over his cheeks, and did not care. He cried out once more in disbelief and anguish, and ran uselessly forward into the grass, casting about, hopelessly searching, calling their names, still unconsciously weeping. Then suddenly he stumbled and pitched forward, rolling over with a great crashing and waving of grassheads, choking with the pollen they shed.

It winded him and calmed his panic a little. For a moment he lay still. But no sooner had he begun to rise, spluttering out grass-pollen and shaking back his hair, than he heard an excited yell, and looking up saw something throbbing towards him black out of the sun, and he shouted and writhed aside. Barely far enough he moved, for it swept his shoulder, but his breast it missed. It drove itself into the ground a little behind him, and stuck there quivering; and it was a spear.

'Harai! My aim was true! I threw and did not miss! Hai, come and see!' A boy on a pony charged up through the grass—coat, trousers, high boots, all were of leather. His saddle was a fleece, and his pony was unbitted. He flung himself from the saddle, and then saw Oliver. As he slithered to a halt his rush of words choked and died. He was slight and dark, his black hair plaited into a single pigtail, his slanting eyes stretched wide in amazement.

'Mor'anh!' he whispered: then cried urgently, 'Father!'

Oliver stood wordless, staring numbly at the boy. He could not accept what his presence implied; he could not yet admit what had happened. His mind kept returning to the picture of transparent wood and earth, of a dissolving world. He pulled the spear out of the earth and looked at it. The shaft was thick and smooth; puzzled, he stared at the head for a long time before he realized that it was skilfully shaped stone.

As one or two faint rustles made him look round, he saw that the rest of the hunting party had come silently up through the grass, and now stood in a wide circle about them. There were about thirteen in all, including two more boys. They all had the same dark slanting eyes and sombre mouths as the first boy and they were dressed like him in high boots, leather trousers, and open leather coats—though many had discarded the coats. They were armed with spears and bows. Their faces were unreadable; some of them showed a faint curiosity, but only the boys betrayed astonishment. None of them gave any sign of hostility or suspicion. They were silent, looking at him, and he prickled all over.

Then a man came through the circle, plainly their leader. He gave Oliver one brief, hard look, and said 'Mnorh!'

The boy half turned, looking from Oliver to his father and back again, and croaked stammeringly, 'Father, look at his clothes!'

The man ignored this, merely saying severely, 'My son, you know what you have done, and what punishment you deserve.'

'Of course—yes, I know, but—yes, but—father, *look*—but father—! Yes, sir.'

A soft growl of laughter ran around the circle. The chief nodded curtly, and motioned Mnorh out of the way. Then he walked up to Oliver.

He was not tall, but he was deep-chested and strong looking, his dark hair streaked with grey. There was pride and strength of will in his bearing, and command carved in his mouth. A curved sword hung at his side, and he wore many ornaments—rings, ear-rings, bracelets, even necklaces. He had no beard, but a long moustache, and seen closely his face, deeply graven with lines, was older than his deep powerful voice had suggested.

'Have you seen them?' Oliver strove to keep his voice calm. 'I don't know where they've gone: my brother and sister. Have you seen them?'

'Be welcome, guest of the land, to the tents of the Hurnei,' the man replied with unhurried courtesy. 'I am Silinoi, Lord of the Hurnei, and I greet you for the Tribe. We have seen no strangers save yourself.'

'But they must be—they came with me—they ...' His voice died, as he saw again the picture of them, blowing away.

'How came you here, stranger, weaponless and so strangely clad? Where is your horse?'

'I have no horse. We came on our—on our—I came on my . . .' He struggled for the word. He could visualize the machine, but there was no word for it. He clenched his hands, gripping the spear shaft, and tried to force down a new wave of panic.

'My name is Oliver Powell,' he said loudly, staking his claim to what he knew. 'My brother is Nicholas and my sister is Penelope. I left them sitting on a gate by that tree, and they have gone. I don't understand. What is this place? Where am I?'

'Gate? But there is neither wall nor gate in the Khentor

lands. You are on the Northern Plains, O'li-vanh, in the Realm of Kedrinh, in the land of Vandarei.'

'Kedrinh? Vandarei?'

'I, Silinoi, as Lord of the Northern Plains, greet you in the name of Kiron, and offer you his protection.'

'Kiron? Who is Kiron?'

The man stepped back and regarded him in wonder. 'Who is Kiron! O'li-vanh, where are you from, that you do not know the name of Kiron! Kiron is the High King of Vandarei! How have you not heard of him?'

'I've never heard of any of it. I don't know how I came to be here. O God! What's happening?'

The chieftain studied him for a moment, then shook his head.

'Your words are strange to me also, O'li-vanh. Come; we will take you to the Tribe, and Yorn shall speak with you.'

Oliver nodded, too dazed and confused to think any more. And then, past the man's shoulder, he saw something which made him forget for a moment all that had happened. Mnorh came, leading his father's horse.

Oliver stared speechless. Never had he seen anything of such grace and power, such pride and beauty. Without question this was the most magnificent horse he had ever seen or imagined; not only in body but in his carriage, in the spirited delicacy of his movement, in the deep intelligence of his wide brow and dark eyes that seemed to watch and consider all about him. There was a little curl of hair on his lower jaw, adding to his look of dignity, and something in his air declared that he might be a friend, but never a servant. And then of course there was the great, the arresting difference; the single long pointed horn which gored up from the horse's brow. It must have been as long as Oliver's arm, straight but not smooth, twisted and spiral grained. The point was as sharp as a javelin.

After that, he ceased to think. He could no longer deny to himself that something impossible had happened. All of it was incredible; but perhaps most incredible of all was that he should find a unicorn walking the earth in daylight.

Chapter Two

Starlight on Black Mountain

The first thing that Nicholas realised was that his knees were bruised and his hands scraped: the second, that he was bitterly cold.

He forced his head up and his eyes open. Sight was slower to return than the ability to feel pain, it seemed. Everything appeared dark, with white flecks in the darkness. Then he saw that he was on hands and knees on a path of black rock. It was night, and the flecks were snowflakes.

Penelope was a few feet away from him, sitting with her back to the rock face, her feet tucked under her. Her face was very white, and her eyes big and round; her mouth hung slightly open, and she had no expression at all.

Nicholas crawled over and sat down next to her. She clutched his arm with both hands, convulsively, shaking him, almost hurting. She was staring beyond him, telling him with nods and little gasping noises to look too. He turned and looked, and felt sick. The path was only six or seven feet wide. Beyond it, the snow whirled away into empty darkness. He had been kneeling on the edge of a precipice.

Heights terrified him. He pressed himself back against the cliff shaking, digging his heels against the rock. 'Don't look, Penny,' he said hoarsely, his own eyes fettered. Then it seemed that the sound of his voice broke the spell on hers; she gave an odd little moan and began half speaking, half sobbing.

'What happened? Where are we? Nicky, tell me what has happened? Where's Oliver? Where are we? I'm frightened! How are we going to get home? Nicky, help me; Nicky, I'm frightened! How did we get here? Where are we? *Nicholas!*'

Her voice grew wilder, though she spoke in a whisper. Her

10

sobs climbed the scale. When she spoke his name, it was in a suppressed scream.

He fought back his own panic in pity for hers, feeling all at once much more than just two years older than her. He pulled his arm away from her hands and put it around her shoulder, holding her firmly against him.

'All right, Pen, all right. Calm down. We'll be all right.' He deliberately kept his voice clear and firm. 'No, don't start crying, you'll make your face sore. Oh, come on Penny, it's all right. I'll stay with you, please, Penny, don't cry . . .' His voice cracked and he stopped abruptly, but she had calmed a little.

'Where do you think we are?' she said huskily. 'And where's Oliver?'

'Well, I don't know. Let's have a look round.' He struggled to his feet, keeping back against the face, trying not to look at the precipice. The width of the path seemed to have shrunk to nothing, and it seemed to slope irresistibly; he felt as if his eyes were pulling him over the edge. But he ought to see if Oliver were there—because if he were, then nothing was so bad.

'Oliver?' called Penny, in a quavering, doubtful voice. 'Oliver?'

'Oliver!' called Nicholas more loudly. 'Hey! Oliver.' He listened to the silence, and sank back down by Penelope.

'Oh, Nicky, what shall we do?'

'Well, for one thing, we'll stop whispering. And we'd better not sit still for too long. Come on, let's have a proper look at this place.'

'What is there to look at?'

There was not much. The path seemed to wind along a mountainside, with the precipice on one hand, and on the other the rockface against which they sat. It was all the same smooth, shiny black rock, streaked thinly with white where the snow had found somewhere to lodge. Mostly the rock was too smooth for it to settle, and it floated in whorls along the ground as the wind blew it. They sat in a little bay in the cliff; that and the rattling skeleton of a dead bush saved them a little from the wind, but where it blew on them it was bitter. They were both shivering violently already, and their hands were growing stiff. Nicholas was sure that if they did not move soon they might never move at all. But where could they move to?

He was just about to stand up and start Penelope moving too, when she caught his arm. 'Listen!' she whispered.

He held his breath and listened, and his heart lurched. For through the dark silence and the moan of the wind he heard voices and footsteps. Just below the bay the path turned out of sight. Around the bend a light was flickering; someone spoke, there was a sudden laugh, and then they turned the corner.

A Princess led them. So tall she was, so beautiful, proud, and gay, she could have been nothing else. Her hair was very long and black as jet, blowing out behind her; her face was pearl-pale, and her lovely laughing mouth the colour of amber. They saw no jewels, only a plain cloak wrapped her; but her royalty needed no trappings. Then she saw them, and stopped laughing.

She exclaimed in wonder, her eyes widening, and coming forward dropped down before them, gazing from one to the other. She had black brows and lashes. Her eyes were a dark sea-green.

'Kinsmen!' she called, 'Only see what is here!'

The men with her came crowding up. They were very alike, and like the Princess; all tall, with long waving black hair, green eyes, and very fair skins. Their faces like hers were proud and nobly carved, but theirs were sterner. They all carried torches knobbed with blazing pitch, holding them so that the light fell on the children; and as they did so the warmth of the flames fell on them too, so that they turned their faces gratefully up to it.

'Children!' said one of the men. 'Up on Black Mountain!'

The Princess took each of them by the hand. Her hands felt exactly as they ought: delicate but strong, smooth as silk, and warm.

'How came you here, children?' she said gently. 'What are you called?'

Penelope hung her head and nudged Nicholas. He looked at her, then stammered, 'Powell. I am Nicholas Powell and this is my sister Penelope. Please, can you tell us what's going on? I don't know how we got here. You see, we were with our brother Oliver, and he told us to wait on this gate, and we fell off it, I think, then everything went grey and peculiar and we were here. And—and—I think it's a bit cold for Penny.'

The Princess smiled and nodded. 'I think you are right, Ni-ko-las. Neither you nor she is fitly clad. Well, your names are strange to my ear, though you speak our tongue. Are you Vandarin?'

'Sorry? Are we—what? No, I don't think we can be.'

'Have you ever heard of Black Mountain? Or the Harani?'

They both shook their heads, bewildered. She knelt before them, still holding their hands, looking seriously into their eyes. A stillness crept over them, and they did not look away. Nicholas quivered and sighed, and felt the fear go out of him. Penelope wriggled and ventured a shy smile.

'No,' said the Princess at last, 'you are not Vandarin, or of this world at all; that is plain. You have been flung from your own world into ours, and I cannot yet tell why. But I sense a strong enchantment, and not without purpose.'

There was shifting among the men, and one of them leaned forward.

'Madam, the time passes. We dare not linger.'

'I know. Attend me a moment more, I pray you.' She looked at the children again, gravely. 'Are you alone?'

'Well—well. Oliver was with us—we hoped he was here— he might be somewhere. Did you say something about— about your world and our world? What did you mean? And how will we get home?'

'Forgive me, I have not time to explain now. Come with us for the present and we will talk later. Oliver you say your brother is called? I will remember and ask of him. Never fear, we will see that you get safely home. Kiron will help you. Of that you may be sure, I give you my word.'

It never occurred to them to doubt her. When she rose and held out her hands they struggled to their feet. The Princess put a hand against Penelope's cheek, and shook her head indignantly.

'I could wish that those who had sent you had sent you better prepared! You are half frozen. Hairon!' The youngest of the men stepped forward. 'Cousin, carry her within your cloak. Nicholas, walk here by me, and I will put my cloak about us both.'

So they set out, Penelope borne by Prince Hairon's strong arms, lapped in the folds of his thick cloak, and Nicholas inside the Princess's cloak, which came down to her ankles and was full enough for them both. Their way was along the winding path, ever higher up the snow-veiled, wind-swept mountain, and save for the wind and an occasional splutter from a torch, they went in silence. After they had been walking for about half-an-hour, Nicholas found courage to ask a question.

'Excuse me,' he said, 'but where are we going?'

The Princess turned to him with a smile, but it died from her lips, and she looked grave.

'We are going to see the Eagles fight,' she said.

He waited, but no one explained this. He looked up at the Princess, but she seemed to be thinking of something else again.

'Oh!' he said, making it as clear as possible that he did not understand. It seemed that no one took any notice, until he heard a chuckle behind him and looked back to see laughter on the face of the man who carried Penelope. The Princess also looked behind and smiled, shaking her head at Hairon.

'Nay, but there is little we could tell you, Nicholas. You will see soon enough.'

But it did not seem soon enough to Nicholas. He grew very tired, constantly climbing as well as struggling against the wind, and enduring frozen cheeks and ears. The rest of him was quite warm, but his face felt as though a hard blow would chip it. The climb did not appear to worry their companions, but though they went slowly, he found it increasingly difficult to keep the pace. He sensed early that at the first sign of him flagging one of the lords would pick him up and carry him, and that made him set his teeth and force himself not to falter. Also, the rock was shiny—whether this was ice, or just a smooth surface, he could not tell—and his feet kept slipping.

All in all, he was glad when they halted. Three of the torches they propped still burning among some rocks, the rest they quenched; then they went around a last corner on to a wide ledge and gathered into a group.

Penelope came and stood by Nicholas. The men stood so that they sheltered the children from the wind, and one of them took off his cloak and draped it around them. The Princess now stood out in front of everybody, still as a statue, holding her cloak about her. She appeared to have forgotten the existence of her companions.

In front of them, away off to the right, was a sheer cliff of rock, as if once a mountain had been sliced in half. It was black like everywhere else and scattered with snowdrifts; at least so they thought until several of these snowdrifts launched themselves away from the crag and drifted about before it. Then they saw that they were birds; and when one came beating from his place to land on the Princess's outstretched arm, they saw that it was a white eagle.

Her arm dipped like a tree-bough when the mighty bird first settled, but after that it did not waver, nor did she flinch at the flexing of those cruel talons. The eagle looked unblinkingly at each of them in turn with his fierce golden eyes. The Princess spoke to him for several moments, seemingly greeting him. The eagle made no sound. When she had finished he bobbed his head once, and plunged off. He circled for a moment, then swept past them, tilted one wing in salute, and glided noiselessly back to the crag.

Away to the left of where they stood, opposite Eagle Crag, the mountains stood forward to fill the sky, and two great peaks, side by side, reared twin darknesses before them all. Between them was a deep cleft through which the mackerel clouds showed silver-grey, as if a strong moon shone behind them. Those peaks, the Crag, and the mountain on which they stood formed a rough enclosure of rock. Nicholas, sensing that the well between them was probably filled with other mountains, was unwilling to look down. So he looked up. Then he gasped.

The wind drew away the tattered curtain of cloud, and the stars were unveiled. The crowding constellations were strange; but that was no surprise. What shook him was their size, and number, and brilliance, so that he gaped and dug Penelope in the ribs.

They were like great motionless snowflakes, like frosty flowers. It was their light, and not the moon's, which had silvered the cloud. The biggest and brightest star in our sky is nothing to those; a hundred thousand such pepper the background, dim and unconsidered. The smaller ones sparkled; but Nicholas knew no word to describe the stately way in which the great ones swelled and sank, bloomed, dimmed, and bloomed again.

The mountains, however, shut off most of the sky from sight. When he looked back at them he saw them not as a presence, but rather an absence, a void of darkness by comparison with the life and movement above them. He tried to imagine what the whole sky, seen from an open place, would be like; but there was nothing in his memory to help him picture it. He felt awed, and drew closer to his sister. She turned to him, and he saw that her eyes were as huge and amazed as his own must have been.

Their companions were becoming restless, glancing from the peaks to the eagles and back again. Now and then one of them would speak in a low voice, though not often; but Nicholas could see frowns deepening dark between their black brows. The Princess turned to the oldest of the men, who stood behind her.

'Ah, by the Swans, my Lord Horenon,' she sighed, 'I know not whether it is a mood of prophecy on me, or I am craven, but I feel a dread of this night's work greater than any I have known before.'

'Let us trust, Madam, that it is not prophecy. Yet even if it is not, there is none would not hesitate to lay a craven spirit to thy charge.' There was a growl of agreement from all the men. She bowed her head.

'Ah, my Lords, but yet I am shamed; for one of my kindred ought not to fear, and the danger tonight is not even to me. Yet much as I dread the coming of this thing, the waiting for it is worse!'

'It will not be long,' said the Lord Horenon.

'It is now,' said Hairon. 'Look!'

Chapter Three

The Battle of the Eagles

In the cleft between the peaks there was a glow like fire. As they watched the moon rose, and with a shock of horror and disbelief the children saw that it was red.

Penelope cried out, and Nicholas felt as if he had been jolted in the stomach. It was not a nice red, even—no warmth or bravery about it. It was not even the red of the setting sun, but a dull copper colour, all unworthy to share the sky with those fiery stars. They could both have wept; but they were not given long to mourn, for as soon as the moon appeared something else happened.

Round the peak out of the moon swooped a black procession of birds. One behind the other they came, their silent wings beating as one; and to the line of them there seemed no end. They flew directly towards the little group, and then they saw how far away the peaks were—for fast as the birds flew, it was many minutes before the leader came close enough to be seen clearly. For a moment it seemed he must fly among them, and then at the last moment he tilted and swerved away. Nicholas saw the spread of the enormous wings above him, and the splayed feathers of the wing-tips, and realized that these too were eagles. Neither was it only being silhouetted against the moon that had made it look black; black it was, from beak to talon, save only the eyes. Those were without a black pupil, and without the blaze of the eyes of the other eagles; and they were of the same red as the moon.

One by one the other black eagles flew up, and then the children saw how many there were: at least three hundred, gathering in a black cloud above them. They were far larger, too, than the white eagles. Looking up, Nicholas saw the

Princess's face was even whiter than before; and the men looked as grieved as they were grim.

The last black eagle joined the flock. For a moment there was utter silence. Then with a scream of hate and defiance the King of the White Eagles leapt from the crag upwards at his enemies; and all his people followed.

The Black Eagle answered with a harsh cry, and dropped towards the other, and the black birds followed in a swarm. Then began the Battle of the Eagles, to see which the Princess In'serinna had journeyed many miles, and two children been brought out of another world.

The two sides met with bruising force. There was no noise of impact, but the very silence as the feathered beasts and great wings clashed set Nicholas' teeth on edge. They had screamed at each other before the battle began, but now they made no sound save for a low harsh 'kaak' in their throats. They reached for each other with snapping beaks and raking talons, tearing at throats and striking at eyes, and occasionally one rose above his opponent and bit his neckbone.

Penelope gave a low cry and covered her eyes. Prince Hairon gathered her up at once, and she hid her face in his shoulder. But Nicholas could not look away. The very savagery of the conflict fascinated while it frightened him, and his eyes seemed chained.

The red moon cast its dim light over all, giving the Crag and the black eagles a sheen of sullen crimson, and flushing the others with a soft rose, quite out of place in this scene of strife. It gave little light, however; as well as being red, it was only half the size of the moon he knew.

Though fewer and much smaller, the white eagles were much faster, and at first seemed to be winning the battle. The huge dark shapes of their enemies were slow and, Nicholas thought at first, rather clumsy. Gradually black shapes began to drift downwards, and he raised a faint cheer; but then he saw the men's faces, and he looked again.

The eagles he had seen as rather ineffective he now realized were not taking part in the fight at all; as yet. Slowly they were folding inwards, closing round behind the white eagles; and then when they struck there was nothing clumsy about them. Instead of thinking it dull and stupid, he now saw their slowness as a hideous deadliness, and white feathers began fluttering in the air.

'There are so many!' cried the Princess, 'So many! How, how has he grown so strong!'

The night absorbed her words as soon as she had spoken them, and the silence seemed unbroken. No one replied to her; they all watched quietly.

Small details began to separate themselves from the main battle, and Nicholas saw them more clearly. Only the white eagles made any sound: the others were dumb as they fought; and to Nicholas that and their slow deliberate movements seemed somehow connected, connected also with the empty horror of their eyes. His skin crawled as he watched them.

The white eagles were beginning to fall back.

There was no failure in their courage or their ferocity, but they were being borne backwards by the unevenness of the fight. They were having to strike upwards, against a larger foe; the black eagles were above them, striking down. And when the black ones struck their sheer size and weight jarred and wearied the white eagles, so that Nicholas did not wonder to see the Princess cry out softly and beat her hands together. The fight was beginning to look ragged; the white eagles were being divided, broken into small groups. It was plain that their enemies were trying to force a way through the midst of them, though Nicholas could not for a time see why; and it seemed that they would succeed.

The Princess took a deep breath and twisted her fingers into a knot; then she stiffened, drew herself up, and tossed her head so that for a second her black hair came leapingly alive, while deep shadows and pale starlight ran like water through the curves of it. Her chin went up, and as he looked at her face, Nicholas thought he had never seen such stern pride. Her eyes flashed like green fire over the whole scene, and the boy thought that if he had been a black eagle, surely he would have died from a look of such scorn. Then she stepped to the very lip of the rock, so that her skirts were blowing out over the void; and she spread her arms and held out her hands to the White Eagles, and called out to them in a language Nicholas did not understand. It was a language of cold, pure sounds; a language of words harsh and sad. It brought visions of bare shining rock-scapes, of high lonely peaks, of wintry solitudes through nights of splintering cold and days of piercing light. Every word seemed to come across vast gulfs, gulfs wider than space and deeper than time; one soul speaking to another across a schism made in the very beginning of the world. Nicholas' whole body shuddered as he listened.

Her voice wavered and sank. The whole speech—it was more than a speech really, yet not quite a song—had sounded very like a lament, although it was not. But there was the same keening note in the reply of the Eagle King, fierce and chill; and at the sound of it all his subjects broke off their fighting, and turned from their foes, and fled back. They formed a close band before the Crag, and turned at bay again. The Princess dropped her arms and stepped back.

The battle began again, but now the worst seemed to be past, and the white eagles to be holding their own. Nicholas several times heard soft delighted exclamations from the men about him. They looked approvingly at the white birds, who were now fighting in a closer formation, and one of them unbent so far as to tell the boy what he had begun to guess; that the Crag must be held from the black eagles, and they had come near to forcing their way to it.

The defenders had grown used to the greater size and greater numbers of their enemy. They had begun to turn them to such advantage as they could, fighting close together so that the black eagles were forced to crowd each other. For a time the fight steadied, and Nicholas' hopes and spirits rose. But it was still desperately unequal. Many more black eagles than white were dying, falling crumpled and oddly unbirdlike into the darkness; but the loss of four black eagles made less difference than the loss of one white eagle, so heavily were they outnumbered.

Twice, small conflicts within the greater came towards their ledge. The first, a black and a white eagle slowly drifting away from the main fight, talons forward, beaks wide, snapping and striking in utter silence, seemed likely to go on for a long time. The white eagle was young and valiant, quicker and fiercer than its foe: the starlight turned its plumes to silver fire, and its eyes blazed black and gold. Nicholas suddenly felt that he loved that bird; and it seemed that his companions felt the same, for the men looked at it with the grim pleasure which he was beginning to recognize as their approval, and the Princess struck her hands together with delight and admiration. But the end was sudden. Silent and dark, another shape dropped from the sky on to his back. A black head reached forward, a black beak bit into the back of his neck, and it was over. The creamy head dropped forward, the great wings stretched upward, and he stiffened. The splayed feathers of his wing-tips reached for the stars like groping fingers and slowly, so slowly, he fell, only his head moving, his body rigid, as he spiralled like a sycamore seed into the blackness. The starlight followed him like a last salute until he was smaller than a snowflake, too small to look like a bird. Then the shadow swallowed him, and on the ledge there was a silence sadder than tears.

By now, the faces around Nicholas had become anxious again; and many times they glanced with furrowed brows at the cleft where the moon had risen—black again now, for the moon had climbed above it. Nicholas was dimly aware of a black shape and a white mounting above them, but he was unhappily counting the defenders, and making their numbers barely more than twenty, less than a quarter of their original force. Then there was a soft flurry of sound, a weight striking his shoulder, and the long cool sweep of a wing dragging past his cheek, and he was looking down on an eagle lying at his feet. One spread wing covered the feet of the nearby men, the other hung half out over the precipice. The bird lay folded in them as in a shawl. There was a red stain growing on his snowy breast feathers; his feet were limp already. He twisted his head round, his beak gaping open, reaching for air, and thrust his neck in a curve backwards, the neck feathers loose and open. As he turned his head Nicholas looked for a second straight into his eye and saw with a faint shock that there was no hint there of weakness or fear, only a burning rage. Then his whole body, tail to wing-tip, gave a last stretch and loosened, and his eye dimmed. Nicholas stared in horror; and the lord next to him, after watching a moment in silent grief, knelt down by the dead bird, gathered his wings about his body, and settled the head under one of them.

'Wren or eagle,' he said, 'they can sleep no other way.'

Now Nicholas saw that the white eagles were yet fewer, and the fight went forward with a silent fury: and now for the first time he sensed a ripple of dread through the company. The Princess beat her hands together, and cried,

'How long? How much longer, my Lord Horenon?'

'I cannot tell,' he replied.

'Is there no help we can give? Nay, I know there is not.'

'Thou hast done all possible.'

'Ah, that! But I did it too early.'

He shook his head. 'No, Madam. Any later would have been too late.'

She fell silent. Horenon after a few moments spoke softly to the men near him, and they nodded; and a murmur and nodding of heads rippled along them all. Then there was a soft scraping noise and when Nicholas looked, each man held in his hand a long, cold-gleaming sword. Then he knew that they were preparing to defend the Princess, and Penelope, and him, against the black eagles; and his heart sank.

Again the Princess cried out, 'O brothers! My brothers!' and then again a little later, in fierce triumph. 'But they are not defeated yet; see—still they hold them off!'

A slight quiver ran through them all, and heads looked as they had before, from cleft to crag and back to cleft. The eagles seemed to feel some urgency, for the battle grew bitterer than at any time since it was joined, and now the whisper of 'How long?' went from mouth to mouth. Then a strange hope seemed to rise in the Princess, and she called to the eagles again, 'But a little longer, my brothers! Hold firm—they shall flee you yet!' And the birds fought with yet greater heat and savagery, and the men grew yet more taut and expectant, and again and again she put her hand up to her face to brush back hair that was not there. But then she spoke for the last time; and for the first time, Nicholas heard the sharpness of real fear in the desperate protest, 'They cannot hold it!'

Indeed it seemed they could not, for the survivors now fought with their backs to the crag, and the attackers drew back for the last onslaught and the kill. But as they swooped, suddenly their shadows leapt sharp and black on the rock face, and the white eagles shone; and all at once there was so much light that Nicholas was dazzled.

From the ledge arose a great roar of triumph, and from the black eagles a wail of dread and despair; and they turned from the rock and fled. Nicholas turned to see what had happened, and Penelope took her face out of hiding; and then they both gave a cry of gladness that was only a little for the rout of the black eagles. For into the cleft had risen the bright and gracious Lady of the Night, a moon all silver, almost four times as large as the other and many times more brilliant, bathing the world in a cool radiance that soothed as it lit.

There was another cry of triumph, and all the men lifted their swords and whirled them about their heads like white fire, and through it all came the Princess's laughter. The black eagles were flying headlong for the mountains' shadow, out of reach of the light. A few of the white eagles—the young and the little hurt—pursued them for a while; but it was not long before they turned back, and most of their comrades clung exhausted to ledges on the cliff face. The Princess looked at them, and her eyes lost their laughter, and her face sobered.

'Well may we cry our triumph at the victory, my Lords,' she said, 'but let us not rejoice overmuch. For see, the cost was very great. Let the fallen not be forgotten, while the victors are saluted.'

Then the King Eagle came again from his place to the Princess; but now he did not swoop. His flight was heavy and slow, and they heard the breath in his throat tearing him. As he landed on her arm he was unsteady, and keeping one wing open leaned with it on her shoulder, and they saw that he held one foot close against him. And he looked steadily at her from one of his golden eyes, for the light of the other had been darkened for ever. She returned his gaze in silence for a while, then spoke softly.

'Great are the people of Merekarl. Great are the White Eagles of Black Mountain. Proud am I, that men call me Sister of the Eagles.' Then she added something in another strange tongue, not the one she had used before.

Then Nicholas and Penelope had the biggest shock since they had arrived, for the eagle opened his beak and spoke, not with a human voice—it was the same eagle's voice as in his battlecries, harsh and almost toneless—but now they understood him.

'A bitter struggle, Little Sister.'

'A bitter struggle indeed, King Merekarl. Yet you are victorious.'

'This time we were victorious. It is in my mind that next time we may not be.'

She did not reply for a moment, then she sighed and bowed her head.

'Alas, my heart fears you may be right. They were very many.'

'Very many indeed. Mighty he grows. I, even I, Merekarl, who never spoke so before, I say this: I fear the next Night of Two Moons.'

'And if Merekarl fears, the stars know how we tremble.'

Merekarl dipped his head, and stood silent for a moment, taking breath. Then he looked up again.

'What will be done?'

She sighed, and her eyes clouded.

'That I do not know. I must carry tidings of this battle to the High King. I believe there will be many powers to hear the news I bring, and that they will take counsel concerning what must be done. For I am now sure that we must do what we will do soon, or fail; but how this will come about I cannot tell, nor do I know how Fendarl can be destroyed.'

The eagle's voice as he replied was as gentle as an eagle's voice could ever be.

'Do not grieve, Little Sister. The decision is not yours. It belongs to the King in the White City, and I do not expect him to fail. To us, this enemy seems terrible; but it is in my mind that he may seem much smaller to the one who sits in the Hall of Banners and wears the Emerald. Let you think no more of such things, for a while. Now, I and some of my people need your help. My leg is broken.'

Her head came up again, and she smiled.

'I thank you, King Merekarl. Nothing consoles grief for an evil beyond our strength like one that we *can* remedy. Let you and those of your people with hurts that will not mend of themselves come here, and we will take them back with us.'

Merekarl rose into the air, and sent a harsh cry to the rock; and while he watched Nicholas felt himself lifted, and turned his head astonished to look into the smiling face of one of the Lords.

'I thought that if I asked if thou didst wish to be carried, thou wouldn't refuse; so I do not ask. Nay, do not protest. I will not set thee down until I may do so in a better place than this.'

So he did not protest, and was only grateful for the

warmth of the cloak, and the rest. He had not realized how weary he was. They descended the mountain in silence, and without torches, for the moonlight made their way plain. The Princess went in front as before, and under her cloak she bore King Merekarl. All the other men carried eagles also— some carried two. Sometimes a bird made a low throaty sound, sometimes a stone rattled. But mostly the only sounds were regular footfalls. Ahead, Nicholas could see the shining tumble of Penelope's head on the Lord Hairon's shoulder; it never moved. Surely she slept.

His own eyes grew heavier as they went on, and his head drooped. After, his recollection of the journey was patchy. He remembered only one moment. As they passed the place where he and Penelope had been found he woke fully, and turned his head to look over the precipice. Below and away stretched a tumble of peaks, sharp white and deep black in the moonlight, fold on fold of hills. He shuddered, and looked away.

Once, much later in the night, he cried out and struggled in his sleep, tossing his covers about; for into his dreams came the dread and madness of empty crimson eyes. But Penelope slept smiling and peaceful, and did not move once.

Chapter Four

The Fire of Gathering

The amber firelight leaped and flickered, and for every slight movement a hundred monster shadows fled away into the night. The fitful light danced on the massed attentive faces of the Hurnei and glowed on the figure of their leader, who stood like a speaking statue of copper.

Oliver was weary. He had come from mid-afternoon to a place where it seemed to be early morning, and had begun the day again. He wanted to sleep. As he sat between Mnorh and the chieftain's place around the evening Fire of Gathering, time after time he had swayed forward asleep, only to jerk back when Mnorh jabbed him. Now again he straightened, blinking and gathering his wits. Silinoi had almost finished speaking. He squared his shoulders and put his hands on his knees, looking about.

He eyed the cushions beside him longingly. They sat—the more privileged of them, at least—on rugs and skins, with cushions to lean on, and beside him Mnorh reclined on one arm, chin in hand. Around the fire the men sat in a dozen positions, each one more comfortable than the one he had chosen, cross-legged and stiffly upright. But he knew that this was the only way to keep awake. Once he got at his ease, nothing would rouse him.

He huddled the cloak of fleece-lined leather they had given him closer, and yawned; then tried to swallow the gesture. He closed his eyes, feeling the warmth of the flames on his cheeks and closed eyelids. For all the sunshine the day had been far from warm. He had not ceased to wonder at the number of men who went bare-chested in the cold. With a cloak over his jersey and shirt, he had not been too warm;

yet it seemed that even without the cloak, he was wearing more than they ever did.

He shivered at the thought, and looked about him. Across the empty chieftain's place, the firelight bronzed the thin, weather-beaten face of Yorn the Priest, making his white hair blaze the colour of a tigerlily. The skin was stretched over the bones of his face, and the fire highlighted the high cheeks and wide forehead, the low-bridged nose and deep, hooded eyes. There was a faint smile flickering on his mouth as he knelt there, hands on knees. He wore a robe of shiny dark-brown leather, supple as water, unsewn. There was a hole for his head and a belt at the waist, but that was all. It came down to his ankles, but the wind might whistle through the sides as it pleased. Oliver wondered how they had obtained a single hide large enough, for Yorn was tall—head and shoulders above most of the other men. Oliver had really had to look up when he had been taken to him, and Yorn had looked down, with that faint smile, and the deep steady gaze of his eyes had not wavered from the boy's face all the time Silinoi told how they had found him. And when the chieftain had cried almost indignantly, 'He does not know Kiron; and where in all the world have they not heard of Kiron?', he had only said, 'It seems the world is wider than we thought.' And just for a moment it had seemed to Oliver that the priest's eyes had laughed, though his face had not changed; and he had felt comforted, drawn within the warm safe circle of his humour.

A low murmur brought him back to the present moment, and he looked up again. Silinoi had finished speaking, and returned to his carved seat. Yorn rose and stepped forward. The murmur died, and the eyes that had turned to Oliver looked back at the tall priest. His hair hung about his shoulders; tongues of flame where the fire lit it, smoke in the shadow. Yet he was not really old, for all his bleached hair. His voice, when he spoke, was strong and musical, almost mellow—a spell-binding voice.

'Brothers; do not doubt a great honour has been done to us, of which we must strive to be worthy. For see, one has come among us from beyond the bounds of this world. Dear to the gods is he, for he was found on holy ground, close by the Tree of the Dancer. Grey-eyed as the guardian is he, clad in true-red of the Avenger; a name of omen he bears, for its meaning is Crowned Victor. Surely Marenkalion stands at his shoulder, and Ir'nanh leads him by the hand! And to the Hurnei has he come. What have we done, to be so honoured? What shall we do? Sons of Kem'nanh, what welcome will you show this stranger?'

His voice as he finished was a cry and a challenge, and for a second there was a silence that rang with it. Then on the far side of the fire a young warrior sprang up.

'Lai!' he cried exultantly. 'Harai Hurnei! Harai!'

And he flung his spear flashing into the air. Then as if at signal the whole tribe were on their feet, crying 'Eu-ha! Harai Li'vanh! Hail the Guardian!' And the men flung up their spears so that the tips, borrowing firelight, became a galaxy and a rain of flames; and the women clapped their hands and tossed their hair and added their voices to the outcry. Oliver was dragged to his feet and drawn to stand between Silinoi and Yorn where the firelight fell full upon him. And then such a roar they gave that the smoke wavered and the horses, startled, joined in with shrill neighs. 'Li'vanh!' they thundered, 'Li'vanh!' And with that name surely the mountains echoed, and they were a thousand miles away. Then their voices went again into ragged cheering: until one of the girls stepped out and began to clap in a rhythm and sing in a sweet wild voice; then others joined her, and the men quietened.

Someone began beating softly on a drum, and the girls sang and clapped, and then came slowly winding out of the crowd in a chain, a dancing skein. Around the fire they danced, stepping delicately, their skirts swaying, their dark hair tossing, their high clear voices rising and falling together. Then the men began to sway and stamp, and to sing quietly; and more drums joined the first. Now the men too stepped out and began to dance, casting their own circle around the wreath of girls, and their deep voices joined the song. And the voices of the men were the dark sea, while the voices of the girls were the flying white foam; or the vast dark plain, and the silver light that ran rippling over it; or the wind-brought rumour of thunder, and the shimmering levin-light. And the drums rumbled and throbbed and passed into the ground; and the sound became the very heartbeats of the Earth herself, beating up through their feet into their blood, into their brains, into their very bones. Then through

all welled the liquid richness of a horn, distilling the praise
and the thanks, the strength of the men's song, and the
sweetness of the girls', and the wildness of the drums into the
clear glory of its own music, climbing above the singing and
the dancing, the smoke and the firelight, the tents and the
herds and the vastness of grass, away high into the great dark
firmament, bearing its song far away above the lands of men,
until at last it pierced the cloud and wound up towards the
flowering stars.

Oliver awoke next morning on a bed of hides and fleeces,
with a rippling ceiling above him. He lay staring at that for a
moment, then slowly looked about him. On his left was a
leather wall pummelled by wind. On his right the floor of the
tent opened out. It was a rough circle, the ground covered by
rush matting, with one or two skin rugs. There was hardly
any furniture: another bed like his, two stools with seats
which curved up to form armrests, and one box. Some spears
with stone and bronze heads stood in a rack around the
king-pole.

He raised himself on one elbow, puzzled. He had felt as he
woke that he was in a strange place, but now he was unsure.
Certainly he could not remember having seen this place
before; but when he tried to recall where else he should be,
he could not. He could not think clearly; his mind would not
focus. He was naked, too, which felt strange, though what
anyone would ever wear in bed he could not imagine. His
skin tightened, and a cold fear touched him; then he shook
his head. 'I'm still half asleep, that's my trouble,' he thought.

Just then Mnorh ducked through the tent-flap, with a heap
of clothes over his arm. He regarded Oliver almost with
disappointment.

'Oh! You are awake. I was just going to come and kick
you.'

'As well for me I am awake, then!' With neither doors nor
windows, the light was dim, and it was hard to judge the
time. 'Late, is it?'

'Mid-morning. You slept right through the Dawn Drum
and the Salute. Look, Li'vanh, I have brought—I am sorry,
how should I say your name?'

'Oliver. Ol-iv. . . .' He hit himself on the head. 'Of course!
Fool! My name is Oliver Powell, my brother is Nicholas and

my sister is Penelope.' As soon as he said their names it was
possible to recall them, and then he could think backwards,
find the faces of his mother and father, his home, his grand-
parents. He laughed with relief. Only then came the questions: where were they, then? where was he?—and the inevi-
table memory of Nicholas and Penelope, sitting on the gate,
dissolving like mist. He sprang away from the thought as if
burned, his mind snapping shut, cutting off all memory. He
stopped laughing abruptly, and Mnorh watched him fascinated, tossing the clothes to the floor.

'Yes, so you told us. Your names are hard to say, O-li-
vanh. Look, my father told me to bring you these clothes,
because we think—well, because Yorn said to do so, really.
He says the clothes you were wearing should be put away.
We borrowed them to get the sizes right. That scarlet—well,
jerkin—the woollen thing; how is it made? It is not woven.'
Oliver tried to find the right words, and seeing him at a loss
for an answer Mnorh said hurriedly, 'No, if it is a secret
craft of your people I should not seek to know. I think these
boots will fit you.'

The leather trousers were comfortable and the coat,
though it did not fasten, was unexpectedly warm. They fitted
him well, though it took him a while to get used to the way
in which they creaked faintly as he moved. Mnorh gave him
the cloak, and watched as he swung it inexpertly round his
shoulders, grinning a little as he dropped one side before
managing to fasten it.

'Lai-ee, you will learn. What do your people wear, if not
cloaks? What is that you wear around your neck? Is it the
image of your god?'

Oliver looked to see what he wore around his neck. It was
so familiar he had not noticed it; besides, usually it was under
his clothes. It was a silver disc on a silver chain, portraying a
bearded man leaning heavily on a long staff. Water foamed
about his knees, and he bore a small child on his shoulder.
Oliver studied it frowning. Mnorh peered at it with interest.

'It is skilful work. Look how his cloak is flapping; and his
hair. You can see it is a storm. Why is the child there? Is the
man your god?'

'No,' said Oliver, slowly, half-knowledge teasing his mind.
'No, he's only a man. But I can't remember properly what

it's about. But I should be able to!' He bit his lip. 'Let's try those boots.'

They were comfortable, but as soon as he stepped forward his foot twisted and he almost fell. The boots had a high bronze-shod heel, and as soon as he tried to walk they threw him first one way and then the other, wrenching his ankles unmercifully. Mnorh watched him, astonished at first, then trying vainly to smother his laughter.

'Lai, Li'vanh, enough! Come, I will find you some breakfast. I will walk slowly. Bring a spear to lean on, if you like: or shall I offer you my arm?'

Oliver made as if to throw a spear at him, so that he scrambled out yelping in mock terror, then followed. The boots added less than two inches to his height, but he felt at least a foot taller, stalking carefully through the camp. All the tribespeople had plainly been at their work for hours. As they passed the men called out and saluted them and the children ran up. The women straightened from their work and followed them with their eyes, bowing their raven heads; but they did not speak unless greeted first. The girls were not so self-effacing, and when a group of them swirled by in a rush of skirts and bare feet and flying black hair, one of them spun away from the others and stood in front of the two boys. She wore a knee-length laced overdress of leather and underneath a white shift. She carried a bow and quiver. It was the girl who had begun the dancing last night. She regarded them, hands on hips, her head on one side, and Mnorh groaned.

'Good morning, My Lord Li'vanh,' she said with a little bow; then, less civilly, 'Good morning, Mnorh. Derna was looking for you. He has the other boys at weapon training. Javelins. He said you were in need of practice.'

'Oh, very funny. What about you. Aren't you missing yours?' Turning to Oliver he explained, 'This is Mneri, my sister. We were born at one birth—though I was born first, which she seems always to forget. Just because I will not be a man for two years, and she will join the women in the autumn. But you wait, madam. You will get your tongue shortened then.'

She laughed, swinging her skirts and looking at him provocatively. 'The more reason to use it now, then.' Her narrowed dancing almond eyes glanced sideways at Oliver, and he grinned back. Mnorh scowled.

'Are you going to Derna?' she enquired sweetly.

'Of course,' he replied haughtily. '*After* I have seen that Li'vanh has eaten. So run away and find your friends, there's no point in waiting, and don't think that I can't see through you!' For a second she looked taken aback, then rather annoyed, but finally laughed, dancing to his side. 'I'd never be so foolish, brother,' she said, and giving his plait a friendly farewell tug ran in pursuit of her friends. Oliver turned to look after her, still smiling, then turned to encounter a suspicious look from Mnorh. He straightened his face. 'Food?'

Mnorh nodded, but was silent as they began walking. After a few minutes he said grudgingly, 'Oh, she's not bad for a girl—not a nuisance usually—I wouldn't want another as a sister—but she's cheeky!'

'She's very pretty,' said Oliver, then laughed at Mnorh's expression of disgust. 'Well, I can't help having eyes, can I?'

'Oh, she's all right,' he admitted, adding, 'But I won't tell her you said that. She'd be unbearable! That would be a thing to boast of to her friends.' He met Oliver's amazed stare with a puzzled look. 'But, Li'vanh, you must realize what a great thing your coming is? Nothing so wonderful has happened in longer than a lifetime! We will all tell our children's children of you, and boast of having known you!'

Chapter Five

'A Stranger in Our Midst'

Oliver sat on the river bank, his knees drawn up to his chin, and gazed abstractly across the river. In the middle the current was swift and silent, but by the banks the water swirled and fussed; plainly the level was far higher than usual, for he could see beneath the surface of the water the bent backs of the swept reeds. Behind him he could hear the voices of the boys at target practice, and the deep growl of their instructor. Downstream women were washing clothes, treading them in the water and beating them on stones; the wind brought the sound of splashing laughter and a continuing undercurrent of conversation. High above and in the reeds birds sang. From far off came the sounds of the herds, and from all sides the noises of children at play. The wind stirred the reeds, making a background of their rustling murmur that the other sounds pierced, sounding jewel-clear but remote.

Oliver himself was lost in a deep silence, trying to make sense of all that had happened. But he could not, or not unless he abandoned all his notions of what did make sense. It admitted neither explanation nor denial; he could not begin to comprehend it, and yet it was.

Yorn and Silinoi had utterly confounded him, for they spoke calmly of magic. Even to hear it mentioned as a serious possibility would have been incredible enough; to hear it spoken of as certainty turned the world inside out. He could not, *could* not believe; yet, as Yorn had said, how else was he there? Try as he might to explain it, the fact remained: in some unnatural, inexplicable way he had been torn from his homeland and deposited in—Vandarei. Vandarin he understood as if it were his native tongue, and his

33

native tongue he had utterly forgotten. He could even read and write Vandarin. What was this, he asked himself, if not magic?

He was still battering his brain for understanding; he could not yet learn to do as Yorn told him, accept facts and trust in the wisdom of the power which had brought him. He had been found on holy ground, said the Priest, for all trees were sacred on the plain, to Ir'nanh the Guide. 'He must have brought you. Without doubt he had a reason, and without doubt he will guide you back to your home. In the meantime, O'livanh, you are welcome.'

He shook his head wearily. If only he could. If only he could relax, run with the tide and give up trying to fathom it. It would be so simple; yet so hard. To attempt it was like trying to fall asleep: the more he tried, the more he failed. And like waiting to sleep, conscious and wide-eyed in the dark, waiting for oblivion it was almost frightening. Better to cling to his confusion, he thought, than to lose himself. But then he felt that if he did not stop thinking around the same circle soon he might lose his sanity.

There was so much he did not remember. He kept reaching back into his memory, pulling out the people and the faces, forcing himself to restate all he knew, and then as soon as he stopped concentrating they were gone again. And every time it was harder, and less came back. It was a cold, lonely feeling, as if he stood with unguessed-at dark gulfs at his back, as if all behind him were a roaring void. All the more reason then surely to go forward to the warmth and welcome of the Khentors, to yield and forget and have faith in his fate.

So Ir'nanh brought me, did he? he thought angrily. Well then, all I can say is that Ir'nanh had a ruddy nerve. But what right did Ir'nanh bring me? What affair was I of his?

And that was another thing. Magic he might possibly accept; he had no choice. But Ir'nanh was spoken of as a god. Of many things he was uncertain, but he was fiercely sure that Ir'nanh was no god of his, and he would not worship him.

Mnorh's voice recalled him, calling good-bye to his friends and walking over to him. Oliver stood up, and Mnorh stopped. He began pushing his javelins into the ground, staring thoughtfully at the river, and cocked his head at Oliver.

'How about a swim?'

'Swim! That water looks icy!'

'Well, it isn't very warm at this time of year, but it's that or stay dirty. We bathe in there morning and night. Still, we'll leave it till this evening when everybody else goes.' He grinned. 'That might give you time to gather courage.'

Oliver launched a blow at him, and he swayed away laughing, then threw aside his remaining javelins and sprang in. Oliver had the advantage of Mnorh in height and weight; but it seemed that only the next second he found himself flat in the grass, with one of Mnorh's knees in his back, an arm crooked around his throat, and another in possession of his wrist. 'I submit!' he croaked, beating the ground, and Mnorh gave a whoop of triumph and let him get up. He rose feeling his throat gingerly, and laughed ruefully. 'This is a dangerous place I've come to. When you're not spearing me or freezing me you're breaking my neck. And I thought I was welcome! What do you do to your enemies?'

'Oh, I won't frighten you by telling you. But you're not very quick, are you, Li'vanh? I didn't expect you to go down like that. I'm not even a marvellous wrestler.'

'Well, congratulations on having met a worse one. In fact I'm not a wrestler at all, though I did think I wasn't bad with my fists.'

'What is that? You do not know how to wrestle?' Oliver shook his head. 'Oh, then I am sorry, it wasn't fair. And that was stupid of me, for how could you know? Only the Khentorei have the art, and we will not teach it to anyone else.' He grinned. 'They are all bigger than us, you see. We must keep something in reserve. But we will teach you. Come, I must put these javelins away.' He pulled them out of the ground and Oliver picked one up, examining it interestedly, feeling the point and edge of the dark flaked stone.

'Mnorh, this is one thing I don't understand. You have bronze; I have seen bronze swords, and spearheads. Why are yours of stone?'

'Because I am not yet a man. Bronze is the man's metal, for warriors only. While I am still a boy, I must use stone only; when we are taken into the tribe as men, our fathers give us spears with bronze heads.'

'But are not some of yours bronze already?'

'No. None.'

'But there are some bronze spears in your tent.'

Mnorh hesitated before answering. 'Those are my brother's.'

'I didn't know you had a brother!'

'Ah—yes. I have.'

'He's older than you, then? What is his name? Why have I not seen him?'

'He is called Vanh. Yes, he is older than us by many years. He has been a man for a long time. He is the Hunter—or he was. For stalking especially, for going silently and living hard, there is no one to match him.' His voice was very even, and Oliver glanced at him in surprise.

'Vanh? That's almost the same as you call me. That's funny. And I suppose I've got his half of the tent? Where is he?'

'He spent the winter with his grandsire, but he is gone from there.'

'Where is he now?'

'We don't know.'

'Don't know!' Oliver felt a sudden curiosity about the man whose place, it almost seemed, he was filling. 'How is that?'

'He . . .' Mnorh hesitated, then continued hurriedly, 'he made a—request of my father, and got an angry answer. Then we got a message saying he was following the wind, and did not know when he would be home. The wind!' he laughed sourly. 'In his right mind he would not have spoken so. We know what he followed, and it was not the wind.'

'What was it?' asked Oliver, after a pause, but Mnorh remained silent. After a moment he tried again.

'You said *his* grandsire, not *ours*. Why was that? And why did he spend the winter there? Surely, he is a tribesman?'

'He always spends the winter there. And he is not our grandsire, only Vanh's; or really his great-grandsire. Though we have met him, and he likes us, especially Mneri. Vanh is the heir to his kingdom.' He turned and saw Oliver's face and stopped, laughing a little. 'Come, sit down. I will tell you.'

'My father has had two wives; Vanh is the son of the first, and Mneri and I are children of the second. They both died early. So Vanh is really our half-brother. Now, a great many years ago, before anyone in the tribe alive now was born, a man of the Harani came to our tribe, the heir to a kingdom far away by the sea. I do not know his name—he was called here Dha'len, Prince, for that is what we always call them. Many of the Princes come here for a while; this one stayed long. He took a wife from the women of the tribe, and left his great castle for a tent, and became a tribesman. But when he had been here about ten years, his wife died, and I think the Prince grew a little lonely—Harani depend more on their wives than we do. Then his father far off fell ill, and called him back. So the Prince took his children, and took his leave, and went. Some while later it was heard that he was a king, and there he lives now in his stone hall by the sea, and he has never been to the plains since. (He is still alive, Li'vanh! But the Harani live for ever, almost.) That is the grandsire I spoke of. But when his son came to manhood he found that the lands of his childhood called him, the wind in the grasses and the thunder of the herds: Khentor blood is strong. So he, in his turn, left his father and returned here, to rear his children in the tribe. And *he* was Vanh's grandfather.'

'Why is Vanh the heir, when your father is still alive?'

'Because our father is nothing to do with the Prince; it comes to Vanh through his mother. Truly, the Harani have some strange laws! Because she was the firstborn of her father, even though he had sons, she, had she been alive, would have received the crown. Imagine! A woman succeeding to a Kingdom! Anyhow, Vanh is the heir. And since he became a man—that is seven years ago now—he has spent his winters with his grandsire, learning the ways of the kingdom. But this spring he has not come back.'

He fell silent: Oliver waited a moment then said, 'Why not? Does he like the castle by the sea so much?'

Mnorh laughed unhappily. 'Oh no, its not that, though the Harani blood runs strong in him, to be sure. No, he was a wise counsellor, a great warrior, a mighty hunter—but the Plains are forgotten like a dream. The Woman of the Swans has stolen his wits. My brother is spell-bound. The Witch of Rennath has him.'

On the next day, Silinoi and many of the tribe went to the Tree where they had met Oliver, to sacrifice to Ir'nanh—a

bloodless sacrifice of song and dance, since he as the Lord of
Life took no delight in shed blood. They asked him to go
with them, but he refused, determining to start as he meant
to go on. Instead he spent the morning with Argai the
Horsemaster.

Argai was one of the oldest men in the tribe, older by
about five years than the Lord Silinoi. His hair and beard
were almost entirely grey. Yet even so, he was not old as
Oliver would reckon it, he was still strong and supple. Khentors, it seemed, were not long lived. There were no men in
the tribe, and very few women, older than late middle age.

It was towards noon when a young tribesman came gal-
loping up to them, plainly ablaze with news. 'Argai! Argai!'
he called, 'Argai! Come and see! Lord Li'vanh! The wind in
your face, Lord Li'vanh—come also! Come and see!'

They went, as swiftly as they could. It seemed that half the
tribe was running in the same direction, and from those in
front there was a great commotion of voices, a strange thing
from people usually so silent. A way was opened for Oliver
and Argai to pass to the fore; and then they stopped, awed.

Those who had been to offer at the Dancer's Tree were
returning. And before them cantered a horse.

He was horned and his body was like old bronze, gleaming
darkly; but his mane and tail, both long and shining, were
golden indeed—almost flame-coloured. He was not one of
the horses of the tribe, yet he did not look like one who had
spent his life running wild on the plain. Not that he looked in
the least tame; but his coat was too glossy, his hooves too
polished. There was no speck of dust or mud on limb or
flank, no tangle in mane or tail. Oliver, little as he had yet
learned about horses, felt that; but what he felt far more,
fierce and sure, was that here was the most beautiful thing he
had ever seen in his whole life. Kingdoms could be whistled
down the wind for a horse like this, and the price not
grudged. Cities could be burned for him, war could spring up
between brother and brother, friend and friend, for the
possession of him—and all in vain, for he was not made to
be possessed.

Mnorh rode up to Oliver and sprang from the saddle,
gasping, 'He was beneath the Tree! Li'vanh, have you ever
seen anything like him? He suddenly trotted round, from the

far side of the Tree. But those who were round there say that
he did not, that he came first from our side. Is he not
beautiful? No one can approach him. He drives them away,
or knocks them down. He nearly speared Hunoi. But,
Li'vanh, if only you could have seen! He trotted past our
horses—they were in a line at the back; I was with them, and
I saw. He trotted by them, and they bowed their heads! It is
true! No, Argai, it is true! As he passed, I tell you, they
bowed their heads, right down, like reeds where the wind
passes. They touched their horns to the ground!'

Oliver watched spellbound as the horse danced and sidled
alone in the midst of the circle that had formed, plainly quite
unafraid, enjoying their attention. A young man stepped
forward from the crowd and began to walk towards the
horse, warily, gently, and the horse watched him come. The
man circled slowly. The horse turned to keep watching him
and Oliver caught a glimpse of his eyes. A thrill of wonder
tingled through him. For they were thinking eyes: lively,
intelligent. He had never seen such eyes in an animal before.
They almost laughed, mocking the plainsman who thought to
lay hands on him. Had not others tried? And this one would
find the same welcome. A little charge, and a flourish of his
horn, and the man sprang aside; a quick turn, and he was
flung sprawling to the ground, rolling furiously out of reach
of the hooves. The watchers laughed, and one or two ap-
plauded. The horse pranced and dipped his head, acknowledging them with the grace of a dancer. Oliver drew a breath
of wonder and delight, and unthinking stepped forward.

'Li'vanh, don't be a fool!' cried Mnorh, and caught at his
shoulders. But his plea went unheard, Oliver shrugged his
hand away. The men fell silent, and the horse stopped preen-
ing and spun to face him, his head turned a little sideways.

Oliver looked into one of the dancing eyes, and it beckoned him on. He had walked forward without thinking, and
went on without will. The horse watched him come, moving
a little away as he approached, luring him on. His eye glinted
both warning and encouragement, calling him forward, almost teasing him. There was not a sound around them.
Mnorh was biting his tongue, Mneri watched Oliver with her
hands pressed to her face. No one dared call to him or pull
him away. Plainly he was entranced; and it is dangerous to
the victim to break a trance.

Then he stood right before the horse, his hand stretched forward. For a moment they were motionless; then the horse moved one pace nearer. The spell was broken. The crowd gasped with relief, and Oliver ran his hand down the satin neck.

He could hardly believe it. A creature of such power and beauty who had spurned the horsemen, now standing quiet beneath his hand, butting his shoulder with his muzzle, whinnying low in his throat. But as soon as the others came up, the horse showed that his gentleness was only for one. An angry whickering and flashed teeth greeted one attempt at friendliness which he seemed to regard as impertinence; the second made him rear and flourish his hooves. When they scattered he came down and nuzzled Oliver's hair as if in apology.

'Open out,' said Silinoi, 'and let him be. Li'vanh, do you see if he will be brought to Yorn. He is no common horse, for sure.'

When Oliver moved forward the horse stood his ground, then tossed his head and snorted imperiously. Oliver turned; the velvet-dark eyes, glinting with deep-sunk green and gold, met his challengingly, demandingly. He hesitated, unsure of what was expected, then the horse tossed his head and gave a little nod. Words could not have said more plainly, 'Ask me nicely.' Oliver laughed aloud.

'O stranger, be welcome,' he said. 'Honour our tents.' He laid his right fist to his left shoulder and bowed low, in the Khentor manner. The horse made a graceful gesture with his horn that nearly made Oliver laugh again, and followed. The tribespeople followed in a wide, straggling procession, and massed again behind them as they reached Yorn's tent. As soon as they stopped, and before Silinoi had called to him, the curtains parted and the priest stepped out.

Silence fell. Silinoi did not speak, and Oliver's explanation died on his lips. The horse and the priest held each other's gaze with their wise eyes.

At last Yorn spoke.

'You have come, then, as was foretold to me,' he said, 'to bear a mortal burden for a time.'

The horse lifted his head, and the wind came and rolled his mane of gold out on the air. He looked proud and suddenly terrible, more real than anything or anyone about him: and his horn wound up from his brow like a spear of light.

'Foretold?' said Oliver, 'You knew he was coming?'

'In a way I knew,' replied the priest, 'Enough to recognize him.' He looked at Oliver, drawing him into his eyes. His voice came low but clear to the boy, speaking to him alone. 'Didst think, then, that this was a son of the earth, beaten by wind and rain, rent by frost? No: above the moons, behind the sun was he foaled, in the land where the grass is royal green and the sky is silver. His brethren graze among the stars, and drink at the Dancer's Fountain. Earth Mother knows him not; he is not of her children. Hornblower has not heard his name. Here before you, Li'vanh, is one of the Immortals.'

Sudden cold crept over Oliver's body. His hair stirred. He looked again; but to see, there was only a horse, great, glossy-coated, his breath misting out of his nostrils, his withers shuddering to shake off a fly. Surely he breathed in, he breathed out, his heart drove his blood around his body; he was a horse, he was flesh and blood—or—was he?

Yorn looked back into the deep bright eyes. 'Meet then your fellow-warrior, your appointed burden. As you, far has he come, a stranger is he in our midst. Li'vanh, the Chosen One.'

Oliver gasped and twisted to stare at the priest. Mnorh and Mneri both burst into speech.

'*Me?*' exclaimed Oliver. 'For me to ride? Is he mine?'

'Yours?' Yorn smiled. 'As much as you are his. You are his rider, he is your horse—for a time. He is appointed to bear you a little while. For you will have need of him.'

'Mount, Li'vanh!' cried Mnorh, 'Mount!' He made a stirrup for him of his hands. Oliver hesitated a fraction of a second then sprang up. Self-conscious, high above any of them, he sat as if throned; and the tribe cheered him.

'What will you call him?' asked Mneri. 'He must have a name. What shall it be?'

Into the suggestions that flowed from her and from Mnorh, Yorn's quiet voice cut. 'He has a name.'

'Oh.'

'What?'

He stepped forward, laying his hand on the horse's nose, but his eyes looked at Oliver.

'His name is Dur'chai: the Endurer. For he shall stand fast in a place where no other would.'

Chapter Six

The Shadow on the Land

'Well,' Nicholas observed, gazing critically up at the mountain, 'it certainly is black, anyway.'

The clouds were thick and low, heavy with more snow. It lay drifted deep everywhere, save on the grim sable crags above them. Stark and unsoftened, they stood harsh against the white sky, even the peaks bare. The pale sun cast behind them faint shadows, which their native darkness engulfed. There was a faint sheen on them, as if they were wet; Nicholas remembered how slippery they had been to walk on. Not a bush, not a blade was anywhere to be seen on their flanks—not even to the lowest slopes did any earth cling. From root to crest they were bare rock. On the very closest Nicholas could see a faint silver tracery, a cobweb of snow that had found some tiny ripple in which to lodge, but this flimsy veil could not relieve their darkness. Being so black, and so shining-smooth, the mountain had rather the appearance of coal. But in coal there is always the promise of warmth, while this was dead of all promise, black with a million nights of frost.

The boy shivered and looked away. Down in this hollow the snow lay deep and the crust sparkled with ice, but the pavilions of the Princess and her attendants were jewel-bright, and the air had not the dead stillness of the Mountain. He turned to the Lord Hairon, looking up at the dark head so far above his own. When he first woke, he thought he had dreamed a race of giants, but their height was no dream. Maybe Hairon was not a giant, but he must have been seven feet tall; the Princess was barely less than six.

'Is it ever warm here?' he asked.

Hairon laughed, and the air smoked with his breath. His

43

hair glittered where crystals had frozen into it. 'Once this was a land like other lands,' he replied, 'Summer came with its glow, and autumn with its pomp. Elsewhere even now the sweet spring is unfolding, but now winter always clings to the skirts of Black Mountain.'

'But what a horrible place to live! Why do you stay here?'

'We do not live here, Nikon! And certainly we will not stay longer than we need. Leaves are unfurling in Rennath, and would I were there, far from this evil place. No, we came only to see King Merekarl and his people in their fight.'

'Evil!' cried Nicholas in astonishment. 'Places can't be evil!'

'No,' sighed Hairon, 'but the powers that dwell in them can, and then a shadow lies on the land, and even the fairest things are tainted. A dark power rules in this place, and summer shuns it.'

'What do you mean, shuns it? Surely summer just happens —I mean, isn't it when we're close to the sun or pointing at it or something? How can it not come?'

'And have your people this sweet surety always, then, Nicholas? It is not so here, alas. There are some things shunned by all that is good—but not only that, the ruler of this land himself hates summer, and it is by his art that it is ever bleak here.'

Nicholas swallowed. He remembered the Princess crying out against someone's strength, and the Eagle King saying, 'Mighty he grows'. Mighty enough to command winter? He shuddered, and huddled into his cloak.

'Who is it?' he asked, awed; but Hairon did not reply, for at that moment the sound of a bugle pierced the air, and he took hold of the boy's shoulder and steered him towards the Princess's tent.

'We are summoned. I think Her Highness will welcome you and your sister.'

Outside the tent he paused and twitched Nicholas' clothes into order. They had taken away his own clothes, which were far from being warm enough, and dressed him in their own style. When they went in the first thing he saw was Penelope, also transformed, in a long skirt, long sleeved blouse, and vividly embroidered bodice, her hair brushed out loose over her shoulders, waving excitedly.

'I've got seven skirts on,' she informed him. 'And long

trousers. What's more I can walk without treading on them. And I've got boots on. Nicky, you do look different; and isn't it all peculiar?'

'Yes, very,' muttered Nicholas, trying to hush her. No one else was talking, and Penny's clear voice seemed unnecessarily loud. He looked at the men with a mixture of apology and defence, but they seemed not at all put out, even showing an amused pleasure. Then the curtains parted, and the Princess came in.

She was robed in silver and bright green, like dew on young grass. From her shoulders swung a cloak dark as holly; her hair was roped with pearls, and round her brow was a coronet of silver. She took her seat on the carved black chair and stood upright before her a great sword. Two-edged it was, cold and shining, and the hilt was twisted of a dark-green metal. She rested her hands on the guards; on the little finger of one hand was a small ring of silver in the shape of a nine-pointed star. On her breast, by a chain of silver, hung a great pearl mounted in a grip of the green metal. Proud she was, proud and stern and beautiful, child of a line of Kings.

'Let the strangers stand forth,' she said.

Nicholas flexed his fingers, and his hand closed on Penelope's. They stepped forward to stand before her.

'Be welcome to Kedrinh,' she said, 'to the Starlit Land. I greet you in the name of the Harani, in the name of the Council, and in the name of Deron my father, King of Rennath, Watcher of Bannoth. His protection I offer you, and claim for you also the protection of Kiron the High King. So speak I, In'serinna, Daughter of the Stars, Princess of Rennath, and Enchantress of the Star Magic.'

Nicholas felt Penelope's hand move, but himself felt hardly any surprise. He thanked her, he hoped without stammering too much, and bowed hesitantly. Penny bobbed a curtsey, rather to his amazement, and then they stepped back.

There was a brief silence, and the Princess laid the great sword across her knees. She gazed at it for a moment, and then looked up.

'Well, my lords,' she said, 'we have much to think on.'

There was general rustling and relaxing, as everybody found stools and cast off their cloaks. When they had all settled the Princess said, 'Let me first explain a little to the children.'

She turned to them, leaning forward in her throne. 'We are now in what was once the kingdom of Bannoth,' she said, 'whose ruler was once one Fendarl. Fendarl was one of the Children of the Stars—a man like my kinsmen whom you see here. He was not only King of Bannoth, but also a Star Enchanter; but he came to love knowledge and power more than honour, more than his virtue; and in his hunger he searched where he ought not, and dealt with powers which should have been his enemies. Indeed, his enemies they had once been—but the evil powers also can forgive, and are ever willing to make allies of their foes. So it happened that he practised the forbidden arts, and fell, and became a Black Enchanter.

'Had he been discovered early, maybe that would have lessened the ill. But he was clever and cunning, and honest men are very often too trusting. This place was the centre of his kingdom; and here in Black Mountain long he wove his spells undetected. And when he was at last exposed he had grown very strong. He could not be destroyed, for he had armoured himself with dark enchantments. Also it was in the time of Hundreth II, and the Magic itself was weakened at its heart. But at last, though he was himself indestructible, in the new-found power of the Emerald he was cast out, and banished to the Mountains Beyond the Sea. There has he dwelt ever since, with great power, it is true, but with no way of enjoying it. Thus a respite was won; but all knew it was only a respite. Still he searched and still he learned, and still his power grew; and ever he sought a way to re-enter the Starlit Land. Many trials of his strength has he made; last night's battle was one. And I am afraid it may prove true what we have long feared—that his strength is enough now to defy the ban, and return.'

In the pause that followed Nicholas knew himself, for the first time in his life, to be afraid—really afraid. Penelope moved uneasily.

'Return?' she whispered. 'Now?'

In'serinna smiled.

'We are not in danger this very minute—or I think not. But the clouds gather, and here most. Never fear, we will see that you are taken to safety.'

'Indeed, we should leave Bannoth without delay,' said the Lord Horenon. 'It is become more dangerous than I dreamed. Only moonrise saved Merekarl and his people last night. Has word been sent to Kiron?'

'He has been told. But as to leaving. . . .' She grew serious and looked down. 'I would ask you to let me delay—a little.'

There were frowns. Plainly the idea was not liked. Several of them shook their heads.

'How long?' demanded Hairon at last.

'Two days. My reason is good, cousin.'

'If it is then share it with us.'

'Not far from here is Bannoth's place of seeing.' She looked around at them. 'If I wait two days—no more—in two days I will be able to see what it has to show.'

The men looked at each other. They were worried and doubtful but reluctant to refuse. The mountain was more than unpleasant, it was dangerous. They were there to guard the Princess, but she to do anything she could against Fendarl. She was the Enchantress. Hers was the greatest power; they ought not with undue caution make her task harder. Yet she was young, and a woman, and their responsibility, and the greater her power the more rigorously ought she be guarded. The Lord Horenon smoothed his hair uncertainly.

'It is a risk,' he said at last, 'Every hour is a risk.'

'Yes,' she agreed.

'Is it worth it—really worth it?'

'Yes, I think so. You see, this is a very ancient place. Of old, it was the heart of Bannoth. Great power was put there in the past. Since the fall of Fendarl none have used it; yet possibly the power remains. I am all but certain that it does, and that having avoided it our enemies will not have corrupted it. It is theirs. To them it will turn. I think I will be able maybe to see something of what they are doing, and that would be even better to carry to the High King.'

'Dangerous, cousin, dangerous!' cried Hairon. 'Be careful lest you draw their gaze to you!'

'No need to tell me, Hairon,' she replied. 'I am in a very proper state of terror whenever I think of him, I assure you. But I promise I will only look. Have I your agreement?'

They exchanged looks again. Horenon glanced at each in turn, and they all nodded briefly except Hairon, who shook his head emphatically.

'I am no faint-heart,' he declared. 'I fear this place, but I swear fear alone will not drive me out. But I am convinced, I am certain, that if you do this misfortune will follow. My voice is for No.'

'You are out-numbered,' said Horenon. 'Princess In'serinna, here you are our liege lady; and you are an enchantress. If you think this thing is worth doing, then it is not for us to hinder you.'

'Thank you.' she said, 'I promise I am not acting without thought. Now, is there anything else, or shall we part?'

'There is something else.'

The speaker was a young man from the very back. They all turned to look at him. He pushed through to the front, flushing a little, and bent his knee before the throne.

'Madam,' he said, 'I fear we may be watched.'

There was a hiss of consternation as they all drew sharp breaths. The Princess tightened her hands. Nicholas and Penelope looked at each other in dismay, feeling themselves prickle with the unpleasant thought that a black wizard might swoop on them at any second.

'Tell us what makes you think so, Captain Emneron.' The young man looked troubled.

'I have no proof to offer, and little reason: only an uneasiness, and a feeling between my shoulder blades. I have felt thus ever since we left Rennath.'

'Have you ever seen anyone?'

'Never a man; but a man may find it easier to hide himself than his horse, and twice in Rennath I saw a horse grazing at night—that is, once certainly, and almost certainly another time.'

'But Captain, horses are many!'

'True, Madam; but here the davlenei of the plains are not so common—and this one was superb, a re-davel indeed! All black and silver.'

'Many men go to the plains. And the Khentorei . . .' just for a second her voice quivered oddly, ' . . . the Khentorei are great wanderers.'

'All this I remembered, your Highness, and not being certain that I had seen this re-davel more than once, I would not have regarded it, save that I do feel that we are being watched, and today—today when I went the rounds of the camp and visited the horselines, our horses were restless.

They were all quivering and stamping and turned one way, with their ears cocked and their nostrils flared, whinnying quietly. I could see nothing. But horses of course smell much that we do not.'

'Were they in fear?'

'No, not fear. More like excitement. As if they were welcoming a friend, or a kinsman . . . and there came into my mind the re-davel I spoke of. I am sure there is something— and whatever it is, it seems to have reason to hide.'

There was a long tense silence. The Princess looked at her ring, and at the great pearl; and the men and Nicholas watched her. So did Penelope, for a minute; then her eyes wandered, and she noticed something which she remembered, much later. Behind the Princess's chair stood her two ladies— one tall and pale, with curling light-brown hair and apple-green eyes, the other slight, dark, and graceful. And the dark maid turned to the other, and nodded at her and made a face which said quite plainly 'I told you so,' and the other smiled and shrugged.

Then In'serinna raised her eyes slowly.

'I have not felt any evil thing come near; and the horses were not afraid. I think—I do not think that this can be one of our enemies. Yet we ought to be secret, so keep a watch Captain Emneron—all of you. But if you should see anyone, do not harm them, though bring them here if you may. Now kinsmen, go your ways.'

Chapter Seven

The Borders of Peril

The two days under Black Mountain were strange, still, unbreathing. The Harani watched the mountain and the sky, their hands never far from their swords. The Princess paced the snow alone at night, watching the clustered stars and wrestling in her mind. Merekarl and his people healed, slowly, save two. Even the clouds held back their snow and waited.

All was in readiness. In the White City by the sea Kiron gathered his strength and summoned his forces. South he looked, to the busy careless cities, north and east whence there was no help, and west to the borders of peril, and he sighed. On the plain the wind blew free and the grasses danced, and among them danced and wrestled the Chosen One as if a Khentor born. In the heart of Black Mountain one watched and prepared, taking his orders. And in other mountains more dreadful yet another watched, and planned, and waited. In heaven the all-seeing stars wheeled and spun, treading their own ordained measure and telling those with eyes to see that the hour was near. Night and day the princes, for all their vigilance, were watched by one they did not see, nor even a mark of him.

In those two silent days the children alone were unaffected. They made the frosty quiet ring with their shouts and laughter, and scarred the white breadths with their criss-crossing footprints, their snow forts and their fights and their snowmen. Often some of the younger lords would join them, glad enough it may be to forget their vigil in noisy games. They are a strange, proud, high race, the Children of the Stars, and there are plenty to call them haughty and forbidding, but children they love. Hairon was their companion almost all the time. He took them to see the chariots and the horses. Small horses they are by comparison with the great ones of the plains, but yet splendid, graceful and strong, swift and hardy, bred to run under the yoke-poles of princes. Even when grazing they wandered in the threes in which they were driven. Hairon bade his charioteer call his own horses to them and they gave them tit-bits, and the horses touched their cheeks and brushed their fingers, gentle as kittens. They dropped their satin noses to be stroked, and nudged them and sniffed their clothes for more plunder. All three were black with a white blaze, and one had white socks also. He was the team leader. 'They are princes, all three,' said the charioteer, 'but that one a king.'

Hairon they greeted as a friend; but it was the charioteer's voice they came to and his chirrup that sent them wheeling quietly and trotting away. Hairon watched them with a half smile 'I am their master,' he said, 'they only are to serve me. In my hand is their keep and their very life; but they care nothing for all this. To them, Vadreth is their lord, the light of their eyes. They would run with my hand on the reins, for they are well schooled and willing, and proud too—they will break their hearts before their paces. But for him they would dare fire or flood, or a gallop headlong down a mountain.'

'That doesn't really seem fair.'

'I do not grudge him that; no better comrade had any man, or one better with his horses. And for my part I think a charioteer deserves any honour he is given, by men or horses. I would not be one, not for one of the stars of the crown. To drive a battle-chariot in the van—to stoop there with no shield, knowing yourself a target for dozens (for kill the driver and you have the warrior) and with nothing in your hand but some leather straps, no shelter, no weapon, no defence—it sets my teeth on edge to think of it.' He shook himself. 'Enough. Come and see my chariot.'

It was heavier than they had expected: they had thought of chariots as shells on wheels, but this was strong, with sides that would turn a spear. The wall dipped low at the front where Vadreth would stand, so that he could be out over it to reach his horses at any time, but at the sides it was four feet high. Hairon showed them the floor of three layers of woven leather straps, the scabbards and rests for his sword and spears. It was lacquered dark green, with an inlay of silver.

'It's lovely,' said Penelope, 'but shouldn't it be gold, as you're a prince?'

'Gold?' said Hairon, 'Gold? Would you choose gold above silver?'

'Well—yes, I suppose. I mean, it's more precious.'

He sighed. 'Not here, little one. Gold is for merchants. Gold is for common men. Gold is the bane of all we love. Where gold waxes, honour wanes, and in it lies the death of magic.'

They were surprised, not only by his words but by his earnest way of speaking; but when they looked about they saw this view seemed to be shared by everybody. Jewellery there was in plenty, on the men as well as the women, and on the horses too; but all of it was silver, and now and then the dark green metal called kamenani. Jewels enough to dazzle, and ropes of pearls, and copper worn by the Lady Arleni, the Princess's dark maid, but never a wink of gold.

Two days—and then the Princess went up on to the mountain.

The men were striking camp at the same time, and Nicholas and Penelope seemed to be in the way everywhere. There was nowhere to be in comfort or even peace, and they felt lost and lonely for the first time since meeting the Harani. So when they saw the Princess preparing to set out they begged hard to be taken with her. They were sure she would refuse, so they pleaded the harder giving her no time to say no. But when at last she silenced them, she said, 'No need to beg; I will take you. I was about to send for you to come.'

'You *were*?' Penny, open-mouthed. 'You *are*?'

'Why? We never thought you would really, only it was worth asking.'

'I do not know why myself, Nikon. I was told to. Go up on to the mountain by all means, they said, but take the strangers or it will be of no use. So. I am not one who can ignore them, though I do not see why you should come. A long walk, and a cold wait, and a long walk again, and not so very safe. But come you, as it is commanded.'

'Who by?' asked Penelope, losing grammar in interest.

'She means, "who is them?",' corrected her brother, rather doubtfully.

'Why, those I asked,' she replied, her eyes glinting. 'Those who see most and farthest. Come, let Arleni and Berethol give you food. It will be a long day.'

They had pouches on their belts, which the ladies filled with food—more than they would eat, they were certain. Nicholas found that his hung heavy, and hesitated whether to take some out; but fortunately did not. In'serinna made them both put on thick cloaks and gloves and fastened them well, but she herself only put a heavy green and black shawl about her shoulders. It was very large, hanging over her arms and down over her skirt at the back, clasped with a brooch in front; but still her head and arms were bare.

'Aren't you cold like that?' asked Nicholas, as they set off. 'I'm not terribly warm even with all this on; but you must be frozen.'

'No, I am not cold, Feel.' She put her hands against their cheeks.

'They're still warm!' said Penelope, astonished. 'How do you manage that?'

'I cannot remember when I was last cold. I never am now. Never cold, or hungry, or tired.'

'Why? Is it because you are—because of your magic? Is it a spell? Can you work it on us?'

The Princess laughed at her, but they caught a sadness beneath.

'No little one, it is not a spell—though it is an effect of my magic. You see, feeling cold is a matter of contrast, of being warm within and cold without, of being accustomed to warmth. But everything has its price; and the price of the Star Magic is this, that we forsake warmth forever. All warmth. So that is why cold has no power over me.'

'It doesn't sound much fun to me,' said Nicholas reflectively. 'Don't you eat, either, like other people? Or go to sleep?'

'Not often, and not a lot. Come, do not let us talk of it. We have a long walk before us; tell me of your home.'

A long walk it was, up along winding mountain paths, the air glittering with cold, the ground treacherous with ice, and the wind tugging at them all the way. But it did not seem too hard for the Princess had a hand for each, and it was fun to walk beside her and talk to her, to hear of her home and tell her of theirs, and make her laugh. She had a clear ringing voice, clear enough to be understood half a mile away, and strong enough to carry too. The mountains seemed to hold their heads higher just to hear it; but she kept hushing herself and looking guilty.

How many hours the walk took them they did not know, but the sun was climbing towards noon when the path rose steeply around a corner and twisted between walls, and stopped where tumbled rocks and two leaning trees made a gate. Here the Princess released their hands and turned to them, looking very serious.

'This is the place. Beyond here I can only go alone. Wait here for me. I do not know how long, but you are out of the wind at least. I am sorry I can not leave you a fire, but it might be too dangerous anyway. Do not go away and do not come in. Do not even look.'

With that she turned from them and passed through the gate.

Nicholas squatted on a low rock and Penelope sat down on the ground, tucking her skirts warmly around her. They began their wait.

They were out of the wind, true; in fact the air was almost unnaturally still. They did talk, from time to time but their voices sounded so loud and intrusive that they were quelled. Even a whisper was a sliding serpent of sound, going past them down the path and—who knew where? To what ears? They ate a little, but the silence was too dampening. So they just sat; and gradually the mountain caught them in its still trance.

Nicholas closed his eyes. The trees behind him, he thought, were the first he had seen green since they had sat on the gate. In fact they were the first growing things of any kind. He tried to remember what a wood looked like, but he could not get his mind the right colour. It was all black with white speckles, funny, swimming, and something tasted bitter in his mouth, and his shoulder hurt. I'm leaning on a stone, he thought; but it was not his shoulder, it was his legs, they ached, and suddenly his memory had come right and he was looking up at tossing green with the sun beyond. Hurray, he tried to say, but no sound came. That was what they were doing, they were opening their mouths but no sound was coming out—no, they were not opening their mouths but there was sound coming out—there was. . . . Then the picture changed and it was moving again, jogging, and there was green before his eyes, then deep blue, then nothing again. Then there was the smell of salt in his face, and the white water curved back and the white towers shone, but then it slipped and he was back in the swimming blackness with the hoarse harsh breathing and the pain in his shoulder. Their teeth, of course, and he woke with a struggle and a cry.

The pain was not in his left shoulder, but the right, where he had been leaning on the rock, and his voice and his boots on the frozen stones were loud in the stillness.

Penny was lying on the ground in a huddle of skirt and cloak. Her face was hidden but her hand twitched. She wanted something, she was cold, she was hungry, but the Princess was saying 'No don't eat, you mustn't eat,' but she would, and the Princess was tugging at her hands, and her face was before her and she was crying, 'Open your eyes! Open your eyes!' But they were open, she could see, see her face, see *that* face start back in sudden terror, and a young man's face, not one she knew, not Prince Hairon, and not Nicholas, though she could hear him calling, sharp and afraid, 'Penny, Penny!' Then she saw another young man coming forward, a stranger, and yet his face tugged at her brain; then she knew him and ran forward. But she slipped, and the grey came back, and everything was sliding under her and Nicholas was crying 'Penny, Pen!' But all her fighting was nothing, she was a mouse in a wheel; then that moment was unbearably close, pressing on her, stifling her, blocking all out, and she twisted and writhed and sobbed, and Nicholas was calling her again but he had hold of her this time, shaking her. . . .

'What do you want?' she said, 'Stop pulling me about!' Then she remembered, and sat up and clutched his shoulder and screamed faintly.

'You were having a nightmare,' he said, his face worried. Penelope never had nightmares. She blinked and gave him a wobbly grin.

'Ho, don't be silly, don't you mean a daymare?'

He tried to smile too, but he was shaky and so was she. Not just dizzy from waking but somehow off balance, as if the dreams had taken them on in space and time, more than just a few minutes, so that Nicholas even felt a little uncertain about the length of time that had passed. It was darker, certainly; the sky was a thicker grey, and the mountains' shadow chilled them.

'She's a long time,' said Penny. 'Is she?'

Nicholas nodded. 'I think so.' He sat silent, thinking. Penelope began gathering little heaps of pebbles, humming to herself. Nicholas watched her, frowning. Nothing every worried Penelope, or not for long. She had been frightened until they met the Princess and the Lords; now she had someone in whom to place her trust and a promise that they would go home, she was quite content. He envied her.

'Pen,' he said slowly at last, 'Pen, why do you think we came here?'

She looked up, almost surprised. 'We fell off the gate, didn't we? And then we came by magic. Isn't that what the Princess said? It was magic, and we would go back quite soon.'

'Yes, I know all that—only she didn't say anything about quite soon—you made that up. I didn't mean on purpose, silly! But that's not what I meant. I *know* we came by magic. That's *how*. I said why?'

She stared at him puzzled. 'What do you mean?'

'Well, magic can't just be flying around loose, can it? I shouldn't think so, anyway. It must have someone working it. So if we came by magic, someone must have made the magic to bring us. Mustn't they?'

'I suppose so. Yes.'

'So if it's someone. . . .' He paused to straighten his thoughts. 'Someone must have done it on purpose. And if they did it on purpose, they must have done it for something. Mustn't they?' She nodded doubtfully. 'I mean, if they dragged us here on purpose, they must have had a good reason—or they ought to have a good reason, or else. . . .' His voice quivered suddenly. 'Or else they shouldn't have done it, that's all.' He stopped abruptly, blinking hard, and Penny came over to him.

'Nicky, what's the matter? Don't you like it?'

'Penny, that's not the point! It's not bad—it's quite fun; but. . . .'

'Well, we can't do anything, can we? And I like the Princess and Prince Hairon and the others. They'll look after us. Don't worry, Nicky, we'll be all right. Won't we? Do you think we won't then, Nicholas? We will be all right, won't we?'

He heaved a little sigh; there was a troubled note creeping into her voice, so he smiled with some difficulty, and nodded. She looked at him gravely for a moment, then smiled brilliantly and went back to her stones.

He sighed again. He should have remembered, he thought, that it would do no good to frighten Penelope too. Much as she admired the Harani, if Nicholas told her that they were wrong she would believe Nicholas. Well at least she was easy to reassure. But it meant that he could not speak to her about the fear that gnawed him most deeply.

He had had three days to think, and all his thinking had led him to one conclusion. They had been brought, by someone, with a purpose; so there must be something for them to do, or something to be done to them. And if it warranted bringing them from an alien world, surely it must be important. Nothing had happened yet in which they had played a part, so it was to come. And the thought of what it might be troubled Nicholas deeply.

Then he turned at a sound, and his heart failed him.

The Princess had swept the trees apart, and stood there in the entrance; but how changed she seemed. She looked years older. Her face was pinched, her eyes were drawn and cold, her mouth tight-lipped, grim. She looked over and past them, rigid, and they quailed to see her.

'What is it?' whispered Penelope, 'Oh, what is it?' But the Princess did not reply, or even seem to hear, and Penelope suddenly gave a sob of fear. 'Nicky!' she wailed, 'Nicky!' and scrambled to his side.

Nicholas was near panic himself, but at Penelope's desolate cry the Princess seemed to recover. She shuddered and then looked slowly around, faintly puzzled, until she saw them. Her face was back to normal, only sadder, and more worried.

'Ah, I am sorry,' she said, 'I did not mean to frighten you. But quickly now, we have no time to lose. I have seen that which fills me with fear.'

She held out her hands, and they got stiffly to their feet. 'What was it?' asked Nicholas, as they hurried beside her, 'I mean, I thought you *were* scared—filled with fear, rather—

anyway, I thought things were already bad enough. What else is there? Something new?'

'It begins,' she said. 'There can be no more doubt. It has begun. Soon Fendarl himself will quit the mountains and dare to come here. Who shall withstand him? Who can cast him out? What will become of the Starlit Land? What I have seen is the first stroke, the first spear-cast; but yet, I fear, not the least telling.'

'What? What did you see?'

'The Kelanat. The Kelanat are massing against us. They have a great army and they will leave their mountains at the Ford of Danamol, and they will bring war into Kedrinh. And it is my own land, it is Rennath, that lies in their path. Blood and death they will bring, and worse; for though they know it not they are but driven by Fendarl's servants. Evil will enter with them as a charioteer in a chariot. Oh, we did not fear anything from them! They have no part in this!'

'Who are the Kelanat?' said Nicholas, 'Why are they against you?'

'Are they bad?' asked his sister.

'No, they are not bad,' sighed the Princess, 'but they are not wise. They see only one thing at a time. They are a people of farmers who live in the mountains, simple and honest enough but lacking wit. They have no great bent to follow evil, but neither have they any great virtue in them to resist it. Indeed, often they do not even recognize it. Why are they against us? I do not doubt they could tell you reasons. I do not doubt their masters have made sore old wrongs or given new ones. Or maybe it is only that they think while we are troubled among ourselves they may reap some benefit.'

'You mean *steal* from you?' cried Penelope.

'That is the other way to say it.'

'But I thought you said they were honest, they weren't bad!'

'Bad they are not. They are just not very good either. As to honest, very few Kelanat would steal on their own, but they somehow feel that things which are wrong when one man does them are not wrong when many do them together. What is this?'

Her voice sharpened suddenly; and they saw why. For as they turned the next corner they were met by a wall of mist. Dim and grey the path continued. The Princess looked right

and left, but there were no other paths. She looked back, and
hesitated a moment; but even as she paused the mist crept by
them and began to dim the way behind them. She looked
forward again, and her face was troubled.

'This may be natural,' she said, 'It just barely may. But oh,
by the shrinking of my heart, I fear not!'

She held them more firmly and drew them closer to her.
'Now at least you need not hurry,' she told them, trying to
smile. 'We will go slowly, carefully. I must not miss the way.
Anyway, perchance it is only meant to slow us.'

Nicholas doubted it. Penelope did not really believe it. But
they could not go back, so they both tried to make their steps
down into the haze as firm as they could.

More quickly than they would have thought possible, it
thickened pale about them. Greyly damp, it hung their hair
with diamonds and chilled through their clothes more depressingly than the fiercest cold. It was thicker than they had
expected; Nicholas on one side of In'serinna could barely see
Penelope on the other. The Princess seemed able to see a
little better, but they went slowly, a few steps at a time, her
peering about them. Sometimes they would stand stock still,
and they would feel her searching, although not even her
eyes moved. It was as though she turned some beam in her
brain back and forth, probing through the blind day.

A few steps, then stop. Then a few more. Then wait. A
grey cell walked with them and silence cloaked them. Nicholas was no coward, but after a time he began to feel the
panic of the trapped, to have the wild fancy one moment
that they had not moved at all, and the next to feel just as
desperately that their friends were there, only yards away,
not more than a few steps, only hidden in the fog. He hated
with a sudden intensity the quiet. He wanted to yell and
scream and stamp his feet just to shatter it. He longed to
run. If the Princess had not held his hand he might have
done so—that was what he wanted, to run fighting into the
mist. He took a hold on himself, and began to draw long
shudders of breath, forcing himself to stillness, terrified lest
he lose control of himself and make it worse for the others.

Penelope was less racked. She was cold and she was frightened, but fear made her miserable, not panicky. She was one
not to flee, but to freeze, in fear; so to stand cold and shivering was all she could think of to do anyway. Besides, she had

put her trust in the Princess, and where Penny trusted she trusted implicitly.

They had been going on in this way for perhaps half an hour, when the Princess first looked about with the sharpening of despair in her eyes. 'Heaven forfend,' she murmured, 'that I should lead you to disaster.'

'Are we wrong?' whispered Penelope. Nicholas swallowed and was dumb.

'I do not know. I hope not. Come this way. Oh, a curse on this mist! Oh, for a wind, a wind!'

They went again, and after a few minutes In'serinna breathed a hopeful 'Ah!' and they went on more swiftly and confidently for a while. Nicholas' spirits began to rise, and Penny grew quite cheerful—until the Princess stopped so suddenly that she jerked on their arms.

They turned to her in surprise at first, but one look at her face and dread killed all surprise. She was looking through the mist, it seemed to them, but plainly there was something there to see, for now her eyes held despair indeed.

'Oh children,' she whispered, 'oh children, I beg your pardon. I have led you all amiss.'

As she spoke, the mist seemed to break and thin away; and looking in spite of themselves, they saw them. A horror stole over them. They felt rather than saw them; but there they stood on all sides, still and forbidding. They were at the mountain's foot, the walls of rock were no longer close about, there was room to move; but now numb, cold terror chained them.

Penelope gave a little whimper. And at that the Princess seemed to find new strength.

She dropped their hands, and thrust each of the children in the back. 'Run!' she commanded. They started uncertainly, and she cried more urgently 'Run! Stay not for me, nor for one another! Flee for your lives! One of us *must* escape!'

Then there was a movement in the waiting figures. She gave them another, harder, push, picked up her skirts and darted away.

The stunned moment was over. Penelope's fear suddenly tore at her, and Nicholas gave way at last to his longing to flee. He heard Penny give a high cry behind him, and calling out to her leapt forward. Something lunged at him. He darted aside then dodged another and swerved from a third, yelling all the while. The mist was definitely parting. He could have seen his way, but he did not look. A true panic filled him, a madness of the gods, and he did not feel his feet striking the ground.

The Princess had drawn the main pursuit after herself, but there were enough left to capture them. Nicholas had hold of his sister's arm, then it was gone again, though he felt her behind him. Then he saw a slope swell up before him, and leapt at it. It was a scree of large but loose stones; twice his feet plunged into them, and the third bound brought him to the top. Before him a firm path stretched away; he heard one of his pursuers give a yell of anger and, laughing breathlessly, turned back to wait for Penelope.

She had come also to the slope and, trying to follow him, sprang at it. But her legs were shorter and hampered with skirts, her leap was ill-judged and fell short, and the stones were disturbed already. She struggled halfway up with them rustling under her feet, then they gave way and slid down, taking her with them. She clutched at them with her hands and screamed. Nicholas, turning, saw in horror her slithering down and Them coming, and turned back. 'Penny!' he shouted, 'Pen!' But she cried, 'Run, Nicky! Run! Run! Get away!' and picking herself up veered away on another path.

For a second Nicholas wavered between fear for his sister and fear for himself, between the shame of fleeing and the uselessness of going back; until he seemed to hear again the Princess say 'Stay not for one another; one of us *must* escape!' And then the frozen second was over and one of the monsters was scrabbling at the foot of the slope, and return was impossible. Nicholas turned, and sprang down the far slope.

Chapter Eight

The Wind Among the Grasses

Oliver Powell was gone.

In a very short time, he would not even have recognized that name readily. Li'vanh was his name, and he also came to know himself by others. Tuvoi, the Chosen One, was he to Yorn and most of the men; Prachoi, Favoured One, to the rest, and the women. Few called him merely Li'vanh. They stood too much in awe of him.

He had forgotten, at last, without even realizing it. Unless he struggled hard against them, the mists came swiftly to cover all the time before he came to the plains, and he soon ceased to remember that there had ever been such a time, bound every day closer into the life of the Hurnei. He no longer feared to lose himself in forgetting; rather it seemed that every hour he was discovering more of himself.

The day after Dur'chai's arrival they had taken him to Derna the weapon master, to see what skill in arms he had. Derna had stared at him impassively while Silinoi had talked, and Oliver, though his stomach had worked itself into a cold knot of nerves, had looked back with his own expression betraying nothing. Already he wore a Khentor face, inscrutable eyes and mouth settled in silence.

Derna had made no attempt to teach him. He had merely given him a weapon to defend himself and then attacked him. Oliver was awkward at first. He felt that they were playing like children, was hideously embarrassed, and wished fervently that Mneri had stayed away. To look foolish before Mnorh was one thing; to look foolish before Mnorh's sister was, he felt, quite another.

Then slowly he began to forget himself. A rhythm began to emerge, and to make sense to him. He was filled with a

cool delight in the way in which his mind and body blent, all
bent to one purpose, to keep the glancing metal from his
flesh. His head felt light and clear. It seemed he was transformed into what was only a greater weapon, no more than
the brain of the striking arm, a limb of destruction. All his
attention was bent on his opponent, watching and judging,
hearing only the ring of bronze, his mind oddly unclouded by
fear. He did not feel noticeably that it was a sham fight.
There was nothing unreal about the glittering edge of Derna's
weapon slicing the air by him, and several times only a twist
of his body saved him from bloodshed. It was real enough to
be headily dangerous, yet he knew that neither of them
wished the other any harm. It was battle without malice, and
he loved it.

After, he had stood, cruelly roused from his trance, await-
ing the judgement. He prickled with heat, he was out of
breath, and his arm ached. He looked almost fearfully at
Derna, who stood gnawing his moustache. Yorn, Silinoi and
Mnorh all looked at the weapon master also, but Oliver knew
that Mneri's eyes were on him, and that was bad enough.
Then Derna looked at Silinoi, and each read his thought in
the other's eye, and nodded. Derna had walked to Oliver, and
putting his hands on his shoulders gazed at him.

'Horse of bronze, eyes of flint,' he said. 'You are a warrior, young tiger. A warrior in ten thousand.'

It took time to believe. He returned to the words and the
thought at night, savouring them, telling them to the stars—
he soon abandoned his tent. Or lying in the river he repeated
them to himself. 'A warrior, young tiger. A warrior in ten
thousand.' He would laugh, then, for the strangeness of
finding himself so great among them; Chosen One, Favoured
One, the rider of Dur'chai, and a warrior in ten thousand. He
remembered how they had been impressed to hear that his
old name meant Crowned Victor; omens had been set on him
at birth, they declared. He had laughed in disbelief but all
the same, a chill had touched him. Was it possible? Were
men fated?

Within one course of the moon he forgot that he had ever
doubted it. Fatalism came, with all the other lessons which
hid Oliver, the crowned victor, within Li'vanh, which means
the Young Tiger. He stopped calling it coincidence, that
there had been a meaning in their mispronunciation of his

name. He became what they called him, one of them,
Li'vanh of the Hurnei.

He rarely noticed that he changed. It was not only that
Dur'chai's back was home to him, that he would not have
slept within walls for silver, that he spoke little, not only the
lessons, the fighting, the herding, the dancing; not even that
he *would* willingly stand up with the other men and dance.
Beneath it all lay the fact that he was one of the men. So
they regarded him, so he was to them, and not a boy. It was
true enough that in years he was the equal of many men, and
in height the equal of most—but it seemed that Dur'chai had
chiefly decided the matter. Dur'chai was a horse, a re-davel.
Boys rode ponies: to win their manhood they must go alone
into the plain and return with a horse. As those who had sent
Oliver a mount had sent him a horse, they plainly regarded
him as a man. He had a man's part to fill, and scarcely
knowing he changed to fill it.

One thing which he did notice was his voice: before, it had
been breaking, but it suddenly settled, deep and true—deeper
than his father's, only he did not remember that. Silinoi, who
had stood before the council fire and given him his spears
claiming him as his own blood, Silinoi was his father, and
beside Silinoi's bass rumble his baritone was light. His beard
grew faster, too, and instead of shaving with much pride
every two or three days he shaved daily and thought nothing
of it. Shaved his beard, at least. Only a few of the very old
men grew their beards, but as soon as a boy cut off his
pigtail he grew his moustache, and so did Oliver. In other
ways he changed physically. He ate less and slept less, and
soon did not notice the cold. He grew a very little more, and
put on some more muscle. Also he went brown, which
amazed and amused his friends highly. They, though they
went half bare almost all the time, never changed colour. He
wished he had not tanned. Never seeing his own face, never
seeing any face that was not slant eyes dark beneath a cap
of black hair, high cheeked and small nosed, with a proud
sombre mouth, he forgot that he did not look like them. The
changing of his skin was something that marked him out
from them, and it both hurt and angered him. He saw beauty
as all else, through the eyes of a plainsman. Mneri, though he
thought her pretty enough, no longer seemed a beauty to
him.

Mneri was a dancer Mnorh, to Oliver's surprise, proved to be a poet. After a hunt it was their custom to honour the spirits of the dead animals, which he thought touching but rather amusing before he had seen it, and nothing of the sort after. The carcases were flayed, and the whole skins with the heads set up on poles, before the Tent of the God. They worshipped many gods—the only thing in which Li'vanh refused to join them, holding out against their protests hot with apology, defiance, and embarrassment; they were surprised, and even more surprised when Yorn supported him, but they accepted it at last. They had Nadiv the Great Mother, Ja'nanh the King of Heaven, Ir'nanh the Dancing Boy, Keriol Hornblower, Marenkalion whom they regarded as Li'vanh's patron, and Avenel, Goddess of the Silver Moon; but whenever they just said 'the God', they meant Kem'nanh. Kem'nanh was theirs; they were Kem'nanh's. He was king of the wind, the plains, the sea, horses, men—anything fierce and free, anything Khentor. It was he whom, hailing him as Lord of Herds, they would thank in song and dance for their good hunting, for the game driven towards their spears. Then after the thanksgiving the hunters would stand forth, and act the story of the hunt. It surprised him, the first time, that they told little about their own part; their praise they lavished on their quarry, telling how cunningly it had evaded them, how cleverly it kept watch, how only with the help of Kem'nanh the Hunter had it been killed. Then the women came out and they amazed him more, for they danced slowly towards the mounted skins with their hands spread beseechingly, and begged the dead animals' forgiveness. They had only hunted them because they must, they pleaded; their gifts would not be wasted.

After that, they would burn some of the body in the fire, as they would with their own dead, to free the soul; and usually that was the end. But at the first of these 'funerals' that Oliver saw, at this point Mnorh stepped forward and began to sing. He sang how the animals would be rewarded for their self-sacrifice, for they had not died as others died. They had had their earthly life cut short so that others might eat, and in recompense they were already reborn into Kem'-nanh's great plain, where they would roam for ever in the full splendour of their prime, knowing neither age nor weariness nor fear of the hunter, immortal and glorious. They had died for the sake of others, which was the royal sacrifice; and so like slain kings they were rewarded, and honour and triumph were their due.

Such was the content; but the language pierced Li'vanh with its beauty and something in the certainty, the faith, stung his eyes. He truly felt grief for the dead beasts, but led through it and freed of it. When Mnorh came back to his place, he asked whether they sang that song every time, whether it was very old, praising its beauty; and the boy did not know where to look, his face afire with pleasure and dismay.

Nor was this ceremony merely ceremony, as he saw later; but before that the tribe had moved.

He had heard of course that they were wanderers. He would probably have guessed anyway, from the tents and the wagons. But it had not meant very much to him. He had listened to them talking at the evening fire of the state of the grazing. He had seen the mighty horse grazing among his mares, the bearer of the title of King which they gave to no man, and saluted the horse too and taken him pungent herbs and licks of salt. Yet all these things did not make a whole, until one evening, halfway through the telling of a story, the air was torn by a terrible scream.

His flesh nearly started from his bones and he leapt to his feet, seizing, already by instinct, his spear. All around men stood poised and tense, waiting for it to come again.

An instant later it ripped at them again, and that time he recognized it. Somewhere out in the herds a horse was screaming, a sound to loosen the teeth and set the feet running; yet not a scream of pain or fear, but anger and impatience.

'It is the Dhalev,' said a quiet voice, 'The King.'

The tension was broken; everybody stirred and a small group of men ran off towards the herds. Silinoi rose and walked over to the Tent of the God. Before it the tribal banner hung, a long banner mounted on an upright and a crosspiece. The fringes which trailed from its point were knotted about the staff. He pulled them loose. The banner quivered, shook, hesitated, then gave a flap and streamed out down the night wind. A ripple went through the people, and a sigh.

'What does it mean?' asked Oliver, though he felt in his heart that he knew.

'The King Horse has spoken,' answered Mnorh, 'We must strike camp.'

The following morning early they broke camp. It gave Li'vanh rather an odd feeling to see the tents which had been in their places since he arrived—that is, for all of his Khentor lifetime—billowing to the ground, their shapes gone, changing before his eyes into mere bundles of folded leather. The fires were out: the circled wagons which had limited and shaped their transient setttlement were trailing out into lines. The herds, instead of being scattered over the surrounding grassland, were gathered for driving, milling, and casting up dust, making a continual undertone of lowing, bleating, and the wilder noises of horses. Those lanes and alleys between tents, those back doubles to the river or the wrestling ground, he had known them as well as he had known the streets of his home town; and in less than a morning they were utterly gone. For a while he felt how far, how very far he still was from the Khentorei, and understood much about them which he had not understood, until then. How little they cared for possessions, since they could not own anything more than they could carry with them; their restless moodiness, the driving energy fiercely leashed in their dances, the aching yearning in their songs, their passionate devotion to their tribe. They were rootless. Any ties they had held them not down, but together.

Also for the first time he began to understand their treatment of their women. On the trail the wagons were in a triple line, driven by the women. The men divided the work of droving and roaming up and down the column to guard it. They were armed and mobile; their women were utterly helpless, tied to the slow-moving wagons filled with their children and their homes. At night they slept in the wagons, but the men did not sleep, patrolling against prowling wild animals—Oliver was himself one of a group which drove off a small band of wolves. To a nomadic people on the move the women were no more than baggage, completely dependent on the men. He understood how the girls who were at the moment riding their ponies with the men could turn almost overnight from the wild, headstrong tomboys they

were to the silent, obedient, unobtrusive women—as soon as
they were tied to a wagon.

Imagine Mneri like that, he thought, laughing; and then
looked troubled. Mneri would be like that soon enough; and
yet not soon enough for her. She had given up fighting her
brother when he said mockingly that she was growing up—
she had given up fighting her brother. Mnorh was loud in his
surprise, Silinoi sighed, and Oliver was silent. For he had
begun to realize that although he still thought of himself as a
boy, Mnorh's sister saw him as a man. If Mnorh asked her to
fetch something she would still tell him scornfully to get it
himself, but she would wait on Oliver unasked, silently,
almost unnoticed; and sometimes as the weeks passed he
would feel her eyes on him, not with their original bright
friendly interest, but with a new look, dark and thoughtful,
which he did not understand and did not wish to understand.
So he would call her little sister then, and laugh at her
determinedly, and ask how her archery went; and she would
toss her hair and laugh defiantly and become a hoyden again
for a while: but he had seen the puzzled hurt in her eyes, and
his heart sank.

They travelled for four days. This was no choice of theirs,
but the dictate of the Dhalev who led them. He was released
and his herd loosed after him, and then the tribe followed,
Silinoi bearing their banner before them. The horse chose
their new camping place where there was grass and water in
plenty, and where he stopped they stopped.

The new camp was much farther north, but the spring had
advanced with them, so save that the river was nearer its
source and more chilled with snow they noticed little difference.

They moved once after that, and it was at the third camp,
farther north yet, that he saw how seriously they took their
code of hunting. One of the tribesmen had been found to be
killing animals he did not need.

There were two methods of punishment. One was physical:
a man would be beaten, which was shaming, as there were
few things that were private in a Khentor camp. But this
man was to suffer the other, far more serious penalty.

They stood him before the council fire, and the men stood
round in a circle, cutting off the women. They stripped him
of all his trophies, all his hard-won honours, even his brow-

band embroidered with the mark of the Hurnei, in a dreadful implacable silence. Three spears lay at Silinoi's feet; the spear this man had been given when he became a man, the spear he had given his wife's father, and the spear he had given his brother-in-blood. Yorn for once had no smile. Silinoi's face was grim, and he named the crimes of which the man had been found guilty. He had twice killed a doe in fawn, twice animals less than a year old, and had even killed more than he could carry back, and left the others on the plain to rot. The chieftain repeated to him the law of laws of which he had broken: 'Accursed be the man who kills without need'—and cried that because of him the whole tribe might have been put under a curse. He had sinned against the tribe; he had sinned against the Laws of Mor'anh; he had sinned against Kem'nanh. Had he any excuse?

The man jerked his head twice, to mean no. His eyes were wide and wild, but set. His face was taut, his mouth hard. Oliver shuddered, wondering what he feared.

There was a moment's quiet. High above them a hunting falcon screamed twice. Somewhere a small doomed animal cowered.

'Hran, son of Der'inh, of the Hurnei!' cried Silinoi, and the man's eyes lit with a strange strained hunger. The chieftain picked up a spear and broke it across his knee; the sound was sharp and jolting. He threw the pieces into the fire, and the man Hran's eyes followed them desperately. 'Hunt evermore alone!' cried Silinoi, and another spear snapped. 'Call yourself no more Hran son of Der'inh; you have no kindred! Call yourself no more Hran of the Hurnei; you have no tribe! As one of the dead are you to us, or as one unborn. Neither brother nor friend have you, and no place at the fire. Leave us and never return, Hran the Outcast!'

The last spear broke, and the fire received it. The man's mouth jerked, but he said nothing. Yorn stepped forward, a knife in his hand. He cut off a lock of the outcast's hair and dropped it into the fire, to show he was dead and gone to them. Then he made a short slanting cut in his forehead, to mark him out, and turned away.

The man stood still for a moment, the bright blood streaking his face, then slowly, stiffly, looked from side to side. Behind him lay all he could take with him: his saddle, weapons, waterbag, and such essentials. He bent and gathered them up, then looked dazedly about him. The men opened the circle for him, and he walked stiffly and unsteadily out and away, towards his horse. From among the women came sudden wild weeping; it was his wife, who had now to choose between taking her four young children out of the protection of the tribe, or forsaking her man.

Oliver found that his skin was clammy and he was trembling. The circle broke up and the men looked at each other, white and silent. No one spoke, but they held together in groups, valuing each other more, each remembering the marked brow and the look in the eyes of their one-time brother as he left them. He was young, he was strong, he could fend for himself. He would not die; but a man who was cast out of the tribe was cast out of life.

Oliver was shaken and chilled. It was a grey day, the sky tumbling with clouds; but that was not the cold wind which he felt. Alone, he thought; out-cast. He looked at the spearheads glowing red in the fire. In this vast land what was one man? Where was he without his tribe about him?

He felt like a child who has played long in the sunlight at a cave's mouth, and suddenly hears from within it a bear's snarling, I never saw the harsh side before, he thought. Now the game is over. Now they have done with treating me gently.

Chapter Nine

The Daughter of the Stars

When Penelope felt the fingers like stone close on her shoulder she screamed once, shrilly and wildly, then bit her tongue hard. She felt sick and blind with terror. Her captor turned her roughly round and marched her back along the path, too fast for her, so that she slipped and stumbled, but did not fall, for the terrible grip on her shoulder never slackened. She felt her eyes burning and her throat jerking in sobs. She wanted to scream 'Help, help, help!' but could not even cry out, so tightly did fear lock her throat. And besides, there was no one to help: even Nicholas was gone.

Then her guard pushed her around a corner, and before her she saw the Princess.

She too was a prisoner; four of the monsters stood around her, with weapons drawn. Yet all the same Penelope felt a sudden leap of joy, as if everything would be put right now, and a sharp relieved cry escaped her. Not for nothing was she called In'serinna, 'gladness of heart.'

She looked at the little girl, and then at the creature who held her. There was a cold blaze in her eyes, and a new sternness to her mouth. 'Filth,' she said, contemptuous, 'take your hands from her!'

Scarcely believing, Penelope felt the fingers slacken, hesitate, then let go. With a wail she sprang away from him and flung herself against the young woman, burying her face in her skirt, so that she need no longer see the men who were not men, the almost human faces whose eyes did not show a human soul. She uttered a few sobs then quietened herself. The Princess did not seem afraid; well, she could be brave too—she hoped.

In'serinna held her close for a moment, defying their

captors to come nearer, then lifted Penelope's face. 'Come, sweetheart,' she said sadly, 'There is no help for it, we must go with them. And that is my fault, and I cry you pardon me for it. But now let us bear ourselves bravely, and show them scorn.'

Penelope shuddered once, then gulped and raised her head. 'Like Grandad Powell says,' she said huskily, 'Shame the Devil.'

The Princess laughed, but she sounded troubled. 'A good saying,' she said, 'but now, I fear, all too true.' She took Penelope's hand, and the creatures formed a hollow square about them. They began to ascend a mountain path.

'Why?' whispered the girl. 'Are these—you know—that one you said—are they his lot? That—er—wizard.'

'I think so, though I do not think—I *hope*—we are not going to meet him. He has his allies here, his descendants; I think we are being taken to the chief of them.'

'Oh!' said Penny, not very encouraged, then 'What—what do you think will happen to us?'

'To you, nothing,' replied the Princess grimly, 'Not while *I* have any power—and I have a goodly amount, Penelope. No, it is for your brother I fear most. For your brother, and my father's kingdom. Who now will warn them? They will never fear an attack from the Kelanat.' She shook her head suddenly, and tossing back her hair looked up at the diamonded sky. 'Marenkalion!' she cried, 'Shining Ones! Come to our aid!'

Her voice rang off the mountains, echoing from side to side, then died into silence. She sighed, took Penelope's hand again, and walked on.

Their path twisted round the mountain's flanks and dipped across valleys. The way was very long. Night deepened around them, night and another shadow. It seemed to Penny that the air became thicker, greyer, like a film on her eyes. She thought, 'It's because I'm tired,' and blinked and rubbed her eyes, but it did not pass. She turned to ask the Princess what it might be; and caught her breath in wonder. Around her, there was no dull shadow, but a faint, soft glimmer of light, so soft it was hardly more than a clearing of the air: yet it *was* more than that. A halo faint and frail as starlight clung to her, and for the first time Penelope really believed that she was an enchantress.

The journey seemed to go on for hours. Penelope began to stumble, and when their captors made to prod her on In'serinna turned on them fiercely. 'She is tired, you fools!' she raged, 'And she is only a child! She can do no more!' So they drew back, for they were afraid of her, and she bent down and gathered Penny into her arms as if she were no more than an infant.

Penelope was woken, there was no knowing how much later, by some sound that had frightened her in her sleep; but by the time she had struggled over the border of wakefulness it was gone. She jerked up in the Princess's arms, looking about, muttering on the edge of speech, then looked at her protectress.

'What was it?'

'You will see,' she replied. 'Do you mind walking, now?'

'Oh, of course not!' said Penelope contritely. 'How long have you been carrying me? I am sorry.'

She smiled a little, and shook her head. 'Not too long; but I think we may have to do some steep walking in a moment. There lies our path.'

They were going down a mountainside. Across a narrow valley lay the most massive mountain yet, darkening nearly all the sky. Yet there was something a little different about its shadow; it took Penelope a few minutes to see that its slopes were covered with trees, and her heart leapt.

'Trees!' she gasped, 'Real trees! They are the first ones I've seen on this mountain at all—oh, except for the ones at that place. Is this better, then?'

'We shall see. Among those trees, I believe, goes our path. You may judge then for yourself.'

Down they went. Penelope had thought that the valley would be easier than the treacherous rock paths glazed with ice, but it was drifted deep with snow and proved to be hardest of all. Weary as she was it was a struggle to force a way through, or else to pick her feet up high enough to step over it. Earlier she had been thankful for the enfolding warmth of the Harani clothes. Now she noticed only their weight and the way they hampered her legs. Once she slipped and fell into a snowdrift; the guards just stood and waited, not helping, but she was glad of that. She could not have borne those hard cold hands upon her. In'serinna helped her up and brushed the snow from her. Penny shook her skirts and tried to laugh, but in truth she had never felt nearer to tears. She was so cold, and so tired; and so afraid.

They began the climb up the other side. In one way it was easier; there was less snow and the ground was not quite bare rock. It was covered in most places by a blanket of earth which felt like cushions to their bruised and aching feet. But with every step dread weighed more heavily; and the darkness which was not night, which had been deepening steadily all their way, seemed to grow very thick. Now the Princess's halo was clearly more than a mere purity of the air about her: it was very obviously a faint light, a shimmering silver aureole, as if a young star walked the earth. Penelope clung to her hand and stayed very close to her side.

They were being taken up a gully, a road with high-banked walls on either side; it did not look entirely natural. On one side the mountain stood high above them; on the other side the dark fir trees leaned over.

'Do you think we're nearly there?' whispered Penelope, 'This looks like . . .'

She stopped. A freezing wail came down the wind which had suddenly risen, and died into wild, great sobs. Penny froze where she stood. A moan came next, and a shriek, vast noises, too much for a human throat, filling all the night, and suddenly the air was in agony with them, sighs and weeping, groaning and howling, every sound of grief and pain that man had ever heard of uttered, lamenting down the wind.

Penelope stood stock still, stiff, her head down. She felt a wave of sickness rising and bit hard on her lips. She clenched her hands until her palms hurt, and tried not to scream or run. Her eyes stung with tears. 'I can't go any farther,' she thought. 'Not even if they hit me. Not until it stops.'

She felt the Princess's arm around her shoulders and turned her pleading eyes up to her face. The young woman looked at her compassionately. 'It is not as bad as it sounds,' she said. 'I have heard of this place. Come on a little and see. Do not give way now. There, that is better. Yes, I have been told stories of this. This is Kuniuk Bannoth, which is sometimes called Kuniuk dol Rathen, Castle Lamentation. It is no living throat which cries out like this—look!' She pointed. They had reached a turn in the path, and before them it ran up to a crest. Beside the path, mounted on a height of rock, stood a castle. Black were the stones of the castle walls, and its windows were lit with no friendly light. About it the wind wailed like a lost soul. And on the battlements—Penny blinked. The battlements were uneven with strange shapes—funnels, pipes, stone horns, turned all ways, so that the wind passing over them woke a fell music.

'How horrible!' Her voice was husky but indignant. 'Did *he* do that? Just to frighten people?'

'No, no. This was done long, long ago, before the time of Fendarl, by Fendarl's grandfather. His wife died young, and he built those instruments because a mortal voice was too weak for his grief. Even her home wept for her, and he forsook it, because he could not bear to stay without her. So however slight the wind, Kuniuk dol Rathen always weeps, lamenting its lost lady. Well may it weep! He was a noble man but his descendants were not, and it is through their evil art that the stones have grown black which were once silver-grey, and now the home of the great House of Kendreth has cause to grieve indeed!'

The wind sobbed twice more, and died for a moment in a vast sigh. Their captors thrust them, and they wearily moved forward again.

But after all it seemed all too soon that the great gate-house loomed over them, and the icy flags of the courtyard were under their feet.

There was something even more crushing in being at last within the walls of their enemy's stronghold. Penelope felt hope bid her farewell at the gate, and even the Princess's halo seemed dimmed.

Across the court they walked, and through a dreadful guarded door, and a passage like a dark throat lay before them. So they were driven on, the child and the shimmering enchantress, farther into the heart of Kuniuk Bannoth.

Penny felt as though she had passed right through fear and out on to the other side. All there was left was something small, still, and miserable where her heart had been; and every time she thought of Nicholas, or the Harani they had left behind, or Black Enchanters, she felt it become stiller and smaller. In'serinna walked along with her head up and her back straight, with nothing to betray her bleak despair.

They arrived before another door, huge, studded with dark metal, and every stud was an eagle's head. Penelope kept her eyes on them, so that she did not have to look at the guards.

All the eagles eyes were coloured red, and every beak was sharpened. She shivered, and was more than ever glad that she had not watched the battle.

The door opened. The Princess put a hand on her shoulder, and from behind there was a harsh command. They stepped forward.

The room which they entered was plainly the Great Hall. The raftered ceiling was high above them, and from the walls poles thrust out into the room. In better days they would have been hung with banners. About three-quarters of the way down the hall was a bench. The walls were lined with soldiers. At the very end of the hall was a dais. On this there was a throne.

Penelope and the Princess were led to the bench. It was hard and uneven. Also, being stone, it was cold. But Penny, folding gratefully on to it, thought it the most comfortable seat she had evern known. She rubbed her legs, and felt the ache in them grow less, and almost laughed with relief. She turned to the Princess to share this with her, but she was sitting erect and still. No one would guess, thought Penny, that *she* had just walked about fifty miles; then she remembered what the Princess had said: 'Never cold—or hungry—or tired', and shivered a little.

Suddenly the sound of a gong shuddered through the hall and she looked up. More of the creatures came through a door at the far end; but she was slowly learning the trick of stopping her eyes just short of them, and did not notice them quite as much. Then a man came in, climbed on to the dais, and sat on the throne.

He was about as tall as the Princess's kinsmen but even broader, and his legs were short and bowed with the weight of his body. He was dark and grim, and his hair was very long. It fell to his thick waist before and behind. If the length of his legs had matched the rest of him, he would have been a giant indeed. As it was, when seated in the throne he towered frighteningly. He was terrible in a different way from his servants. They were terrible because they were made so; he because he chose.

He curled his fingers around the arms of the throne and smiled at them, a cold and dreadful smile. Penelope swallowed. In'serinna took a firm hold of her hand and stared unflinchingly back.

'Greetings In'serinna, kinswoman,' said the man.

'Greetings also to you, Kunil-Bannoth, no kinsman of mine,' she replied coldly.

'For sure we are kin, madam. All know we have ancestors in common.'

'And all know that the blood of kings is running thin in your veins. I have even heard that the blood of mankind grows weak. Also never think we will admit kinship with any of the servants of your master.'

He laughed. 'Then I greet you as a guest,' he said, 'That greeting at least you may not refuse.'

'Be very sure I would if I could!' she flashed angrily, then bit her lip and looked annoyed. Kunil-Bannoth laughed again.

'Rumour lied of you, In'serinna,' he mocked. 'I heard that your speech was as courteous as your face was fair; but the face is a thousand times fairer. Still, you are welcome to my halls. I have waited long for you to grace them. I am glad indeed to see you here. Long may your life here be.'

Penelope felt the Princess flinch a little; then Kunil-Bannoth spoke to her.

'And you, little one,' he said, his voice as pleasant as it could be made, 'you, I greet as a friend.'

'Friend?' she cried, and almost looked at him. In'serinna tightened her arm about her. 'Take no notice,' she whispered fiercely. 'Do not believe him!'

'Why, yes,' continued the troll king, 'you have been a friend to me. You have helped me. You see, child, we have long wanted the Princess In'serinna within these walls, for three reasons: for her beauty, for her wisdom, and for the great love her father Deron King of Rennath bears her. Now she is here, and the doing is yours.'

'Mine?' whispered Penelope, hardly daring to listen.

'Of course yours. Do you think we could ever have taken her captive alone? No, child, she is too strong for that. Only because you were with her was she taken. Indeed, perhaps it is true to say that she was not caught at all, but only you. We brought you to Kuniuk-Bannoth; In'serinna came with you. Alone, she could have escaped.'

And Penelope bowed her head and hid her face for shame, for it was true, she knew it was true, and it was no use In'serinna saying 'Do not listen,' because that made no difference at all to the fact that she had betrayed her Princess, and she felt her heart would break.

But Kunil-Bannoth laughed again, delighting in his cruelty, and raised his hand. 'Few do so great a thing in all their lives!' he cried, 'Seek not to live longer!'

Penelope saw his hand, the middle finger pointing, and heard him speak; yet lost in her misery she hardly knew what he meant. But the Princess flung up her head, and the green fire leapt again in her eyes, and casting her shawl around Penelope she cried,

'Have a care, spawn of darkness! For prisoner or no, I am one of the Children of the Stars, and you had best think hard before you harm this my friend!' Then she took a deep breath, and summoned her power. 'Anoth ilenu!' she said.

And as she spoke the words of power the glimmer that had clung to her leapt out, huge and bright, to the very walls. Penelope felt a searing, a burning without heat, and was pierced by a wonder like pain. The troll men shrieked and fled back from it. Those caught within the light fell shrivelled, and where it touched the walls and floor they were again soft silver-grey. Then the flash sank back, to form a globe of clear silver light, in the centre of which sat In'serinna and her charge.

The troll king had started back and flung up an arm to shield his eyes, though the light did not seem fierce to Penelope. He bit his lip and glared at the Princess.

'Try now to reach us with curses,' she said, 'Or see which of your creatures is hardy enough to approach us. None may pass these walls of star-glow and live, and well they know it.'

'A cast weapon may!'

'Yes, it may—but before you seek the child's hurt, be warned of this. I also can make a weapon for throwing of this star-glow—a weapon that cannot miss. If you would live, Kunil-Bannoth, guard your prisoner's life well.'

For a moment he stared at her, his mockery consumed in a rage of hate, plainly groping for a way to strike at her. Then he spun on his heel, turning his back to them.

'Take them away!' he shouted.

Only one or two of his servants moved forward, and they hesitantly. But In'serinna rose to her feet, drawing Penelope with her, and went proudly through the door. Then their captors took courage a little and harried them through the corridors, though they never came too close. To a tower room they drove them and there locked them in. Cold it was and bare; all the furnishing it had was sparse straw upon the floor. Yet, being free of Kunil-Bannoth and his subjects it seemed very fair to them.

They raked the straw into one heap and sat down where the moon's light fell, huddled close for warmth. The Princess sighed, leaning her head against the wall, and closed her eyes. Then she opened them and turned to Penelope.

'How are you? Have you taken any hurt of my star-glow? I am sorry to have been brought to it, for it is perilous to mortals.'

'I feel all right. It did sting a bit, but only for a minute. It felt a bit funny though, sort of hot and cold at the same time.'

'Then that is well; and well, too, I think, that you are so young. A little older, and I think you could not have endured it scatheless."

She sighed again, and brushed at her hair. Penny looked at her in sympathy.

'What's the matter? Are you still worrying about your father? Perhaps they will know. Someone might tell them, or they might see it too.'

'Indeed they may, and I pray they do. But that is not all. Wars are won by numbers as well as valour, and brave as my people may be, they are few. We need allies: warriors of might in plenty. We need our friends, and they do not know.' She raised her voice in anguish. 'We need the Khentorei: and they will not come. They will not come!'

Chapter Ten

Through the Glittering Desert

Nicholas ran.

Once, just after he fled, he heard Penelope scream again; and fear, which had until then been half heady and half unreal, rose sickly in his throat. He set his teeth in his lower lip, stretched his legs, and ran.

The sounds of pursuit, hideously near at first, grew fainter, and farther, and ceased at last; but he did not notice. For though he had escaped the thing he feared, the fear itself he could not out-distance. That he bore with him, like a crow on his shoulder. Indeed it seemed to swell and darken with each stride, a huge cloud groping just behind him, and he fled in a blind panic terror.

Nicholas ran.

The mist soon thinned away, but that proved little help for now the day was blind with whirling snow. He had no idea of his direction. The stony ground was uneven; one time it would seem to rise up at him and his foot would strike it unexpectedly soon and hard, another time it sank from him and his stomach would lurch and his head giddy as his foot plunged an extra four sickening inches. But always it was slippery, flinging him first to one side and then to the other, and always it was hard, bruising and jarring him at every stride until his teeth, yes, even his brains seemed loose and rattling, and all his bones hurt. And still he ran.

The mountains gave way to meadow land and fell back; but he did not know, only feeling dimly that something of menace and something of shelter was gone. He was floundering now, through blanketing snow, and the wind blew more directly into his face, so that his cheeks were whipped raw; yet he did not slacken his pace. And now to the horror of

darkness and fear was added the torment of pain. His feet
were bruised, his face wind-torn, his finger stabbed with cold;
but pain worse than these was growing in his shoulder, in his
chest, and lodging like a little spiked nut under his arm. His
legs ached to the point of torture. He had bitten both cheek
and tongue. His veins seemed like to burst with his pounding
blood. As he ran he moaned and cried out. But still he ran.

The brief northern day was darkening already into night,
and far above him the fair stars flowered. He paid them no
heed, for the darkness around him was all too full of white
whirling stars; and his eyes were darkening. Yet he was
half-conscious that a more compassionate power was present,
and now the wind suddenly blew less fiercely, and shifted a
little so that it was not quite in his face.

But still he was very wretched, for by now to the torment
of fear and pain had been added the misery of weariness. He
could scarcely be said now to be running. He tottered desperately along, barely able to keep upright. His chest was bursting. His head spun. He ran on with buckling knees, his arms
stretched groping in front of him, his tongue hanging out. His
breath came and went in small harsh croaks. His whole body
cried agonizingly for rest, but unheeded. He no longer had
any will to stop. The motions of his legs, the rise and fall of
his feet, had become mechanical. His body's anguish meant
nothing to his mind. Those things were happening to some
other Nicholas, some machine of blood and bone who must
suffer and be silent, for all Nicholas' consciousness had
shrunk back into his brain, obsessed by the fear of his
pursuers and the chill horror of feeling that he was trapped
in a cage roofed, walled, and floored with white snow,
wherein he struggled and could not move.

Fear held him to the path: fear, and the power of a will
not merely his own. But be fear and will strong as they may,
flesh and blood can bear only so much. At last all his strength
was exhausted and his limbs could bear him up no longer.
With a desolate cry he pitched on his face in the snow.

After a moment, he turned his head to one side; and after
that he did not move for some time. His eyes were black; his
ribs had become a cage of spiked iron against which his heart
hurled itself, and a lance transfixed his left arm. He tried to
breathe because he felt himself choking, then tried not to

because it tore him. His legs ached and trembled, his stomach quaked and churned. The cold began to pierce his overheated body with arrows of ice. He pressed himself down, gasped and whimpered, and waited for it to pass.

At last it did pass. His breathing eased, his eyes cleared, the pain and trembling ebbed, leaving behind only a monumental heartbreaking weariness.

Oh, it was comfortable, lying there, all the contours of the ground rounded and softened by snow. Now that he could hear that the hunt was not on his heels, he had neither the will nor the desire to move. His limbs were like logs of wood; snowflakes began to nest in the curls of his hair. His cloak, spreading out as he fell, covered him from shoulder to ankle, fleecy-warm and beginning to be heavy with settling snow. He really had not the strength to move, he told himself. It was silly to try to pretend he could just get up and go on. . . . His head felt muzzy and heavy. His eyelids drooped. He knew better than to go to sleep in the snow, of course he did! But he would not stop for long . . . just enough to get his strength back. It was so white . . . like pillows, and sheets . . . new soft blankets . . . warm bath-towels. . . . And he was so warm . . . not for long. His pulse slowed. He yawned. Silly, to push yourself. . . . The wind sang low, moaning and crooning; lie still—rest—sleep. . . . He nestled his head on his arm. His eyelashes fluttered and sank to his cheeks. His breath quivered out in a long sigh. He stretched and relaxed. Sleep, sang the voices sleep, sleep. Noise and struggle never come near you, trouble and effort leave you for ever—worry no more, fight no more, come to the place prepared for you, safe in the arms of the White Queen, Ice Queen . . . Great Mother, Cold Mother, Dark Mother. Here is balm, weariness for ever banished, warmth and quiet and rest eternal . . . rest now, wake never . . . sleep, sleep in the snow. . . .

His eyes were closed, his breathing light. His mind was being charmed away into the singing dark. His blood chilled and thickened. His outline began to blur into the snow; soon no one would know a boy lay there. . . .

Nicholas slept.

The wind rose to a last wail, of triumph or grief, and sank. And into the sudden silence came a sound, faint and far but harsh and cold, that pierced the dim clouds and touched his wits. His eyes twitched open and he listened, but could hear nothing more. Still he was uneasy and at last, muttering in annoyance, he dragged himself to his elbow and looked back. . . .

His heart leapt to his throat.

There were three of them, running low over the snow, swift and tireless. Their breath streamed behind them, and their tongues lolled. From nose to tail-tip they were white as curd, but he saw the red blaze of their eyes. Though they were some way behind he could see them, and even hear their snow-muffled footfalls, quite clearly. Then as he watched in fascination the leader flung back his head and loosed his cold, lonely, savage cry on the air.

It was a strange cry, midway between howling and baying. But it was a cry that said, as plain as words, 'There he is!'

Nicholas leapt to his feet with a shout of alarm, and took off like a hare.

He was wide awake now, and wild again with fear. It was no longer a sick, nightmare fear of the horror he had sensed in those figures in the mist, but a very hot, real, down-to-earth fear—fear of hot breath and cold noses, scraping paws, lashing tails, wrinkled snarling muzzles and hard white teeth clashing at his throat. It did not numb and darken the mind as that other fear had done; but it gave wings to the feet.

Nevertheless, he was tired when he began. This flight could not last as long as the other, and very soon he knew it, and his thudding heart came into his mouth with terror. He realized also that they were not merely chasing him, but driving him; bearing steadily to the left. He began to think there was purpose in this; but he dreaded to guess at it. Not that he could spare the thought. There were just two thoughts in his mind: the first that he had to get away, the second that it wasn't *fair*.

The noises of their breath and their running feet began to sound closer and closer behind him, but he put it down to his imagination and refused to look back. Then again that freezing cry rose into the night, and he could not help it, he had to snatch one glance over his shoulder.

At once he wished he had not.

They were running tirelessly, with no sign of strain or

flagging. Only half the original distance lay between them and Nicholas. No, less than that: barely a quarter.

He gasped and groaned, struggling to go faster. The thick snow dragged at his feet as he churned a path through it. Ah, but they drove him hard now. He could feel the heat of their breath and hear their low snarling. He dared not look back. He floundered on, his legs shaking, and his heart failing him for fear and despair. And then at last the end came.

Suddenly before him the ground dropped away. Instinct jerked him back; then thrust him forward again. He dared not go back. He could not go on. He tried to swerve aside; his foot slipped, caught under a stone, and threw him forward. He flung out his arms, and with a bitter reproachful cry toppled over the edge.

It was not a long drop. He landed uninjured on his back and lay with breath knocked from his body, waiting almost gratefully for the end.

Almost in the same second as he landed, they leapt out from the cliff. The three shapes at full stretch soared over him and landed a few yards beyond. He saw now that they were wolves: thick-pelted, lean-flanked, mighty-shouldered, great white wolves. He saw again the blood-red, scarlet blaze of their eyes, and trembled as they touched the ground.

But they did not turn back. On they loped, without a pause or a sound or a break in their pace. He turned to watch them, feeling silly with surprise. They could not have missed him; they could not! Then the leader swung his head back and looked at him, and he knew it was no mistake. Once more the wolf lifted his head and howled, but this time it was different. There was no longer menace in it, but satisfaction.

Then they gathered themselves and made a great spring into the night, and vanished.

He lay staring after them for a few minutes more then shook his head. He was too tired and dazed to think about them. Sleep urged at him but he knew he could not sleep where he lay. Yawning and rubbing his eyes he sat up and looked about him.

A few yards away a jumble of rocks leaned up against the cliff, and he crawled in among them. In there, at least he would not freeze to death. There was no snow at all on them, and they were shelter against the wind. Indeed, for a few minutes he felt almost warm, curled as small as he could inside his thick cloak; and he was asleep before he knew.

The sun on his face awakened him and he tried to stretch. But his rocky nest was too small, so he crawled out and looked about him.

Dawn had not long since broken and the sky was still flushed, lending a little of its colour to the snow, so that its white looked blue in the shadows and faintly pink and gold towards the east. His rock shelter faced east and slightly south; also to the north-east was a twisted bunch of small trees. These had sheltered him from the bitter wind. He scrambled up the rocks until he could see over the cliff edge. Stretching back north-west he could see the unsteady track he had churned through the snow on the previous night, and at the end of it stood Black Mountain, looking an impossible distance behind him. Nicholas would never have dreamed he could travel so far so fast, and looked back with awe. Feeling a new respect for himself he turned and climbed down; then a thought struck him and he clambered back and looked again. There were no animal tracks in the snow.

Standing on firm ground again, he considered what to do. It was of no use, he decided, to stay where he was. No one would come looking for him. Penelope and the Princess were, he presumed, captives. Prince Hairon and the other lords, even assuming they were still safe, would think he was a prisoner too. And they were the only people who knew that he existed.

It was a terrifying thought and for a moment he fought panic, but the moment passed. 'I'll have to keep moving,' he thought, 'and while I'm at it I'll jolly well get as far from that place as I can.' And so as Black Mountain lay directly behind him a little north of west, he began to walk south of east, directly towards the sun.

He knew that he would have to be careful not to turn as the sun turned, but by checking to see that his track kept straight and the Mountain stayed in the same position he steered a fairly consistent course. There was still some food in his pouch from the previous day; he rationed himself carefully, feeling very intrepid and efficient, so that his hun-

ger was at any rate quietened. Drink was his real problem.
He did not have much with him, and had gulped half of it
before he realized that he did not know when he would find
more. He stopped himself, muttering angrily; but what was
gone was gone, and the worst was that his thrist seemed
almost unabated. Resolving not to drink before he positively
must, he pushed the flask behind him and marched forward.

The day was sunny and there was no wind. The sky arched
above him glittering blue and at first Nicholas rejoiced. But
as the time passed he changed his mind. Partly it was because
the air was so clear that however he walked Black Mountain
seemed to stay the same distance away. Partly it was because
he felt so exposed. But mostly it was the cold. It did not
attack him as the blizzard had: there was no need. It was a
still cold, infinitely patient, slow and cruel. For all his boots
and gloves, for all his thick clothes and heavy cloak, he knew
he was helpless against it. He knew that it would eat through
everything he wore, growing on him little by little, steady and
implacable. Around him the snow glittered; if he kicked at it,
the soft snow he overturned had a crust of ice before it had
settled. Remembering something he had read, he spat; and
heard the warm spittle crackling into ice as it touched the
snow. Above him, the limitless crystal heavens sparkled with
cold. He would have given anything for a blanket of cloud.

At mid-day he ate half his remaining food and rested a
little. He dared not stop long, both because of the cold and
because he wanted to get as far as possible: he dreaded to
even think of having no shelter that night.

He felt more and more lonely, and from time to time he
would be overwhelmed with the hopelessness of his plight. He
had a normal appetite for make-believe, but no more. He
could not hide in it for long. Every now and again he would
be swamped with a wave of despair; he was not a spaceman
on the moon, or a cowboy on the prairie, or a daring
explorer. He was Nicholas, a ten-year-old boy who was *really*
lost in the snow desert, with no one even knowing he was lost
and help beyond expectation. And as if that were not bad
enough, he was lost not only in a strange country but in a
strange world. At such moments he would almost succumb to
his aloneness and his fear; but he learned the trick of relaxing
his mind, acting as if it *were* a wave, letting himself be
carried resistless until it broke and dropped him. He went on

doggedly, not with any hope, but because there was no point in doing anything else. 'O.K.,' he thought, 'very likely I'll drop dead sooner or later of starving and cold. But anyhow I'm warmer walking.'

Once he cried a little, but not much. There was no point and anyhow it chapped his face. Then during the afternoon his water ran out. His raging thirst had got the better of him, yet when the water was gone the thirst was unslaked. He tried snow; but when it melted it did not really amount to much liquid, and it made his teeth and throat ache. Then he began to feel really frightened. It was all very well saying to himself, 'Reck'n we'd better go easy on the water, pardner,' but this was real, now. He was desperately thirsty and he had nothing to drink.

He had almost given up, when at last as he came to the top of a rise he saw something other than snow all around. The farthest horizon was uneven, and green.

His heart leapt, then he tried to steady it. He did not know what it was, he told himself. But at least it was not snow. And it might be shelter.

He set off with a new eagerness: so much that, when the next rise obscured his vision, he broke into an awkward run. His cold limbs felt stiff and heavy at first, and he could not keep it up for long; but from then on his plodding was interspersed with short bursts of running. After about half an hour he could see that the green strip was a forest.

His spirit soared, and he gave a faint hoarse cheer. Down the next slope he plunged whooping—cold, weariness and thirst momentarily forgotten. A forest was trees—shelter—most likely a soft place to sleep; almost certainly water. He felt triumphant, elated, lucky almost. In fact looking back, now that he had hope of escape, he was inclined to feel he *had* been lucky. After all he might have taken another direction and never come up against this forest. Or he might have broken his neck when he fell over that cliff, or been eaten by those wolves; and he nearly *had* slept to death in the snow. And it had been a near thing, too, back at Black Mountain. He might easily have been caught, and that would have been terrible. . . .

He stopped. There had been another reason why he had run: not just fear. What was it? Something the Princess had said . . . 'One of us must escape.' He went on again, but slowly, thinking. Why had she said that? Something had been worrying her. . . . Of course! Rennath . . . Kelanat . . . an army invading her home—Danamol—someone to give warning!

He found he was shaking. There's only me, he thought. Only me, who's free and who knows. I'll have to tell someone. It's up to me.

Chapter Eleven

A Wood in Spring

Nicholas squared his shoulders and marched on with renewed determination. He was glad he had remembered his responsibility: the knowledge that his survival was of vital importance to someone else was a comfort. He did not feel quite so alone; and it was pleasant, even at such a time, to feel important.

He soon saw another thing which puzzled him. The forest was green; the trees were not winter trees, all bare black branches, nor did they look like pines. The green was too bright and fresh, and he saw the sun rippling over the tossing leaves. Yet in this harsh winter landscape how came a forest in leaf?

His bouts of running became fewer. For a long time he seemed to make little progress, and his goal stayed depressingly far away. Then suddenly it seemed to rush towards him; every hill-crest brought it bigger and closer. His heart began to thump uncomfortably. Then as he climbed the last hill and saw that only a long slope kept him from the trees excitement swept away his weariness, and he broke into a run.

One moment he was struggling through deep snow, then for a second he was slithering in slush that splashed up at him, then without warning he could see his feet again pounding up a gentle slope of grass, and he was beneath green branches.

He stood dazed and bewildered.

It was spring.

The air was soft around him, and the spreading trees whispered above. The sun came slanting over his shoulders, sending his long shadow among the trees and lying deep gold on the young grass. It was warm on the back of his neck.

Low clusters of pale blue flowers were scattered between the trees, so that in the distance it seemed that the ground lay beneath a soft blue mist. Birdsong filled his ears. The woods quivered with life.

For some time he stood gazing, almost stunned with delight and wonder, then woke a little and began to walk slowly farther in among the trees. He wandered aimlessly, just gazing and breathing, his eyes alight and awed. Perhaps it was the relief of leaving Bannoth's winter behind; but there seemed something specially wonderful about this spring in these woods, as if it were somehow not merely spring but the essence of spring, as if the world had been caught and held forever in the first moments of life's waking. A cloud of garnet butterflies skimmed his head. He glanced up at them startled, then continued to watch in fascination. They were no bigger than his thumbnail; as they danced down one of the paths they drew him charmed behind. Then suddenly they lifted away, up between the branches until he could no longer see them. He peered up after them for a while and then gave up. Suddenly he laughed, for pure lightness of heart. It seemed so long since he had felt like this—at ease, unworried, enjoying, yes, enjoying himself. At the sound of his laughter a quiver ran away among the leaves, as if the forest itself shook a little with inner delight. He hallooed at the green deeps. His voice broke a silence which seemed a hundred years deep—yet he did not feel guilty, nor did he feel that the forest grudged him.

After a while he came to a stream, and then he did remember that he was thirsty. He drank deep of the cold water, then leaned over the edge looking at his shadow on the stones. The water was so clear it looked to be about six inches deep, but when he dipped his hand in his arm would have gone to the shoulder if he had not hurriedly drawn it back. He shook his hand laughing and dried it on his cloak, then whooping took a running jump at the brook and cleared it. A small dark-brown animal sprang away from his feet, squealing 'Aark! Aark!' in almost human cries of startled anger. It looked more like a rabbit than a squirrel, but it shot without hesitation up the trunk of a tree where it hid, scolding and grumbling at him from shelter. He laughed again, and began prowling round the tree imitating it and making every animal noise he could think of until the unfortunate animal was nearly choking with rage.

So intent was he upon this noisy pastime that he did not hear the gathering rustles around and above him. And as he did not look up, neither did he see the forms poised among the branches—not until the tree-rabbit fell silent with disgust and he began to walk away did he see them. For then a figure swung down right into his path.

He stopped short and stood staring. Before him stood—what? A boy? A young man? He was somewhat taller than Nicholas, and very slender. One hand still grasped a bough above him, the other rested on his shining belt, worked of some strange metal. His head and feet were bare and he wore only a short, almost sleeveless tunic, patched and streaked with different greens so that at first Nicholas thought it was stitched of leaves, and only on looking closer saw that it was cloth, of a kind. Brown hair swept back from his brow. His skin was fair, his eyes were a green-gold slanting under winged brows.

In an instant Nicholas saw all this, and before he could speak there were other soft rustles and he saw maybe a dozen beings like the first slipping out of the trees on all sides, coming towards him with a wary, curious grace. Not all were the same: all were youthful and slender, and all had the same air of stillness, but while some were clad as the first others wore long dresses that swept their feet, many had long sleeves to their tunics, and one or two wore only short kilts. Mostly their hair was russet and brown, but there was one whose head was covered in curls the colour of clear honey; another, in a short tunic like woven gossamer, whose hair swirled about her like a silver cloud; and one who was dark as night. All were very fair, and their hair seemed to be lifted by some breeze Nicholas could not feel.

The one with dark hair came through the circle; he seemed to be a lord among them, for a pale shining circlet was around his brows and a silver belt about his waist. His tunic was dark blue, and he spoke to Nicholas without looking him in the eyes.

'Who are you, man-child, who enter Nelimhon, and not by the road?'

Nicholas stood quite still and his voice died. He felt cold

with shock. For though he had heard the words the speaker's mouth had remained closed and silent.

The lord waited a few moments then said again, very courteously, 'Who are you? What brought you here? Who gave you leave to pass? In fashion of dress you are like to the Swan Lords, but never have I heard of Harani with hair like leaves in autumn.' His lips did not move once.

Nicholas fainted.

Coming on top of his hunger, his thirst, his hours of cold, on top of such struggle, such weariness and such fear as he had endured in the last day or so, this strangeness was more than his mind could bear. He crumpled to the grass.

He opened his eyes on green leaves quivering in the last of the sun's light. About him he could feel the concern of the woodfolk, though they were still silent. One of them was supporting his shoulders; it was he who had first dropped from the trees. The dark lord was kneeling by him, holding a flask to his lips: the liquid was sweet and strengthening. Nicholas noticed with relief that their hands, though light, were warm. When they were sure that he was recovered the lord began to speak again, this time with his lips. His speech was a little slow and careful; his voice was like the stream, deep and clear. He still avoided Nicholas' eyes.

'Do not be afraid,' he said, 'I am sorry to have alarmed you. I had forgotten that men speak thus; it is very long since one was here. We are nothing to fear. We are called the Nihaimurh by men. Once we were many, when trees clothed the world; but trees have dwindled and so have we, until only here do we now dwell in numbers. Through men our fall came; wherefore a ban is on men entering Nelimhon unbidden. That is why we came upon you. But truly we mean you no harm, and if we can help you we will.'

Then Nicholas remembered, and 'Kelanat,' he said.

Some of them frowned, and the air seemed to quiver. They looked from one to another. It was then that Nicholas noticed another peculiarity of theirs: the innermost hairs of the eyebrows, the two either side of their nose-bridges, were lengthened, curving back over their brows. Sometimes they would dance a little, pricking at the air.

The Lord of the Nihaimurh looked down again. 'The name you speak is known to us,' he said. 'Tell us what trouble is coming.'

So he told them: all about the Battle of the Eagles, and the Princess's vision, and the invasion of Rennath. 'The Princess said her father's kingdom was in danger,' he ended, 'but no one knows. Oh, if you can do anything, please do, and quickly!'

'Never fear,' came the answer. 'Before tomorrow's sun is high the help they need will be on its way. We know well the Swan Lords; they are a noble people, and lovers of forests, and we are glad to show friendship to them. Him that ruled once on Black Mountain we know too; and he is one that hates every living thing and we hate him. The Nihaimurh are not warriors, but we will bear your news to those that are. The Wind Children we will tell; for they too love the Harani well, and though they do not care for forests they are gentle with wild things. So we do not account them enemies. Go with these folk now, and they will find you a place to rest. Farewell, man-child.'

He turned and walked away, and three of the Nihaimurh followed him. Others helped Nicholas to his feet and began to guide him through the trees. They still avoided meeting his eyes and this annoyed him a little. He began to try to outwit them and catch their eyes, but when he succeeded he wished he had not. For though in face and form they seemed to him like youths and maidens of maybe fifteen summers, their eyes were a thousand years old.

After a while the journey began to seem a little confused. It grew dark slowly. Nicholas' eyes grew heavy. The wood-folk were shy of talking to him, though they were quick to guide him if he did not notice an obstacle. He looked at their bright calm faces, and wondered if they ever slept. The lord had talked of finding him a place to rest, but he suspected that to him 'rest' was only a word whose meaning he did not understand. He stumbled after them, and they stepped unfalteringly on their light tireless feet, but bit by bit he began to drop behind. He did not feel the bitter tiredness of the night before, but he was sleepy. Often his feet faltered, and then he would have to hurry to catch up with the wood-folk. But he never quite caught them before he failed again and stopped to yawn, or just to rub his sticky eyes, and then they drew away again. Several times they stopped to wait for him, but never for quite long enough. Then came a time when Nicholas peering drowsily ahead could not see them. He

listened, but the whole company had made less noise than a
cat on a carpet, and he could not tell which way they had
gone.

'Well, good-bye,' he thought, 'Nice meeting you and all
that, but I've found a place to rest, thanks very much.' And
he lay down at the moss-cushioned root of a tree, and slept
straightaway.

But the Nihaimurh girl with the gossamer hair had lingered, waiting for him. And when she saw him sleep she stole
back, and slipped softly up into the tree, where she sat gazing
down on him. Presently his comrades noticed that he was
missing and the woods quivered to their voiceless call of
dismay, but the long hairs of her brows danced and they
went on reassured. Back to their place they went, whither
they would have taken Nicholas; and so he missed the chance
of going where no mortal had ever been. But nightlong in the
boughs above him watched and guarded the silver-haired girl
with the ageless eyes.

To his sister in Kuniuk Rathen too, sleep had come at last,
after her forced journey and her meeting with her fell host;
though a sleep too often broken by the voices of the castle
and shapes of fear in her mind. But it had not come to the
Princess In'serinna. Weariness had no power to still her
mind, and never had she known more bitterly that this was a
mixed blessing. All the hours of darkness she stood at the
window, watching the stars, weighing their peril. And too
well she knew how great it was: greater than she had dared
tell Penelope.

Again and again she had tried to reach her comrades of
the Star Magic: over and over she had called them, hurling
the power of her mind against the barriers of Kuniuk
Rathen. But it was useless. Fendarl himself had sealed his
fortress behind a wall of spells, thick, dark, and heavy, and
she could not break out. In vain to cry to her kin for help;
she could not reach them. Kiron could break these defences,
and maybe a few others. But they did not know the need.

As a caged animal paces before the bars of its prison,
refusing to believe in defeat, so her mind coursed desperately
back and forth. She knew the reasons for her capture. Firstly
they wanted her power: they hoped to persuade her to help
them—well, they would fail there. She curled her lip scorn-

fully at the thought, and then remembered Penelope and almost groaned. Suppose they threatened her? She clenched her fists and tears stung her eyes. No, not even then, she told herself. I am sorry, little one, not even for you can I help such as these. But while there is breath in me I shall defend you. They will have to kill me before they can harm you; and I do not think they want that.

No, she thought, they wanted her alive. Because if she would not help them herself, still she might be a weapon in their hands. Deron her father, and all his people, loved her dearly. And she was of high blood, first cousin to the High King. At the very least the loss of her power was a blow. At most she could be a valuable hostage.

Willingly she could have cursed Kunil-Bannoth; with all her heart she prayed that none would treat with him for her. She was all but certain they would not, for it was the oldest of their principles, to have no dealings with the evil powers for any cause. But even this certainty, though it gave her bleak satisfaction, was small consolation. For behind the greater fears hid one more: she knew Kunil-Bannoth's mind, and quailed at the knowledge. Aside from the commands of his master he had long watched and waited for a chance to trap her. Not because of her power did he desire her, or because of her royalty, but for her beauty—that she might be his and never again leave his grim home.

She shook her head violently, and struck her knuckles on the stone in anger. I will die rather, she thought; and then remembered Penelope again. She felt that the blame for their plight was her own. If there was anything—anything—she could do to defend the child, she knew she would do it.

There must be another way she thought, and again her mind began its pacing, searching for a gap. By force she could not break out, neither force of arms nor magic. Rescue? There was no hope of it. She could only pray her little escort would not try, for they would certainly be destroyed. An army would be needed to take the castle, and with war at hand an army could not be spared. She leaned out of the window and her glance strayed down the wall. Escape? She did not waste time on the thought. Even if she herself could scale the wall Penelope never could, and while the child stayed she must, to give what protection she could for as long as possible.

For as long as possible . . . and so her mind had come full circle to the heart of her fear. How long would it be possible? Her power was not the same at all times. She had been sent to Black Mountain because her own star was rising; but the Great Dance was never still, and soon, now, soon, her star would sink—and what then? And what of the moons? She raised her eyes to them and her heart chilled. The red moon in Kedrinh is the sorcerer's friend, and the silver moon his foe. From the silver moon she could draw strength—more strength to fight Kunil-Bannoth, more strength to defend Penelope. But they had been full together on the night of the Battle of the Eagles. And though seven-and twenty days is the full cycle of the silver moon, so that in nine nights it would be dark, yet between the full and the dark of the red moon lie thirty-seven nights. So when the silver moon was gone and could not help her, the red moon would still have almost its full strength to lend her enemy.

A chill crept over her and she faced at last the thought she had refused for so long. Was she beaten then? Was there nothing left to do but to die in Kuniuk Bannoth? I have failed in all things, she thought. I have not taken back my tidings and I have brought Penelope to ruin with me. Well then, I will die if I must, but I will not betray my magic.

Proudly she made her vow, but her spirit sank and still her heart rebelled, for she was young and eager for life. A year before she would have said that she hoped for no better end—to die in defence of her magic. But that time was a year gone. Since then she had found many new things in the world, and though her resolve was unchanged she did not want to die. She raised her face to the sky again and stretched out her arms, crying in her strong young voice 'Marenkalion, Shield and Defender! Help us!'

But the night received her call in silence, and leaning against the window she hid her face in her hands. Tears that she had never shed for her own grief until now spilled through her fingers. And the name, formless as a sigh, that she breathed then in a soft agonized voice, no one heard—not even she herself.

Chapter Twelve

The Rising Wind

Li'vanh Tuvoi lay by the river, his eyes closed against the sun. For just over three months now he had been one of the Khentors, though it seemed to him far longer. His brother was travelling strangely companioned far to the north. His sister lay prisoner in Kuniuk Bannoth. Yet little he knew; his frown and set mouth were for another cause.

'By the Spear of Heaven, Mnorh,' he was saying, 'I *will* go on the hunt tomorrow if I have to sit on Rehai's head all night to make him take me! Why won't they let me? Why?' He leaned up on his elbow, looking furiously at Mnorh. 'And if you say once more that he can't take everybody, I'll choke you. He's picked just about every able man and boy in the tribe over and again, but never me. He's even taken *girls*— but not me. Why not?'

'You have not been taught the hunter's skills.'

'Mor'anh!' exploded Li'vanh, 'And neither have half the boys. You took me for quarry once, if I remember, but you've been hunting twice since then . . . at least twice.'

'Well, Li'vanh, they are teaching us.'

'I know they are, bird-brain. Why don't they teach me, that's all I want to know? I don't mind admitting I'm a beginner. Do they think I'm so proud I will demand to lead the hunt? All the same, I don't think I'd be an actual hindrance. With bow or spear, I don't often miss my mark.'

'It's not that, it's the stalking and the . . .'

'I know, I know what it is! All I'm saying is, I'll never know if no one teaches me, will I?'

'Yorn said it was more important to teach you weapon-craft.'

'Yorn said! Yorn said! That's all I ever hear!' Then he

cooled a little, and added rather guiltily, 'Well, no, I didn't mean it like that exactly. But I'm getting tired of just swords and spears every day. Well, not tired, but I'd like to do something else too.'

'Lai-ee! And have you not learned dancing from us, and wrestling, and horse-craft, and . . .'

'Mnorh, be serious! Dancing! And no one ever learned horse-craft except where I learned it—from my horse. All right, all right, I know dancing is worth learning—and wrestling—but that's fighting again. Derna teaches me nothing but war. Which is all very well, but when am I going to use it? Unless Father is thinking of picking a quarrel with one of the tribes, which he wouldn't. But hunting—hunting is *important*.' He tugged moodily at his browband.

'Well, maybe you'll be released before long,' said Mnorh peaceably. 'I heard Derna telling Father that there is not much more he can teach you.'

'Did he?' He was diverted for a moment. 'Truly? What did he say?'

'Only that. And the usual, that you were a great warrior and that sort of thing. Do you really beat him, mostly, now?'

Li'vanh nodded absently, wondering what would happen if Derna really could teach him no more. He moved restlessly. A feeling of faint foreboding came over him again; he felt the coming of some change.

He had not felt comfortable since the out-casting of Hran, five days before. It was as if a chill wind of the spirit had arisen then and not ceased since. He had been uneasy and, he knew, short-tempered for days. Then two nights since he had had a troubled dream: a voice he knew had called to him for help, but he could not place the voice. She spoke strangely, in the tongue of the Khentors, but with a strange accent. And he did not know where the cry came from, or why. Time and again he told himself it was only a dream, but it bothered him. Something was wrong somewhere, he felt. His carefree life of the past months had left him, and he could not recapture it. Even Dur'chai had, he fancied, been giving him strange, ironical looks. He felt tense, tiptoe, a-quiver, prickling inside as if his heart had gooseflesh.

Suddenly he shuddered, then scrambled to his feet, looking restively about him. Mnorh sat up staring in surprise. Dur'-chai lifted his head and his eyes glinted in amusement.

Looking at him Li'vanh almost laughed, and tugged at the grass still trailing from the horse's revolving jaws. 'Why don't you come right out and talk?' he demanded. 'Laziness, that's all it is.' He ran his fingers through a tangled lock of mane, picked up his saddle and swung it high on to the horse's back.

Mnorh had risen with alacrity, and was saddling his pony also. Li'vanh saw his face, full of curiosity and suppressed amusement at his sudden change of mood, and then remembered what they had been talking about. He put on a dark scowl for his friend's benefit.

'I will go on the hunt,' he declared. 'I'll not stay behind to be the mock of women and maids!' He finished with a grandiose gesture, congratulating himself on his phrasing; but Mnorh hooted.

'The mock of women and maids!' he cried, 'The Mock! O Great Mother, may I live to see the day! The mock!' He made some mincing steps and fluttered his hands, in intended caricature of girl dancing. 'Oooo, Li'vanh Prachoi!' he fluted, 'Favoured Son of the Lady is Li'vanh Pra-achoi! Mighty among the mighty is Li'v—gurk! Ahg! Enough! Enough!'

He beat the ground with his hands; gone were the days when he could master his friend at wrestling. He continued crying his submission while snorting with laughter. 'Li'vanh, let me up, I'm breathing in ants!'

'If *I* had a voice like a girl's still,' remarked Li'vanh grimly, '*I* wouldn't show it off. I won't let you up until you apologize.'

'What, for saying you were mighty among the—yow! I apologize! Yellow dog, you're breaking my back!'

Li'vanh released him, and grinning he scrambled to his feet, brushing dust from his coat.

'Not but what you are—I mean mighty among—all right! All right! You strange man; can't take a friendly compliment!'

'Child,' said Li'vanh loftily, swinging Dur'chai round towards the camp. 'Your tongue betrays you.' He quoted a proverb. 'The small stream chatters loud, but who hears the voice of the river?'

Penelope woke, yawning and rubbing her eyes. She was cold and uncomfortable; then suddenly she remembered why.

She promptly relaxed and curled up again, trying to pretend that she had never woken. For a few minutes she lay with her eyes closed, breathing softly, trying to think herself back to sleep. But it was no use. She was too stiff, too cold, and much too hungry.

When she remembered that she was hungry she came full awake and opened her eyes. It was broad day. The cold pale light lit their prison without cheering it. Penny was lying half in and half on the heap of straw. Her own cloak and the Princess's heavy shawl covered her, but she was not warm. In that room nothing could be warm—only more or less cold. In'serinna was standing at the window again and the girl wondered, as she had wondered the day before too, whether she had been there all night.

She sat up. 'Princess?' she said.

The Princess turned. 'Penny?' she said. 'Good morrow. How are you this morning?'

'All right,' replied Penny, not quite honestly. 'What sort of day is it?' She walked over to the window, and peered out. It was a clear cold day, as the day before had been, and the day before, and ... 'Oh,' she sighed, 'I'm almost forgetting what summer is like!' She looked up at her companion, who smiled faintly at her, but all at once Penelope was shocked to see how her face had changed. Her eyes looked smudged, and tired—but she never gets tired! she thought. But this was not a tiredness that sleep could cure, it was a weariness of spirit. The arrogant cutting edge of her beauty was dulled, and she was muted.

Penelope shivered a little, and swallowed. In'serinna, brought back to mind of her, looked down and smiled—her old smile, that lit her face with warmth. 'You look troubled, little one.'

'Well, you seem so worried.'

'Oh, Penny, do not ...' then she laughed. 'Listen to us, each so earnestly surprised to think the other is worried, and me about to say there is nothing to worry about! Of course we are worried, and of course we have reason. Let us speak of it no more, and try to forget it.'

But that was something which even Penny could not forget. She leaned on the window sill, gazing down on to the tops of the snow-mantled trees. The wall beneath the window fell sheer, unbroken by door, gate, or window. They were on a side of the fortress away from the road. If Penny leaned out and twisted her head round she could look up to the battlements; but it made her giddy, even giddier than looking down. There was no living thing in sight, not even a bird. They seemed to avoid Kuniuk Bannoth. Penelope did not blame them.

'Do you think Prince Hairon will come and save us?'

'Hairon? He might well wish to try, especially as he knows that you were taken; but it will not rest with him. The Lord Horenon commands my escort. Penelope, do not hope for them to come. Pray that they will not try. They could not save us. To take us they would have to take the castle, and Kuniuk Bannoth was not built to be taken by a handful, however valiant.'

Penelope's heart swelled with protest. She almost cried out, 'How will we get away, then?' but fear of the answer stopped her. She swallowed, and framed a different question.

'Why did Kunil-Bannoth call you kinswoman?'

'He presumed too far!' There was a fierce hardness in her voice. 'But he spoke a travesty of the truth. We are kin from afar.'

'*Really?* How?'

'Do you remember, I said that Fendarl was one of the Children of the Stars? There are Nine Houses of the Starborn, and we all count ourselves kin. But more than that, Fendarl's house, the House of Kendreth, and mine, the House of Andereth, are descended from twin sisters, Elineth and Valunna, and our kingdoms have been closely bound through all our history. We have intermarried often—as have all the Starborn houses, of course, as we are bound to do.' Her voice was all at once strangely husky.

'Bound to do? Why?'

In'serinna looked down, her voice low. 'Only we Children of the Stars may wield the Star Magic. It is our duty no less than our right. Not every one of us is an enchanter or entrantress, but even those who are not have their part in the magic. I am an enchantress, so my part is great. I wear the Pearl of Rennath and sit in the Council. But as for your question: if we marry one who is not of this kindred, then we lose both our right and our power. It is too hard a fellowship for strangers.' Her voice died away, and there was silence for a moment. Penelope shifted uncomfortably. Then In'serinna flung up her head again.

'So that is why Kunil-Bannoth called me kinswoman, and that is why I am sometimes called Sister of the Eagles, for the House of Kendreth were called the White Eagles after their banner. Alas for Bannoth, and alas for Rennath! We were halves of one whole, but we must seek their destruction. For Bannoth death is the best that can befall, and for Rennath at most a crippled life. Alas for the White Eagles! And oh, may the doom appointed find Kunil-Bannoth soon!'

'What does that mean—the doom appointed?'

'Chiefly, it means that I hope there is one appointed! But there will be. Like Fendarl he has armoured himself within his magic, even though his power is less. But not even the strongest of spells will guard for ever. They always leave a weak link, an undefended spot. There is always some condition that limits them. So for Kunil-Bannoth, too, it is said that he has never taken a wife for fear of an oracle. But for him also, there will come one day—Penny!'

She suddenly caught at the child's shoulders, staring at her as if she had never seen her face before. Penny jumped with surprise. 'What? What is it? Princess!' The enchantress was silent, lost in thought; her eyes gleamed and she almost laughed. Penny caught her arm and shook it impatiently 'Princess, tell me, please! Have you thought of something?'

She took the child's hand, laughing a little. 'Maybe I have. If I have, it relieves me of one fear of my own! No, Penelope, I cannot tell you; I must think on it more. I may be wrong. But if I am not ...' Her eyes shone, and she smiled at Penelope almost exultantly, as if they two were in a plot together. 'Well, if I am not, we shall see soon enough.'

Li'vanh found he was included in the hunt after all, without needing to sit on Rehai's head all night. He told the young hunter, laughing, that his had been the fate prepared for him, but the man only grinned faintly, looking at him almost apologetically as if acknowledging that he appreciated the effort. Everyone was trying to cheer him. He had not smiled for days. They closed around him almost protectively, but still it was no use, and they knew as well as he that the more they rallied to him the emptier seemed the space at his side. Rehai had been brother-in-blood to Hran the Outcast.

'It's very hard,' remarked Hunoi, one of the hunting party, to Li'vanh just before they set out. 'Rehai's wife and baby died in the winter, you know, Tuvoi, and now to lose his spear-brother. . . . A man would think the Gods had cursed him. Yet you will never find anyone to say ill of Rehai.'

Li'vanh nodded. He remembered Rehai before Hran's going. He had not been happy then, with his other loss so new, but now. . . . He was sorry. He liked the man. But his reflections were cut short as there was a call from the front and they surged foward. He turned to grin and wave to Mnorh, and then seeing Mneri come out of her tent included her. She returned the wave without smiling. Just for a moment he felt the faintest twinge of resentment, as if his day might be spoiled; then he shrugged it off and turned back. Ahead he saw Silinoi turning to scan the faces at the back of the party; catching his foster-son's eye he beckoned him forward. Li'vanh nodded to Hunoi and touched Dur'chai lightly with his heels. The horse snorted and leapt forward, tossing his fiery mane.

Li'vanh arrived beside Silinoi, and they rode in silence for some three miles. He had vaguely expected that someone—Silinoi or Rehai—would outline to him what to do, but no one spoke. For a moment or two he had a wild dread they would leave him in charge of the horses: their hunting was always done afoot. It was not done to use horses in the hunt, because horses too were the hunted and not the hunters, and they would then be traitors to their kind. Loyalty was the strongest law they knew. Once, long ago, this had surprised him. Once he had thought that their hunt was a chase, and been foolish enough to say so to Mnorh. Mnorh had been so disgusted and insulted that he was almost speechless. 'That would be to be like the Kelanat!' he had choked at last. 'To hunt like the Kelanat! The Kelanat are savages. They hunt with dogs. And they hunt like dogs. They do not stalk, they let the dogs find a scent, and then they run the animals down. We—we are not like that. We are the Children of Kem'nanh, we are the true hunters. We hunt not like the dog, but like the cat. To stalk silently and strike swiftly—that is the way for a man to hunt. Chase, indeed! Why, we have a saying that if you are a really good hunter your quarry does not know it is in danger until it is dead.' He had paused, and added in a lordly tone, 'Of course, I don't expect you'll be a really good hunter.'

'Well, thanks! Very nice I'm sure.'

'Well, Li'vanh, a man cannot have two such great gifts. At least, he rarely does so. Warriors are not hunters, and hunters are not warriors. You are a great warrior, Derna says, so why should you be a hunter too?'

'And why can a man not be both?'

'I did not say he cannot. But he hardly ever is. It would not be just of the gods, to give two such skills to one man.'

'I see. So your brother Vanh is a poor warrior?'

'Vanh is not a poor warrior! Vanh is the best of fighters!'

'How? When he is Vanh the Hunter?'

Mnorh had grinned reluctantly. 'Who taught you to turn a man's words back against him? Eu-ha, maybe you too will be a hunter.'

Li'vanh grinned, remembering. It seemed a long while since he had made the mistake that had brought Mnorh's anger on him. He was amazed at himself now. Now he believed with the rest that only a savage would use dogs to hunt, and to hunt for sport was to be lower yet, less than a savage. He no longer saw anything strange in their genuine love of the animals on which they preyed. It was necessary, they could not avoid it, but it was an instinct with them to be as merciful as they could. The idea of taking pleasure in their pain was intolerable. Once it had made him wonder, to hear them call themselves the 'kerivh meni', the gentle people, for between themselves they were anything but gentle. Passionate and violent, to one another they could be barbaric; yet to their animals they were never so—never rough or angry, always using them with an odd tenderness; they even believed that man had only been created to guide and care for the beasts. 'The Khentors, at least,' they had amended. 'There is no knowing why such as the Barelonh and the Islanders were made.'

They had ridden for about seven miles when Rehai, who was riding ahead, gave a warning cry and held up his arm. The men surged to a halt. Rehai turned and looked at Silinoi, and nodding to Li'vanh to follow the Lord rode forward.

They arrived beside Rehai together, and looked where he was looking.

After a moment Silinoi said, 'So. Today, we have no need to seek our prey. Today, the prey seeks us.' His rumbling voice was nearer than he had ever before allowed to betraying amazement.

Coming towards them, though still a good way off, they could clearly see a proud-antlered stag. He swept swiftly through the grasses, plainly making deliberately for them, as directly as was possible.

Li'vanh half laughed, incredulous, but Rehai shook his head.

'Look again, Terani. It is not the stag who seeks us.'

Silinoi narrowed his older, less keen eyes, and after a moment exclaimed softly, 'It is the falcon's sight you have, Rehai. Li'vanh, do you see? It passes belief.'

And just then Li'vanh did see.

Sitting sideways on the stag's back was a young man, his hands resting on the antlers as if he were parting the branches of a tree.

'Mor'anh!' whispered Li'vanh. 'What is this?'

Silinoi and Rehai both shook their heads. All three sat in tense silence, as stag and rider swept gracefully up to them, and then stopped.

Slender, bare-armed, bare-legged, beardless, the stranger looked a stripling. Yet as his grave, shadowed, unseeable eyes passed over them, Li'vanh's nape shuddered. He looked at them each in turn, considering, stroking the neck of his strange mount. He had the look of one who lived in a sheltered shady place, clear-skinned and delicate as a windflower; yet they each flinched instinctively from meeting his eyes. At last he spoke.

'Where are the riders of the Northern Plains? Where are the sons of Kamenon? Arm now, Wind Children, for the Golden Ones arise, and there is war on the bounds of Khendhalash. At Danamol, at the fording of the river, there will they strike, and the Swan-king of Rennath has need of his friends. Now is your might needed. Now must the Khentorei prove their faith. Arm, Lord of the Hurnei, Lord of the Northern Plains. Lead your tribes to war!'

Chapter Thirteen

'The Child Death-eyed'

Nicholas was awakened by, of all unlikely things, the smell of cooking. There was that and wood-smoke tickling his nostrils, and when he opened his eyes there was a small fire burning near him and a man standing over it.

He was growing used to strange sights, and yet the man made him stare a little. He was of medium height and stocky build, with shaggy dark hair, beard, and whiskers. He wore clothes like the Harani, but rougher, and in woodland brown and green. His skin was weatherbeaten and wrinkled; the backs of his strong hands were thatched with hair.

Strangely, it troubled the boy that there was so little about the man that was odd. He did not have the lordly look of the princes, or the frankly inhuman look of the Nihaimurh. He looked fiercely mortal—even earthy. Perhaps that was it: he looked too alive to be real. Then more lines appeared in his creased brown face and his merry eyes danced as his thick, almost coarse lips curved into a smile.

'Will you know me the next time we meet, do you think?'

His voice was the best thing about him. It was deep and splendid, heavy with laughter as a tree may be heavy with fruit, and underneath all the time was a rich rumble. When it went to its deepest note the forest quivered in response, as sometimes the walls of a church tremble to the note of an organ. Nicholas grinned a little, but could think of nothing to say. The man saw this, and laughed again.

'Hungry?' He got an enthusiastic nod to this and turned back to the fire. Nicholas threw off his blanket (and found he could not because it was his cloak) then scrambled to his feet and followed.

Breakfast was hot crumbly cakes, honey, cheese, and

water. Nicholas found that he was ravenous, and his companion too ate heartily. He talked to himself continuously, in a soft growl which Nicholas could not follow. This might have been due only to his accent, which was quite unlike the speech of the Princess's kinsmen, for all it was the same language. He did not take very much notice of the boy, but in some strange way he was a very satisfying companion. Nicholas, full at last, leant back against the tree behind him with a satisfied sigh.

Though the man did not look at him Nicholas felt at once that he had all his attention. In a moment he said unhurriedly, 'Well now, suppose you tell me what brings a stranger into Nelimhon?'

It took quite a long time, with hesitations and explanations, and telling some things twice, and not really liking to tell some things at all; but at last all was recounted and his tongue had brought him over the borders of the Forest to his meeting with the Nihaimurh.

'. . . . and so he went off to tell—the—wind-children I think it was—anyhow he said they'd help, and he sent me with some others to get some rest . . . only they left me behind. I mean, not quite like that, but I was so tired, I couldn't keep up, and they didn't wait . . . so I stayed here. And here I am. And who are you, please?'

The man laughed a little, then looked thoughtful. 'Blame not the wood-folk,' he said, 'They would not have meant to leave you, but mortals are as strange to them as they to mortals. They have heard that men grow tired and need rest, but they do not understand that weariness makes the feet and mind slow. Besides, one of them stayed; did you see her? She watched over you all night, the pretty one, and did not go until I came. Now, who am I? Well, well, what a question. I can tell you my name, if you wish to know it, though it is long since it was used. The name of my house I know, but do not tell. Or there are many other things I am called by men. But who I am? That is too long a tale, and not yet finished. Even you, young as you are, could not tell me who you are in a few words. Perhaps you do not even know yet. We are more than our names, boy.'

Nicholas was rather taken aback. 'Well, all I meant really was, what shall I call you?'

'Well, now, of all the names I have been given, which shall

I choose? The Borderer, I think; it is fittest, yes, and I like it better than most. Yes, call me the Borderer.'

Nicholas stared. 'Are you *sure*? It doesn't sound like a name. It doesn't sound—well—very polite.'

The man gazed at him for a second, then flung up his head and roared with delighted laughter. 'Polite! Oh, boy, you are my friend for ever. Polite! Shades of my house, do you hear?' He shook his head, looking at Nicholas with his face alive with merriment. 'You think respect due to me, then? Thank you for that, boy. But call me the Borderer. It is well enough.'

Nicholas blinked a little, then thought of another question. 'Who are they? The Ni—Nihaimurh, I mean? What sort of people?' Then, as the Borderer began to shake with laughter, 'I'm sorry, have I asked a stupid question?'

The man shook his mane of hair. 'Not stupid,' he chuckled, 'but so big! And so loose! and so without an answer! They are just the forest folk, the dwellers in the wood; just another sort of people, as men are just men. They live by different laws, that is all. They are the Companions of Iranani—some will just call them the Companions.'

'Companions of—who?'

'Iranani.'

'Who's that? Or is it what?'

'The answer to the who is just Iranani, and the answer to the what is that he is many things; but one of them is the Lord of Wood and Water. In his quiet moments I do not doubt he takes pleasure in the clear streams and cool glades of Nelimhon.' He looked at the boy thoughtfully. 'Well now— what did you say you were called? Nicholas? Well, Nicholas, you have told me enough to set me thinking. Merekarl nearly swept from Black Mountain, and your sister and the Star's Daughter the prey of Kunil-Bannoth, and the Kelonat going to war and the Khentorei coming to meet them, and a boy hunted by the Inkalyei—oh yes! I have heard of your wolves before! And you have a brother, too? I wonder, now, I wonder. The Starlit Land has not been quiet this long time past. Men may call me strange, but I am not blind nor am I deaf, and I can smell more things than galya with my nose. Things are stirring—stirring.'

'Well, it was funny—the snow, and then the spring here.

But I'm glad I got here. I think this wood is—is the happiest place I ever saw.'

The Borderer smiled. 'Maybe you are right,' he said, 'but if so, now you must learn how happiness comes only in small doses. For I think the sooner I see you in the White City the better. You must leave Nelimhon.'

Nicholas looked startled. 'Why? I mean, I'd like to see this City, I've heard enough about it, but is there so much hurry? I like it here. Why must I go right now?'

'Because Nelimhon is no common wood. Do not forget, either, that it is banned for men, and this is partly for their own good. Already it casts its spell of peace over you, and you have not strength to resist. Nelimhon is a fair place, a good place, but perilous. Strange things happen to those who breathe its air and drink its water, and walk long beneath its trees.' He saw the look on the boy's face, and smiled. 'Those like me? That is what you are thinking? That strange things have happened to me?'

'No; only you reminded me. Men aren't allowed in. Why are you here?'

The man laughed aloud. 'True, and I have no good answer. Except, Nicholas, that I am an exception to many rules.'

That day in Kuniuk Rathen, Kunil-Bannoth sent again for his prisoners.

They came, the Princess cold and proud and stern, Penelope weary and miserable. Hunger was growing on her: all the food there was the Princess gave her, but it was not enough. It was three days since she had had a proper meal, and the hungrier she was the colder she felt, and hunger and cold both came between her and sleep. So as they went into the hall she held her companion's hand and leaned against her arm, wretched and even a little sullen.

She did not listen to their talk. She would not look at the throne. Her shining hair was rough and tangled from three days without combing; her unbrushed teeth made an unpleasant taste in her mouth; she felt dirty and untidy and not at all bold or defiant. So instead she looked at the carvings on the walls, and the designs still faintly visible in the worn stone flags. There were swans there, and eagles: they did not look like the black eagles—more like Merekarl's people, bold and

rash. She remembered the Princess talking about lords before
Fendarl, and wondered how old the place was. The strong
stonework, the high arches—Kuniuk Bannoth: Bannoth Castle.

She closed her eyes half drowsing, thinking of the castle;
and all at once she seemed to see it as it had been. A border
stronghold, the fortress of a lord on the marches of a
kingdom, holding a mountain pass against Kiron's deadliest
foes. Summer bloomed on Black Mountain; green flowed up
its foothills and into its valleys, and the black snow-pied
heights above looked grave and benign, not cruel and cold.
Birds dipped and sang about the towers; above the grey walls
floated the banners bearing the White Eagle of the House of
Kendreth. Within, in the raftered hall, the proud banners
swayed above the heads of the household. The King of
Bannoth sat in his chair, and behind him were spread three
standards; one for his house, one for the Veduath, and
one the nine-starred standard of the Enchanters. . . .

Almost she heard the talk and laughter, almost she smelt
the food, felt the fire; if she opened her eyes surely she would
see them, the graceful ladies with white hounds leaning
against them, the tall lords with falcons on their fists. . . .

'Open your eyes!' the Princess whispered fiercely. 'Open
your eyes!'

She started forward and up in a glad movement, her eyes
flying wide, and looked about her. She saw In'serinna's lovely
face for a moment as part of her dream, and turned to see
the bannered wall and the King. And on the dais the present
Lord of Bannoth stood staring and received the full force of
her vivid gaze, and with a cry flung up his arm and fell back
in sudden terror.

O, eyes are called blue, and pass for blue, and are nothing
of the sort, or poor weak spiritless ghosts of the colour. But
Penny—Penny had blue eyes. Startling, clear, they were blue
as summer skies, blue as new-opened flax, blue as chicory, as
chalcedony, as the mantle of Keriol Hornblower. And in
Vandarei blue is the colour of death.

Kunil-Bannoth's shriek startled Penelope out of her bright
dream, and she leapt back to the Princess's side, clutching at
her. In'serinna cast her shawl around her shoulders; but her
eyes were on their captor, and suddenly she laughed fierce
and harshly triumphant.

'Yes!' she flung at the huddled figure on the throne, 'All your watch and ward was vain, and the child has come at last! Oh, you have feared, you have guarded, but against your own evil even you had no defence! Your own black heart has betrayed you, for by your own act the one you feared is within your walls, and you have brought your fate upon yourself as an unwilling prisoner!'

He shrank from her words, pride, arrogance, even hate for the moment gone, nothing between him and knowledge of the blinding truth. 'Fear a child in your halls,' the oracle had said, long long ago, 'Fear the coming of the child death-eyed.' And all these years he had taken care, until he had almost forgotten the flaw in his defences. Never in all his life, not even when the Princess had blazed her star-glow across his hall, had he known such dreadful shock and anguish as when the colour had leapt at him, like gay lighting flashing from Penelope's small, pale face.

Pain twisted in him and he leapt up. 'Kill her!' he yelled. It was the second time he had threatened her with death, and this time she was too bewildered to be afraid. As soon as he spoke, the Princess's voice pealed out.

'Take care!' she cried, 'Take care, Kunil-Bannoth! Release the death in her eyes, and who can tell where it will fly?'

Rage and fear fought in him. He did not believe the Princess's words, he did not believe the death in this child's eyes would fly anywhere, but—but. . . . Fear won. He cast them a look of hate, then flinched away lest his eyes should meet Penelope's.

'Back to their room!' he commanded.

Penny stumbled along almost in tears. The Princess's words had frightened her more than anything that had happened. They kept leaping in her brain—'the death in her eyes'—in her eyes—death, death in her eyes—it was horrible, horrible! And what did it mean? There was nothing she understood, and it was all frightening, and now the Princess had frightened her too. She did not even want to look at that bright, fierce, good face. She wanted her mother, she wanter her father, she wanted Oliver, Nicholas, she wanted to go home. 'I-don't-like-this-game-let's-play-something-different.' Only it was not a game, and she could not stop, and she didn't *like* it. 'Kill her'—'death in her eyes'—she didn't *like* it!

Penelope burst into tears.

When her weeping subsided, much later, she was sitting on In'serinna's lap, clasped in her strong arms, leaning weakly against her and gulping jerkily for breath. The comforting nonsense that the young woman had been crooning over her head gradually sorted into sense. 'I am sorry, I am sorry, little one. I did not mean to frighten you. But I did mean to frighten him, and I dared not tell you. I was not sure that I was right, but I think now we have scared him. I almost pity him. . . . Why, what is it?'

'You said—you said . . .' Penny's voice wobbled. 'You said there was death in my eyes. . . .'

'Ah, truly, there is no need to weep! It is only that they are blue, and with us blue means death or mourning. No, that is not an omen, I am not ill-wishing you. But many years ago Kunil-Bannoth was told that his magic would protect him against all he feared for a long time, but this time would end with the coming of the 'child death-eyed' into his halls. So now he sees you, he is in terror, for in you is gathered the menace of everything he has ever feared.'

'Oh!' Penelope brightened a little. It was something, anyway, to frighten Kunil-Bannoth, even if she could take little credit for it. 'I bet he could kick himself now, for making me come here . . . it's nearly funny.'

'Oh,' the Princess replied, almost grimly, 'he could do worse than kick himself. He has destroyed himself, and he knows it. . . . So perhaps there is hope for us after all. I had almost given it up, shame on me. . . .' She did not say aloud that she wondered what it would be like, to be the prisoners of a frightened gaoler. 'If he is afraid,' she thought resolutely, 'Then that is the worse for him. And worse for him must be better for us.'

They soon discovered how much better.

Next day they were sent no food at all.

Until the call to arms, Li'vanh had rarely remembered that his foster-father was Lord of the Northern Plains. His visits to Kiron, the arbiting between tribes, the settling of disputes—these things were usually the work of winter, when the tribes gathered in a fairly small area. There was rarely need for his authority to be displayed in summer. But on the day of the hunt the chief produced from his tent an amazing number of maps, drawn on skins and marked with routes and landmarks wholly invisible to Li'vanh, and worked out routes and distances and days needed, where tribes might be encamped, and where they should muster. On the same day ten riders were sent out bearing the 'rashev r'munhan', the summons to war. The Wolf Spear many called it, because of the white wolf-tail tasselling the blade, gripped there by a narrow collar of dark green metal. The spear butt was stained red.

'Red for war, of course,' explained Mnorh, 'and the metal at the neck is kamenani—the royal metal, to show that father's authority comes from Kiron. The wolf-tails are in memory of Mor'anh Mer'inhen, who is sometimes called the White Wolf, and who first led the Tribes to war ... also because the white wolf is called the Hound of Marenkalion; it is said he always keeps a pack of three to do his bidding—we call them the Inkalyei.'

Li'vanh was filled with a queer tingling excitement, half pleased and half afraid. He was going to war. It was only a phrase as yet, only words whose sound had not yet acquired meaning. Going to war—the vindication of all those hours of practice with Derna, a familiar pastime, but now filled with new and dreadful dimensions of death. Going to war—for him, it belonged to stories still, and he found it hard to make it seem real. This would be a battle of spears and swords and charging horses, meeting the man who meant to kill him hand-to-hand, face-to-face. And this, whispered apprehension, would put Derna's judgement of him to the proof. This would be the touchstone; this would show whether or not he was indeed a warrior in ten thousand. He felt even more restless than before, though less short-tempered. When the stories of the heroes were told, he hated to hear the cowards scorned, for he thought 'What if I find that I am a coward?' He brooded much on this: what if he should find that he loved his life more than his honour? He examined himself, and came to the reluctant conclusion that there was little, very little, less than he would have thought while it was just a question of thinking, that he loved more than his life. . . . So it was with rather mixed feelings that he made his preparations.

Mnorh, on the other hand, was quite certain of his delight. There had been a short unpleasant space when he thought he might be left behind, but he had besieged his father with pleas not to be parted from Li'vanh, claiming the position of

squire, weapon-bearer, boot-boy—anything—until told that
he might go with the host. Quite a few boys would be going
with them, to watch over the things the men might not want
to take into battle. These things would usually be their
falcons or their lithe hunting cats, and because of a command
of Yorn's Oliver had neither of these, but he was very glad
Mnorh would be with him.

Mneri also was in no doubt of her desire to accompany
them, but she had not pleaded with her brother's noisy
conviction of success. She had begged her father quietly at
first, then when he had refused implored him with an intensity which she had never shown before, startling Li'vanh by
dropping down at her father's feet, clasping his ankles and
laying her brow to the ground, pleading desperately and in
anguish, so that the sight hurt Li'vanh and he went hurriedly
away.

But still her father refused—or so Li'vanh guessed when,
passing a wagon later in the day, he heard a choke and a
wild gasp that sounded very like someone trying to smother
their tears. He was seized with a desire to run, but pulled
himself up sharply with a stern reminder about cowardice,
and looked around. Then he bent and looked under the
wagon, and there, in the Khentor's age-old refuge, huddled
the daughter of Silinoi.

The urge to run became even stronger, but feeling at the
same time a half-guilty wish to help, he crawled under the
wagon. There was a pause while he wondered what to say,
and Mneri tried to pretend she had not seen him; then he
said, 'Foster-sister, why do you weep?'

The floor of the wagon was so close above that it made his
voice sound heavier, deeper, startling him for the first time in
weeks by its manliness. He felt himself blushing hotly and
scowled. Mneri, keeping her back to him, snuffled for a few
more minutes, then said in a thick shaky voice, 'Because
my—because our—because Father means to leave me behind.' Her last words trembled on the edge of a sob. He tried
to think of something suitably manly and scornful about
women weeping and the uselessness of it, but could not
remember ever hearing one of the tribesmen say anything
like it. Then he remembered uncomfortably that Khentor
women never, never cried. They lamented, but they did not

cry, not like this. So he said as briskly and lightly as he could, 'Does it matter that much?'

'Yes!' she wailed passionately, 'of course!' and then for all her gritted teeth began to sob again.

Had she really been his sister—had she been Penelope, or even his cousin Margaret—he would have put a comforting arm around her; but now he did not. Besides, he excused himself, the axle was in the way. He was desperately uncomfortable. The wagon floor was the height of his shoulders so he had to kneel stooped. He wanted to get out from every possible motive, yet he had to stay.

'Well, I don't see that it matters much,' he said as reasonably as possible. 'It won't be for long. Everyone will be back soon. And there'd be nothing for you to do. And no one for you to be with,' (Oh, you idiot!) 'and I should think a bit dreary all round. I'm sure you'll be better off here. After all, Father would never let you fight. And I think we'd rather eat our own cooking!' he ended, with a desperate attempt at a joke. But she did not laugh. She whispered. 'I want to come'.

He felt uncomfortable and foolish, and suddenly annoyed. *'Why* do you, for goodness' sake?' he demanded, exasperated; then cursed himself in an agony of remorse, and bit his tongue savagely.

She stiffened, then slowly turned towards him. Her face was dusty and blotchy, and puffed with tears, but somehow he did not notice. He felt hot all over.

'Li'vanh,' she said, with an odd forlorn dignity, 'I do not believe that you do not know.'

And of course he did know. So he evaded her eyes and crawled out, abandoning the field defeated, leaving her to cry as Khentor women never cried, as though all were over, and not even hope left.

Chapter Fourteen

Wanderers and Captives

Nicholas was the first to begin his journey to H'ara Tunij. On the day he met the Borderer, while his sister was bringing fear to Kunil-Bannoth and his brother hearing the drums of war, they began their walk.

'How far?' said the Borderer with a chuckle. 'How far? I don't know. But I reckon that we will have to walk for about fourteen days—if we wish to keep you in one piece, that is, and I suppose we do. What do you make that face for? Why, to walk through such a lovely place in such a lovely season—what could be better?'

Very little, it seemed. There seemed to be no great hurry. They wandered along, often in silence; the Borderer sometimes told a rambling story, sometimes they talked about the country. And it was indeed most beautiful country. The part of Kedrinh through which they passed has no mountains, no very grand or awe-inspiring sights, and it is far from the sea, but it is rich in all the gentler beauties. Mostly they were crossing the northern limit of the downs, where they are lower than farther south. Broad, shallow green valleys and tree-patched crests, deep river meadows and sunny pastures—such was the country which rolled before them. It was very quiet. The soil is poor there and of little use for farming. Sheep and cattle are grazed on it, but because of the harsh winters they are not kept there all the year, and when Nicholas and the Borderer passed through the shepherds and drovers had not yet come. The Borderer explained this; Nicholas tried to imagine a harsh winter there, or anything harsh, and failed. The spring days followed in mild succession, not all sunny but just right for walking. Nicholas lost

116

count of them. He did not care how long they took. He was enjoying every minute.

But of course Nelimhon had been best. They had spent barely a day walking through it, but it had been a rich day. Not all the forest was the same: there had been places where their path led them along the small valleys of streams, where low graceful trees leaned from the banks. In other places the trees stood tall and close, and on either side of the path the wood stretched deep and dim. There were flower-ringed pools, and glades as broad as meadows, places where the path almost disappeared into a thicket, and one stretch where it was so overhung and bowered with trailing creepers white and gold with blossom that to walk it was like going through a tunnel. But best of all were the broad walks where the trees stood with room between them and the grass growing deep, trees bathed in sun and cool with shadow, each distinct and proud in its individual glory, yet all joining to make a greater beauty.

'It's—it's—it's like a choir that's all soloists!' exclaimed Nicholas at last, after striving for quite a while after a description. 'And—oh, look at that!'

He pointed to two great trees, one either side of a bright stream, leaning so that their branches twined. One tree was covered in blossom, the other hung with fruit. The Borderer looked, and nodded.

'Always something in bloom, always something in fruit. Nelimhon, where the flowers never fade.'

'I think it's—well, I suppose this is what heaven must be like ... do you think?'

'No!' The violence of his voice startled the boy. 'Do not start thinking like that! Walk faster! Like heaven? Maybe— but this is the shadow, not the substance. This is no place for you! Ageless Nelimhon! Well for those who can walk its paths—but *you* are not one. You are a man, and men are not ageless, men are not timeless. You would lose yourself here, dreaming away fifty years as if they were fifty days, and then where is your life? No, Nicholas! Come on!'

The Borderer was right; yet in one way Nelimhon was good for the boy in a way nowhere else could have been. He had been much tried, frightened, lonely, in danger; and he had not the nature which forgets easily. But the graceful,

calm, timeless happiness of the Dancer's Forest cured him as
nothing else could.

Penelope, unlike her brother, was one to forget easily what
she did not wish to remember. So she could not afterwards
clearly remember her fourth day of captivity in Kuniuk
Bannoth.

Even while the day lasted it was hardly real. She had
woken with her stomach aching with hunger, feeling weak,
and trembling. Then later, as it slowly dawned on her that
there was going to be no food, she crept down into the pile
of straw and tried to vanish. In'serinna did not try to rouse
her. She just stood by the window unhappily, after tucking
her shawl around the child. For the rest of the day Penelope
just lay and shivered. She could not stop—not even when the
Princess took off all her own petticoats and put those over
her too.

The fifth day dawned duller. There was cloud in the sky,
and when In'serinna leaned out of the window she could not
see the trees below for mist. Penny did not move, though she
was awake. The Princess stood silently by the window staring
out over the lost world. The mist thinned a little. By mid-
morning she could see the tree-tops. She was watching them
when the doorbolts scraped.

She turned in a flash. Amazingly two food-bowls were
placed inside the door. The straw rustled as she picked her
way warily up to them, her senses alert ... then her heart
sank. She had feared this. They felt bad; not stale, but
wrong. To all appearances the contents of the two bowls
were quite normal, but she knew beyond all hope that this
was troll food, and no fit meal for humans.

She pulled her mind up on the edge of cursing Kunil-
Bannoth savagely. She felt quite sick with anger and hate,
and not at all inclined to pity him. Nothing could be worse
than to eat this; but very nearly as bad would be taking it
away from Penelope. Quickly, before she wakes, she thought;
and picking up one bowl took it to the window. She hurled it
furiously as far as she could, and stood watching it for a
second in fierce satisfaction. In those seconds, Penelope
acted.

Since she had seen the food she had lain quite still; so the
Princess did not dream she was awake. When she saw one

bowl taken to be thrown away, she did not believe it for a moment; then she thrust aside her shock and horror and decided she must reach the other quickly. She got soundlessly to her feet and went to the bowl at a tiptoe run. The Princess turned just as she siezed the food, and ran to her with a cry.

The next few seconds were a nightmare. She was struggling to get the food to her mouth, and In'serinna was pulling at her hands. Penny heard her saying 'No, don't eat, you mustn't eat it!' but she was desperate. She fought, she heard herself wailing, she thought she kicked, then the bread broke and somehow she could not hold it ... then she was fighting to pick up the pieces but the Princess was still holding her wrists. She heard their voices, heard herself calling the Princess names, shouting, and then heard the Princess's voice crack ... and suddenly there was another noise, a thin hum, then a light tap and rattle, and something dark flashed by them.

There was a short silence. Penny stared blankly at the Princess and saw that she was crying. In'serinna knelt still for a few minutes, gasping with sobs, then shook herself and stood up. She wiped her eyes, then gave Penny her hand, helping her to her feet.

'I'm sorry,' whispered Penny, struggling up. 'I'm sorry, Princess, I didn't mean it, really I didn't.' In'serinna shook her head.

'It is not your fault, sweetheart. It is far more mine. I am sorry to have brought this on you,' she replied huskily. 'Now, what was that noise?'

Lying where it had bounced, a short way from the foot of the wall, was an arrow. The Princess picked it up with a soft exclamation, blinked and wiped her eyes again, and said, 'There's something tied to it.'

'I don't think it's something tied on,' said Penelope, recovering more quickly. 'I think it's just a string—look, it goes right out the window.' She picked it up, and it twitched in her fingers. She dropped it with a cry of surprise.

'There's someone on the other end!'

In'serinna gave a gasping half-laugh. 'Yes, there would be.' Her voice shook oddly.

'Oh, of course!' Penny laughed, then looked at her curiously. 'Is something the matter?'

'Nothing! Well, if they are outside, they are the more likely to be our friends. I wonder who . . .' Then the thread twitched again, several times. She hesitated, then said, 'I ought to pull it up, I suppose.'

'Yes, go on, do!' Penny's excitement was mounting. She wondered what was the matter with In'serinna. Her cheeks were at once pale and flushed, and her hands trembled. 'I expect it's your escort—Prince Hairon, I should think.'

'Oh!' said the Princess sharply, letting go the cord and then snatching at it again. 'Y-yes—yes of course—it must be.' Penelope wondered at her. It sounded almost as if she had not thought of that—as if she did not like the idea. She shook her head and picked up the arrow interestedly. 'It's *quite* long,' she said, 'but I did think they were longer than this, I think Oliver said once they were a yard long. This isn't.'

The Princess stared blankly at her, then exclaimed, 'Oh, the arrow!' Penny looked at her in consternation.

'Are you all right? You do look funny. I didn't say anything very bad, did I? I didn't mean it. Or are you just feeling hungry now, too?'

In'serinna smiled suddenly. 'No, no,' she said, pulling the cord steadily, 'but tell me; has the arrow a metal head?'

'No-o,' said Penelope, examining it. 'I don't quite know. It's ivory—no, people don't make arrows out of ivory, do they? It's. . . .'

'Bone,' supplied the Princess. 'Bone. It is a Khentor arrow.' Her voice mingled triumph and alarm. Penny stared; but at that moment the cord became a rope of leather, and she forgot her questions.

The Princess pulled the rope to the door, knotted it tightly to the ring, hesitated, then jerked again.

There was a squeak as the door-ring twisted and stood out from the door; the rope went taut. Whoever it was had a long climb before him. The Princess clenched and unclenched her hands, watching the knot fearfully for any sign of loosening. Penny watched the window, her legs trembling. They both stood still and tense. Then suddenly a hand grasped the window sill.

Penelope gasped. In'serinna made a small noise, almost protesting. The hand shifted, gripping the wall. It very plainly was not the Prince Hairon, or any of the Harani. Their hands were graceful and long-fingered; this was an oval hand, at once smaller and stronger. There was a bronze bracelet around the wrist, and for a second Penny had the wild notion that this was a woman. Then, with a last heave and twist, a young man sat astride the sill.

He was dressed entirely in dark green leather, save that his boots were black. His straight black hair grew out from the crown of his head over his brows. His dark eyes slanted, his cheek-bones were high, his nose was low-bridged, and his mouth unsmiling under a curving moustache. His skin was at once dark and pale, and his strongly arched brows were drawn down a little. He looked, thought Penny, very foreign. She took in every detail, fascinated, as he swung his other leg over the sill and stood up. He had long legs and broad shoulders, and was nowhere near as tall as Prince Hairon—in fact, he was about the same height as In'serinna. Somehow he managed to look at the same time graceful and compact, yet rough and almost wild. She was not at all sure that she liked him, until he looked at her. For a moment his intense eyes looked almost fierce; then he smiled. It was like daybreak. Penny smiled shakily back, and then, almost hesitantly, the stranger looked at the Princess.

Penny looked too, and blinked. The Princess had retreated as far as she could, and was now pressed back to the wall as if hoping that would open for her. Her cheeks flamed with colour. In a voice which sounded quite unreal she said 'My Lord Vanh!' then gulped, and added 'How—how do you do? Penelope, this is the Lord Vanh!'

'Yes,' stammered Penelope, fascinated. 'Is it?'

In'serinna laughed at that, though weakly, and stepped forward and looked a little more like herself; and the young man laughed too, though with restraint. The Princess looked at him, a strange expression in her eyes.

'So you have come to rescue us?'

Her voice was light; but his dark eyes were grave and his voice low, as he answered, 'Did you doubt that I would?'

She avoided his eyes and tried to laugh again. 'I dared not think of rescue! Do you think we can escape?'

'I think we have a good chance—if we hurry.'

She coloured at that, and bit her lip. 'I take the hint. Penny, do not look so puzzled. If you do we will have to start explaining, and I have just been scolded for delay.' She looked uncertainly at the Lord Vanh, then flushed. 'And now you are thinking how much I talk, are you not, my lord? Very well, I will stop.'

His lip quivered just a little. He looked as if he had indeed been thinking just that—as had Penelope. The Princess swallowed, and almost visibly composed herself. 'How—what must we do?'

The Lord Vanh went to the door and checked the knot. 'I shall go first, to keep watch and steady the rope at the bottom. The child to follow me, and you come last, my ...' he stopped, and scowled for a second. 'Your Highness. Starwind my horse is among the trees. It will be best to make all the use we can of the mist.'

Then Penny, who had been looking out of the window, said, 'I can't.'

They looked at her. Her legs shook; they felt as if the bone in them had melted. Tears pricked her eyes. 'I can't,' she said.

There was silence for a moment, and then the Princess came and knelt before her, taking her hands. 'What is it?' she asked gently.

Penelope gulped. 'I just can't. My arms are all wobbly and my hands won't hold on and I'll go giddy. . . .'

'She is quite right. How could she? She is faint with hunger.'

But that raised a small uneasiness between them. Penny swallowed, and impelled by honesty said 'It's not that; I'm scared. When I'm high up I just go sick and screw up.'

The Princess looked at her in amazement, but suddenly the Lord Vanh laughed, as if in relief. 'Never mind, it is just as simple. Madam, you must go first, then I will pull the rope up, make the child a safe sling, and lower her down. You may go as stiff as you like, then, Peneli—the stiffer the better. Will that be all right?'

She blinked at him, wondering how he knew about the stiffness, and deciding suddenly that she liked his deep voice, less ringing than the Harani voices—'Sort of furry,' she thought. She liked his strange accent too, and his odd, light shortening of her name. She smiled and nodded. The Princess stood up.

'I go first then. You can make Penelope's sling more comfortable with my shawl . . . over there.'

'This?' He picked it up, and then picked up something else,

something white, and looked at her with a suddenly mischievous grin. 'What about these?'

'That—what—Oh! My petticoats!' She blushed scarlet and snatched at them. He laughed, swinging them out of her reach. 'Lai! They would make it even more comfortable!' She took no notice, but seized them and, almost flouncing to the window, dropped them over the sill. 'Oh!' she said, between shame and laughter and fury, tossed her feet indignantly over the sill—and slipped.

She did not slip far. She clutched at the stones, and he was across the room gripping her arms before Penny had drawn breath to cry out. He took her weight while she found and grasped the rope, and when she had it he still held her. They looked at each other for a moment, both deathly pale.

'Be *careful*, woman!' he said harshly.

The Princess nodded meekly, the lord let her go, and she climbed slowly down out of sight. Penelope peered after her, but it looked such a horribly long way down that she drew back hastily. She turned to the Lord Vanh, who watched her with a little twisted smile, and wriggled.

'I'm sorry to be a nuisance, but I couldn't climb down. Honestly, I would just let go. It frightens me just to look. I ...' He cut her short with a gesture and a smile.

'Do not distress yourself. I will be the last to blame you, Peneli. Come, here is the rope.' He began knotting a sling for her, while she watched apprehensively, then gave her a merry secretive look. 'Shall I tell you something? I am glad I will be the last—because then there will be no one to see how long it takes me to gather courage to climb over the edge.' Penny looked at him in wonder, and then remembered how pale he had looked when he first climbed in. 'Oh! So that's how you knew about going stiff!'

'Yes ... and why I understand you not wanting to climb. Now, sit in there. Comfortable? Good.' He took the belt from around his coat, and put it round her and the rope. 'There, now you are safe as can be ... sit on the ledge ... don't look down, look at me ... look at my eyes ... now wriggle off; I've got you ... go on ... there, I said I'd got you. Now, if you bump against the wall push away with your feet. I am going to let you down quite fast, it is better that way—there you go.' His re-assuring voice faded away above her. Penelope took a breath and held it, thinking how lucky

she was that she did not have to climb, how much luckier
than Vanh—what a funny name—there was hardly anything
to it. She was determined not to think how far there was to
go, and her only support one pair of arms. Of course in the
mist you couldn't see the ground, that was a good thing—but
ugh! when you were in the middle you couldn't see anything!
Then she went down several feet with a bump, her throat
swelled suddenly, she shut her eyes ... then she felt the
Princess take hold of her, and she was down, and untied, and
feeling quite tottery with relief.

'I am sorry to leave the rope,' said Vanh when he joined
them. 'I only hope we have no need of it. ... Come now, my
horse is over this way. We will get as far as we can from
Kuniuk Rathen while the mist lasts, but then I promise you a
hot meal, Peneli. Hoi, Starwind my brother, did you think
you had lost me?'

Penelope stared speechless at his great horse, black with a
silver mane and tail. It was her first re-davel, and she was as
staggered as her brother had been. The Lord Vanh helped
the Princess to mount, tossed Penny up before her, then
turned to gather the weapons he had left on the ground.
Penny stared at the ground and clung. In'serinna turned and
looked up, and gasped.

'I cannot see our window! How did you aim your arrow?'

'I climbed a tree. But it was not one of the tallest, and
then I had to wait for a gap in the mist.' He slung on his
baldric, while the Princess looked at him in wonder.

'That was a mighty shot, then.'

He looked up at the tone of her voice, and then smiled; a
slow warm smile. Penelope suddenly felt she was not included, and turned aside.

'A man can do much,' he said softly, 'when he has such
good cause.'

She flushed, then looked away. His smile faded, and the
glow in his eyes died. His face looked shut and fierce again,
as he took a grip on the stirrup.

'On, Starwind!'

The horse surged forward; it began to canter, he to run.
Penelope gasped and shut her eyes; In'serinna bit her lip and
sighed. The mist surged together behind them.

Chapter Fifteen

The Border-dwellers

The hooves of the davlenei spurned the miles behind them.

Li'vanh was glad that they were on their way. The last evening in the camp had been oddly uncomfortable, impatient; all preparations made, no one could settle to an ordinary gathering around the fire. There were no women there anyway, which made it seem strange, because they had all gone away on their own, out into the plain beyond the wagon-circle, to dance and pray to the Good Goddess that she should send their men safe back. It made Li'vanh wriggle with discomfort, because none of the women had made any protest that he knew of—well, hardly any of them—but had submissively accepted the war; and now the snatches of their music and impassioned singing that the wind trailed back to the men sounded almost like laments. It was an unpleasant thought, that with so many prayers some must be unanswered, and he shrugged it quickly away. Few of the other men seemed disturbed. Silinoi said impassively that it made no difference, Keriol Hornblower knew each man's hour and his name . . . but that was not really much better. Anyway, it was not anything to do with him. Keriol Hornblower was no god of his. And he was riding a splendid horse across the plains in company with friends, and summer was just beginning, so what more could he want? He took a deep breath of the grass-scented air and sighed with satisfaction, then frowned again a little. It seemed that they would not be going back to the Plains after the battle, but on to H'ara Tunij . . . which was all very well in its way. Li'vanh wanted to see the city of the High King of course, but on the other hand he did not want to miss the plains in summer. And that

125

thought took him full circle to Mneri, and the women, and their wailing 'Rahai! Rahai!'

'Rahai' was the lament, the death-cry; it was also the men's war-cry 'Harai!' turned inside out, which was an uncomfortable thought. He balanced them in his mind, the men's voices fierce and triumphant, the women's lingering and grief-stricken ... what was that song? 'Rahai! My heart knows there will be no returning; Never, from the Blue Sea and the funeral burning. . . .' Oh, shut up, for crying out loud, you rotten coward!

But he was not a coward. Fear of death was not the fear that haunted him. It was a dread more unexpected and more unnerving: the fear of killing. He kept remembering the sharp-honed bronze of his sword, looking at his gleaming spear-heads, thinking, 'These are weapons. Weapons are made for killing men. These are your weapons. You are going to fight in a battle. In this battle you will use your weapons: you will use your weapons to. . . .' But still he could not make himself believe it. He could not picture that sword, veteran of a hundred fights with Derna, really shedding blood. He wondered if it ever would—if suddenly, when the fighting began, it would all become real—and if so what he would do, whether he would be able to make himself strike in earnest. 'I suppose,' he thought, 'when they are going for me to kill me, I'll do it by instinct.' It was not a pleasant thought.

In after years it was the walk with the Borderer which Nicholas never forgot. When Merekarl's eagles were only a quivering echo of valour, when the Inkalyei were rare nightmares, the memory of Kedrinh in the spring stayed with him. Never quite remembered, never quite forgotten, those cool green miles wove themselves into the backcloth of his mind, something that would belong to him always ... for they did seem to belong to him. Because there were no houses, because they never saw a man or any sign of one, he felt as old pioneers must have felt, crossing new continents and claiming all they saw.

Once they came on a road. As he reached the top of a rise he almost stumbled over a low white stone, such an unusual sight that he stopped in surprise. Looking about him he saw that there were two long rows of them, very wide-spaced and some half-concealed by grass. Between the two rows the grass grew, but there was a slight difference—maybe it was very slightly shorter, more stunted and tougher than the other, as if it had had to fight its way through harder packed earth. The road cut at an angle across their route, running roughly northwest-southeast. Nicholas was staring up and down it when the Borderer reached him. He had just noticed that here were very faint lines in the road, shadows almost, but tracing one to his feet he saw that it was a shallow groove. He looked up at the man.

'What is it? Where does it go?'

'A branch of the old North Road. They do not use it much now—they say the new one is easier to supply—but in the old days this was trodden all too often. This road goes to the Marches, and the King's armies made this path.'

'Armies!'

'Yes, armies! Can you not see the marks of their chariot wheels? The soldiers left less trace; but that is the way of things. The works of men outlast their makers. The feet of men beat out this road—so many feet, so many men. Emneron the Young himself must have passed this place. Now Emneron the Young is fallen and the armies march no more, but the road still runs to the same end as ever.'

The Borderer spoke calmly, but his words disturbed Nicholas. The road seemed suddenly alive; not merely a strip of hard-trodden earth and stunted grass, but something with a mind and will of its own. It went where it had always gone, heedless of the fickleness of the men who used it no longer, caring nothing for their favour or neglect, flowing past the milestones like a patient serpent who never came to the end of himself. He shook himself, and so much by instinct that he did not even notice, looked right and left and right again before hurrying after the Borderer, almost as if he feared to be trodden down by the tramping feet and run over by the rattling wheels of ghost armies.

'Did they have battles here, then? This seems such a peaceful place. It doesn't go, somehow.'

'Yet most of the worst battles of our history have been here. Not far from this place Emneron the Young died ... yes, these downs are peaceful. But they are the last of the lands of law; the very edge of peace. Beyond their borders has always been the threat at least of war. Yet I agree with you, these hills are more tranquil than anywhere else in the realm. It is strange, but common, that things seem best when most in danger. The sun is never more splendid than at his setting.'

Nicholas wriggled. There was a sadness in the Borderer's voice that somehow recalled Black Mountain and all that had happened there. The howl of the Inkalyei rang in his mind, and he felt chilled.

'Are we—is it—is there danger now?'

'Oh yes! Kedrinh never enjoys any but a defended peace, and in these days of Fendarl's rising, great is our peril. . . .'

For Penny too this was an interlude of calm. There seemed to be hurry but no danger. She supposed vaguely that they would be pursued, but that was no affair of hers. Vanh and the Princess would see to that.

She did not see much of their descent from Black Mountain, except that the ground was usually steep and there were plenty of trees, because the mist persisted. The Lord Vanh merely said that this was good, as it made escape easier, but the Princess was jubilant. She said that it showed that Kunil-Bannoth must be much disturbed to let the weather change. Penelope gasped.

'He doesn't run the weather, does he?'

'Why else is it winter and a hard frost on Black Mountain, and spring elsewhere? He keeps it so; he or Fendarl. I would guess at Fendarl, but he must work through Kunil-Bannoth at the moment, and if his mind is in a turmoil so is his master's magic. And we know whom to thank for that.'

'Me? Good. I hope I have upset him. And I hope he gets even more upset when he finds us gone. Ha ha serve him right.'

Vanh laughed. 'And I hope that my tokens give him pause—a Khentor arrow and a Khentor rope. If he knows enough to recognize them.'

'You've talked about Khentor things too, Princess. What do they mean? What's funny?'

'Not things, Penelope, the Khentors are a people. My maid Arleni was Khentor. We Harani and the Khentors—we are the Border-dwellers. Some say that we are unlikely yoke-fellows, but of all peoples in the world we have the firmest friendship . . . have we not, my lord Vanh?'

'It is good to think so, Madam.'

There was nothing remarkable in his tone, but again Penelope had the feeling that he had said something which she had not heard. It was often like that, when he spoke to the Princess. Sometimes it was quite strange to hear them. Often they would talk almost without words, understanding leaping between them as if they were the oldest of old friends. At other times they would be so distant as to seem almost total strangers. And they changed from one mood to the other with no warning: suddenly in mid-sentence all the warmth froze, and often Penny found herself the only one left talking in a silence grown suddenly knife-edged. Now, this time, she determinedly carried on.

'Are you a Khentor, then, Lord Vanh?'

'Mostly, Peneli. I am a miserable hybrid. Part of me is Vanh the Hunter a Hurno of the Northern Plains. The other part is Prince Vanh, heir to the Kingdom of Lunieth. And the Boy knows what will become of me.

'Which boy?' asked Penelope. But neither of them answered her.

That night, full and warm with food, Penelope lay for long on the border of sleep without crossing it. And in this half-awake state, she began to be aware of the Prince and Princess talking, not as they usually talked but carefully, almost stiffly, as if trying to make a firm bridge between themselves. She did not listen; but without really knowing it she was hearing.

'How did you find us?'

Kuniuk Rathen is not hard to find. It was only a matter of not being seen.'

'And how did you know I—we—were there?'

'Where else would you be?'

'But how did you know we were captive? Did you—have you seen my kinsmen? Do you know if they are safe?'

'When you did not come down the mountain they went up. Maybe they tried to win you back by force of arms. I do not know. I did not wait to see them return. I came to Kuniuk Bannoth by the fastest way I could.'

'You *were* there! Captain Emneron—he *did* see something! It was you!'

'Yes, Princess.'

'But how—why were you—what brought you to Black Mountain?'

There was a small, still pause. Then he said, his voice very even, 'What else but you, In'serinna?'

The Princess made a faint noise, but said nothing. After a moment he said, 'I followed you from Rennath. And little enough cover there was, too. I think your Khentorji saw me.' There was another pause, and then apparently the Princess began another question, for Vanh said quickly, almost roughly, 'And do not you ask me again "Why?" You know why; you must! Surely you must!'

'How should I? You never said . . .'

'. . . anything. I know—oh, I know; I kept my tongue between my teeth. But surely you realized? I know I have hung my heart on my bridle all these months; if you could not see, you were the only one. You *did* know, and I will swear it did not displease you! Yes, I will swear there was a time when you were glad of what you saw!'

'Enough for that! Why, you scarcely even spoke to me!'

'In'serinna!' There was a sudden movement, and opening her eyes, startled, Penelope saw that he had sprung to his feet. 'I am a plainsman bred, and little used to talking. Also they all said to me 'Hold your peace!' All—my friends, your friends, my grandsire, even my father—yes, even he said I was a fool, that I should consider you were a Daughter of the Stars and remember my place. But all bade me hold my tongue. Well, I will speak all you want now. I have had my fill of silence. They were all wrong—all of them. Even my father—"Remember your place!" *He* is the one who does not know my place! I know it now, lai, and yours also. In'serinna, my heart. . . .'

He took a step towards her, and then suddenly she was scrambling to her feet, pointing upwards, saying in a high, almost panicky voice 'Look! The stars! I had nearly forgotten—I must speak to Kiron! Pardon me, my lord—I must speak to Kiron!'

And she turned and fairly fled from the firelight. Vanh stood frozen absurdly for a second, too taken aback to protest. Then he stepped back and sat down, and drawing his knife, his lips moving in unheard curses, began to hack savagely at the cold ground.

As time passed Nicholas began to notice that the Borderer seemed uneasy. He talked less than at first, and often the boy heard him muttering to himself. He frowned often, his eyes searching the countryside, and several times in an hour he would stop, prickling like a dog at a scent. When his young companion pestered him to show what was the matter he grunted only, 'Things are stirring—stirring.'

'You've said that before.'

'Aye, and will again. Those who once knew better have sounded a strong blast to call their friends, and many things have heard. Again I say, boy, things are stirring. And things are stirring that are best sleeping.'

But Nicholas could notice nothing: peer and sniff as he might for a whole day, he could find nothing that seemed unusual to him. Though when he said so to the Borderer, he got only the reply that seemed the man's motto: 'I am not blind, nor am I deaf, and I can smell more things than galya with my nose.'

At last, one time when they had just come through a patch of trees and Nicholas was about to run ahead, the Borderer caught his breath sharply and clamped a hand on the boy's shoulder.

His grip hurt; Nicholas twisted and almost cried out, but the man hissed 'Quiet!' and pointed. And the boy looked, and was quiet.

Down in the valley before them the earth stirred, and then there appeared the figure of a girl riding a pony; and they waded through the green earth as though it were a river.

The pony was stocky, earth-coloured, powerful looking; she too was sturdily built, square and strong, with a broad, rather sullen, peasant face, and weather-beaten skin. Yet still there was something eerie about her, something witch-like. She wore a long crimson skirt, but otherwise her fire-gold hair was her only garment. She did not so much ride the pony as let it bear her, and she turned to one side, one hand resting on its quarters, looking about her. Her eyes passed over the travellers, and Nicholas shuddered. He could not see their colour, but she felt their fierceness. A slow, deep savagery moved in them, and as she rode heat rippled from her. Not warmth—heat. She was coarse, she was primitive, she was frightening—and yet she was beautiful. She was beautiful in a way he had never dreamed of, did not understand, yet seemed to remember. And looking at her, everything that he had ever called beautiful faded, paled, seemed but husks beside her, and the very thought 'beauty' re-shaped in the mind until it fitted her; for it had been made of her, and for her, and now all at once it seemed a richer, brighter, more terrible thing.

Girl and pony seemed to move at a walk, but before the boy and man knew it they were past, more swiftly than seemed possible. The earth flowed and splashed from them, a wash and wake of brown soil churned and swirled behind them, and then slowly dissolved and sank back to unbroken green. And Nicholas breathed again, and looked at the Borderer, who stood shaking his head.

'Did she see us?'

'Nay, we are not real enough. We are not solid enough for her eyes. She saw only earth, and growing things.'

'Who is she?'

'She is one of the oldest spirits of the earth. She knows no law but one, and it is better for all that she should be under the earth and not over it. Vir'Vachal she is. Vir'Vachal! Oh, Vir'Vachal! Deep have they delved indeed, to wake the earth magic!'

Chapter Sixteen

The Wind and the Stars

It took the Hurnei four days to reach the place appointed for the muster. On the third day away in the east Li'vanh saw a tangle of low hills that someone told him were the heights of Kunoi Len Vanda; but apart from that the country was the same plain all the way. Two tribes were before them at the muster and four came after, giving them a host, Li'vanh judged, of about six thousand spears. And in the dark of the moon they rode out.

During the first day they crossed a wide river, which Silinoi told Li'vanh was the border between Khentorash and Khendhalash. 'Now we are in the country of the princes,' he said. Li'vanh could see the difference at once. The country was tame; the hand of man lay upon it, light but firm. They began to see farms with houses of wood and stone, 'rooted' houses the tribesmen called them. Once they passed a village. Li'vanh watched it with curiosity and a faint unease. This country he knew could not be familiar; yet he could not feel that it was strange. It touched a faint chord in him, as if among foreigners he had met a man who though not of his tribe was yet a plainsman. It was not recognition, but acknowledgement.

From all these works of settled men the plainsmen kept themselves almost fearfully, but so large a host could not go unnoticed and many times they were hailed and asked what brought them. The blood in those parts is mixed, and none of the men who spoke to them was pure Harani, but Li'vanh was still struck by the difference between them and the Khentorei. He avoided them; they woke the same echo of memory as their country, and he disliked it. To all who accosted them Silinoi returned the same answer: that Deron

King of Rennath was being attacked by the Kelanat, and all who had help to bring should bring it to the Ford of Danamol as soon as might be. So gradually another, Harani, army grew, and followed behind them. But the Khentors did not ride with them. Outside their own lands now they clung grimly together.

The night after they had seen Vir'Vachal was the dark of the silver moon; and Nicholas woke to see the Borderer standing stiffly above him, every nerve tense and every sense alert. He began to sit up, questions forming on his lips, but the man waved him fiercely down. Thinking there must be some danger he lay down flat and quiet; but nothing happened, and when he woke again it was morning and the Borderer was cooking their breakfast.

'What was it?' he asked, struggling free of his covers. The Borderer glanced at him. His eyes were troubled and, Nicholas thought, rather angry. He did not answer for a moment.

'What was it?' the boy repeated.

'Nothing!' he said. 'Or something. How should I know? Is it any concern of mine? Am I not of the Tenth House, having no part in the Magic? I cannot be certain that it was anything at all. I can only guess.'

'Well,' said Nicholas, taken aback, 'what did you guess?'

The man's face relaxed a little, and in a moment he smiled unwillingly. 'I am sorry, boy. There was no need to visit my House's grievances on you. No, I am troubled. In the night, I am sure I felt something ... and it was dark of the moon.'

'What do you think?'

'I think ... I think I must make more haste to see you in H'ara Tunij.' He went on slowly, 'I think—I fear—that Fendarl has re-entered Kedrinh.'

Nicholas sat still. A prickle of shock and fear ran over him.

'Where—where would he go?'

'He would go to Kuniuk Bannoth. It was his home of old. The Eagle will roost again in Black Mountain.'

'Black Mountain! But my sister is there! Oh no—oh— Penny—Merekarl—Hairon—the Princess. . . . Oh, Penelope!'

He scrambled to his feet, panic in his heart and face, unheeded tears in his eyes.

'Hush, now. Hush! If Fendarl is there at least the eye and mind of Kiron will be on them. There is nothing we can do. Be calm; I will see if I can discover any more tonight. Now eat, and then walk!'

It took Penelope and her companions four days to reach Rennath. They could have done it in less, but Vanh was careful to lead them by a way, he said, hard to follow; although In'serinna said that they would not be pursued beyond the bounds of Rennath. And when they had crossed into her father's land, somehow they seemed to travel more and more slowly.

It was not a comfortable journey. The Lord Vanh talked to her and the Princess talked to her, but they rarely spoke to each other. They seemed both to be trying to pretend that the other was not there; yet a tight cord of pain ran between them, and even the child felt its restraint.

The Lord was merely proud and silent; but the Princess was troubled and miserable, and Penelope grew unhappy watching her. She would sit on the horse with her head drooping, arguing endlessly within herself; and then suddenly fling her hair back and laugh defiantly, and start talking with fierce gaiety. But that was always the signal for Vanh to fall silent, or to give curt answers. Once or twice her temper flashed, and they almost quarrelled. On the whole Penelope preferred the Princess to be silent. She was so changed, so strange and moody, that the little girl would sooner talk to Vanh. He told her about his tribe, about his father and brother and sister, about his life on the plains. Sometimes Penelope would become aware that the Princess, though she made no sound, was listening eagerly, which she thought strange as they disagreed so much. She would watch him too, Penny noticed. If he looked at her she would turn haughtily away, but when he did not notice her eyes were often on him.

The evenings were better. There would be little talk, but Vanh would sing the strange, achingly sad songs of his own people, and sometimes In'serinna would add some of her own. But more often she would wander away from the firelight—'Star-gazing,' said Vanh with anger—and he would tell Penny stories until she fell asleep. Often In'serinna, who slept beside her, woke her in the night with her restlessness, and once the child woke to see her sitting with her arms around her knees, and her face turned up to the stars which silvered the tears sliding down her cheeks.

For a moment she did not believe it. Then she sat up, and put a timid hand on the young woman's arm.

'Princess?' she whispered, 'What is it? What's the matter? I thought we were safe now.'

'Yes,' she answered in a low voice after a moment. 'Safe enough. But I would sooner be in the blackest danger of my life, than in this torment.'

'Why? What is it?' There was no answer, and after a moment she said hesitantly, 'Don't you like us being with the Lord Vanh?'

Her face twisted as if for a second she felt like laughing; but she just shook her head, whether in answer to her question or not Penelope could not tell.

'But don't you like him? I do. I thought you did at first. Have you quarrelled with him?'

At that the Princess did give a laugh—of sorts. 'No, Penelope, we have not quarrelled. And I do not dislike the Lord. It is only. . . .' She stopped again, then gave a shaky laugh and suddenly hugged Penny fiercely. 'Oh, I am being foolish, and there is no need to bring you into my—my worries. Go back to sleep, and do not trouble yourself.'

'No, that's not fair! I am already, and now you won't tell me anything. You never tell me anything. And anyhow, you owe me something for the eyes bit.'

In'serinna looked baffled for a moment, then smiled. 'Oh yes, maybe I do. But you are so young—I do not think I can—it is only that I should—that I wish. . . . Anyway, I cannot. I cannot!'

'What not?' said Penelope, thoroughly confused.

'Desert,' she answered miserably.

'Desert? What do you want to desert?'

'Oh, I do not know what I want—but I think I am learning. But it would be. Peneli, what would you think if, knowing there was a war and too few soldiers, one of these soldiers laid down his weapons and said, 'I'm tired of fighting, someone else can do it.' Would he not be a coward and a traitor?'

'A what? I don't know. You called me Peneli just then.'

'Oh!—Oh, it is no use, little one. You cannot understand yet, or help me. Lie down.'

'Well, I wish you would say something straight out! Why were you crying?'

She was silent, then put an arm around the girl and drew her close to her.

'I will be as plain as I can. You know I am an enchantress. Well, I love the magic—so much, so very much. The power and the high peaks and the battle—can you understand that?'

'Oh, *yes!*'

'Well, do you remember me saying that everything has a price? I have always known this, or thought I knew. If you remember, the price of the Star Magic is to forsake warmth forever—all warmth. I thought I could pay this price—oh, easily. But—it is just that I never knew until now how cold I was.'

Penny was silent; and the Princess sighed. 'Lie down now, Penelope. Good night.'

'Good night,' muttered Penelope, and lay down. But she still looked up at In'serinna, and saw her draw out from within her tabard the Pearl of Rennath in its eagle-claw grip, and cupping it in her hands look at it, sighing. Then she let it fall. And the last thing Penny saw before her eyes closed was the Princess pulling her shawl up around her shoulders and with a gesture wholly unlike her usual movements, huddle into it.

All through the next day she was very quiet, and if the Lord Vanh ever spoke to her at all angrily—as he did fairly regularly—instead of flashing back herself she answered almost meekly. It seemed to work. Vanh seemed to grow ashamed of his own moodiness, and as the day passed became much better tempered.

'Tell me what this place is like, that you are going to be the King of,' persuaded Penelope, during the afternoon. 'Is it like this place?'

'Like Rennath? A little; but it is hillier, and warmer. We grow good fruit there—at least so my grandsire tells me. I have never been there in summer. But there are some good ponies there, as well as sheep and cattle. I could make them something worth having. And one thing it has that Rennath lacks: the King's castle is called Kuniuk Emneth, and it looks on the sea. I have seen it, once or twice, on a warm day of early spring, when the snow has gone, and the flowers begin to bloom, with the seabirds swooping about it ... I think a man would have to go far to see anything as fair.'

'I like the sea. Come on, Princess, what has Rennath got as good as that?'

'The borders of Rennath run up to the mountains. that is worth something, for those who love mountains. But I believe the Khentorei do not?'

'Not as we love the wide spaces and the windy places ... but we can see their beauty. A place that is lovely, but where we do not wish to be.' The Princess laughed, and he looked pleased, his rare, splendid, smile coming to his lips. 'But what need has Rennath to boast of her mountains when she has other, greater riches, which Lunieth can never equal ... and is ever the poorer for lacking?'

They travelled late one day. Once the Princess exclaimed 'Look! The Melneth Tree!' pointing to a very ancient growth. It was almost entirely rotted, covered in thick ivy, and through the trunk was stuck the corroded remains of a sword.

'That means we are within four hours journey of Rennath Castle.'

The Lord Vanh looked at the sun. 'We have an hour or less to sunset. But we can do it before we rest if you wish.'

The glow on the Princess's face died, but she made no protest. So after sunset they went on, though they were passing through woods and it soon grew very dark, and the rising wind moaned coldly through the trees. Penny said once or twice that it was all very well for some people, who did not get cold or hungry or tired, but they took no notice. And then very abruptly the woods came to an end at the top of a high hill, and the wind snatched at them suddenly, so that the two girls gasped. But Vanh stood all at once spellbound, his gaze held by the massive moonless arch of heaven, and the blazing stars.

'Look!' he breathed. 'Look at the stars!'

'The wind!'

'Ah, but look! How beautiful they are—and how high and calm.' He sounded suddenly almost ashamed. 'The winds that shake the grasses cannot trouble their majesty.'

And then all at once, the Princess's face, gazing on him,

changed and stilled and her eyes grew soft, and she gave a sound between a sigh and a laugh, as if bonds had fallen from her.

'Then it is well for them,' she said, 'But for my part I am here, and the wind is certainly troubling me.' Her words made a sudden stillness; then the Lord turned and looked up at her, wonder and disbelief and gladness fighting in his eyes. And she laughed down at him, her expression gay and tender and rueful.

'My Lord,' she said, softly and a little shyly, 'could we go down from this height? For I' she said 'feel cold.'

Chapter Seventeen

Dancer of the Streams

So in the third hour of the night the Porter of Rennath City was summoned to open the gates in the name of Deron the King, and great was his delight and wonder to hear the voice and see the face of the King's daughter, and much did he wonder at her companions. There was shouting and noise of feet as the guard of honour turned out, and the clatter of hooves as a messenger was sent to the castle; then one or two folk whose houses looked on the road pushed back their windows to see what caused the commotion, and they saw in the torchlight the face of their lost Princess. The news spread like flames through the city, and even the children were brought from their beds to cheer her through the streets. So they passed to the castle amid rejoicing, and there at the Great Gate stood Deron her father, and his three sons behind him, with Prince Hairon and the Lord Horenon, dazed with relief. She slipped from Starwind's back and went to her father, and the people cheered; but the King took his child in his arms and held her to him without a word.

That night Penelope slept in a canopied bed, in a small tower room whose walls were plastered white and painted with flowers, after a bath in a wooden tub in front of a log fire. She woke far into the morning to a breakfast of porridge and milk and honey, and they dressed her in fresh clothes, a blouse of white silk and a skirt of dark green, the stiff sleeveless tabard embroidered with bright yellow flowers. Then the Princess came to her, clothes all in white and gold, and kissed her and asked her how she liked Rennath; and she answered that she liked it well. And In'serinna led her down and took her to her father and presented her. Penelope curtsied, the king raised her and greeted her gravely, and courteously, and presented to her his sons, Argerth the Throne Prince, Prince Veldreth, and Prince Garon. They smiled on her and bowed to her, but the Prince Hairon laughed and swung her up over his head, tickling her and saying had she given the old devil something to think about then?

She giggled, and squealed and kicked and wriggled until he put her down, and In'serinna laughed at him and said 'While I remember, Hairon, I give you your due. You were right to say danger waited up the mountain. But I think I was right to go, and we have suffered no lasting harm. Penelope, my father has had news of Nicholas. He is in safe hands.'

'It seems your brother made his way to Nelimhon,' said King Deron, 'and there met with one who is some sort of kin to us. One of the Dwellers in the Wood brought me word of him: though I did not then know who he was. Then Hairon came, to say that you and my daughter had been taken by Kunil Bannoth.... We were near despairing of rescuing you, and then came help unlooked for. Vanh, son of Silinoi Lord of the Northern Plains, Hunter of the Hurnei, Throne Prince of Lunieth, our thanks to you are beyond expression.'

Vanh bowed; but he turned the talk to the coming battle. It was only a day later that the hastily summoned army of Rennath was led out by Prince Argerth. All of the Rennath princes rode out: Hairon, handsome Veldreth the Enchanter, and merry Garon; and Vanh rode with them as a kinsman.

For during that day, Vanh had sought out the King, and had asked him for the hand in marriage of his daughter In'serinna. The King looked on him gravely, and said 'You are a noble man and a brave one. You brought my daughter safe out of the fortress of her enemy, and restored to me that which is dear to me above all. My debt to you is past knowledge. If you can win my daughter's consent, and the consent of Kiron, then you have mine.'

'Having given him my heart, father,' said In'serinna, 'I would sooner not withhold my hand.'

So they pledged one another, and the Princes embraced him and called him brother; but King Deron did not yet give them his blessing, nor did they exchange bracelets after their custom. For they could not be called betrothed without the consent of Kiron—and that was still to be won.

After the night of the dark of the moon, the Borderer hustled Nicholas on more quickly. He reassured him all he could about the fate of Penelope and the Princess, but in the end only weariness of heart stopped the boy's worrying. There was nothing at all that he could do, and after two or three days he reflected that if anything awful was going to happen to them it had happened by now. So he schooled himself not to think, and on the whole succeeded.

They had been walking along the bank of a river for some time; not very broad, but deep and swift. Then suddenly it turned, and they stood on its brink.

'Do we cross it?' asked Nicholas, wondering if his swimming would serve him, and doubting it.

'No,' said the Borderer, 'It is time to turn east, and the river is our swiftest road. We must reach the sea before the last of the King's ships leaves harbour. Now we can rest our legs, Nikon; here we take to the water.'

'We do?' He looked up- and down-river, but there was no sign of a boat. 'How?'

The Borderer laughed. 'Wait here. I will be gone a while.' And with no more explanation than that he left him.

Nicholas sat and waited. He watched the river birds, and trailed his arm in the water. It was icy cold, and even by the bank pulled on him fiercely. He crawled along the banks peering into the reeds and laughed to see how the water-fowl had moored their nests, weaving the rooted rushes into them on the downstream side so that the drag of the current helped to keep them safe and still instead of sweeping them away. The water was very deep and the banks were steep cut. He was glad he would not be asked to swim.

At long last, just as he was beginning to wonder if his friend had forgotten him and if he was going to be left to walk to the sea, he heard a familiar deep voice singing a familiarly unintelligible song. He looked along the banks, but the Borderer appeared in midstream.

Nicholas gaped. Where on earth, he wondered, had he managed to find a boat at this notice? A trim boat, too: narrow and light, with upcurved prow and stern, a small tent amidships, and a small steering deck that was hardly more than a foothold. There were two dark blue sails: a square mainsail, and a triangular sail rigged from the mast to the stern. The Borderer sat with the tiller under his arm, and when he saw Nicholas' face of amazement he laughed and guided the boat to the shore. 'Quick!' he said, 'Wind and water call her; she is high-tempered, my lovely, and fretful to be gone. Jump in!'

Nicholas seized the prow and sprang. As soon as he had landed in the boat the Borderer swung his craft back into the centre of the river and, with a cry of encouragement, seemed to urge her forward. The wind and the river took her and she sped downstream.

Nicholas crawled through the tent and emerged by the Borderer's knees. He was sitting on the tiny deck and grinned at the boy. Suddenly he seemed less deep, less earthy; the wind ruffled his shaggy hair from behind, and his laughter split his beard. Nicholas stared.

'What do you think of her, my bird, my beauty? Eh?'

'She's marvellous! Is she yours?'

'What, would I take another man's boat? Though if another man owned my treasure, I would be tempted, boy. No, she is mine, I built her with the help of a friend I have, so I named her for him. *Dancer,* I call her, my dancer of the streams. Her keel and her mast are made of irvelhin, the tree that dances in the wind, the Irananitree; and *Dancer* hates to be still.'

'How come she was so handy?'

'Ah, she is never far when I need her.' He chuckled again, and Nicholas eyed him askance.

'You're about the oddest man I've ever met,' he said accusingly. 'I sometimes wonder if you're a man at all. *Are* you human?'

The Borderer's face stilled a little. 'Oh, yes, Nikon, I am a man. But I cannot help my strangeness. All my family are strange, for we are all always—strangers. We are inconvenient nuisances, but it is not our fault. We fall between two worlds, and neither can fit us in.'

'You are—! Why?'

The man was silent a moment, leaning back. Then he said 'Listen, then, and I will tell you.'

'The Harani have not always lived here. They came over the sea more than a thousand years ago. Before that they were a poor farming folk; but the High Lords chose them out for a task that was to be done, because they are like no other men in the world. To guide and to rule them and to bear the brunt of the battle that was to be waged the High Lords purposed to bring high blood into them. So they sent the Starborn, the nine children of the Shining One Tinoithë, to them; Alunyueth and his eight sisters. Alunyueth married Garinna, the King's daughter, and his sisters the eight worthiest men of the land. Alunyueth ruled the people. A son was born to him and Garinna who was Emneron the White, and a son to each of his sisters. And daughters also were born to his sisters, and to one of them twin girls. But Alunyueth's daughter was born last, late and unlooked-for, and some say should never have been born at all. Then after a few years the Children of Tinoithë departed as they had come.

'The years passed and the children grew up: nine Starborn lords, but ten Starborn maidens. And each of the lords took one of the maids to wife. Emneron became the King. But Garinna his sister, youngest and loveliest of the Starborn, had no husband. She was wild and fierce and proud, not easily to be won, though there were many to try, for Garinna Emneleriath was the most beautiful woman the earth has ever seen, and she was the daughter of Alunyueth royalest of all.

'Then the word came to Emneron, to follow the swans, and the people came to Vandarei, to the Starlit Land. Then it was that Garinna was won, by Indaron the helmsman of her brother's ship. Now each of the Starlords founded a city, and from those nine lords and ladies descend the Nine Houses of the Children of the Stars, the wielders of the Star Magic. From Emneron, of course, descend the Kirontin and the High Kings. And from Garinna descends the Tenth House.'

'That is what you are! You said . . .'

'That is right. Now, though Garinna was Starborn, her husband Indaron was no more than mortal. *We* say that Indaron our forefather was a worthy enough man, and Garinna's birth should have outweighed her husband's. Her brother was the High King; and was not her father Alunyueth the Prince? But *they* say that we are of common blood on one side, and not Starborn. So we are denied part in the Star Magic, and place in the Council of Enchanters, and must play a solitary part in the great war. For we *are* of their blood, and we *cannot* make ourselves mortal, and it has been ordained that though we can never be more than we are, the centuries will never make us less. So the Children of Garinna are as you see me: strange wanderers, half magicians. The power of our foremother's blood is in us, but not the lore of ages.' He fell silent and sighed, watching the river. Nicholas glanced up at him but did not find anything to say. He had never seen the Borderer looking sad before. It hurt him and he looked away, half ashamed. After a few moments the man looked back to him and saw his troubled face and laughed again, suddenly.

'There, Nikon, do not think it is such a grief! Well, well, enough of old grudges. At least none of my high-born kin have the strange friends that I have; and none of *them* are free as I am, to fly with *Dancer* down the river!'

Chapter Eighteen

The Ford of Danamol

At the Ford of Danamol a spur of the mountains runs right down to the river, making a low rampart of hills screening it from the north. The Khentor host was pausing to eat about two miles away from the Ford; Li'vanh and Mnorh had gone away from the rest about a mile, to the top of a low rise, to keep a watch. They were lying very flat in the short grass taking it in turns to keep an eye on the land before them. And it was during Mnorh's watch, while Li'vanh was looking back towards their own camp, that the enemy first showed themselves.

Mnorh kicked his brother. 'Look!' he hissed.

Li'vanh breathed in some pollen in his surprise, and choked. 'Be quiet!' snapped Mnorh, thumping his back. Li'vanh spluttered indignantly, rolled over, and looked along Mnorh's pointing arm.

'Kelenat!' hissed the boy.

Some way away, between them and the Ford, the head of a column of men appeared from the trees clothing the hill. They were on foot, which was a shock: he had forgotten that some armies marched. Much closer to them—the nearest less than a hundred paces away—were some single men. 'Scouts,' whispered Mnorh, 'Well, there's the Kelanat.'

Li'vanh felt his stomach turn over; he did not know what to say. It was like meeting the half-Harani, but far worse. He had never met a Kelanat. They were strangers, foreigners, and he knew them.

He knew those square, bony faces. They were familiar—their height, their weight, their firm slow tread. They were big men—big, not just tall; heavy with muscle. They wore tunics and sandals and their limbs were red and brown from sunburn. He looked at the bright fair hair curling on their necks, and knew without seeing that their eyes would be grey-blue. 'And probably,' he thought with sudden fury, 'they have thin lips and big hands and hairy chests and flat feet!'

But this did them less than justice. They had their own beauty. Certainly the young man closest to him would have been in many places thought very handsome indeed; he was tall and powerful, clear-eyed, blond, and tanned. Siegfried, Apollo, Galahad, the hero of a hundred forgotten fairy-tales walked the grass near Li'vanh. But Li'vanh quite literally hated the sight of them.

It would not have been so bad if he could have held the memory they roused and understood it; but when he would have grasped it, it slipped from him. A fear that was almost panic mounted in him, and he had to look away. Something about them was reaching out to claim him, and he shrank from it, and because of this, and because of the horror that filled him, he felt a sudden fierce dislike of the Kelanat, and a pitiless anger against them.

'Come on,' he said harshly, 'We'd better go and raise the alarm.'

They seized their horses and scrambled on to their backs, heading back to the host at a gallop. Their approach was seen; Silinoi and the lords of the other tribes were waiting.

'About a mile and a half away,' said Mnorh, 'and heading for the Ford. The numbers I cannot tell.'

Silinoi turned, calling brief commands; and all at once horns and drums began their compelling music. It was a call Li'vanh had been taught. 'Arm!' it said. 'Take your weapons. Mount.'

He raced through the camp, a sense of unreality filling him. He seized his spears and pulled on his baldric— Khentors wear their swords slung from their shoulder across their body, not on a belt—straightened his clothes, checked his horn and knife, illogically combed his hair and moustache, and ran back to Dur'chai. Hunoi grinned at him, Derna clapped his shoulder in passing. He ran by Rehai the Hunter, who was slowly and methodically clasping necklaces and pushing on bracelets. He thought as he mounted, 'I'm sure I've left something behind.' He felt no fear. He did not believe in any of it.

Mnorh suddenly surfaced beside him; but he had miscalcu-

lated, and found himself trapped by his father's stern gaze.
'Go back,' commanded Silinoi, 'All the boys are to stay with
Yorn.' Mnorh made a face, but no protest. 'The God be with
you, my father,' he said, then turning to Li'vanh clasped his
hand. 'Good hunting, my brother,' he grinned.

Li'vanh nodded, but could think of no reply. Suddenly his
mouth was dry. What could one say? 'If I don't come back
you can have my blue rug?' For the first time a cold spasm
clutched him.

He glanced over his shoulder. All over the host men were
nodding and clasping the hands of their comrades, wishing
them luck as casually as if there was no chance that this was
for ever. Rehai the Hunter he saw, inclining his head and
giving his brief uncertain smile, and saying something to
Derna. Derna punched him affectionately. 'Get away, you
fool,' he said.

Li'vanh moved Dur'chai up to beside Silinoi, who had
mounted and was holding the banner. It took him a minute
or two to realize that someone was calling his name, then he
turned. Rehai was behind him. 'Tuvoi!' he said, his still dark
eyes holding Li'vanh's. 'The wind in your face always, and
may the gods ever love you as they do now.' Then before the
startled Tuvoi could make any reply, he crossed to Silinoi.

'Terani,' he said, 'the banner?'

Silinoi looked at him startled, then thoughtful. Rehai
watched him seriously.

'Let me bear it.' His quiet voice was intense. 'It is my
right, Terani. Your son would have taken it, and I have
taken his place as the Hunter. Let me take the banner.'

Silinoi hesitated. Rehai gestured. 'Do you not think me
worthy?'

His chieftain drew breath and looked at him steadily.
'Rehai the Hunter, Rehai son of Yaln,' he said, 'I account
you worthy of any honour the tribe can give. Take the
banner and bear it to victory.'

Rehai took the banner and his back straightened. There was
a light in his eyes; he almost smiled. The host drew together,
and fell silent. Silinoi said to Li'vanh, 'We must cut them off
from the Ford.' Li'vanh nodded, running his tongue over his
lips. Yorn stood out before them and, raising his arms, cried
out the prayers to the gods. Li'vanh looked firmly at his

saddle; he tried to think of a prayer for himself, but all he could manage was 'Help!'

Then suddenly his father's voice beside him bellowed, 'Harai!' And the voices of the tribe, his own among them, bawled back 'Harai Hurnei!' and then in their turn the other tribes, and then the whole host was yelling together, 'Harai! Hai-ai-ai! Harai Khentorei, hai-ai-ai davenei!' and all at once were surging forward.

'It's happening *now*!' thought Li'vanh, his heart jumping; then, 'No, we've nearly two miles to go yet!'

But two miles, he thought, was not far; and it seemed even less with the horses stretching from trot to canter to gallop, and the sound of the charge roaring in the air behind him. A wordless sound was rising from the throats of the tribesmen, a sound not unlike the belling of hounds—a cry part to their horses, part to themselves, part to their enemy. They swept over the rise where the boys had kept watch, and Li'vanh saw the Kelanat force shift and quicken as they joined the race for the ford and at the same time prepared for combat.

Li'vanh set his teeth and moved his grip on the reins. He felt quite sick, but with a cold growing excitement. He levelled his spear and gripped it, but his right hand was sweaty and damp and did not seem to hold well. He clenched it under his arm, against his side, but had to relax it after a minute or two. 'I am afraid!' he thought triumphantly, as if it was something he had always wanted to be. Some men were yelling and waving swords. He thought, shook his head, stuck to his spear. In front of him rode Rehai with the banner. He was singing; and Li'vanh saw with sudden, almost indignant disbelief, that he had no weapon ready. He seemed not to know he was going into battle; he was just riding and singing, his free hand caressing his horse's neck.

Then he saw that they were at the Ford, and the race was won. He gave a yell of triumph, and then, not even waiting to see what anyone else was doing, wheeled Dur'chai and charged the Kelanat.

He had heard of battle-madness—in that moment it seized him. Afterwards he thought it had been not unlike panic, except that he had raced yelling towards the enemy and not away from them. He was aware of Silinoi beside him, of Rehai before, now with his sword drawn and ready, not singing, not yelling. Behind him he heard a man laughing fiercely. Then the two forces clashed, and at once all was confusion.

He lost his spear; it was wrenched out of his hand almost at once. He snatched another saw someone strike at him, swung with the spear to ward off the blow and, of all things, dropped it. Suddenly he found this very funny, and laughed aloud as he swept out his sword. Then the fighting became close and grim. He could see nothing but his own little patch, and not much of that. He had no time to think ahead; it was all he could do to keep up. 'Watch his eyes,' Derna had said, but he did not have a single enemy, there were no eyes to watch, only arms and weapons. Spearheading the charge as he was, he met a continual succession of fresh men, and he had to fight like a madman merely to keep alive. At one time he became suddenly aware that he had a spear in his left hand and a sword in his right ... at another time that there was a burning pain in his left leg. Then he began to feel that the ground was rising steeply: he shifted his seat and gripped harder. His leg shot again. He flinched, put his hand on it, and took it up wet with blood. 'Mine,' he thought, and for no reason laughed savagely. He thought 'I'll go to the top of the hill and have a rest'. He had always thought it an odd thing to do, when he heard of it. Now it seemed natural and sensible. Then a commotion suddenly burst on Dur'chai's right flank. The horse leapt aside. Li'vanh yelled and struck out, but it was nowhere near him; then something struck his wounded left leg. He shouted with pain and sprang about. There was a small knot of Kelanat beside him bending over something, a riderless dark grey squealing with fear bolting out of the confusion, and the banner of the Hurnei knocking past his knee. He stared at it for a moment, then saw it begin to slide down, to fall. So he snatched at it and dragged it up. Then he went on to the top of the hill.

First he straightened out the banner, which had become tangled and twisted, and set it firmly in his empty spear-bucket. Then he turned in his saddle and looked over the battle.

He was struck at once by how few the Golden People were, and puzzled. The Khentor host was overwhelming them. Already they were curling back on them like a break-ing wave. He rubbed his head, not noticing it was his bloodied hand, and frowned. Had they really thought to invade a kingdom with that handful? It was difficult to judge the original force now, but it could have been no more than four thousand ... still, if they had not expected the plainsmen ... he suddenly felt desperately tired, and lay for a moment on Dur'chai's neck, letting his arms hang. Then, yawning, he turned his head, and looked down the other side of the hill.

There was a long road, and down the road an army was hurrying. It was a rather small army, of between one and two thousand men, mostly foot and—why, *chariotry*. They had obviously heard the sounds of the battle, for they were coming at speed, and one look at the man in the leading chariot told Li'vanh he had seen a Son of the Stars at last. But between him and this army, at his feet on the north side of the hill, lay in ambush along their road another army—a Kelanat army, at least six thousand strong. Here and there in it were men—men?—who appeared to be in command, men who wore darkness like a cloak.

He grew still and cold. They can't see them, he thought. They'll be massacred! Then that lot will come over here on to us. But Mor'anh! they could have done it with half that number, and given us more trouble ... perhaps they didn't know. Perhaps these are the ones they want. I wonder what makes them so important? He looked again at the leading chariot, at Prince Argerth. I've got to do something. But what? What?

His mind raced. If I just yell and wave, probably they will think I am asking them to hurry. If I could shoot that Black Captain there, it might help ... but I have no arrows, and no bow. Keep calm, you fool.... Under the pressure of his knees Dur'chai danced. If I charge down yelling I shall never get through, they will kill me at once ... and I would be no help to anyone. But that sounded like the ghost of a good idea ... then the shadow-man he had called the Black Captain turned and saw him. Li'vanh saw him touch an archer's shoulder and point, and an arrow sang by him. He pulled Dur'chai back from the crest. But he knew what he had to do.

He gripped the standard and raised it, and put his horn to his lips and blew, wildly, anything he could, he knew not what nonsense. Out of the corner of his eye he saw Derna fighting a young man who looked familiar—the scout. He blew on and on—it was the 'Arm and Mount', but it did not matter, as long as they looked.... Then he let the horn fall and drew his sword, waving that and the banner. 'Hurnei!' he yelled, and for the first time in months his voice cracked. 'Hurnei!' he yelled again, and his voice rang true, bugling over the battle. 'To me! To me! Harai Hurnei, Hurnei, hai-ai-ai-ai-ai. . . .' He saw some faces turn to him, swept frantically with his sword arm, brandished the banner and with a last yell charged over the hill.

The next few moments were horrible. The banner hampered him, he was completely alone, and he was not even making much stir; but there were at least twenty men turning on him. Had they not been hampering each other, he must have died. Just after he burst among them he thought quite calmly, 'In a minute or two I will be dead.' Then thinking stopped. It was eye and arm, sword and brain, Dur'chai was lashing and bucking, fighting with hooves and horn and teeth. He was yelling, slashing, there was pain in his left arm, blood in his eyes, and he was not even sure anyone had seen, anyone would follow ... then there was a shout behind him and a chorus of voices and O great god Kem'nanh they *saw*!

Nothing was quite as bad after that. More and more of the host stormed over the hill, more and more of the ambushers had to turn to engage them, until they grew so close-packed that the front of the ambush was forced forward and burst across the road ... just in time to receive the charge of Prince Argerth and his chariots.

Li'vanh cheered hoarsely and reeled with weariness. He struck out at a Kelanat, missed, and thought of the scout. 'Hope he gets away,' he thought illogically. Then for the first time he realized that Rehai had taken the banner and now he had it so Rehai—Rehai must have fallen. 'O gods, I am tired,' he thought.

It was a won battle, a rout for the Kelanat. For Li'vanh Tuvoi it was his first and almost his last. For he was unhorsed, how he never remembered, but he was weary and wounded, and his enemies closed around him. Yet he struggled up one last time and staggered to a rock, set his back against it, gripped his banner, brandished his sword, and yelled defiance in a faint and husky voice.

'This is my lot,' he thought. 'It couldn't last.'

But someone challenged his assailants from behind, and

they turned to meet them. Only one remained, and Li'vanh
was just trying for energy to fight him when he too vanished,
struck down by Dur'chai. so there was no one attacking him,
and he lowered his sword because it was too heavy, and there
seemed no reason to stand up. So he sat on a boulder and
closed his eyes for a second. And when he opened them there
was a tall young man before him, and on all sides the Golden
People were surrendering.

'Hail!' he said, 'Was it you who took those Kelanat away
from me? I think I owe you my life, then. Thank you. There
is something familiar about your face.'

The man smiled. 'I am not quite sure, but almost, that
many of us owe our lives to you, stranger. I thank you.'

'Grey your eyes and great your courage,' said another
voice, and he looked into the face of the kingly charioteer.
'Surely the Guardian favours you. I am Argerth, Throne
Prince of Rennath, and I owe you life and kingdom both.
May I know in whose debt I stand?'

'I am Li'vanh Tuvoi, of the Tribe of the Hurnei,' he
replied, 'And I am called the son of Silinoi, Lord of the
Hurnei, Lord of the Northern Plains. And I greet you.'

The charioteer looked at the other young man in wonder,
and he laughed amazed.

'Then we are brothers,' he said, 'For I am Vanh the
Hunter, the first born of Silinoi, Lord of the Hurnei. And I
greet you, and say, well met, Young Tiger!'

Chapter Nineteen

On a Cold Sea-shore

The aftermath of battle was in many ways worse than the battle, but Li'vanh saw little of it. Argerth and Vanh put him on Dur'chai's back and led him down to the Ford, leaving him with the other wounded. Then they went back to the field, and Vanh was reunited with his father, and they embraced.

'And I have met a brother I did not know I had, father,' he laughed. 'Great honour he brings the family.'

Silinoi looked at him anxiously. 'Is he safe?'

'Wounded. But walking wounded. He is at the Ford.'

'Good. Go seek Mnorh; he is here, and will be glad to see you. I think,' he said, 'he may have need of you.'

Mnorh was never so glad to see anyone. He was shaken to his soul by the ruin of the battlefield. Yorn was directing the boys, keeping them as far as possible from the worst sights, but Mnorh had never dreamed that those bright and glorious deeds of song could leave such chaos, such unheroic untidiness behind them. His throat was tight and his eyes hot, but he did not weep, not even for the horses, the lost lordless horses. There were many horses left riderless but hardly any horseless riders—largely because a Khentor unhorsed is fairly easy prey to the big Kelanat. But he was pale and stiff, walking to the river, when his brother met him.

When their greeting was over Mnorh, wiping away tears he had never meant to shed, said, 'Vanh: have you seen Li'vanh?'

'I have met him, yes. He is at the Ford.'

'Is he all right?'

'Fairly. In no danger. Why?'

'Derna—Derna wants to see him.'

154

'Derna?' Vanh frowned. He had been taught by Derna himself and knew his ways. 'Won't it wait? Li'vanh is tired and has lost much blood. Couldn't he go in a while?'

Then Mnorh's throat swelled again, and his eyes swam. 'But Vanh,' he said, 'Derna is dying.'

So they took Li'vanh to him, and the old weapon-master's eyes lightened to see his best pupil and he laughed grimly.

'The fool I was,' he said in a voice that, however weak, was Derna's old scornful voice, 'thinking because I was a teacher I had nothing else to learn. It was the prettiest stroke—something like this—' he demonstrated, 'though I could show you better on my feet.' He looked at Silinoi, his eyes suddenly bright and anxious. 'While I remember—my horse?'

'He is a sea-horse: he reached the Blue Sea before you.'

'Good. Together is best. He can bear me.' He looked at Li'vanh, and his eyes wrinkled in a smile. The youth thought he had never seen him look so carefree and so kind. 'And to think I laughed at Rehai. I was sure we would meet again at this evening's fire.'

Li'vanh found his tongue. 'You were not wrong, Uncle,' he said softly, using the respectful address. 'Rehai was a little before you, but if you hurry, you will catch him.'

'So? Then I will hurry. He was a good man.' He stretched and moved restlessly, then looked intently at Li'vanh. 'They tell me they have given you the trophy, First Spear of Danamol.'

'They tell me that, too, Uncle.'

'So?' His face creased with pride, and he jabbed the boy in the ribs, laughing with all his failing strength. 'Did I not say so?' he whispered. 'A warrior, Young Tiger. A warrior in ten thousand.'

Of all things in the world, Nicholas decided he liked boats the best.

He had thought nothing could be better than walking through Kedrinh with the Borderer; but sailing down the river through Kedrinh with the Borderer in this gayer, lighter mood, proved him wrong. He was allowed to take the steering paddle, to reef the sails, and even to cook. But there was not much work, and mostly he just lolled in the boat watching the river.

Dancer swept on, swift even without the help of wind or river. By and by the river slowed and broadened, and they were at the mouth.

The wind brought the tang of the sea, and gulls cried about their mast. *Dancer* quivered and slowed and her sails slackened. The Borderer sighed and guided her to the bank.

'Here we must leave the river,' he said, 'And you must say farewell to *Dancer*.'

The boy looked at her, her slender grace, her dark-blue sails, black keel and mast, and silver-bloomed sides. He put his hand gently on the curve of her prow, and fancied that she pushed a little against his palm. But perhaps it was only the movement of the water.

He turned determinedly away, and put his hands in his belt. 'Where now?' he asked.

The Borderer smiled, and led him on to the top of a cliff. 'Only as far as this, now,' he said, 'But in a while, down there.' He pointed, and Nicholas came beside him and looked down.

He gasped. A little beyond the place where they had left *Dancer,* the river turned, then poured itself out into the harbour. This harbour was below them now: a small town, a fishing village, and a long waterfront with many quays. And seven ships riding at anchor.

They were quite small ships, not over long, and fairly narrow, high prowed and with high bulwarks. They were of wood and their sails were furled. The largest had three masts and the smallest only one. But they seemed to gleam in the setting sun, throwing long shadows out to sea, and from their mastheads floated black banners worked with the silver swan of the Sea-Kings.

'Oh boy!' he remarked with restraint, '*Sailing* ships!'

The Borderer laughed. 'What else, in these seas? Rowboats? They carry oars but they rarely use them. These are the last. In the autumn twenty of the Royal Fleet were here for refitting, and they were caught by the early winter. This harbour is ice-bound half the year. Most of them have gone back to H'ara Tunij. I am glad to see we are in time for these. Tomorrow morning I will take you down there, and you can sail with them.'

'I can! Oh, boy!' His eyes sparkled. 'Do you know their names?'

'The largest is the *Kedrinhel*—that is the name of a city. I do not know the names of the next five. The smallest is called the *Impudence*.'

'Bags I her.' He looked down on them with longing. 'We're staying up here for now though?'

'Not quite here.' He looked at the clouds sweeping in from the northeast, and pondered. 'There is something I would like you to see, and I think that you may have the chance. Come along a little.'

He led Nicholas south along the cliffs for about two miles, then stopped and prepared them some food. The sun set. The Borderer leaned on the grass in silence. Nicholas lay back.

After some time the Borderer asked, 'Do you hear anything?'

Nicholas had been half-thinking that he could for some time, but had disbelieved himself. 'I thought I could, on the wind.'

'What?'

'A sort of cracking noise; and a booming.'

'That is right. Do you know what it is?'

'No?'

'Ice. Away north the frozen rivers are reaching the sea, and melting and breaking up. The great ice-castles are snapping off and floating out to sea. Great cliffs and crags of green ice. Very, very beautiful.'

'But dangerous! What about those ships?'

'I am not skilled in sea lore. It doesn't seem to bother these sailors. But I have seen the ice-castles, and they are beautiful.' At that moment a few spots of rain hissed into the fire, then the shower swept by and the moon gleamed for a moment. The Borderer sat up. 'There is a chance! This is just such a night as they love!' He crawled away towards the cliff edge.

Well, it's not just such a night as I love, thought Nicholas, following him. There was rain in the wind, and the moonlight was fitful. At least the air was not too cold—just cool and salty. He slunk on his stomach and collided with the Borderer's boots. He muttered, and the man chuckled.

'If they should come, be very quiet,' he whispered, 'and do not show yourself.'

'If who should come?' But he got no answer.

They watched for some time. Nicholas grew stiff and cold

and rather sleepy. The hushing of the incoming tide lulled him, and the dark white-marbled water kept blurring before his eyes. He had forgotten that he was watching at all when the Borderer suddenly caught his breath and gripped the boy's arm.

'Look!'

He blinked and peered, but at first could see nothing. Then a patch of moonlit sea broke and glittered, and a head rose out. Then another beside it . . . and another. They waded slowly to the shore and came warily up it, looking about. And all at once the surf was full of them, tumbling out of the waves on to the sand and shingle, springing up the beach, making a strange haunting music with their mouths.

He did not believe it, he thought. Nothing will ever surprise me again, he thought. Ever.

They were dancing over the sand. They were small, smaller than the Nihaimurh—only about four feet tall. Their limbs were smooth and pale; but once or twice in joints and hollows he thought he saw the sheen of scales. Their rippling hair was dark—dark green, he thought, but it was hard to tell in the moonlight. They leapt and spun, flinging their arms out to the rain and wind and cool silver light. They were silent except for their low strange humming, moaning almost, like the wind over a funnel. Pale and supple and coldly wild; he saw their small upturned faces, and their dark deep eyes. Their wet hair lashed their pearl-white sides. He saw the sparkle of salt on them.

'What *are* they?' he whispered.

The Borderer wriggled a little back from the edge. 'The Teraimurh. Some say they are but a sailor's tale, but I have seen them now three times. But they are not like the Nihaimurh: you cannot talk with them. If they see you they spring back into the waves like diving gulls. They are shyer and wilder than the Forest Folk, and even more strangers to men. They are the Sea People—the father's people their name means—but then the Khentors who gave the names call the sea by a word near to father. Now and then the wave riders will come out of the water to play, as they are there. But they come out only on damp nights like this. Sailors say that a full moon brings them to the surface, out at sea. They say too that they sometimes follow ships, calling to them. But sailors say many things.'

'Why aren't they as friendly as the Nihaimurh?'

'I did not say they were unfriendly. But they are shyer. They are so easily hurt, and men are rough. Also I have an idea that the heat of our bodies hurts them ... and anyway, Nikon, at least we can share a little with the Forest Folk. We know trees and woods. But the Teraimurh know nothing of the haunts of men; and what do men know about the Green Halls of Kamenon?'

In the morning he took Nicholas down to the harbour. The boy did not like the town very much—not that there was anything amiss with it as a town, but it was so full of people. There were women in rough bright clothes, fishermen, harbour officials, and children who stared. He felt shy. He had grown unused to people. He shrank close to the Borderer's side; but the Borderer himself did not seem very comfortable. Among men he seemed somehow to shrink a little, to become more what he seemed to them—an oddity, a tramp, a weather-beaten vagabond. Nicholas held his arm.

They went down to the waterfront. Here it was less crowded. The sailors were busy on their ships; there were a few children busy watching them, some of whom silently turned and watched the strangers, but not with the critical, half-scornful eye of the adults. Near the big ship *Kedrinhel* stood a knot of men: officers in green and black and silver, the swan on the shoulder of their cloaks. They had silver knots on their jerkins. One had more than the others, and looked the oldest. The Borderer led Nicholas up to them.

'Captains!' he said.

They turned to him. They were Harani pure, men like Hairon and Horenon, though perhaps a little less princely looking. Beside them the Borderer looked stocky and shaggy, rough and uncivilized. Nicholas suddenly felt fierce in his defence. 'He is of the Tenth House of the Starborn!' he thought, 'His ancestor was Alan—someone—and he's better than any of you!'

But they greeted him courteously, and the Commander shook his hand. 'Vulneth Emneleriath!' he said, 'Is it you?'

The Borderer smiled. 'Perhaps,' he said, 'but rarely by that name. I bring you a passenger to take to H'ara. It is time he had company, and an easy passage. Except for a short way in my riverboat he has walked from Black Mountain, and I doubt not can tell you many marvels if you ask. Farewell Nicholas, I thank you for giving me your company.'

'Fare—you're not . . .' stammered Nicholas: then realized that the youngest captain was exclaiming, 'You *walked* from Black Mountain!'

'No, I ran. Borderer . . .'

'What were you doing on Black Mountain?' asked the Commander sharply. 'It is an ill place. Vulneth . . .'

But the Borderer had gone.

'Where's he gone?' cried Nicholas. 'Why? Why isn't he coming with us?'

'To H'ara Tunij?' The Commander laughed. 'That would not be to his liking. He does not like men in crowds. With reason, maybe.'

'But—shan't I see him again?'

'That is not in my power to tell you. I am sorry, but would you tell us why you were on Black Mountain?'

'I—I can't say how I got there. Princess In'serinna was there—and eagles . . .'

'Princess In'serinna! In'serinna of Rennath?'

'Yes. And the eagles had a battle, and the black ones nearly won; then the Princess went up the mountain, and found out about a war, and someone came after us, and they were caught . . .'

'Caught!'

'Yes. The Princess and my sister. And I ran, and ran, and then the wolves . . . Then I got to a forest. And I met the Borderer. And then we walked, until we found *Dancer* . . .'

'Dancer! What has *he* to do with this?'

'She. It's a boat. We stayed with her until we got here; and we saw the Teraimurh last night. The Borderer said I was to go with you. Can I look at the *Kedrinhel?*'

The men laughed. 'You may sail in her,' said the Commander. 'We sail on the mid-morning tide. Then you can tell me your story more slowly.'

'Oh. Can I have a quick look at the *Impudence*, then?'

They laughed again, and the youngest captain swept his arm at him. '*Impudence* yourself! How do you know the name of my ship, sprat?'

'The Borderer knew. He knew a lot.' He felt suddenly lonely. 'I wish he hadn't gone.'

But there was no help for that, and Nicholas was learning

not to waste his time in futile regret. So he devoted his time to examining the Harani ships. *Impudence* was very neat, but he was only on her for an hour or two, and some of that was taken up with breakfast. *Kedrinhel* was far more complex. He did worry, just as they cast off, whether he would be sea-sick; and he thought of the Borderer with another bitter pang. But as they reached the centre of the harbour, suddenly the length of the river came into view, and away against the horizon he was sure he saw two dark blue sails.

And so Nicholas was the first to reach the White City. Just after dawn on the second day they sighted her, crowning the cliffs, catching the first light of the young sun, with clouds flying like banners of grey and gold above her. There were sea-swans rising from the waves and beating in before them, and the white water curved back and the white towers shone, and he came at last to the fortress of Emneron the White, city of the Kirontin of old; the Pearl of the North, H'ara Tunij of the Sea Kings.

Chapter Twenty

The Hall of Banners

Penelope left Rennath as official maid-of-honour to the Princess In'serinna, and progressed through Kedrinh in the train of King Deron. They passed through Nelimhon by the road, without a glimpse of a Nihaimurh, and crossed the downs in an ever-growing cavalcade, for all the kings and princes of Kedrinh were riding to the council which Kiron had summoned. Penelope came to the city on the afternoon of that day whose dawn had seen Nicholas' arrival and there was much gladness at their reunion, and much telling of news after.

The Khentor host did not set out for H'ara Tunji until two days after the battle. On the first evening they burned their dead. Silinoi lit the pyre for Derna and his grief was bitter, for they had been sworn spear-brothers all the days of their manhood. Vanh put the torch for Rehai, and wept for him, for they had become men in the same year, and were both hunters and men of like mind, and after Hran the Outcast Vanh had been nearest to Rehai in friendship.

All through the night the funeral fires burned, and long after the last horn salute the drums beat on in slow grief, as when anguish is exhausted heartache remains, without rest or comfort. The fires glowed in the dark, flameless, but smouldering hot and red, a dome of dusky light arched over them. The stars and slim silver moon looked pale and very remote; only the echoing flare of the red moon seemed real. The smoke, the smoke smelling of more than burning wood, the smoke whose smell Li'vanh could never forget, was everywhere. It burned his eyes as he lay wakeful, looking towards that sombre radiance. When the drums were silent the fires made themselves heard with faint snaps and shiftings and

rustles, and sometimes sounds like soft sighs. Li'vanh thought
of the men, well fitted for their lives, skilled in horsecraft and
hunting, deft with their hands and lithe in dance, each the sun
of another's life, who had risen that morning whole and
strong; and in this manner they laid them down, all their
skills and their loves and the years that would have been
theirs crumbled to ash in the flames.

The rising sun quenched the fires' glow, revealing them as
low mounds of pale ash and charred embers; and with the
dawn came the wind to scatter these last remains. All the
morning it was as if a white mist rolled before the wind,
drifting southwards, so that maybe some reached the plains
again. But by noon the wind had strengthened and all the
ashes were borne away, and none could say where they
would rest at last, if ever.

The fame of Li'vanh Tuvoi went to H'ara Tunij before
him, and he was now given two new titles. They called him
Tan R'munhan, Lord of Warriors, and hailed him as First
Spear of Danamol. They had presented him with the trophy
spear of the battle, which it was thereafter Mnorh's pride to
bear for him, and with many gifts of honour, necklaces, and
rings for arm and finger, and ornaments for his horse. Very
much the Lord Li'vanh he looked now, as he rode with Vanh
and the younger Rennath princes at the head of the army. 'It
is good to be among kinsmen,' said Hairon sentimentally,
'even when one of them is Garon.' Garon exclaimed indignantly, and Veldreth the Enchanter, usually quiet, laughed,
for in the past he had often been Garon's chief victim. 'It's
all jealousy,' Garon told Li'vanh. 'Hairon used to be called
the wit of the family, till I took over. Of course he wasn't
much of a wit, but then he hadn't a hope of being the
beauty, with Veldreth about.' This brought the wrath of both
his brother and his cousin upon him. Vanh laughed, and
remarked, 'I wouldn't say that the beauty of the family was
Veldreth anyway. He doesn't impress me all that much.'

It had amused Li'vanh to hear the cause of Vanh's exile
from the tribe, and the Harani princes shouted with laughter
to hear In'serinna described as the Witch of Rennath, though
Mnorh looked sheepish; he had decided to forgive her, since
it seemed that she was to marry his brother after all. Yet
strangely enough, though Li'vanh heard often from Vanh of

the Princess's little foreign maid, though Hairon had much to say about her and her brother, though Garon described her quite accurately and they all agreed that Peneli was a strange name, he never felt once a twinge of remembrance.

They struck northwards to the road through Nelimhon and then turned east across the hills, riding at an easy pace—for many, like Li'vanh, had wounds not yet healed. Then on the thirteenth day they saw something hazy and vast on the eastern edge of the world, and looked at last on H'ara Tunij, going like a white waterfall down to the sea.

So last of all came Li'vanh Tuvoi to the High King's hall. And now the High Lords took the threads which they had spun, and plaited them into a single cord.

Outside the city the Khentors made their preparations. They groomed their horses until they gleamed, and polished their weapons. Li'vanh had washed his hair the previous night, and trimmed it. Now he put on his best coat and trousers, and the boots which Mnorh had brushed for him until they looked like velvet. He put a ring on each hand, two bracelets on each wrist, and several necklaces, including a splendid pectoral of carved ivory. He belted his coat firmly about his waist, and slung on his bronze-studded baldric that had knobs of amber in the studs. The band for his horn hung the other way across his chest. Then he put on his cloak. Mnorh had taken trouble with that too; the bloom on the folds gleamed softly. It was lined with vivid scarlet wool. He did not fasten it, but pushed it back over his shoulders so that the chain stretched over his chest. Then he pulled his brow-band straight and looked anxiously at Mnorh. 'How do I look?'

Mnorh looked at him silently a moment, then shook his head.

'Yi-i,' he said, 'If Mneri could only see you!'

Li'vanh laughed and went for him. Mnorh struck back, and he leapt away. 'Don't you put a hand-print on my cloak!'

'*Your* cloak, who brushed it anyway?' But then they heard the signal for them to mount, and Mnorh realized that he was only half ready himself. Li'vanh did what he could for him then went and admired Dur-chai. The big horse gleamed metallically, bronze and gold, and his horn was burnished. The sheepskin saddle, newly washed, looked like fresh curds,

and the ornaments against brow and breast and bridle rang
softly as he moved.

Mnorh came racing up to him to take his Spear of Danamol, and Tuvoi mounted. He looked about him at the
tribesmen who were coming to the Palace in their barbaric
splendour; soft suede and shining leather, bronze and copper,
amber and ivory, necklaces of teeth and claws and quills—
and had a moment of pride in being of their company.

They rode back to the Harani nobles, who seemed to have
done no more than brush down and comb their hair. 'But
then,' he thought enviously, 'they always look magnificent.'
Prince Garon looked at him in silence, then made a face.
'How I suffer, here's *another* one to put me in the shade.'

They rode down to the city and the gate-guard saluted and
stood back. They entered the streets, and were deafened by
the sudden clatter of hooves. Li'vanh shuddered and prickled,
and a ripple went through all the Khentors, a quiver of
wariness and defence. For most of them this was their first
experience of a city, and Li'vanh felt all at once tense, with
the walls and gates and narrow streets confining him. There
were people turned out all along the way to cheer them. The
Harani acknowledged them, but the plainsmen never smiled—
they were too occupied with looking guardedly about them.

They came at last to the Palace, the ancient stronghold of
Emneron changed almost beyond recognition, and rode under
a gatehouse pealing with trumpeters. Yet this was not the end
of their journey. They went farther and farther, down streets
and alleys, across courtyards, under long arches shadowed
from the light of day, a chamberlain leading them. Deeper
and deeper; Li'vanh had never dreamed a building could be
so big. In fact the Royal Palace now fills the walls which held
the whole of the first city. At last they came out into a
courtyard bigger than any before, and the sun dazzled them.
Before them was a great four-towered keep of massive white
stones. Banners floated from the battlements, and standards
hung at every window. The ramp to the door was lined with
buglers. They dismounted; the buglers blew a salute, the
doors opened, and the Captain of the Veduath came down
to lead them in. They marched forward.

The cavalcade entered a Great Hall, high with dark beams
and the sun slanting through windows near the roof. The
sides of the hall were massed with nobles; the floor gleamed

like smooth water. Brilliant banners swung from their poles
high on the walls. From the central beams hung nine magnificent standards—for the Veduath, for the Enchanters, for
the Kirontin, and for the other six Starborn houses which
remained. There was a dais at the far end with steps
thronged with lesser royalty, and in the throne sat Kiron.

He rose when they entered, and while the chamberlain
announced them they looked at the High King of Vandarei.
The first thing to amaze Li'vanh was Kiron's age: he was so
much younger than he had expected, surely no older than
Prince Argerth. Li'vanh had expected some venerable sage,
not a man in the flower of youth. He was tall, very tall, and
straight as a young tree. His dark hair swept back from a
stern and royal face. His clothes were splendid but sombre,
black and silver—save for the magnificent cloak which fell in
silken folds to his feet, lay in a glowing tumble behind him,
and fell over the first step. That was a glorious deep green,
dark and shining as holly, royal green. Kiron's face was the
face of a king carved in alabaster: handsome, dignified, and
still. His eyes were clear green, reserved and even a little sad,
with the loneliness of kings. He wore no crown; but on his
right hand was the Royal Ring, and on his breast hung by a
chain of silver the King's Emerald.

'Welcome, Silinoi, Lord of the Northern Plains; welcome,
Argerth Prince of Rennath.' His voice was deep and clear
and grave, greeting courteously the princes and lords, and
the lord of even the smallest tribe by his name and his father's name.

On the second step of the dais stood Deron King of
Rennath. Beside him stood his shining daughter, and behind
her her attendants. At least, they were supposed to be behind
her. But Nicholas was peering through the King's elbow—all
he could see was Kiron, but of that sight he never tired—and
Penelope had crept around the Princess's skirt.

She looked at the strangers with interest, once she had
satisfied herself that the Rennath Princes were there, and
Vanh. They were very small, she thought. They made the
Lord Vanh look tall. And very strange-looking, savage and
unsmiling. That oldish man, with the drooping moustache—
that must be the Lord Silinoi, Vanh's father, strange as it
seemed—and there was a boy. Behind the boy was a man

who did not look quite like the rest, a very splendid figure; she blinked at him, a little puzzled.

Silinoi was speaking about a man whose name had been unknown to the Princess—Li'vanh Tuvoi, Tan R'munhan—but Penelope could not follow his deep voice and his accent. She stared at the young man again. He bore himself with superb confidence, like a king, but there was something in his face that tugged at her memory. I can't ever have seen him before, she thought. He shifted his stance from time to time with the lithe grace of a plainsman, as if uncomfortable on foot. His strong tanned hands rested lovingly on his sword. His face is familiar, she thought. But how?

Then a lost memory stirred, and came back to her. If he had been younger, he would have looked like Oliver.

Just a little. Just the shape of his face—not the way he looked, or those withdrawn eyes, or his mouth—maybe it was his nose. He would look quite like him, though—if his hair was cut, and he was much younger, and had no moustache. In fact, if he had no moustache and looked only a little younger . . . in fact. . . .

'Oliver!' she squealed, shattering the dignity of Kiron's court. 'Oliver! Oliver!' And shouting her brother's name she leapt down the steps and across the floor, and hurled herself against him.

Chapter Twenty-One

The Young Tiger

Li'vanh Tuvoi heard a strange voice calling a strange name: then the world reeled, and he was someone else, and the name was his own. The voice was the voice of his sister, and shaken and confused he was holding her shoulders and saying 'Penny. Penny. Where's Nick, then?'

Nicholas was at his side almost as soon, and they were both shouting questions and news at him at once, so that he could not hear one from the other, nor could he have understood their accents anyway. He stood bemused, weak with shock; and then Prince Hairon put a hand on the shoulder of each and said, 'Nicholas. Penelope. Quiet for a moment.'

Nicholas obeyed, but Penelope bounced on for a moment, squeaking, 'It's Oliver! It's our brother Oliver we told you about. He's our brother. Princess, this is Oliver!' Her voice was wild with joy. Li'vanh winced at every sentence. But finally she too subsided, and, becoming aware of the amazed silence of the court, he looked up at Kiron.

The High King stood on the edge of the dais, unmoving. His eyes dwelt on them consideringly, with the calm unsurprise with which he had watched the whole episode. Then he began to laugh.

A ripple of relief ran through the hall, and then a wave of amusement. Hairon suddenly snorted with mirth, and all at once a surge of delight swept the room. Even Nicholas grinned ruefully, and Silinoi gave the twisted scowl which with him took the place of laughter. One large king on the dais bellowed and slapped his knees. Kiron did not move, he stood straight and splendid, but he flung up his head and his laughter ran among the banners. Only Li'vanh Tuvoi stood bewildered and unsmiling.

'Well,' said Kiron when he stopped at last, 'save yourself further trouble, Silinoi my friend. I think I know now who he is.'

Remembrance was agony.

He looked at his brother and sister with the eyes of a stranger. These fair foreign children in their Harani clothes were alien to him: he could not follow the strange accent of their quick, easy speech. And yet those faces, those voices, were cruelly familiar, painfully dear. Their kinship laid hold on him and would not be denied, shaming his forgetfulness, waking every moment more echoes of a world to which he no longer belonged. The warmth of their welcome, their delight in seeing him, were anguish and reproach, for he could not respond in equal measure. He loved them; but they were so far away. They did not know him; they were greeting some lost Oliver of their memory and thinking they had found him. They cried 'Do you remember? Do you remember?' recalling a life which was nothing to him, dredging up memories which he fought away. Yet they were real, and his, binding him against his will through them to the world they still remembered. It was as if the love he undoubtedly had for them put hooks in his flesh, tearing him every time he felt it, hurting him as it held him.

The first adjustment had been hard enough; this was worse by far. Yet he did not want to rebuff them and hurt them by his coldness. He must try to be pleased to see them. He met Nicholas' puzzled brown eyes and forced a smile.

They had both told him their stories, and Penelope was demanding to know what he had been doing. He was at a loss for an answer. 'What have I been doing? What should I be doing? I have been living, learning. I have a horse—you must see him; Dur'chai is his name. Oh, and we fought in the battle; there was that. They gave me the trophy.'

'*You* fought in the battle?' said Nicholas, impressed and faintly shocked. 'Really fought?' He stared at Oliver as if trying to see him anew, with an almost horrified curiosity. 'Did you kill anyone?'

'Nikelh!' He shied away from the question, almost repelled in his turn, not noticing Nicholas flinch from the name he gave him. 'Well, I do not know. It may sound strange, but I do not. I suppose that I must have.' But that was a conclu-

sion he did not like, and it was a relief when Penelope said
'Are you going to shave off that moustache?'

'Shave my moustache?' He stared. "Why should I?"

'It makes you look different.' Nicholas sounded uneasy.
'And you talk differently, too.'

'Compared with what?'

'With the way you used to talk,' Nicholas had intended to
say; but Penelope laughed, and said 'With the Harani.'

'Well, I *am* different. I am a Khentor. And I find you hard
to follow when you speak quickly.'

Nicholas swallowed a sudden lump, and said, 'You are a
Khentor?'

'Of course I am a Khentor. What do I look like?' There
was an almost angry note in his voice, but he saw Nicholas'
face and calmed himself. Penelope looked from one to the
other, perplexed. The two brothers held each other's eyes
helplessly for a moment, then Nicholas cleared his throat and
looked down at the seat.

'You've been here longer than us, haven't you? I wonder
how. But I expect that's why. . . .' He took another breath.
'Where is your room?'

'I have no room.'

'Oh well, I expect there's still time to get one near us.
We're both in the East Tower of the Old Palace. You'll have
to see the chamberlain.'

'Nikelh!' He bit his lip, annoyed at being unable to say his
own brother's name. 'I won't be in here—inside all this!'

'Why not? What's wrong with it? It's jolly comfortable.' He
checked himself with an effort. 'Where will you be, then?'

'In my tent if it rains, out if not.' He looked at their
stricken faces and gave a strained smile. 'Look, let us leave
this alone. We all have much to get used to. Just two things:
Do not keep telling the Hurnei that my name is O—is
O'li—is Oliver, and not Li'vanh; and do not look annoyed,
Nikelh, or giggle, Peneli, when I call the Lord Silinoi Father.'

'But he's not. . . . All right! Well, what should we call him,
then?'

'Lord Silinoi, if you prefer. Or Terani, as the tribesmen
call him. Or Uncle. Call him Uncle—he would like that. But
I call him Father.' He grinned at Penelope's disapproving
face. 'Come on, come and see my tent, and my Dur'chai.'

They rose and went with him. Penelope, already inter-
ested, bounded ahead, but Nicholas followed more slowly. In
his heart there was a deep bitterness. He did not know who it
was had torn them from their own place and brought them
here, for their own purpose; but he knew that he resented it,
fiercely. To Penelope, this was a holiday; to Oliver, all too
plainly, home. But to him it was neither. Not, he thought,
that there had not been good parts, but they had been well
paid for. The relief of finding Oliver, certainly, had been
bought dear with the bitter irony of the meeting. He had run,
all gladness, to greet his brother, and been met with a look
more of horror than pleasure, on the face of a stranger, a
man, this Lord of Warriors, this Li'vanh, this Young Tiger.

The west tower of the Old Palace is given over entirely to
the use of the Star Enchanters, as the south tower is to the
Veduath, the order of champions. To the west tower, on the
fifth day after the arrival of the army, were called all the
princes and powers of the Starlit Land, to the great Council
which Kiron had summoned. In the great round chamber
they took their seats, and Li'vanh sat among them.

There were the Star Enchanters, many of them; and the
masters of other powers, the Khentor magicians of the Wild
Magic, earth witches, wielders of white witch-magic, and less
definable persons—men and women with tokens of power or
the gift of prophecy, sybils and seers and sages.

There were the priests and priestesses from various tem-
ples, come to watch more than to take part, for Black
Enchanters were little concern of theirs except, that is, for
the priests of Marenkalion, wrapped in their scarlet white-
lined cloaks, who had come to offer their spears. There were
the kings, princes and lords who had answered the call to
arms. There was the Captain-General, and the Captain of the
Veduath. And in the centre of all sat Kiron, combining
warrior and priest and enchanter.

He looked at them for a moment or two, grave as always.
Then he rose to speak. 'My friends,' he began, 'my friends,
my kinsmen:

'All of you know well why I have called this council.
Fendarl has broken the ban. He has left the mountains at the
edge of the world, and re-entered Kedrinh. For many long
years, since the first wielder of the Emerald cast him out, he

has sought to do this, but never until now has his strength been great enough. That now he has power to break the barriers raised against him is bad enough to give us pause. I will not conceal that we are in great peril. He has grown very strong. We were not able to keep him out; to cast him out will be yet harder; to destroy him hardest of all. Yet one of these we must do.

'He sits now in Kuniuk Bannoth and gathers his servants to him. He can call on great numbers out of the deep north, whence our enemies have always marched. In all likelihood he can deceive or frighten a host of Kelanat into joining him. We can be certain that even from lands we thought our own, many will go at his call. Those who serve *his* lord can always be sure of sufficient numbers.

'He must meet us in battle. He cannot avoid this, and knows it; but he does not fear it. I have wrestled with his mind, and found hate and scorn and pride, but no fear. He knows his own strength, and the strength of his Master. It is we, he thinks, who need to fear; and he is right.

'He can choose his own time to come to battle, and we can tell to a night when that will be. It will be the next full of the red moon: the Night of the Sorcerer. Today—tonight—is the dark of the dark moon, so we have seven and thirty days to prepare. Four weeks; no more. Moreover, on that night the silver moon will have little strength to lend; she will be waxing, true, but still very young.

'The number of Fendarl's army we cannot know. I have assumed at least thirty thousand at least, and these will not be all mere men. Less than the third part will, I believe, be human. The rest will be creatures of necromancy, demons and monsters, the troll-men of Bannoth and their like, far worse to face in battle than mere men. Many will have charmed lives. So to be evenly matched, we need double their numbers.' There was a faint murmur from the Harani benches, and Kiron flung up his hand. 'No, it does not sound heroic. In this battle we seek victory, not glory. If we can raise these numbers, why give our enemy any advantage that we can deny him? There is more at stake than our pride; more to be lost than a warrior's reputation. There is more even than our magic, or the Starlit Land. There are those whose safety lies in our hands, whom it is our charge to defend. Shall we betray them for our own vanity? It is our plain duty to conquer.' He smiled grimly. 'Have no regrets, my falcons. If we *should* fall, however gloriously, there would be none to sing of us.

'We can call on no more than are represented here. The Great Plains would send help, but they are too far; so are Halilak and Nevirh. The Islands are close; they might not send of themselves but I would command them in another time. But pirates out of Vala and her neighbours have been growing troublesome of late, and the men of the Islands have taken to their ships instead of their chariots. Little help or none will they give. Of the seven realms that leaves Kedrinh, Kunoi, and Lelarik. Lelarik of the cities cares little, and believes even less. The Temple of the Guardian has sent, but that is all the help we can look for. Kunoi . . .' he smiled. 'the Prince has promised what help he can give, but that may be only a hundred or so. Let us, then, reckon our strength. Our largest hope first—my Lord Silinoi?'

Silinoi rose. 'The Northern Plains can send twenty-five thousand, within the time,' he rumbled. 'More would take longer.'

'That is half the force we need. Truly the men of the Wide Lands are generous friends! Now let us reckon what the Harani can do.' One by one he called the names of the kingdoms, and the numbers they could raise were given. The total was sixteen thousand, making forty-one thousand.

One of the red-cloaked priests rose. 'From the Temple of Marenkalion we can bring four thousand to this battle with this limb of our Lord's old enemy.'

'We thank you, brother.'

A slim hard-muscled young woman was the next to rise. She wore trousers and tunic of embroidered doeskin, her hair fell in a tail from the crown of her head, and a crescent moon hung on her brow. 'Maybe our Sister will be able to lend you little aid, but we the Avenei will bring a thousand. Alas that it cannot be more, but the larger part of our sisters are too far away.'

'Praised be the Warrior Sisters of the Moon!'

Then all at once the chamber was filled with laughter, for a big golden-haired young man rose from the back rank, looking embarrassed. 'We Kelanat,' he muttered, 'understand little of these matters you speak of, but we wish to make amends for our rebellion. So we will send a thousand to this battle, because we are sorry, and we beg your pardon.' He sat down hurriedly, and Kiron thanked him. Then another man rose, even bigger than the Kelanat and much fairer, calmer of face and dressed only in leather shorts and sleeveless jacket. 'The Kerionenei of the high mountains are few,' he said quietly, 'but we wish to strike a blow in this cause. I bring you a hundred.'

So it went. A slight brown-haired man pledged five hundred archers from Kunoi Len Vanda; the Captain of the Valan Guard, a tall man with curly dark-red hair and grey eyes, said he would lead his men with them; and a young negro told Kiron that the King of Humarash would send five hundred. Then the grey-clad Captain of the Veduath rose. 'I will bring the Order of Champions, but we are not at our full strength. I will not be able to lead our "seven ranks of seven".' Suddenly he made a face, and men began to smile. 'To the war the Veduath can send the imposing number of forty-one.' The room exploded with laughter and he sat down smiling. Kiron laughed, then held up his arm.

'Forty-one such as the Veduath are more than they sound.' He turned to his secretary. 'How many now?'

'Forty-eight thousand, five hundred, and forty-one.' There was another ripple of laughter, but Kiron frowned and shook his head. He was silent for a moment, then sighed. 'There is no help for it. I will command the Islanders to send us one thousand men. They can afford such a number, though I do not like forcing help. . . . Well, that gives us a fighting force of maybe fifty thousand. That may be—must be—sufficient to overthrow Fendarl's army. To overthrow Fendarl's magic is another thing, for another council. But here we have gathered all the enchanters and enchantresses of the Star Magic, Lords of the Wild Magic to lend us their strength, and witches of the earth. Have any of you, brothers and sisters, anything to say to the Council?'

A woman rose; dark, slant-eyed, Khentor. 'Only this from us,' she said. 'Old things have woken, powers easier to loose than to bind. We are troubled: this enemy of yours, King Kiron, is too far from the earth for us to reach; but if we can help we will. But our help may be small—maybe only to heal and help those who fight with you. Our magic is not like yours, not a weapon to be wielded, but a well to be plumbed, and its workings are slow. But he has unleashed some of it on to the light himself, with his calling and delving, and this may hinder him. Vir'Vachal and her like are no friends to you either, but they strive for the old way of things, a way dark and maybe cruel, but yet a true and right way. They are not good as you, Starborn, reckon goodness, but they are not evil, and he may find our power too heavy to thrust aside. And I will warn all of you now: to bring these unleashed forces to heel may be a long task, and not without price. . . . This I say now, lest later you blame us for our methods.' There was all at once an odd satisfaction in her voice, as if she had scored a point. 'Blood will have blood and life will have death, as always, King Kiron.' She sat down; and there was a muttering among the Star Enchanters. Kiron thanked her with restraint. Then a dark man of middle age stood up.

'We of the Wild Magic, we are not weapon-wielders either. We bear a power—if we can. It is a chancy ally; but an unpredictable enemy also. We can say no more than that we are with you, for what we are worth.' He sat down again and then a boy, or a very young man, stepped unexpectedly from the background.

'Greetings, Kiron.' He was a Khentor, coatless but with a dark blue cloak, light and lithe as a dancer. 'I come unsummoned, but I have a word to say, of hope maybe. We of Iranani, we have no magic and no strength of arms to offer, but we too are *his* enemies. And if it comforts you I think he may find our power, the power of life and laughter, the hardest in the end to overthrow; too quick to catch, too frail to bind. We cannot destroy him, if you fail; but we can outlive him. I thank you, lords. Farewell.' And while they still stared he turned and slipped away.

Into the silence after he had gone, a young Harani rose from his place. 'Sire,' he said, 'may I ask a question?'

'Ask on,' Kiron said.

'We have spoken of defeating Fendarl's army, we have spoken of defeating Fendarl's magic. But what of Fendarl himself? Who is to face him? Yourself, Kiron; or one of the Veduath? Who?'

There was a sudden silence among the Enchanters, and Kiron sighed. 'I myself will face him. But I have no hope of slaying him.'

'Is he then such a mighty man of arms?'

'Nay! But he is scarcely now a man. Listen, and I will tell

you. Long ago, early in his sin, he fell to the oldest and deepest of fears, and made himself undying. Still, those who do not die may yet be slain, and an oracle told him his life could not be endless. So he brewed himself more spells, and made himself unslayable by man or woman, and mocking asked the oracle what its answer was now. But the oracle said only 'By the young tiger shall your death come'. So more enchantments he made, with more hard-won power, and armoured himself against all that is under sun or moon, against every creature of Khendiol, and went again to the oracle—but this time it was silent. So he can be slain by no creature of Khendiol. None of you could face him; do not try. It would be useless.'

And Li'vanh was taken from the world, and for him all grew still. The talk went on, but he no longer heard. He felt himself to be the pivot of a vast wheel, the focus of the attention of the universe. He stood alone, face to face with a knowledge he did not want, hearing the beginning of a call he wished to flee.

'The young tiger. No creature of Khendiol.' And then another voice. 'A warrior in ten thousand.'

No, he thought. No. *No!*

But he had heard, and he knew, and he was alone in a moment grown deep and ringing, as if echoing to a great gong-note. He did not see the Council; he did not hear the voices. He saw only the choice before him, and heard only the unmistakable summons.

He stood up.

'Kiron!' he said loudly, interrupting in a voice hardly his own. 'I am no creature of Khendiol, and men call me the Young Tiger. I think,' he said, his throat grown tight and dry, 'that this fight is mine.'

Chapter Twenty-Two

The Hard Fellowship

Every face turned to him, but for a long time no one spoke. He stood there, feeling hot and cold and aghast at what he had said, his legs beginning to tremble. Then Kiron nodded.

'Li'vanh Tuvoi.' he said, 'Young Tiger, Chosen One. You are right, my Lord of Warriors. This is indeed your fight.'

Li'vanh sat down again rather abruptly. He was vaguely aware of Kiron dismissing the council, of the circles of the chamber emptying; but he stayed where he was. He was not sure that he could have moved if he had tried. In a short while he was the only one left: just him, and Kiron, and Silinoi hesitating.

'There is no need for you to go my friend,' said Kiron to the chieftain. 'I do not know if Li'vanh wishes to speak to me now, or not. Tuvoi?'

He raised his head, and managed a smile. 'As well now as ever,' he grinned. 'Strike while the iron's hot.'

Kiron smiled down on him. 'Then come to the north tower in an hour,' he said, 'There are one or two other people I need to summon.'

The north tower looked on the sea; in it were Kiron's private rooms and the place where he worked. The room to which Li'vanh was led was round and full of light; he guessed it was in one of the turrets. Silinoi was there, and Yorn, and an enchanter he did not recognize. Against the wall sat the Captain of the Veduath. Kiron leaned at the window, watching the gulls swooping and gleaming past. 'They think I am going to feed them,' he was saying to the enchanter, 'but it's not their time. Go away!' As Li'vanh entered he stood up and came over to him, welcoming him and offering him a seat. Li'vanh declined it—he felt small enough as it was—and leaned on a table. Kiron turned to the company.

'Li'vanh Tuvoi of the Hurnei has claimed the right to meet Fendarl in combat, as you all heard. The question now is, should we consent?' He looked a little grim. 'For Fendarl is very great, and Li'vanh is still new to arms, and has no magic; and he is very young.'

Li'vanh revived a little and looked faintly indignant. He had grown unused to being weighed so light. Yorn, leaning on the window opposite to Kiron, answered at once.

'Who are we to consent or not? The decision was not ours, and was made long ago. Why else was he sent to us, a boy whose name was Crowned Victor, grey-eyed and scarlet-clad, guided to the Tree of the Dancer? Marenkalion the Avenger works in him. Why else was Dur'chai, the Endurer, sent to him, an immortal horse with a name of omen, if not to bear him to this end? He is young? The less chance that evil has a foothold in him. And Fendarl must be slain. Have we another champion to send?'

'I would go myself . . .'

'And you would perish.' The white-haired enchanter spoke. 'And we would be weaker, and Fendarl no less. Against such spells what can we do? Only find a way past them. When the High Lords put weapons in our hands, we dare not scruple to use them. And for his lack of magic—well, if his mind is an unploughed field, it will be the harder for Fendarl to harrow. At least he will be fighting with his hands alone, and not his will; for Fendarl will be less able to catch hold of it. If he is willing accept the gift with thanks, Kiron.'

'As for his might of arms,' growled Silinoi, 'let those who have seen decide. A man I held worthy to judge called him a warrior in ten thousand. But let the Captain of the Veduath try him.'

Li'vanh swallowed, partly from re-awakened grief for Derna, partly at the dawning realization of what he was offering to do, a little at the thought of being 'tried' by the Captain of the Veduath. He looked across at the man, whose dark hair was greying at his brow, and met the considering gaze of his unexpectedly dark brown eyes.

Kiron looked at him and smiled.

'Then, Lord Li'vanh, we accept your offer with many thanks. And this I pledge you: as long as the Starlit Land endures, we shall never forget. No name in song or story, not the name of Emneron the Young or the seekers of the Emerald, shall be greater than yours, Li'vanh Tuvoi, who are the Shield of Kedrinh.'

The High King's cloak quivered in the wind, and he stood dark against the stars. Li'vanh looked at his chiselled features in the silver light. Behind his head the two moons, red and silver, were but the faintest rinds in the sky. Below them the sea boomed among the rocks.

'You wished me to tell you of the Star Magic. I can say but little; but since you are our champion and the chosen of the High Lords, I may tell you some that is only known to the blood. But you must not speak of it, except to the enchanters.

'Some think we made the magic, or it was made for us. That is not so: rather, we were made for the magic. It was a power running wild on the earth, and the High Lords decided that reins were needed on it, and a strong hand on them. So they took us, and put the blood of the stars in us, so that we, the Star-born, can never have the quiet of other men, and gave us charge of this power.

'Not all magics are the same.... But if you wish, I will tell you what we believe to be the origins of the Star Magic. No, more than believe; we know. You wish to hear? Listen then and I will explain.

'Long ago, the One created the Seven to be his servants, and the guides of his lesser creations. Of them we will say no more, save this: the highest and greatest of them grew too proud, and rebelled, and fell. In your world also you must know of this. The power which he had was taken from him, and he was cast down and driven out. He who had been the Thrice Holy, the Prince and the Beloved, was now the loathed enemy, and heaven still mourns. Made to be a mighty servant was he, and even though Marenkalion threw him down he is a mighty foe. The power that had been his now had to find other masters. Much of it was divided among the remaining Six. Of that which remains the Star Magic is a part.'

Li'vanh made a small sound. Kiron smiled grimly.

'Oh yes. It frightens me too. This which is now in the control of a mortal kindred was once the domain of the greatest of gods. It is his own weapon which we turn against him. There is our strength—for the magic is very strong—and there our greatest danger.

'He has no power now of his own. And he cannot make, he can only corrupt. He must work through men, he must win himself strength through them. Of all weapons in the world what so easy or so apt to his hand as the magic which was once his own? It remembers him, it will readily turn to him. We can never be free of him. We are his other side.

'As he was Fairest before his fall, so too is the Star Magic. No power in earth or heaven is so strong and pure, nothing so dreadful when corrupted. The Black Enchanter is our commonest and worst foe.

'We walk a precipice. One slip and we are lost. We dare not stray an inch from our path; we dare not yield a step to evil. Our fall is never farther from us than is our shadow. The other magics have not this fear. They are blunt weapons, hard powers to control, but not so sharp to wound the wielder. This is why our enchanters must be given to it so wholly: why they may not, for instance, take wives or husbands except of the kindred, unless they renounce the magic. We are repaid—never think it is all suffering—to tread the pathways of the stars is a thing beyond dreams; but all things have a price. Our price is warmth and comfort, the small joys of common men. Other things have other prices. You heard the Earth Witch: her magic demands blood, and life for life. The Wild Magic is different from both, but those gifted with that never know peace again. Of all things in the world, we say, only two are given freely: love and the mercy of Kuyorei. And even love to be valued must be paid with love again.'

Li'vanh thought of Mneri and did not smile. 'And Fendarl?' he said, 'What is the price of the Black Magic?'

Kiron looked at him. 'Too dreadful to speak of,' he answered, quelling. 'If you do not know, do not seek to.'

Daron the Veduath Captain was pleased with Li'vanh, and more generous with his praise than Derna had ever been. Others of the Order of Champions came to watch; more and more as the days passed, and they came into the Palace.

Li'vanh was being taught a new method of fighting: no longer with the curved swords of the Khentors, but with the straight Harani longswords, and he had to learn to use a shield to defend himself. These lessons were short at first, for the wounds he had got at Danamol were barely healed. 'What a lot!' Nicholas had admired them—in his leg, in his arm, and on the side of his forehead. 'And all down one side!' wondered Penelope. Captain Daron laughed.

'You can always tell a cavalryman, his scars are always on his left side. Why? Well, Nikon, you cannot defend that side so well. Your sword is on the right . . . all right, if you were left-handed your scars would be on your right side. Brat.'

He told Li'vanh something of the Veduath. 'We are never more in number than forty-nine,' he said, 'but if forty-nine men worthy cannot be found, then we are less than that—we are not just content with the best we can get. A man, to join the Veduath, must have more than mere skill in arms. He must be something besides, a master of lore or a maker of songs, or learned in history, or maybe skilled in many tongues of men. Not all of us are Harani. There are some Khentors—there was an Islander once. But a Veduath has many duties. He must help those who have no other aid, defend the defenceless, uphold the humble. We must never refuse a call, not from weariness of body or soul or because our own lives call us. I am afraid our wives do not like it much. Oh yes, we have wives! Children too. Did you think we were a priesthood? No, we are ordinary men. Some Veduath are noblemen, but others are of common birth. But we have to be sworn against evil. Surely you have heard of this sort of thing?'

'Oh yes. But it's amazing to meet it. How old are you?'

'I trust you mean the Order? Many hundred years—about six hundred. We were formed in the reign of Anderon I, and our headquarters then was the castle of Veduath, whence our name. We were called then the Brotherhood of Veduath, or the Order of the Champions of Veduath; properly speaking, that is our name now. We swear oaths of loyalty to each other, of course, which have never yet been broken. New men can only be elected—or rather invited to join—by the unanimous vote of the whole Order, including those who left because they grew too old to bear arms. But those are few. Our uniform is grey, though we wear a cloak of royal green; our sign and badge and banner is the holly. And I think you will find our name is held in honour. We have many odd privileges: for instance when I am in H'ara Tunij I keep the keys of the Palace; the Queen's Champion is always one of the Veduath. And so forth.' He paused, and grinned with a shy pride. 'It is said, that the eldest son of the High King would sooner have the lowest place at our table than his seat at his father's right hand. But for the truth of that you would have to ask Kiron.'

'The Star Magic is bound by laws, Li'vanh.' Again he walked beside Kiron on the starlit battlements. The red moon was a crescent, but the silver was half full. 'Laws older than the magic itself were made to govern it. These laws—they are not like the laws of men. There is no power that sees them enforced. There is no arrest and punishment for the breaking of them. The keeping of them is between a man and his soul, and the flouting of them cannot always be known.

'Yet they cannot be set aside with impunity, and the prizes for which they are broken have yet their price. These great laws, you might say, cannot be broken, but only twisted, and some day the offender will have to loosen his hold. They are like a catapult, or like a green wand. The more they are bent the more stinging, when it comes, is the backlash.'

Kiron stood alone at a window, looking down on the sea. He was not used to wearing his thought in his face, and no one would have known by looking at him that his heart was heavy. He did not turn as his cousin In'serinna stepped into the room.

'Amnerath?' she said, 'You wished to speak to me?'

He turned then and smiled at her, and said, 'Yes. I think you can guess why.'

She blushed faintly. 'Vanh?' she asked.

Kiron nodded, and stepped away from the window. 'He came to me yesterday. I spoke to your father this morning.'

'Do you like him?'

'Your father? Oh yes. I always have.' He laughed at her. 'No, I know what you mean. Like him? I think I like him. I know I could willingly feed him to the gulls.'

'Amnerath!'

'You are surprised? Why? Surely you knew how I would feel?'

'I thought. . . . Kiron, we are cousins.'

'Yes I know, In'serinna. I do not mean I am angry. I will be more than glad to see you happy, but I would rather have seen you happy within the kindred. You understand that?'

'Of course. I am sorry.'

He was silent for a few minutes, then said, 'You do love this man?'

'Oh cousin, I do. I tried not to. But I do.'

'And you are willing to forsake the magic for him?'

'I was most unwilling, but I can do no other.'

'You have thought of all it means? He is a Khentor, unlike any other man you know. You realize that he is likely to wander off at any time the mood takes him, for who knows how long?'

'He has said that himself. I am not afraid.'

'There is another thing In'serinna. Have you thought—his people do not live long. If he sees fifty he will be unusual. You may have a long widowhood.'

'I would sooner be his wife for twenty years than any other man's for eighty. I know this Amnerath.'

Kiron's smile was touched with bitterness. 'I think you do not know, however, what it is to be lonely.'

'Lord, *any* man may die young. Kiron your father . . .'

'. . . . died aged sixty-seven leaving me High King at twenty-eight. Too well I know. Well I did not think you were ignorant of anything I have mentioned, nor did I think to bring you to renounce your lover. I summoned you to tell you my decision, little one.'

There were many who would have laughed to hear her called such a thing. But beside Kiron she did indeed look slight and young. He walked back to the window.

'It was not because of your high birth that there was any hesitation, but because you are an enchantress. So I concerned myself with nothing else.' He paused. 'The laws say that none may be compelled into the service of the magic. To forbid this marriage would be to compel you. Therefore, with other consents given, I give mine.' She made a glad movement towards him, but he checked her with a gesture. 'With one impediment. Sit down.'

She sank into a chair. He came over to her.

'In'serinna, we cannot spare you.' His voice lost some of its command: it was almost appealing. 'Not now, of all times.

We are barely strong enough at any time, and now, with Fendarl—you must keep your star in the sky until this is over, cousin. After the war go your way with my blessing. But do not take your strength from us yet. Not until *he* is defeated.'

She said nothing for a moment, then looked at her cousin with compassion. 'A heavy burden, Amnerath?'

'Heavy enough. But I can bear it. Will you do this, for me and for us all, In'serinna? I do not want to command you. But do not desert us in our need.'

'I will do it willingly, my liege.'

'That is good!' He straightened, and sighing with relief, went back to his window. Then another thought struck him.

'In'serinna!'

'Lord?'

'This is a very small fear, and a foolish thought for which I beg pardon, but—you are not—escaping?'

'Escaping!'

'You are not marrying this man *because* this would take you out of the magic?'

'Amnerath! Do you think I would? Would you believe it of me?'

He smiled wryly. 'Oh, I did not really believe it. But I could understand it, In'serinna—with no trouble.'

Their shadows lay black on the white flags, and the city below them was pied dazzlingly. The wind brought the scent of the sea, and the white moon was full.

'Every star in the sky has a name of its own: and every star is the star of an enchanter, be he living, dead, or unborn. The name of our star is our name, and our greatest secret. Never will an enchanter tell his star-name; or never while he retains his wits. Who knows our name can call us; they can compel us. To discover them is our enemies' constant labour; their successes serve as warnings. We do not, *not*, reveal our star-names.'

He paused, then looking up at the sky again went on. 'If a man or a woman has practised the magic and served it well, when they die their star shines on. Their power goes back as you might say into the pool. If they have fallen, like Fendarl, that star is a demon's eye—a spy, a bad apple. We have to try to destroy it—a fearful task.'

The crimson sorcerer's moon grinned above the hills. It was half full. Kiron gazed on it, then up again, and sighed. Li'vanh thought, 'He is very full of the stars tonight.'

'Two weeks left,' remarked Kiron. 'How goes the practice?'

'They say I improve.'

'The terseness of the Khentorei! But the stars.' He sighed again. 'They live on after our deaths: but if we desert them. . . .' His voice sank. 'If by some cause, we never come to the Magic . . . or if for some reason an enchanter or an enchantress renounces the magic; then her power is lost and her star goes out. It dies.'

Again he sighed and bowed his head.

'It is a terrible thing, Li'vanh, for a star to die.'

Chapter Twenty-Three

Gathering for War

Riding back to the tents of the Khentors after that day's practice with the Veduath, Li'vanh was suddenly aware of the strange emptiness of the outer circles of the Hurnei tents. It always seemed a little strange, for there were no women and no children, but usually there were some men in view. Today there was emptiness and silence, but as he rode nearer to the centre he heard Silinoi's voice, and then laughter. His interest quickening, he urged Dur'chai to a trot, and arrived at the back of the crowd. Still, being mounted he could see over the heads of those in front, and what he saw made him catch his breath and swear softly.

There was a mill of ponies and girls and young women, mostly Banyei, but some of the women were being reservedly welcomed by their husbands. Silinoi stood before the door of his tent, fists on hips, face and voice betraying his rage. Before him, clasping the bridle of her pony, stood his daughter.

'Who gave you permission to come?' he demanded. 'Who? Who?'

'No one, Father,' she replied meekly, 'But there was no one to ask.'

'How *dared* you leave the tribe and ride two thousand miles alone!'

'But I was not alone! I was with the army!' There was a shout of mirth from the onlookers, and she flushed and looked dignified. 'I was with the Banyei, and the other women. I was quite safe.'

'Quite safe! Maybe you were, safer then than now! Is this your obedience to me? I told you before we left that you could *not* come. What do you deserve.'

'A beating, O my father.'

'True enough! Did you think I would not beat you?'

'Oh no. I was sure you would.' There was such soulful resignation in her face and voice that Li'vanh almost joined the laughter himself, though he was not really in the least amused. He was just deciding to back Dur'chai quietly away when Mnorh wriggled backwards through the crowd and came over to him. He looked up and made a face.

'Sisters!' he growled, with a world of expression.

'Where are the children?'

'Oh, I was teaching Nikelh to ride, still. I left him with the pony, when I saw the Banyei ride in. Before you ask me— General—a part of the army has come from the plains: the first. But some women have come to join their men, and the Sisters of Avenel, and of course *she* wouldn't stay where she was put.' Li'vanh stuck out a foot, and Mnorh vaulted to sit pillion. They rode to find Nicholas and Penelope, with Mnorh still muttering darkly.

When they got there Nicholas was still jogging in circles.

'I've got him to trot and stop and start and all that, but I want him to do the next one up from trot and he *won't*!'

'Keep your back straight. Lower your hands,' criticized his brother.

'Hit him,' growled Mnorh, hitting him. The pony bucked and lashed. Nicholas hit the ground. He sat up and brushed himself. 'Al right,' he remarked, 'I'll walk. Suits me. It's good enough for the Borderer, it's good enough for me. Keep your rotten pony.' He stood up, and grinned at Mnorh. 'What was all that commotion, anyway?'

Li'vanh dismounted. 'You'll see. Peneli, you're so fond of laughing at Nikelh, let's see you get up.'

They had to catch her first, but between the three of them, they hoisted her on to the pony's back, squeaking and struggling. The pony laid its ears back doubtfully.

'Keep still, you're scaring him,' gloated Nicholas.

'If you don't shut up I'll put you on Dur'chai.'

'Mnorh's pony has a vicious streak,' put in a soft voice. 'Do you want to use mine?'

There was a sudden silence. Nicholas, Penelope, and the pony turned their heads. Mnorh scowled. Li'vanh set his teeth.

'Hello,' said Penelope. 'Is your pony nicer than this one?'

Mneri swung off its back. 'Much,' she said, with the manner of one starting a quarrel.

Mnorh bridled. 'That's not true!' he cried. 'She picked *her* pony for its looks—just like a girl. Mine can outstay it any day. And outrun it too. Look at . . .' He began to compare the ponys' points, and Mneri laughed at him suddenly, showing her white teeth. Her pony, a dun with black points, was certainly prettier, but there was nothing to choose between them in any other respect. Both the twins knew it, but they still kept the old dispute going. No one listened to Mnorh. The children stood gazing at Mneri; and at last Li'vanh too turned to look at her.

She looked at him as if she did not dare to smile, almost pleadingly, seeming in fear of his anger; yet she had not flinched from her father's fury. He was helpless. How could he reproach her? So he nodded and smiled a little, and said, 'Did you have a good ride?'

She smiled with relief, and nodded. 'There is a scar on your head.'

'Yeah!' said Nicholas with enthusiasm, '*And* that's not the only one.'

'He is First Spear of Danamol!' cried Mnorh, abandoning his pony's virtues, 'And that is not all . . .'

'Leave it!' said Li'vanh quickly, colouring a little. The last thing he wanted was a paean from Mnorh. 'Nikelh, Peneli, this is Mneri. Mneri, this is my brother and sister. Mneri is Lord Silinoi's daughter.'

'Oh,' said Penelope, 'then you are Lord Vanh's sister. And Mnorh's.'

Yes,' said Li'vanh firmly, 'And mine.'

'Oh sorry, I forgot. We're a big family then, in a way—though you can't really count Lord Vanh.' But Mneri caught her hand.

'Vanh? You know Vanh? Where is he? Is he here? Oh, how is he?' She turned to Li'vanh.

'He is well: never better, I think he would say. Come, I will find him for you. I think he will have quite a lot to say to you.' He saw a guilty expression cross her face and laughed. 'Even after the scold. I think I know one person who will welcome you without reproach though.'

'Who?'

'Your grandsire: the King of Lunieth. He arrived a day or so ago and was sorry you were not here.'

'Oh!' She laughed. 'Yes, I have always been his favourite, even though we have no bond of blood.' She looked at him tentatively, then took a risk. 'Prachoi, you have not scolded me either.'

He was silent a moment, continuing to where Vanh was talking to Prince Argerth, then stopped and glanced at her. She was pacing out some dance steps on the spot, and seemed absorbed in her feet.

He said slowly, 'I am not your father, or your eldest brother, that I have the right to rebuke you. And there is no need to call me Prachoi, as if I were not of your kin.' He hesitated. The little dance had stopped, though she still watched her feet. He added unwillingly, 'I hope the beating is not too bad.'

She looked up at him consideringly a moment, then smiled.

'Oh a beating is soon over. And I got here didn't I?'

The silver moon was waning, and the red moon grew greater. It began to give faint colour to the night. Below, in H'ara Tunij, Li'vanh could see the lines of the torch-lit streets, and occasionally a lamp at window. Beyond the walls he saw the fires of the Khentor camps—one fire for each tribe, the numbers growing every night. Kiron leaned on the battlements.

'Do not over-rate the strength of Fendarl either,' he was saying. 'Even now, he is not as great as some. I for one am stronger than him.'

'Then can he not be defeated by your power?'

Kiron sighed and crossed to the other side of the tower. He gazed down on the ebbing sea.

'It is not so simple, Li'vanh. It is true that I can still call on greater magic power than he can. And if I could use Fendarl's methods, attacking his mind, breaking the holy laws, I could destroy him in an hour.' His voice hardened. 'Kill him, madden him, scatter him. But I cannot. For to use the Star Magic thus for such a purpose—to destroy and not to strengthen—would be to misuse it, to foul the well-spring and corrupt the heart of the fairest power on Khendiol, and the enemy would be strengthened beyond measure. I believe

I spoke of this before. It is a temptation we must all face. But I most sternly, for the centre of the Star Magic is mine to guard, because my forefather was Emneron, first-born of Alunyueth the Prince, first-born of the stars.' He stood straight now, and spoke almost to himself.

'There is our danger. There is our greatest weakness. There is the bitterness: that evil by its very nature can be more powerful than good.'

'Surely not! Kiron, I have always thought it was the other way!'

'You think not? Well, I describe it badly. Say rather that good is more vulnerable than evil. For the like of Fendarl will stoop to compulsion, from which we hold ourselves. And on the side of right there is always the temptation to turn upon evil its own weapons, trusting in the end to justify the means.' His eyes flashed and his voice rang fiercely. 'But the end does not justify the means, nor ever has! And once *we* resort to evil, even to defeat evil, then the enemy has already won!'

It was a cry of warning, anger, and rejection. Li'vanh fell back a pace, then shook his head. 'I do not understand,' he said.

Kiron turned, enquiring.

'What enemy, if you have destroyed Fendarl? Is not he the enemy now?'

The King grimaced and laughed, and shook his head. 'No. He is the present foe, and a bitterer or more dangerous there has never been. But he is like the champion a king sends forth, when he will not himself do battle. He is the servant (though he cannot bear the thought, and bitterly denies it) of a far more ancient and deadly power for evil, He Whose Name Is Taken Away: the Prince of Heaven of whom I spoke to you, whom mortals call Ranid the Thrice Accurst. And there lies our sorrow. It is certain grief if we lose; but not certain joy if we win. For if Fendarl has the victory we are lost; but if he falls we do but live to fight again.'

The length of days before the battle shortened.

There was plenty for Nicholas and Penelope to watch. Every day more men came in—came in, that is, to present themselves to Kiron—then marched out again to camp outside the city. There was no room for them within the walls.

Day by day more tribes from the plains rode in and pitched their tents beside the others. There were twenty-seven fires at last, with their tents about them, twenty-five thousand men and horses.

'Three times three times three tribes,' observed Prince Hairon, who had re-appointed himself their guardian. 'That's a lucky number.'

'What a *lot* of them,' whispered Penelope. 'I never thought there were so many.'

Hairon laughed. 'Oh, this is nothing. If the Great Plains had time to send their host, now, you would see something. The Northern Plains are small by comparison.'

'How are they going to feed them all?'

He grinned wickedly. 'Feed them? Khentors? You don't have to feed Khentors! They don't need food. If they get really hungry they chew their tents. On the march they chew their boots. They can live for weeks on the juice.' They regarded him suspiciously. 'As for the horses, of course, they chew their bits.'

'Fooled you,' said Nicholas. 'They don't have bits—Oliver told us. Just a noseband.'

They went to watch the Island levy disembark. Two thousand men, one thousand chariots, two thousand horses. 'I thought the Islanders were only sending a thousand.'

'One thousand fighting men; that means another thousand as charioteers. You notice they have two-horse chariots only.'

The Islanders were tall men, though not as tall as the Harani, with curly brown hair, pleasant faces, and deep-blue eyes. They had the walk of seamen and an air of prosperity and comfort. Their clothes were like the Harani clothes but lighter, and the white sleeves of their shirts were often intricately embroidered.

'Such are the men of the Islands,' said Hairon. 'The Islands, children, you must understand, are famous for their fruit, their wine, and their people's failure to see why they should do as Kiron tells them.'

'Why should they? Did you conquer them?'

'No! It may amaze you to learn that we have never conquered anybody ... not in that way. No, the King of the Islands many years ago did homage to Kiron in return for our protection, but not all his subjects liked it, roughly half of them in fact—the ones who did not like him. Anyhow, now and again they mutter that they have nothing to do with us.'

The harbour was one good place to be for ships came in on every tide, some bringing troops, most bringing supplies to feed the growing numbers. The road just outside the gates was another, for the troops came along that, or else the fields under the walls where the different armies exercised. They watched the red-headed Valans with their short swords and hard round shields. 'We are friends of old with Vala,' said Hairon. 'This guard is the token of a long alliance. They have a Harani guard in their palace.' They gazed admiringly at the big Kerionenei. 'A strange people. We rarely see them. They live among the peaks of the high mountains in bitter cold; but for all I can tell they only ever wear those shorts and jackets.'

The archers of Kunoi marched in—rather small men, slight, with brown hair and grey or green eyes. They did not mix much, and even their language was a little different, Vandarin with a scattering of strange words. They were rarely seen outside their little realm. Kunoi Len Vanda they called it—the Kunoi a tribe apart—and well was it named.

But the best day of all was when with vivid colour and beating of hand-drums the five hundred men of Humarash came. Their splendid king was at their head, the only king within Vandarei who does not do homage to Kiron, and calls him 'My Friend' and not 'My Lord'. They bore spears with iron blades, the only people apart from the Harani to use the metal, and they were splendid to see: tall and long-limbed, dark with the garnered gold of a million summers, lithe and merry—the Humarei, the Sons of the Sun.

'Look!' said Nicholas admiringly, 'the King's leading a leopard!'

'Everybody seems to like them,' said Penelope, listening to the cheers, 'even the Khentors are smiling. They growled at that last lot, the blond ones.' Hairon laughed.

'Oh yes, they are well liked,' he agreed. 'The beloved of the gods. These men have walked three thousand miles or so to come to us, and to maybe die beside us. They are not even subjects of Kiron, and their country is small. They could not be commanded as others have been. They are far from the danger. And yet we did not even have to ask for their help, it was given so freely!'

Seven of the eight races of Vandarei were to be in the battle. There were the Khentorei and the Harani, the Humarei and the Kerionenei, the Kunoi, the Islanders, and the Kelanat. Only the Barelonh would not be there.

Li'vanh had seen them in the city, merchants usually, though they had more the air of scholars or priests. He had spoken to some of them, and could not help liking them: they were amusing, with a dry ironical wit, and a great deal of charm. They were tall, slender, and pale skinned, with curly light-brown hair which they took great pains to hide, and slanting apple-green eyes. It was difficult not to admire the Barelonh—they admired themselves so profoundly. They watched the world from under lowered lids, with a subtle smile. They looked cool and rather austere, but it was said that they were the greatest of all lovers of luxury.

These Li'vanh learned were some of the men of Lelarik of the Cities. Most Lelariki are of Khentor stock, but few though the Barelonh are—they set the tone of the whole realm. Once their numbers were greater. They had a realm of their own with ten mighty cities. But the Khentorei swept over them, destroying all but one city. The Barelonh were slain or scattered, or fled into exile—many of them took to the sea. It may be that a few reached the far western shores of Avenya, to mingle with the city-dwelling Quaren and build, as some say, Baneros. But whether they lived to teach their cool smiles to that laughter-loving people, or whether they all perished in the salt sea, none know for sure.

Chapter Twenty-Four

Shield of Kedrinh

The sea glittered away until it melted into the hazed cobalt of the sky, and the wings of the gulls flashed as they wheeled about the tower. There in the High King's bright turret room were gathered Kiron, the white-haired enchanter Li'vanh had seen before, a page in royal green livery holding a scabbarded sword across his arms, the Keeper of the Treasure House with something covered in a cloth before him, and the Captain of the Veduath. The boy who had escorted Li'vanh to the room bowed him in and closed the door. Li'vanh saluted the men as he stepped down into the room, wondering again if he would ever grow accustomed to the height of Harani: even the pages were as tall as he.

Kiron greeted him and took the sword from the page. 'Captain Daron was saying that there would be need to forge a sword to your measure,' he said, 'but we bethought ourselves of this. Will you try it, Li'vanh? No new sword could be better, if this will serve you.'

The Harani longswords in the armoury were much too long and heavy for Li'vanh to wield, but this one was perfect in size and weight and he exclaimed in delight at it. It handled superbly. The hilts were of twisted silver, the grip bound with green leather, and the weighted pommel adorned with a moon-stone. The weapon was old, but the hilts and the silver inlay on the blade shone as if new, for in Khendiol it is gold and not silver which tarnishes.

'It could not be better Kiron. The balance is beautiful. Was it made for a Khentor?'

'No, for a boy. This is the sword which Emneron the Young bore into his first battle, so it is not unworthy of your task. It is an heirloom of our house, and so was not in the armoury. But it is a well-forged blade, meant for more than lying among jewels. So too is this.'

He turned to the Keeper of the Treasure House, who drew the covering from the thing which he held. It was a slightly convex oval of dazzling stones; Kiron took it from him and held it up.

'This is the Shield of Adamant. It is one of the ancient treasures of the Harani. Once it was the treasure of one of the Nine Fair Cities. Edunuath was that city, which is now destroyed. It is our wish that you should take it for your use, and bear it into battle against Fendarl. It is lighter than most shields and will turn any weapon, especially weapons of evil, for it is bound with bright enchantments. Iron itself will flinch from adamant, and the presence of this shield will be a pain to Fendarl in itself, for it has a weight that cannot be quenched. But take it, and feel.'

Thanking him Li'vanh took it. The grips hooked over his arm and into his hand as if they knew him; the curve was just right, taking his shoulder and arm in comfort. It was so well balanced it seemed almost weightless. Indeed, it was more than light: it seemed to have a life of its own. He turned it round and looked at it. It was wrought of many stones of adamant cunningly fitted together and it blazed with a white fire. Parallel to the rim, about a handspan within it, ran a line of silver, and in the centre a single silver star spread its slender rippling rays among the jewels. Li'vanh smiled with delight.

'How can I give thanks?' he said. 'It is so beautiful, it seems a pity to be behind it.'

The men laughed. 'But apart from details like that, it is a good shield to be behind,' said Captain Daron. 'We will use it in our practices. You must learn its ways.'

'It seems too light to be meant for hard blows. Is it really so strong?'

'Oh indeed.'

'Then—thank you. Thank you very much.' He weighed it again. 'But who was *this* made for? Surely not for someone my size? But it can't have been for one of you?'

Kiron laughed. 'The treasures of the Fair Cities were remarkable in many ways. There is more to the Shield of

Adamant than its strength, and its beauty. Look.' He took the Shield from Li'vanh and fitted it on his arm. Even the Veduath Captain drew in his breath sharply. It could not be said that the Shield changed, but it fitted Kiron as well as it fitted Li'vanh, and it covered each of them from shoulder to thigh. Kiron laughed at their faces and handed it back.

'It was made by a very great craftsman, Li'vanh, and he made it to be the right size. Whoever the bearer, it will be as if the Shield of Adamant was made for him alone. But do not speak of this property it has, or show it to your friends. Such things should not be made game of, and I did more than I ought.'

Li'vanh nodded, and looked from the shield to the sword of Emneron. 'I thank you again for putting these in my hands. May I bear them not too unworthily.' He frowned a little. 'Kiron, I have often thought: why does Fendarl fight? Why does he not just sit in Kuniuk Bannoth doing all the harm he can? Surely he would be hard to get out?'

'Yes he would. But fight he must. He is come to the last throw, and it must now be conquest or nothing for him. His victory would be our downfall and that is what he seeks: the overthrow of the rule of the Star-born, the end of all dear to us. But he has another reason, and I think that even if he had nothing to gain or lose he would still seek battle. The pride that has made him what he is will not let him turn aside. He wishes to prove himself what he believes he is—mightier than death and destiny. And to do that, he must face them both.'

Next night Li'vanh left the camp quietly and went to sit on the cliffs. The evening fires were gayer now, with girls to dance as well as men; but he did not feel like dancing tonight. Nor was he comfortable in his tent. The Shield of Adamant shone, and the Sword of Emneron gleamed in its light. It made the little house of hide radiant, but not restful. He was proud of them, but not yet at ease with them. So he rode Dur'chai to the clifftop and sat there with his bronze Khentor sword across his knees, dark and earthy and reassuring. He stroked it and remembered Derna and the plains, the smell of grass and the bitter smoke of dung fires, and the careless life he had led there. Here the cliffs grew short springy turf, and the smell was the smell of the sea. But that is still Kem'nanh, he thought, then bit his tongue furiously. The silver moon lay a very faint light on the waves. She was nothing but a paring now. Her rival ruled heaven.

There was a soft throb of hooves behind him, then a light and hesitant step. 'My lord?'

He knew her without turning. 'Foster-sister?' he said.

'May I stay here a while?'

'Stay and welcome.' She did not come to his side, but knelt about six feet away, hands on knees. He looked at her, then back across the sea. She had on her best khechin, of cloth, with embroidered borders. He felt an old pain for a moment. Since she had arrived in the north she had been so withdrawn. She had rarely spoken to him.

'Father tells me,' she said softly, 'that we will go in a short time.'

'We will, yes,' he replied. 'Are you coming, then?'

'Father has given his permission,' she said hesitantly. 'I would not wish to come unbidden—again.' He heard the question she did not ask, and nodded.

'That is good. We will all be together.'

There was a brief silence, then Mneri said suddenly, 'Li'vanh my brother, something is troubling you.'

'Yes.' He paused, then went on in a rush, 'I am afraid, Mneri. Very afraid. Sometimes—I feel so small. And I feel as if he has found out about me, and is—I don't know—putting curses on me.'

'I do not think you need fear that. I am sure Kiron can defend you from that.'

'Have you seen Kiron, then?' She nodded. 'Did you—I mean, is he what you expected?'

'Oh, better!' Suddenly there was life in her voice. 'He is so much younger, and handsomer, and just as strong!' She sounded so admiring that Li'vanh threw back his head and laughed aloud, and she smiled, pleased. Then she said slowly, 'Li'vanh, father told me something about the Council, but— must you fight him?'

'Oh, yes. Obviously. Why else would I have been brought, with Dur'chai, and everything else? I cannot refuse.'

'A man cannot escape his fate. But it seems hard.'

'Not as hard as some things . . . I suppose. I mean, I've just

got to do something, and if I survive it then it's over. I'm
doing it, at least, it's not just happening to me. And in a
week....' He swallowed. 'In a week it will all be over. A
week is not long. Nine days is not long.'

'No,' she agreed, softly, almost fearful. Then, 'And after—
when it is over?'

In the pause which followed he saw the chance to tell her
something which he had long wanted to explain. 'After that,'
he said, 'it seems we'll be sent home.'

'Home? To—to the plains?'

'No. Home. Where I come from.' He spoke firmly, almost
as if he believed it himself. 'Kiron tells me we were only
brought because we were—right for the tasks. Peneli to bring
the curse on Kunil-Bannoth. Nikelh to take the warning to
the Nihaimurh, and so to us, and me to fight the battle.
Because we could be brought—we were the right ages, the
right kind, the right time, or something. I didn't really understand. But when this is over, we will be sent back.'

She had bowed her head, but he could still tell what she
was feeling. 'Do you want to go?'

'Of course,' he said hardheartedly. 'I've loved it here of
course—so many friends—but my father—my mother....'
His voice dried. 'Besides, it makes no difference. I have no
choice.'

'But you belong here!'

'No, Mneri! I do not! That is the point. That is the whole
reason why I can defeat Fendarl, because I do not belong
here. Yorn told me this at the beginning. He warned me I
would not stay.' No, not warned; he had been glad to hear it
then, he remembered, and laughed mirthlessly. 'He told me
something else, too.'

'I am listening, lord,' she whispered.

'I wanted a hunting cat, and he forbade it. He said Dur-
'chai was another matter—he was a stranger as I was and
would go also—but a cat was bound to Khendiol.' He saw
out of the side of his eye that she had raised her head, and
gazed sternly out to sea. 'He forbade me to bind any living
creature to myself. He forbade me to take the oath of the
spear-brother with any man. But it did not arise, Mnorh is
too young. I am in no position to make any promises. That
is what he said.'

There was a silence 'I see,' she said at last. 'I see what you mean.'

'I hoped you would.' He dared not look at her. Illogically, he felt ashamed. 'I am sorry, Mneri.'

'There is no need.' She sounded very dignified—older, he thought. 'It is no fault of yours, Li'vanh, that—not all bonds are made of promises. Nor that I am—older than Mnorh.' Her voice shook suddenly, and with abrupt energy she stood up. 'And I am sorry too that I disturbed you. Good night, my brother.'

He waited until the sound of her pony's hooves was far away before he stood up; then he mounted. But he stayed for several minutes more, looking with a troubled gaze out to sea.

He was sorry, bitterly sorry—of that he was sure. But whether he was sorry for her sake alone, he could not truly say.

For the last time he stood beside Kiron on the starlit battlements of Emneron's fortress. H'ara Tunij below them was almost invisible, a pattern of lights, and a pale red light reflecting from her white stones. Above them the red moon held sway. The silver moon was dark.

'H'ara Tunij,' mused Li'vanh. 'It seems a strange name for one of your cities. More a Khentor name.'

'But it is, it is a Khentor name. When Emneron founded this city he called it Kirontin, and from that our house took its name. But the Khentorei called it the Pearl of the North— H'ara Tunij—with such determination that everyone else came to do so too. Some Harani will still use the old name, but mostly we have discarded it. It is still called Kirontin in the records of the Nine Fair Cities, the cities founded by the Nine Houses of the Starborn. More than half, though, of the cities are fallen; and two of the houses have come to an end. Fendarl is the last of the House of Kendreth; or so far as we can tell. Maybe some forgotten younger branch will come forward to claim the Eagle Banner, but I doubt it. In the way of mortals, we diminish.'

'Is H'ara Tunij that old?'

'Yes, though that is young in the reckoning of cities. There is a city in Lelarik, not quite dead yet, which must be four thousand years old. But H'ara Tunij has changed, since her founding. She has outgrown her walls three times. This is the fourth that now surrounds her.'

Li'vanh nodded. He had seen the discarded walls which divided the city into circles. Boys used them as short cuts.

'We march tomorrow then,' he said loudly, suddenly. Kiron nodded.

'He left Black Mountain today. He turned north, which cheered me.... I did not like to think of him bursting through Nelimhon. It seems he fears it. Perhaps the Boy has come to guard his own. We are prepared.'

We are prepared.... And suddenly the realization of what the morning would bring broke on Li'vanh, and his fear almost swamped him. The night pressed thickly about him, and he was gripped by a terrible loneliness. There was blackness all about him, the sorcerer's moon was watching him, and the darkness between the stars leaned down to gather him in. He ground his knuckles against the stones, shaking in a terror soundless as the flooding sea.

Kiron said abruptly, 'Li'vanh, are you still willing?'

The horror melted, and he was himself again. 'Yes Kiron. Why do you ask?' His firmness surprised himself.

'You know more now. I would not blame you for fearing more. I would not have you—not consenting.'

'I have not changed my mind.'

'I am glad.' He was silent for a while, then began slowly, 'For you have more strength than any other could have. Even if Fendarl had not armed himself against the children of this world, I say to you that no Harani champion, no Khentor champion, could be as strong against him as can you, Oliver Powell. For this is their fight whether they choose or no. Every loss they had to fear from failure, every good they would gain by victory, would weaken them, would weight their arm, would work against them. I do not know why this should be. Some things even I am just told without explanation. But someone like you, Li'vanh, someone who offers himself freely and without need, who has everything to lose and nothing to gain—he is immeasurably stronger. If I may speak of something which I do not expect: even if Fendarl should slay such a champion his victory would not be complete. This I know,' he said, 'but do not understand.

Maybe you do. For it is a little like the Wild Magic. And though I do not think even they could explain it, it is your people, it is the Khentors, who best comprehend the power of the given death—the royal sacrifice.'

Chapter Twenty-Five

The Flight of the Swans

So the Swan of the Sea Kings was borne again into the north; and on the right of it went the Sea-horse banner of the Khentors, and on the left the nine-starred standard of the Enchanters.

Close behind rode the Veduath, forty men and their captain, grey-clad and cloaked in royal green as shining-dark as the holly of their banner. They, as is their right, rode before all.

After them came the vanguard, the first of the Harani armies, three thousand chariots. Each army flew the flag of its own kingdom and after them rode the first of the Khentor host, three thousand cavalry, each tribe following its own banner, led by the Hurnei.

Behind the Khentorei rolled the thousand chariots of the Islanders. Their standard was a golden wheel on a blue ground, symbolizing the sun in the sky, for before all other gods the men of the Islands serve Janar the King of Heaven, Lord of the Golden Chariot.

Following them came the Kelanat, one thousand men under a plain blue flag, marching with long-limbed ease. Their back ranks seemed uneasily conscious of the second troop of Khentors on their heels, three thousand this time, with four thousand Harani chariots behind them.

In the rear of these strode the Valan Guard, four hundred strong, their Captain bearing their banner, orange with three black pine trees, at their head. A handsome sight they made, all big fair-skinned men with the same curly dark-red hair and smoky grey-eyes. Their boots, trousers, and belts were black, and their long-sleeved tunics the amber of their flag. Each man carried his round shield upon his back. The

Kerionenei walked behind them, not marching in ranks: one hundred men. Their thick wavy hair was fluffy silver-fair, and their calm eyes were a clear sky-blue. They had neither badge nor banner and they walked barefoot on the hard road.

Then came the last of the Harani chariots—three thousand —and another five thousand Khentor cavalry.

Next in order came the archers of Kunoi, clad in doublets of green and gold, flying their standard of a stooping falcon. After them the Humarei, flagless, and marching to drum-music, their King with his leopard walking before them.

Then came nine thousand horse: three thousand Harani, six thousand Khentors.

Behind them riding on ponies came the warrior maidens, the Moon Sisters of Avenel. Two tokens went before them, one a disc of polished silver, the other a banner of dark blue silk worked with the starburst in silver, for the Lady of the Night is called Star-Crowned Avenel.

After the fighting sisters came the Harani foot: three thousand men, tall black-bearded farmers with a long easy stride. Country men and peasants were they, with the faces and bearing of kings. Then came another three thousand Khentorei, their long banners proclaiming which tribes were there.

Next came a mighty troop: four thousand warrior-priests of Marenkalion the Avenger, robed in red and white, strong and stern. One thousand horse, one thousand foot, and two thousand chariots, beneath a white standard charged with a scarlet spearhead.

After them rode an army of another sort: the company of the enchanters of the Star Magic, young and old, man, woman, and maid, with the mark of their kinship in their faces, the high proud beauty of the Starborn. Among them rode Veldreth of Rennath and his sister In'serinna beside him. And last came the rearguard, five thousand men and horses, the end of the Khentor army.

So they went, a great host: of horse, thirty thousands and forty-one; of foot, six thousand five hundred; and of chariots, thirteen thousands. There were forty-nine thousand, five hundred and forty-one fighting men with their charioteers and their squires; and the enchanters; and the long train of supply wagons and camp followers behind. Though they set forth at day-break yet the walls of the city were thronged to see them go, shining in the new light of the sun, terrible with weapons and splendid with banners.

Mighty they seemed, but mightier yet was the army which the north sent down to meet them, dark things among it, fell and evil—and nought among all the host so dreadful as its Captain, the last of the House of Kendreth, the Black Enchanter of Black Mountain.

The following days were the most miserable ever endured by Nicholas and Penelope.

They went with the army. They could not have borne to be left behind, yet never had days seemed so long, miles so dreary. All the people they knew were there, but all with their own concerns. No one had time for them. They felt astray, lonely, unimportant, frightened.

Mneri had charge of a wagon of supplies and Penelope rode with her. Until this time she had not known the Khentor girl well, but now she felt closer to her than to any other person, even In'serinna, though she could not have said why. And Mneri was herself comforted by Penny's presence. Anyone so willing to talk about Li'vanh was welcome company to her. Drawn together by a shared love and fear, they became for a little while truly as sisters, even though Mneri always found Penelope's speech hard to follow, and Penelope never understood the true nature of Mneri's feelings.

Nicholas did not stay with them. He borrowed Mneri's pony and rode with the Hurnei beside his brother, taking turns with Mnorh to bear the Spear of Danamol and the Shield of Adamant. Li'vanh liked to have him there. He never mentioned Fendarl. He talked mainly about his riding, asking how to improve it, or told them again of the Nihaimurh and the Teraimurh. He talked often about the Borderer, especially to Oliver. 'You would have liked him,' he kept saying. 'I wish he hadn't gone.'

Silinoi aged before their eyes. Until then he had carried his gathering years unbowed. Now his powerful shoulders sagged, and all the lines in his weathered face drooped and deepened. He was not a young man. Hardly a month before he had burned his spear-brother. His eldest son was as bad as lost to him, and at times it seemed that he had lost his daughter too, for he was no longer first with her. Much though he loved Mnorh he could not see himself in him, only reminders of his dead wife. It was Li'vanh who filled the place in him which Vanh had left empty, and now he feared for Li'vanh.

Nicholas felt a little guilty. He had been jealous of Oliver's affection for the chieftain; he had hated to hear his brother call this man Father, and though Penny had called him Uncle quite cheerfully, he had remained Lord Silinoi to him. But now he saw that Silinoi truly loved Oliver as his son—now he saw his fear—he was sorry, and would have cheered him if he could. If he could—but he had no comfort for himself, much less to share.

Li'vanh rode in silence most of the time, rarely speaking unless spoken to. He was quiet even at the fire at night. The two children slept in his tent and often he would sit in there with them, watching them as they slept. Once he set himself to recall his parents, concentrating until he could remember their faces; but when they came clearly to his mind, they meant nothing—he could do nothing but sit and stare. In the past few weeks he had felt so much that he was numb. He did not even feel fear of Fendarl now. He had talked himself into complete stillness: what would be would be, and there was no more for him to do but play his part.

On the third day he was riding beside Kiron, when the young High King drew rein and said, 'Look.'

Out of the northern sky the swans came flying, one or two at first, then more and more, a huge phalanx darkening the sky. Hundreds there must have been—more than hundreds. Their heads and outstretched necks swayed up and down, their vast wings creaked and whooped. The skein passed them and beat on. Li'vanh gazed after them.

'I never saw so many all at once, let alone all in flight.'

'In flight indeed. In flight from Fendarl. Those are the royal swans, who cannot bear to stay where any evil thing approaches. Our enemy advances.'

The fourth day came, and the fourth night, and Li'vanh looked at the almost perfect circle of the red moon, and felt sick. During that day he had noticed a heavy drabness in the air, and now it seemed to smirch the night as well, so that the stars were paled. It was as if the high dome of heaven were filled with dirty water. The air was heavy and stiff. In or out of his tent, he could not sleep, and when he did sleep his dreams were evil.

The fifth day broke. He woke, and knew what day it was, and fear was reborn.

There was little talking as they began their march that day. The air seemed to oppress everybody, even the Humarei. It had a thick leaden tinge, like the dullness which Penelope had seen on Black Mountain, but much worse. Now all could know one of the Star-born from afar, without needing to see their robes or their rings. The silver shimmer clung to them all, even, faintly, to those of the Children of the Stars who were not enchanters. As for the enchanters, they shed a light on the ground as they walked, and Kiron was more easily seen than was his banner. But the Shield of Adamant was unexpected. It dazzled with its light, and the light shone and grew as they advanced and the dullness grew worse, until the shield blazed as though forged of a galaxy of stars.

At noon Kiron halted them before the brow of a hill, and sent his squire to summon the leaders of the host. Li'vanh waited with him, silent, fingering the little silver medal which he had worn from the first. Often during these last days he had found himself doing this, though most of the time he forgot that he wore it. He looked at it now, and thought suddenly, 'It's like a moon: a little silver moon at the full,' and smiled faintly. He took it in his hand, examining the picture again, finding it oddly comforting. Between the storm's strength and the malice of the water the man was almost overcome, but the child sat with upraised arm, entirely unafraid.

The captains were assembled. Kiron said, 'Beyond this hill is a broad plain. There will we meet him.' Li'vanh let the medallion slip from his fingers. Kiron went on to restate the battle order which they had planned, and the captains nodded their assent. There was no air to waste on unnecessary words. Even the Harani were oppressed by the thickened air; and to the Khentors, who love the free wind, it was almost maddening.

'How long do we have?' asked Li'vanh, wishing his voice did not sound so husky.

'Till moonrise,' said Kiron with a glance of sympathy. 'He

is not far, but he will not advance until his moon rises. Go now all of you; eat, and get what rest you may.'

They separated. Li'vanh rode slowly back towards the Hurnei, where already a few tents were raised. The grey air was as dry as if it were filled with dust; he could feel it against his face as he moved forward, quietly resisting him. With so many thousands gathered there the quietness was unnerving; no one spoke without need. Li'vanh almost felt that he could hear everyone breathing, a low continuous hushing that ground on his nerves.

Mnorh had food waiting for him. He ate, but he had no appetite, and even the drink was savourless. He left both unfinished. The oppression in the air seemed to grow worse. The spectral sun glimmered still high in the hazed sky, and over the horizon rose the ghost of the crescent moon.

He would go and bathe, he decided. His tent had been erected; Mneri and the children were there now, laying out his best clothes and his weapons. But he would not go to it yet. There were still hours to moonrise. He did not want to think about his weapons yet.

Chapter Twenty-Six

The Night of the Sorcerer

Li'vanh stood in his tent.

They were all there: Silinoi, Yorn, Mnorh, Vanh, Mneri, and Nicholas and Penelope. He had bathed and dried himself, and groomed and polished Dur'chai as if in a dream. 'Steady brother, steady,' he kept saying, but Dur'chai was steady. He was an immortal, and his hour had come. Calm and assured, he stood gazing into the north. It was Li'vanh who was not steady. He felt light and hollow, as if fear had shelled him. He seemed but the husk of himself.

They had shaved him. They had helped him dress in his best suit. They had checked his weapons. All he had done for himself had been put on his boots. They had armed him, between them. Vanh had settled the cloak across his shoulders, Penelope had shaken it into folds at the back, Mneri was just tightening the buckles on his baldric. He looked down at the top of her raven head, then at all of them: Yorn his guide, Silinoi whom he called father, Mnorh and Vanh, dear as brothers ... then last at Nicholas and Penelope, dearest to him, looking small and afraid. He felt the bangles on his wrists, the rings on his fingers, touched his necklaces ... he was ready. He remembered the voice of Hairon saying with a laugh, 'Khentors are like trees: they put on all their pomp to die.' I will not die! he thought fiercely.

The Sword of Emneron was under his hand. All he lacked was his shield, and that Nicholas held ready. Mechanically he checked his horn, smoothed his moustache. The wind quivered the sides of the tent. Mneri had finished with the buckle, but she stayed where she was, kneeling at his side. He looked round them again helplessly. In a moment they would be going. The Khentors out to pray to the gods, Nicholas and

Penelope to a place of safety. In a moment he would be alone.

'Forgive me,' he said huskily, 'if I do not speak. . . . I thank you for your help. And I will thank you for it again. After.' He smiled as best he could. Mneri took his hand suddenly, touched it to her brow, and rose and left the tent, silently, not looking at him. The men came: Vanh first, then Yorn, then Silinoi, to embrace him, and Mnorh last of all. Then they went out.

He looked at Nicholas and Penelope in silence, and they stared back. Then suddenly, with a sob, his sister sprang up to him and flung her arms around his neck. He hugged her hard for a moment, then let go and stood back, smiling at her. Nicholas stood frowning and chewing his lip. Li'vanh grinned, and put an arm around his shoulders and shook him a little, then took the shield. 'See you later, then,' he said.

Penelope nodded and turned to the door, blinking. Nicholas began to follow, then hesitated, and turned back. He took out his precious knife and looked at it for a moment, turning it over in his fingers, then thrust it into his brother's hand.

'Here,' he said gruffly, before he fled. 'It is sharp. Prince Hairon sharpened it for me. And it is a good knife. Take it. For luck.'

He was alone.

He gazed after his brother for a moment, smiling faintly, then looked at the knife in his hand. He hesitated a moment, then shrugged and took his bronze knife out of the sheath, replacing it with Nicholas' knife. Then he squared his shoulders, then drooped a little again.

Out there the army was praying to its gods, and he felt a terrible loneliness. He was nearer than he had ever been before to going out to join them, but still he held back. They were dedicating their weapons, too. . . .

He sighed. It was not so easy to pray, alone—or at least he had never found it so. But all at once he felt that he dared not go unblessed—unarmed. What prayer could he make, to the God whom he had refused to forsake, yet could not truly remember? He drew his sword and held it up before him, hoping for words, but none came. The moonstone on the pommel shone faintly in the dimness of the tent. The Shield of Adamant glittered. These two, and me, and Dur'chai; that's all, he thought. That's all there is, to meet him. 'Take us,' he said aloud, 'for what we're worth. It's harder than I thought—and I'm afraid. . . .' His voice shook, but it was the best that he could manage. 'Oh help me God!' he cried suddenly, but silently. Then all at once his fear almost choked him, he bit his mouth and gripped his sword. Don't break up now! You haven't time. It's no worse now than when you took it on—just nearer. . . .

He gave a little gasp and the moment passed. Outside there was a stir of sound. This is it, he thought, and sheathing his sword took a deep breath. Slowly the phantom courage of despair was stiffening him. His heart was frozen like a bird before a snake, and hope was so far as to be a children's tale. I have no courage left, he thought, but I can pretend. Nothing can save me now from this, but I'll go laughing. Well I'll try. He tried out a nonchalant laugh, but the strangled hoot that came from his throat, sounding all alone in the quiet tent, was so funny that suddenly he did laugh in real amusement. And Mnorh, entering then, stared.

'You are merry Li'vanh?' Then he looked sorry to have spoken, and said 'Dur'chai is waiting. . . .'

He went out and mounted Dur'chai. Mnorh handed him the Shield of Adamant, blazing with light. He looked down on his foster-brother's face and again managed a smile.

'I left my knife in the tent,' he said, as he prepared to move off. 'I don't need it. Nikelh lent me his. Look after it for me.'

I hope that didn't sound too much like a bequest, he thought, and laughed a little, hoarsely. The army was drawn up. Kiron was waiting. He smiled at Li'vanh, and nodded to the east.

'The moon is up.'

Indeed, it had risen: a perfect circle, like a shield of copper. It looked at him, bland, ominous. He swallowed and looked at Kiron, grave within his nimbus of silver.

'I am ready.'

Kiron lifted his arm to the bugler, and Li'vanh his to the Khentor with the horn. The bugle first, sharp and vivid, then the horn, sad and fierce. The host, with a lower, quieter version of the strange baying he had heard at Danamol, rolled forward. They surged on, and over the hill.

Across the plain advanced the enemy host, vast and dark,
black and crimson in the light of the moon. It was not so
great as their army but far more dreadful, full of its own
darkness. Before it rode its captains, and Li'vanh shivered.
Against those captains were ranged the mightiest men of
Kiron's host, Kiron among them. But before the captains
rode one from whom the eye flinched, and that was his
enemy.

The armies came on, rolling towards each other, but
Li'vanh had no eyes for anything but that great shape riding
before them all. With a shock he saw that he was mounted
on a horse—that he had not expected. A dragon would have
surprised him less. The banner that went before him was in
mockery of Kendrethon's white eagle, for on a flag of sullen
red a black eagle spread its wings. Fendarl was hooded, and
his cloak billowed behind him, distorting his shape. But
Li'vanh could see how tall, how very tall he was, and gulped.

Then all at once the sounds behind him stopped.

He reined back, startled, and looked behind. The whole
host had halted. All along the line, men urged on their horses.
But the men's hearts were failing, and the horses had
baulked. None of them would go any nearer to Fendarl. Not
Kiron, not even the Khentors could get their mounts to stir a
pace.

Li'vanh looked back, aghast, then forward again. The
other army had also drawn a halt. And Fendarl was still,
waiting.

There was a long moment of stillness. Then Dur'chai tossed
his head and neighed, and very deliberately stepped forward.

'He will stand fast!' muttered Li'vanh. 'Ha!'

But even though the other horses were standing fast and
he would not, Dur'chai was showing his immortal mettle and
earning his name. Now and then Li'vanh would feel the great
horse shudder, but he was too close to his own fear to notice
this. His world had shrunk, small and very tight. Behind him,
Kiron's host and all he loved were growing farther and
farther away. Ahead of him Fendarl drew closer and closer.
Dur'chai was moving with his smooth, almost silent stride,
not too fast; and Li'vanh savoured each bitter second as if it
were a lifetime of pleasure. Yet still he sat straight and
resolute and unwavering, and though he himself was wretched,

yet those watching wondered at his courage. His pride helped to sustain him, and the burning gold of Dur'chai's mane cheered him, and over the rim of the shield he was conscious of a glimmer like moonrise. He rode until the length of four spears lay between himself and Fendarl. Then the wizard raised a pale narrow hand and said 'Halt.'

Li'vanh was half inclined to disobey, but Dur'chai stopped. There was a long silence, in which the enemies gazed at each other.

Li'vanh looked first at Fendarl's horse. It was big and entirely black, save for the eyes, which were of the red of the moon and without a black pupil. It stood unnaturally still. Then he raised his eyes to Fendarl.

He was tall and long-limbed, but his robes hid most of him. There was only his face, and his face was that of a Son of the Stars, handsome still, even in its ruin. His skin was very pale and his features were strongly carved—but he looked old. Strong still, and dangerous, but old and bitter. His nose stood out like an eagle's beak, and his thin-lipped mouth had a downward curve. His hair, which Li'vanh glimpsed, was white. His eyes had sunk deep into his face and they were dark, cold, and haughty. His hands though bony looked dreadfully strong, and on the little finger of his left hand was a ring like a nine-pointed star—black.

'Well?' His voice was quiet, powerful, and cold. He spoke with faint impatience, as if in scorn, and Li'vanh found his voice.

'Fendarl Kendrethon, onetime King of Bannoth, fallen Enchanter of the Star Magic,' he cried, every word clear and challenging, carrying to the hosts before and behind, 'sentence of banishment was put on you, which without Kiron's pardon you have defied. Wherefore I call on you to face me in combat, hazarding your person, and endure the justice of Heaven!'

Fendarl smiled. 'Justice of Heaven?' he queried, and laughed without sound. There was a ringing quality in his voice, so that it had a chill beauty. 'You are young, horse-boy, to be the champion of Kiron.' Then all at once, without warning, Li'vanh felt himself attacked—not by weapons, but by the air around him, which quivered and cracked. The world was buffeted, shaken; he was pulled and torn by the wizard's power, iron hooks dragged at his mind. He gasped and reeled, then suddenly flung the Shield of Adamant before him, ducking his head behind it, and felt the pain lessen. The shield blazed in Fendarl's face; he wavered, and winced; then Li'vanh felt the power prised from him, forced back to the Black Enchanter. He let the shield fall back to his side, and straightened, and looked Fendarl in the face again. He was shaken, and battered, and something had left him, for he was no longer immune to the sorcerer's presence. The dark eyes flickered on him.

'You have a little strength to resist me,' said that calm, splendid, dreadful voice, 'but not enough. It was Kiron's strength which saved you then.'

Then a cold anger touched Li'vanh. 'I called you to hazard your person,' he said, taking a spear and putting it in rest. 'Defend yourself!'

Fendarl smiled coldly. 'So be it,' he said. 'What is your name, champion of Kiron?'

Li'vanh gathered up the reins and looked at him. He said, 'They call me the Young Tiger.'

Just for a moment a tremor of doubt and disbelief crossed the necromancer's face, and fear glanced in his eyes. Then he whirled his horse and rode back a way, wheeling for the charge. Li'vanh followed suit.

He turned Dur'chai, drove his feet into the stirrups, swung the Shield of Adamant before him, pointed his spear across Dur'chai's neck, and drew a breath. It did not seem possible that it was happening at last, that here and now they were bearing down on each other.

They met with a shock. Fendarl's spear, hitting the Shield of Adamant, shattered, but Li'vanh's buried itself in his opponent's shield before the shaft broke. The sorcerer cursed, and reached to snap it short; then they wheeled and charged a second time. This time they did not strike so square: Li'vanh's shoulder was jarred, and his spearhead scored across Fendarl's shield. Once more they charged, and each broke his spear, but both stayed in the saddle. Then they drew their swords and closed in.

Fendarl was not the greatest of warriors. Li'vanh soon found that. But it was hard, harder every second, to stand and face him. There was a sickness in his mind, a darkness, a horror of the sorcerer's presence. He could not concentrate on his fighting. This numb dread kept getting between him

and his sword arm. Time and again he knew he had mis-
judged, felt Fendarl come closer than he need have let him.
He set his teeth and pulled himself together, attacking hard.
Pulled himself together was the literal truth. He felt he was
being broken in pieces ... he could feel the enchanter's mind
grappling for control of his, and knew he had not strength to
resist that. It was well for him that there was so little in his
mind on to which Fendarl could fasten. Concentrate, he
thought, concentrate. His sword arm seemed to be thinking
for itself, for he was sure he was not thinking for it. The
shield, flaming like a white sun, seemed to be flinging itself
before the blows of its own will. He wondered whether he
had fallen into a fighting trance, such as he had heard of.

Dur'chai, immortal horse though he was, could only just
bear Fendarl's continued presence. Li'vanh could feel him
quaking and shuddering, snorting and sweating, not as in
fear, but with a sick hate and disgust. And as for him, his
head was filled with a black madness that wanted him to run.

Strike. Turn. Press. Parry. Thrust. The blows he took on
his shield ached in his jarred shoulder, the blows on his sword
hurt his hand. But he was beginning to master the panic, and
his mind was not under attack. He could not guess why:
perhaps Kiron had come to his aid, wrenching the necromancer's magic away from him, or perhaps Fendarl was just
growing tired, or had abandoned it as useless. Now and again
Li'vanh saw him flinch away from the Shield of Adamant,
but whether it was the light of it or whether it had some
power he could not tell.

The attack pressed on, and then suddenly he felt he had
the advantage. For a moment he could not believe it, but
then Fendarl snarled in rage and hate, and drew back a
second. He drove back into the fight with greater vigour, but
now Li'vanh began to be surer of himself ... and then all
at once the sorcerer leapt from his horse's back.

Li'vanh was taken by surprise. He could not see why. Then
he saw that Fendarl could get on the right of him, away
from the burning light of the shield, and that also there he
could get under his guard. He had a choice: to turn his left
side and make it harder to attack for himself, or to
dismount. He hesitated a moment, wondering why Fendarl
had taken such a chance, wondering that he seemed to fear
the sword less than the shield ... then he made his decision,

and leapt from Dur'chai's back on the side away from the wizard.

At once he felt so small.

Fendarl towered over him, at least two feet taller. His impressive stature was made yet more impressive by his whirling robes. His eyes, aglint with malice, gazed down on his enemy from a face dreadful with triumph. I shouldn't have dismounted! thought Li'vanh desperately. Fendarl's height was too much advantage. He was outmatched. Doomed.

Then Fendarl began to laugh, and raised his sword. But as he did so, he drew back his shield arm also, exposing his left side. And Li'vanh struck.

He struck aside the sorcerer's descending sword, and with a hoarse shout drove his own deep between his enemy's ribs. With all the strength of his arm he thrust, and from the ranks of the host of Kiron went up a great glad cry of triumph.

But Li'vanh did not join them.

For as he thrust, Fendarl did not flinch or waver, and when he would have drawn his weapon out he found there was nothing to withdraw. Only the hilt, and a handspan or so of blade, rimed and smoking. And he dropped his arms. And Fendarl smiled at him cruelly, and then looked beyond to the army, and gave a laugh fierce with scorn.

'Fools!' he cried. 'Fools! Did you not know, had you not remembered that I cannot be hurt by any creature of this world? And though you send against me this foundling boy, yet what is bronze, or what is hammered iron, if not a creature of this world?'

And they were silent, for their shock and grief and shame were too terrible for tears or any sound of sorrow. And in all that vast host there was no movement save sometimes the stamp and shudder of a nervous horse. For a long moment there was silence. Then Fendarl laughed again, and flung up his arms in triumph.

All this while Li'vanh had stood as motionless as the rest. First he had felt sick with disappointment and shame at his defeat. Then he had felt a small chill bitterness against the High Lords. They must have known. They must have known it was useless. Why had they sent him unarmed to fight this demon, to die here? But it soon passed, for what did it matter? He was cold and weary and hopeless. They were all going to die soon: Mnorh and Silinoi, Vanh and In'serinna, Kiron, Yorn, Mneri, Nicholas and Penelope, the Starlit Land itself. And a numb despair lay on him.

And then he heard Fendarl laugh.

At first it was just another knife-twist in the wound; but then he thought of all their struggle, all their patience, and he thought of the Starlit Land, so fair and doomed—and here was this demon, this creature, this *thing*, exulting in her ruin, and mocking with his vile mirth men more brave and noble than his rotted soul could compass, and Li'vanh's friends. And anger, that had been a slow smouldering fire in his veins, leapt into red flame.

He had taken this fight because he felt it was his duty. He had been prepared to kill Fendarl because he was an evil thing that had to be destroyed. But even when he had met the Black Enchanter he had not felt personal hate—only fear, and disgust at his evil, and awe, and longing to be gone from there.

But now, with that laugh, Fendarl had become *his* enemy. A wild rage and hate leapt in him, and dreadful bloodlust that did not weigh what was possible and what was not. Killing Fendarl was no longer just something he must do, it was something he *wanted* to do. And if not to kill, at any rate, to strike.

He gave tongue to a cry of fury and hate and defiance, horrible to hear but glorious relief to utter. He flung away from him the shard of his useless sword, and the Shield of Adamant also, for he no longer cared for defence, and his hand went of itself to his belt, and seized Nicholas' knife. Clasping the knife-hilt two-handed he sprang forward right at the sorcerer, and with another wild war-yell swung down, with all the strength of his shoulders and length of his arms. And the bright-honed blade bit at his enemy's flesh.

And as his blow went home such a shriek arose that all without exception trembled, and Nicholas and Penelope fell to the ground and covered their ears.

O, bitter is the thought of death to mortal men who live with it; but who shall conceive of the anguish of one who thought himself immortal, then feels the pangs he never thought to bear? He had felt himself safe, armoured with dear-bought power against anything the world could send him, yet a champion had been brought out of another creation

to face him, and now he was pierced by a weapon against
which all his power was naught. Deep-delved in unknown
mountains were the mines whence came that strange ore; it
had been forged in no fires of Khendiol, by men who knew
nothing of the Star Magic. It raged in his side like ice, like
white fire, spreading agony to every fibre of his body, snapping the thread of his bewitched life, and crumbling his flesh.
He was dying, who had thought never to die, and he gave
another piercing cry of despair and pain and terror. For the
pride which had brought him to this was useless; the power
for which he had lusted had failed him; to win protection
from this he had sold all of himself that could have survived
it; and now in the final bitterness he saw all this clear-eyed.
Yet he was evil still, and seeing his slayer before him,
standing dazed and surprised, he reached out his hand to do
him some last hurt. But as he seized Li'vanh's shoulder, the
strength left his legs and he fell, dragging the boy to the
ground with him.

Then his grip loosened, and he writhed for a moment or
two. His face was distorted with bitter hate and spite. His
eyes bored his enemy. 'A curse ...' he croaked, but got no
further. Another bitter cry he gave, and died.

Li'vanh, after his blow had gone home, had stood amazed
at the cry, bewildered and confused, not daring to believe.
He had taken the knife because it was the only weapon he
had left, and struck only with the desire of striking, not the
hope of slaying; but could this toy knife do what the best
blade in the armoury could not? Could he, after all, have
destroyed Fendarl? Then he felt the grip of the wizard's hand
on him, dragging him down, and bitter pain shot through
him, and he cried out on his own account. It seemed but a
few heart-beats from drawing the knife to finding himself
crawling on the ground by his enemy's body, retching and
shuddering.

The pain was iron in his bones, and a black sickness filling
him, and now that his anger had run its course his strength
had gone, and the rearing horror of Fendarl's closeness had
returned. He would have fled now if he had been able. But
there was something else—something he did not understand,
that as neither weakness nor pain nor fear, that tore and
buffeted him from within. A roaring in his brain, a thunder in

his blood, a swelling in his heart—a strength within him too great for his weakness to bear.

He dragged himself to his knees and looked about him; and recoiled from what he saw.

To his eyes the world had changed. Much of it had gone smoky and pale, and some had vanished altogether. Above him the sky was lit with a million turning suns, each different from the others. The red moon was a pool of fire. The white moon was a sickle of burning ice. And the people had changed.

He looked at Kiron's army. Much of it he could only see as shadows; but the tribesmen seemed in some way to have sunk together, to have blurred into a huge shared identity. He was no longer aware of them as so many thousand men, each a Khentor, but rather as Khentorei, a vast fire, a dark green blaze of pride, indignation, anger, loyalty—all instinct, all feeling, direct as an arrow's flight. For the first time he guessed at their potential power, and was afraid. They were so fierce, so free. They were like—like anything wild and strong and pure. Like the wind. Like the sea.

With the Harani it was the other way. He was conscious of them no more as a host, but as so many single Harani. He could see them all quite clearly—countless bright warriors— but except that some were brighter he could not distinguish one from another. He could feel differences, and guessed that if he could control it this strange power reached out to minds and not faces.

But they were all remote, dreadfully remote; and there was no sound at all.

He was clearly conscious of Fendarl's army too, but they also were far off and silent. A wall of grey wavering mist seemed to be round him, and the only things close and real were the black heap of Fendarl's body by him and a rioting golden fire a little way off that was Dur'chai, revealed now in his true immortal glory. For as the dying enchanter had gripped Li'vanh a little—a very little—of the power that was leaving him had passed into the boy, and he was now briefly gifted with witch-sight.

But he did not know it was witch-sight, and he did not know it was brief; and it was a gift he would gladly have refused, bringing such loneliness. But he mastered himself—

for was he not the champion of Kedrinh?—and struggled to his feet, and looked up.

And at what he saw then, he dropped again to his knees, and fain would have flung himself on his face, but that he could not look away.

Chapter Twenty-Seven

Princes and Warriors

Beyond him, seeming behind and above Fendarl's army, was one at sight of whom his whole being cried out Worship! Worship!

He filled the sky, and he did not stand, but sat at his ease, as if the very heavens were a throne for him. But it was his beauty—there was no other word—which held Li'vanh riveted. It was the grace of his seated form, and the chiselled perfection of that cool, princely face. There was something in that face akin to the Harani, and it troubled Li'vanh a little; but what it was he could not say. It was not in the features. *His* were formed in a mould more fine and graceful, and though his looks were fair and proud he lacked utterly the sterner nobility of the Sea Kings. His complexion was pale, and he had the appearance of a young man, though the hair that swept back from his face was silver—not white, nor yet gold, but pure, shining silver. His eyes were dark, so dark: black and deep and so cold that Li'vanh shuddered. 'Royal' but debased his majesty. 'Imperial' was nearer. A crown of the living stars would be unworthy of him. He was robed in some long pale garment—not white, but a pale, pale gold—and over it was cast a mantle of glowing purple, the same colour as a ring that burned against his pale hand.

He bent his eyes impassively on the army of Kiron, on the dead Fendarl, on Li'vanh. And though the boy quailed, feeling the touch of a mind and a power too vast to comprehend, the sensuous perfection of his face was untroubled.

Li'vanh never doubted he was seeing a god. But slowly he began to feel afraid; he began to feel there was a pride, an egotism, an insufferable hauteur behind that cool detached face of such fearful beauty, an arrogance that demanded as a

right the homage, the adoration, the obedience—yes, the
worship—of all, only to swell his own glutted pride. And in a
single moment of rending horror he knew whom it was he
saw. Fendarl's master; the great enemy; He Whose Name Is
Taken Away, that Prince of Heaven whom he had always
called Lucifer, Star of the Morning.

He could not bear it. Not the evil, *and* the beauty. Not
knowing who he was, and still wanting to bow to him. He
covered his eyes with a groan, dragged himself round to face
the other way, and crawled forward.

The folds of a mighty scarlet cloak boomed in the wind.
The shelter of a mighty shield was over him. He looked up.
Awe and wonder filled him again, but no terror. He knew
himself safe, for this could only be Marenkalion, the Defender.

He stood above them, straight-backed, with a soldier's
stance. On his right arm was the great shield, in his left hand
he grasped a colossal spear. A helmet shadowed his grave
face, crested with a plume of white light. His face was fair
and stern, his brown hair blew out from the helm, and his
shining grey eyes held his adversary with a gaze of rejoicing
and challenge. Li'vanh saw the command in the grey eyes,
and felt it flow in the air about him, though he heard no
words. You are defeated. Acknowledge it.

A cold, unwilling smile touched the lips of that face of
deathly beauty, and he inclined his head. Then Li'vanh felt
cold eyes grip him; a dreadful energy of fury and spite was
bent on him. He cried out silently, and flung up his hand, and
the great warrior held out his spear in denial.

Do not touch him. He belongs to Him against Whom you
cannot prevail.

And that dreadful malice licked round him, fell back, drew
away, ebbed; and as it went the power Fendarl had be-
queathed him began to die away, draw back towards its
source, until he was himself, mortal, crawling in the cool
grass. The sky was empty of figures, the stars were stars, the
silver moon was frail, the red moon was full; but what did
it matter now that Fendarl was slain?

He shuddered and looked about him. He still felt sick and
shaky, and could not for a moment grasp that the witch-sight
had passed. His shoulder where the dying sorcerer had seized
him still hurt desperately. He turned and looked behind him,

and saw Fendarl lying where he had fallen. That was real, then? He really was dead? He sat back and shivered, and relaxed slightly. 'Then it's all over,' he thought dazedly; and suddenly as he leaned forward to retrieve Nicholas' knife, unexpected tears welled into his eyes.

But Dur'chai came, neighing fiercely and imperiously, pushing and jostling him to his feet. The two armies were preparing to charge. Even as he rose there was a scattering of bugle notes and the mounting growl of the advance. Li'vanh clutched at the horse's mane and looked about him blinking. Dur'chai was snorting and chopping at the ground, all but forcing him to mount. He staggered forward and picked up the Shield of Adamant from where it lay, and the remnant of Emneron's sword also, was a vague memory that it was an heirloom. Then he struggled into the saddle and sat there, swaying and unarmed but erect.

Then Dur'chai gave a neigh higher and wilder than the bugles' notes, and raked the air, and with a snort sprang forward. So Li'vanh Tuvoi, trailing the white fire of the shield and astride a horse fiery as the wrath of heaven, was borne like a bright banner before the army of Kiron; and a dread was he to the ranks of darkness, the slayer of their master and the token of their ruin. They quailed and cried out, and some stood and others fled, but all were overthrown.

For shouting the war cry of the Starborn, 'Tinoithël,' Kiron led the charge. His cloak cracked like thunder behind him, and the sword in his hand was unsheathed lightning. With him rode the Veduath; a small part of the army were they, but so is the spearhead a small part of the spear, and like a whetted blade they clove the forces of darkness, and few who met them lived. Then where the King and the Veduath had passed came the massive weight of the Harani chariots, hewing a broad avenue through their enemies. There fought Argerth Prince of Rennath, and there his kinsman Hairon led his men, fighting with his iron-bladed spears, and when they were spent doing red work with his long sword. Well it is, for all who oppose them, that the Harani are a people slow to strike; for their anger, long withheld, is long remembered. Patient they are but not passionless; strong of purpose but no less strong of arm; and their blows, when they fall, do not fall lightly.

The sorcerer's army was riven by that mighty charge, hurled away on either side like a great bow-wave; then on either flank of the sundered host came the chariots of the Islanders, and of the priests of Marenkalion, and the crushing force of the Khentor cavalry. Stern warriors are those scarlet-cloaked priests, and no strangers to war the Island men; and terrible to meet in battle are the plainsmen, the gentle people. For the wild strength of Kem'nanh is in them and in the might of the storm they smote their enemies—nor did they fight with weapons alone. For wherever there was found one of these foretold by Kiron, one against whom spears were useless and swords of no avail, who scorned javelins and laughed at arrows, in whose shadow the creatures of darkness rallied, there rode the Wild Magicians. They rode unarmed, but dreadful to encounter, possessed by their magic: that power which is hardly to be endured by those who serve it, and cannot be withstood. When they who bore that power unleashed it, even those towers of the Dark Host were swept away in ruin, and the madness which is the curse of the Wild Rider fell on the lesser things.

And after the chariots and cavalry came striding the foot-soldiers; Harani farmers making a grim harvest; dogged Kelanat and resolute Kerionenei, fair giants; bold Valans of the Guard and the warhardened servants of the Avenger. There too came the Humarei, bringing grace even on to the field of slaughter, and the maiden warriors of Avenel, proud and slender, with their smoothed spears and barbless arrows; and there were the silent archers of Kunoi, silent still, letting their bows speak for them. And last of all came the Children of the Stars, not armed with weapons, seeking out those among their foes strong in the dark arts and joining issue with them.

Long and bitter was that battle and grievous the cost, for Fendarl had massed a dreadful host, not easily to be overcome. Kunil-Bannoth turned at bay in his doomed despair, and Kiron was hard put to overthrow him; but at the last he slew him, and thus ended the House of Kendreth. Three of the matchless Veduath fell that night, men of uncommon worth: Inseron the loremaster, Der'inh of the Alnei, and lean scarred Gadreth the singer. The Council of Enchanters was weakened by four who could ill be spared, and nine Masters of the Wild Magic lay quiet upon that field when all was

over, destroyed by the strength of the god they served. There
were many farmers in Kedrinh that year who had sown and
would not reap, many Islanders who never felt again the
deck of a ship beneath them; there were paths in the Kelanat
Mountains watched by fair-haired wives in vain, and many
Kunoi who did not return by the secret ways to their own
quiet land. Young Garon of Rennath got a wound there that
stopped his laughter for many weeks, and the Captain of the
Valan Guard lost the use of his shield arm, and Hairon lost
more. For Vadreth the peerless charioteer had gone into
battle with him, guiding that proud team with skilful hands,
until a spear broke through his light shield and killed him at
his Prince's feet. Many hundreds were the Khentorei who died
there, and many proud horses; and thirty of the Humarei
went into that darkness and never saw their sun rise again.
There was cause made that night for many long nights',
weeping, many dead men and maidens, many maimed lives;
but before the setting of the silver moon all that black host
was slain or scattered. Those that fled yet did not escape, for
Kiron sent out a strong force of Khentors to pursue them.
Then they planted on the field the three standards, the Swan
and the Stars and the Seahorse, and sounded around them
the bright bugles and the mournful horns.

When Dur'chai at last consented to bear his rider back to
the encampment the night was almost over, and Li'vanh was
very weary. In body he was unhurt, for defenceless as he had
been none of his enemies had dared abide his coming, but had
fled in panic wherever Dur'chai had borne him; and his
weakness and confusion had passed. He was whole in mind
and body, but sick at heart.

He was much more than weary: in very truth he was
exhausted; or—utterly spent, worn-out, empty. He had conquered, but his victory had the taste of failure. He was filled
with a corroding disappointment, and a bitter sense of loss.
He felt bereft, although of what he did not know.

The sky was grey with chill light in the east; in the west
the red moon slid towards its setting. It was hargad, the hour
between night and day, the time which Khentors fear. A thin
cold wind stirred the faint mist, the world had no colour, and
the stars had lost their fire. The broken stump of Emneron's
sword was knobbed with a solid white pebble; the Shield of

Adamant, filmed with moisture, was only an oval of hard colourless stones. In this dull cold world, Dur'chai alone was unchanged. Beautiful and untroubled, he cantered with floating grace across the still battlefield, showing an immortal's disregard for the slain on all sides. But Li'vanh looked about him, and the weight on his heart grew. For here where the battle had been won there were none but the losers, and he saw not the scene of his triumph but only men; dead men—dead men.

He tried to think of Fendarl, his evil and his strength; and of his own victory. But he could remember only the death wail of a man in great terror, a man whom he had killed; and killed, in the end, not out of justice or necessity, but in the rage and hatred of his heart. The ache of loss became a pain and tears burned his eyes. Yet in his shame and grief there was a seed of anger, for it seemed to him that in some way he could not understand he had been cheated. He had been ready to make an offering of his fear, and maybe even of his life; but something had been taken which he had not offered, something which could not be regained and would be missed for ever. He felt an oppression, as if part of his life had ended.

So he went at last to his rest, wherein lay the only healing for him. But the thing which he had lost he never did regain, though what it was he could never have said. Perhaps it was his youth. For Li'vanh was one who had looked upon the darkness in his own heart, and he must henceforth live his life in the knowledge of that darkness, and in the fear of himself.

Chapter Twenty-Eight

The Green Grass Growing

Victory, thought Nicholas, came in an unexpected fashion. It seemed that he and Penelope, rejoicing in their brother's safety, were the only people happy; and they felt obliged to take their gladness away where it would offend no one, to hood the radiance of their joy lest it hurt the eyes of others. None of their friends could truly rejoice with them—not In'serinna consumed by fear for her own brother, nor Hairon mourning his closest comrade, nor Vanh learning to believe that Starwind would never bear him again. Even Oliver himself had wanted only to sleep.

He had slept throughout the whole of the day following the battle; slept, and woken, and slept again; and by degrees his strength came back to him. He had escaped both the grim labour which fell to the whole and strong, and the sad gathering which followed it. The pyres were cold before he left his tent. Yet little as honour may profit the dead, to pay it gives comfort to the living; and on the second evening Li'vanh came to the edge of the battle ground.

That plain had never been especially renowned for its beauty, but it had been as fair as most fields, when the grass was green and the flowers blooming. Very terribly was it changed now, and all the grace of spring gone from it. The new-turned earth of the grave-mounds was cold and stark; there were wide black scars where the pyres had burned. A cairn of grey stones had been raised over Fendarl's body, surmounted by his banner: the black eagle shook from time to time in the wind, seeming almost to mock them.

Li'vanh leaned on his spear in silence as he gazed across the plain, remembering that other battlefield where he had mourned for Derna and Rehai. In those days he had never dreamed of the trial that lay before him; and now it was all over. All over. His battle had been fought, and he had not been overcome. His ordeal was behind him, and he was still alive. He sighed and suddenly gave a shudder of relief, leaning his brow against his spearhead. Then he heard a step behind him, and turned to see Kiron.

They had not met since the battle. Kiron, thought Li'vanh, looked very weary, and it seemed to Kiron that Li'vanh's eyes, which had been the grey of silver, were now the grey of iron. It grieved him, but he made no sign of it as he greeted him.

'Hail, Shield of Kedrinh! I am glad to see you Li'vanh. Are you well?'

'Hail, Kiron. I am well enough, I thank you. A few bruises, and my shoulder aches still; but nothing very much.'

Kiron nodded, but said nothing. Looking at him Li'vanh saw that he was watching him consideringly, and felt uneasy. There were some things he did not wish to speak of, even to Kiron. To break the pause he straightened and pointed at the eastern sky, where the red moon had just risen. It had lost the perfection of its fullness, but only just.

'Look, Kiron. It has hardly decreased, and even that only by the passing of two days. For all our striving we did not diminish it in the least.'

'Of course not,' said Kiron calmly. 'Did you expect it? Do you not remember that I said that we would but live to fight again? It is an ancient battle, and the end is not in sight. But we have done our part. We have withstood the foe that was sent against us. And for that we have you to thank. It was a great deed, Tuvoi. I hope that you are as glad in your victory as you deserve to be.'

'Glad?' Li'vanh looked at the cairn with its quivering banner and looked away. 'I am not glad that I killed him. But I am glad that it is over, very glad indeed. And you Kiron?'

'I?'

'Are you glad in your victory?'

Kiron shook his head abruptly. 'I have no victory in which to rejoice.'

Li'vanh looked at him startled. For a moment the High King's eyes were bleak as winter, and his voice as bleak as his eyes as he said with finality:

'If we had truly succeeded we would never have been

brought to this. All our lives we strive against evil with all our strength; yet what does our victory come to? That today we are the conquerors, because yesterday we did more harm to our enemies than they could do to us.'

Li'vanh was silenced. He remembered his own resentment because his victory tasted flat, and was ashamed. But as for Kiron, it was a grief he had known before, and one the Harani always bear. Other men with lesser aims may succeed and rejoice, but it is the doom of the Children of the Stars to strive always after perfection which is not for mortals, and so for them there is always the bitterness of failure.

On the third day after the Night of the Sorcerer, unexpectedly, Kiron gave the command to break camp.

There was general surprise and some protest. They had neither expected nor desired to remain long, but three days was little time to renew their strength. Kiron went himself to the chief of the Earth Priestesses, in whose care were all the wounded, to tell her that they must prepare for the journey. She had hardly slept since the night of the battle and was almost spent with her labours, and many of those labours had been in vain. She was in no humour to bear with a man and a warrior, and answered him shortly that it was not to be thought of. Kiron answered her just as curtly that they had no choice but to think of it, and left her. She watched him go with her dark eyes hot with anger, and returned to her work cursing in her heart all bearers of swords.

Yet many besides her were astonished, for a journey at this time would be a sore trial for many of the wounded, and to take such a thing lightly was not Kiron's way. He must have had good reason, and indeed his face told that all was not well; but this reason he would not share, and that again was unlike him.

Still, Kiron's command had been given, and they must obey: even, finally, the Islanders, whose captain had argued most and longest, and only forborne when Kiron's rare anger flamed. The Khentorei could have been on their way within an hour from the order, but the other peoples were less practised, and there were very many wounded. So for all their haste the sun had set before the column began to move.

Silinoi rode at its head. Kiron intended to remain until the last of his people were away before he would take his place;

and though his face was grim with the expectation of danger, still he would not name his fear. A very few lingered with him, among them the Earth Witch, who claimed care for the wounded as her reason though she waited on after they had all passed; and Li'vanh Tuvoi, who had no excuse but curiosity. Maybe he would have been wiser not to have stayed, but Kiron's determined silence intrigued him. Maybe he was guilty of rashness in taking so lightly he knew not what, but in those days he was beyond command.

They sat their horses at the top of the low ridge on the south side of the battlefield. It was a clear warm evening, and the silver moon, a little less than half full, had risen. No one spoke above a murmur as the long line of wagons lumbered over the hill. The creak of the laden wains, the scrape of the horses' hooves, an occasional gasp from one of the wounded—these were the only sounds. In Kiron's small party no one spoke at all, and apart from the faint chinking of a horse mouthing its bit or shaking its head they waited in silence.

Li'vanh looked down on the ugly, pitiful field and on the campsite, where patches of pallid grass marked where the tents had been pitched. The red moon was just rising when the last of the rear-guard began climbing the slope, led by Vanh mounted on an unfamiliar brown horse. At the crest he paused a moment and looked back, remembering Starwind, then rode on.

The faint moonlight, and the starlight, and the dregs of day, gave the air a strange dim glow. Li'vanh had three shadows, none of them more than a ghost. In this twilight anything was possible. He shivered a little and looked at his companions, the impassive Earth Witch and Kiron in his majesty, then glanced back at the empty plain northward. But it was no longer empty.

He cried out sharply. The rearguard, hearing him and looking where he looked, broke ranks and with a wild drubbing of hooves fled over the hill. Kiron's horse reared suddenly. Only the Earth Witch sat without moving, and her nostrils flared wide.

Li'vanh felt a choking thickness in his throat; his blood throbbed and his head swam. The dusk was thickening blue, but she who approached pulsed with a glow of her own. She was all light and colour, but she filled him with darkness and his senses reeled.

Vir'Vachal's hair, twined with poppies, was the rich ripe gold that sometimes in summer glows at the heart of a cornfield. But the red of her skirt was not the gay scarlet of poppies; it was dark crimson, like blood that wells slowly from a deep wound.

She halted her earth-coloured pony and turned her head slowly from side to side. Her dark savage eyes passed over the blasted field—mutilated, trampled, and withered, scarred by fire and strewn with ash. She looked at the long lines of bare graves, the charred grass, and the grey cairn; and her sorrow went forth like an audible cry while she stretched out her arms in grief. Yet it was not for the slain that she mourned; but for the injured earth itself.

She left the pony and walked forward, her arms reaching out. The whole measure of the dreary field she paced, her slow patterned movements almost a dance. She stepped and turned and swayed, sank low and wheeled and wreathed her arms, bowed her head and bent her knees, moving with ponderous hypnotic grace. It was a dance of ritual grief and heavy anger and entreaty, and the blue night began to pulse to her rhythm. Her skirt brushed the black ashes; a slow flower slid from her hair, and another, and another; and those watching drew a quivering breath of awe and terror.

For as she moved she sank ankle-deep into the earth, and behind her green welled from the hollows her feet had pressed, welled up and overflowed and spread. Wherever she passed the ground woke to life, and grass grew and flourished. The earth brushed by her skirt bore clover, and flowers bloomed where her poppies fell. A slow tide of verdure flowed out from her, and not one yard did she leave untrodden. The fire scars were thick with blossom; the graves were banks of scented growth; a vine wreathed Fendarl's cairn and twined his banner. Surely the dead would sleep more quietly under such a coverlet than in the cold naked earth.

Vir'Vachal stood still at last, looking about her; and nodded, satisfied. Then she raised her eyes, and they swept indifferently across the group along the ridge. And she saw Li'vanh.

His mind sang with shock. He had been told that she could see only earth and its fruit, and plainly she saw no one else. But him she did see. He could not doubt it. He felt her strong eyes meet his and fasten on him, binding him, compelling him; and he looked back at her helpless, mesmerized. Far away as she was, he saw that her eyes were the dark malty colour of rich earth, and when he looked into them it was as if he were gazing down a fathomless abyss into the molten heart of the world.

For a long moment she looked while Li'vanh's strength ran from him; then she hooded her eyes and turned away, and seated herself on her pony. The beast of earth plunged forward, and turned, and bore her away out of sight. The heaving earth sank still and smooth, and the night grew calm; and only the flowering battlefield remained to prove where she had passed.

Li'vanh found his shaking fingers twisted in Dur'chai's mane, while the horse's neck was reared back almost against his chest. He had risen a little in the saddle and was leaning forward; now he sank back, his heart thudding, his breath coming unevenly.

'Why?' he croaked. 'Why did she—what made her—how could she. . . .' His voice failed him.

Kiron shook his head wordlessly; his face was drawn, and he patted and soothed his terrified horse with a hand itself unsteady. The Earth Priestess too was shaken and pale; but when she looked at the High King she smiled with the touch of malice she always showed to him.

'She smelled your battle, Young Tiger,' she said. 'The blood and the burning, and it drew her.'

Li'vanh recoiled slightly, and Kiron's mouth gave the faintest little quirk of distaste. But the priestess saw it, and her eyes leapt with anger, and she turned on him crying fiercely.

'Yes! Yes, you shudder and call this darkness, but who blended that scent for her? Oh, you northerners, you lords of men, with your talk of right and wrong! You put on scorn like a robe and curl your lip, because in our worship blood is shed. Yet in one night you will spill more blood than would we in a thousand years, and no god has demanded this offering! Yes, Vir'Vachal is drawn by the scent of death, and you do not like it. But where she found death, she had left life; and you—what did *you* do, King Kiron?'

Nothing else she could have said would have cut so deep; and the taunt stung Kiron to anger. Their eyes, pine-green and earth-dark, met as the eyes of contending warriors meet;

but Li'vanh only shook his head as if he had not heard, and
waved his hand. 'No, no,' he said, 'I did not mean that.'

He sounded so strange, they both looked back at him. 'I
did not mean that,' he said again. 'I meant—I mean, that
is—after—when she. . . .' They both stared without understanding, Kiron's face puzzled, the priestess's blank and
opaque, as his tongue stumbled over the words. He looked at
them with a kind of despair and struggled once more.

'I mean, I thought it was only grass. I did not know she
could. . . .'

And suddenly the Earth Witch's eyes flickered, and lifted
sharply at the corners, and she drew a quick breath. He saw
that she was on the brink of understanding him: and he was
seized with sudden terror, and stopped.

Now it was his turn to strive with her eyes, and his own
were become like grey pebbles. She waited for him to contin-
ue, but he closed his mouth firmly.

'Well?' she said at last, 'There was something you wished
to say, Prachoi?'

He shook his head. 'I have forgotten,' he said. 'It was
nothing.'

She did not believe him and her eyes fought his for the
knowledge, but he would not yield it. All his instincts told
him he was in deadly danger, though how and why he did
not know. He knew only that he feared this woman with her
intense, almost predatory face—feared her with all the passion
of his blood, feared her as he loved his life.

'Come!' said Kiron sharply, 'What is this? Li'vanh, was
there something you wished to know? Priestess, enough of
this!'

The woman's eyes slanted with fury, but her hold was
broken. Li'vanh looked at Kiron. 'It was nothing, Terani,' he
said steadily. 'It was only—what we must all have felt.'

The High King looked at him perplexed and doubting for
a moment, then shook his head. 'Well,' he said, 'It is past
now.'

'Past!' cried the priestess, 'Past! What dangerous folly is
this from you, Kiron? Past! It is *not* past, nor will it be until
she is bound in her place again! Do you *still* weigh her so
lightly?'

'I do not weigh her lightly, nor ever have! But . . .'

'But! But what? You will still not acknowledge the truth!

Necessity is a stern goddess, Kiron, and we all must bow to
her; and all things have their price, as you are ready to admit
in everything but this. Vir'Vachal is at large and many will
suffer for it. If she is not bound in her place before seed-
time, a bitter spring will the North have, and a bleak harvest!'
Then her voice grew suddenly soft with menace, sending a
shudder through her hearers. 'Kiron,' she said, 'look to your
young men!'

Eight days it took them to ride from the North, and on the
morning of the ninth day they entered H'ara Tunij in conquerors' state.

It was morning of a clear still day; there was a glinting
high tide, and the rising sun drew the mist wreathing from
the meadows about the feet of the victorious host. The
watchful sentries on the walls gave a shout, and raising their
long shining trumpets blew a clear fanfare; and the heralds of
Kiron answered, and the great gates opened for them.

So they rode in triumphant, while the gate-guards shouted
and clashed their swords across their shields, and girls cast
down flowers before them, and the people of H'ara Tunij
cheered them through the streets. The city was hung with
banners and garlands, flags rippled from every gate and roof
and from the masthead of every ship in the harbour.
Trumpeters greeted them at every gatehouse, the hooves
clattered, the chariots rumbled, the feet of the infantry
tramped, the crowds roared, and flocks of startled birds
wheeled and cried above them. The soldiers straightened
their backs and walking with lightened steps laughed, with
gladness to be home and gladness at their welcome. And it
was fitting that it should be so, and worthy were they every
one to be thus honoured, for all that they had endured, the
hard battle they had fought and the host they had overcome;
and none was more worthy or more acclaimed than he who
rode at the side of Kiron—Li'vanh Tuvoi, Lord of Warriors,
Slayer of the Black Eagle, Shield of Kedrinh. They hailed his
prowess and his youth, and he bowed and smiled and waved,
while they hung him with garlands until they made a deep
scented collar about his neck, and he waved, and smiled. Yet
there was a stillness about him, where there should have been
a glory, and it seemed that he did not exult in his triumph as
did his comrades. He did not laugh as he returned victorious,

he who had laughed going forth; for he could not forget the cry of Fendarl, or the face of Ranid, or the eyes of Vir'-Vachal; and all the time through the cheers and the fanfares came to his ears the cold voices of the gulls.

Very lovely in summer in Rennath, smallest of the Nine Fair Cities, with the sky blue behind the sunlit stones of her towers and arches, the city walls canopied from within and without by trees, and the sun glancing on the waters of Eron Nes, the river that half encircles her. So she looked on the day when King Deron gave his daughter In'serinna to Vanh of Lunieth, when all the great ones of Kedrinh rode to their wedding, and Kiron joined their hands.

Lovelier still the city looked by the light of the full summer moon, turned all to silver against the deep blue heaven—silver walls, silver trees, and silver river. The stars were like a spilled treasure chest. Li'vanh was standing at a window looking down at Rennath when he was joined by Hairon, who looked over his shoulder and sighed with pleasure.

'Could any place be lovelier?' he asked. 'Oh, I have seen Nadirh and H'ara Tunij, and I have heard of Conda and Baneros, but I do not believe any of them can equal Rennath. I will never weary of the sight of her.'

Li'vanh moved aside to make room, glancing up at the prince's face. 'How will you like Kuniuk Rathen, then, Kunil-Bannoth?' he asked; for Hairon had been charged with the hereditary wardship of Kuniuk Bannoth and the lands thereof, and was now Kunil-Bannoth—which charge and which title were borne by his heirs for generations, until Garon II made an end of their house. Hairon laughed a little ruefully, thinking of the fortress in Black Mountain, then turning back to the room sighed a little.

'Well, things cannot remain unchanged for long, Li'vanh,' he said soberly, 'and it is said with truth that it is the bright light which casts the black shadow. There is no gain without loss.'

He looked at In'serinna as he spoke, and it was not hard to guess the gain and loss he weighed, for many had the same thoughts. Radiant in white and silver, her dark hair roped with pearls and crowned with galya blossom, her green eyes brilliant, In'serinna was indeed beautiful. But it was a beauty new to her; a warmer, softer, loveliness, not the high shining beauty of the only half mortal Children of the Stars. She was fair and proud and royal, but no longer terrible; and through the rejoicings ran a faint strand of sadness.

She was not unaware of it. Once or twice her eyes strayed to the window and the stars beyond, and then her face wore a look half sorrowful, half guilty: she would glance at Kiron as if in apology then turn again to her husband, and seeing the love in her eyes no one could really believe she grieved.

But at the end of the evening Li'vanh and Nicholas found themselves standing with Kiron, Hairon, Veldreth and the King of Rennath on the battlements. No one spoke; no one moved, save now and again to make room for another arrival. They watched the sky in silence, and waited.

The white moon had set, and the red crescent was no rival to the stars. They pulsed steadily, undisputed rulers of heaven. The watchers grew stiff and cold with their vigil long before Kiron moved suddenly, and pointed.

Away in the south, in the small constellation of the ship's prow, a star quivered. It paused a moment, grew, hesitated, shrank a little, then glimmered larger again. Nicholas caught his breath, and Li'vanh made a faint noise of protest.

If they had expected anything, they had expected the star to flicker and die. But it did not. It grew. It grew as if living its million years in a moment; it blossomed like some fantastic flower of heaven. Its burning rays eclipsed its brother stars. It was the brightest thing in the sky, brilliant, vivid, lighting their awed faces with its fire. It stood above them proud, defiant, pulsing flame.

The star swelled once more then hesitated, trembling with light like a brimming glass. It hurt to look at it yet they would not look away. Then all at once a darkness appeared at its heart, and the star seemed to burst. Faster than their eyes could follow, its rim grew, spread, hurtled across the sky; and there was left only a globe of hazy, pearly, light. Then that too faded, dimmed, and died, and they were left, letting out their breath in a long shuddering sigh, gazing silently at a blank place in the sky.

Chapter Twenty-Nine

Shepherd of Stars

For Nicholas and Penelope, spending that flawless summer with Vanh and In'serinna in Lunieth, this was the good time; but for Oliver it held the bitterest moments of all. For he went home to the plain, and the plain was no longer home.

His only desire had been to go back, back to the unquestioning warmth of the tribe, back to the simplicity of patterned days and a life governed by law and custom, back free of conflict and conscience and doubt. In his longing he had deceived himself, as is all too easily done, into thinking that a return to the place would be a return to the time; and when he found his loneliness waiting for him even there it was the darkest moment of his life. For then he knew with certainty that the change was within himself, and there was no refuge for him.

The first shock came in realizing that he could not hope to return to the tribe he had left. Derna was dead, and Rehai, and a score of other men; from facts like these there was no escape, nor from the truth which he was soon forced to acknowledge, that the change in him had gone far deeper than weariness. He had been a boy still when he left, for all they had called him a man; but he was a man now beyond any doubt. And more even than that, as days passed there grew within him the slow recognition that he was no longer a Khentor.

He resisted the knowledge desperately, but it could not be denied. It was not that he found any fault in them, for it was only in himself that he found any fault. The life they lived still seemed very good to him, desirable even in its harshness, all the sweeter for the struggle that made even survival a constant miracle, and best of all in the strength of the bonds that make it more natural for a Khentor to say 'we' than for him to say 'I'. He admired, envied, loved them; just as ever he longed to be one with them; but it was now a thing beyond his power. Somewhere in his wandering he had left them behind, and he could not return.

For the first time in his life he tasted that grief which has no name and for which there is no cure: grief for the relentlessness of time, the grief which belongs in all creation only to man, who is mortal and knows it. It sometimes seemed strange even to him that this passionate regret should possess him when he was in the very prime of his youth, but though day is long the dew once dried does not fall again.

There has been a camp here before, thought Li'vanh. He let the reins slide through his fingers as Dur'chai dropped his nose to graze, and while he looped his rope around the saddlehorn scanned the stretch of the grass before him. Within a wide ring of darker green there was a mass of little shadows in the grass—it was hard to say how they differed from their surroundings, and probably they were only noticeable at a distance. That will be where the fires burned in front of their tents, he thought, and smiled.

The air was very still and the sky's blue arch quivered with heat. Dur'chai's ornaments chinked faintly as he cropped the grass with quick sideways wrenches of his head. A small blue bird flickered across the deserted camp site, pricking the silence with his call. Li'vanh wondered which tribe had raised their tents here, and where they were now, leaving these traces of their passage like a salute. He was looking for the place where the fire of gathering had burned, and when he saw a wider patch in the grass pressed Dur'chai forward. He moved unwillingly, tearing the grass as he went, and Li'vanh swung his leg over the horse's neck and slid to the ground.

It was the great fire, he thought. Wind had carried away much of the ash, and blades of fresh young grass pushed through the black circle like the ghosts of the flames. He dug at the layer of black with the toe of his boot; it was quite thick, but the grass-roots anchored it. Something small and heavy fell away from his foot, and he stooped for it. It was a little smaller than the palm of his hand, leaf-shaped, its roughened surface vivid with verdigris.

It was the remains of a bronze spear-head; and meshed in the grass roots, close by it at the edge of the fire where Silinoi had cast them, lay the other two.

Horror flooded him. He jerked his hand away from the spearhead as if it were still red-hot as he had last seen it, and stepped back, shaken, scrubbing his hand against his leg. The pleasant sense of fellowship had betrayed him like perished leather. The bird whistled again and the sun burned in his cheek, but he was hearing again the falcon's harsh cry, and shivering in the cold grey wind.

Fiercely he told himself to be sensible: it need not be the same fire, he could not know that the spearheads had belonged to Hran. But that was no comfort, for no one could have thrown them into the fire without reason, and there could only be one reason for such a thing. Hran or not, someone had stood by this fire as his spears were broken before him, hearing that terrible curse, knowing himself outcast.

He shook his head. He deserved it, he thought angrily. He had shed blood.

And then he thought, but so have I.

He stood stricken with the truth of it. At last he understood. This was what had been oppressing him. This was the loss for which he mourned. This was the thing which divided him from the Khentorei. This was the unadorned fact in all its cruelty. There was blood on his hands.

In the clarity of the moment he reasoned coldly against himself. It was useless to plead that it had been necessary for Fendarl to die, for did necessity make the deed itself less evil? It was dangerous to claim that Fendarl had deserved death. And had he slain him only in the spirit of an executioner? He knew he had not. Maybe only a blow struck in passion could have breached the Black Enchanter's dark defences, but he knew that did not justify the striking of such a blow. He knew that if he had not killed Fendarl many would have suffered, and he knew that this did not pardon him. He could argue and excuse all he liked, and it would not make his hands clean. He had killed. That was the truth behind all the trumpets and garlands and songs, and in that moment it seemed to him that all his honours had been bought at too high a price.

He thought of the Khentorei, whose hands were not

stained by the blood they shed, with infinite regret but no bitterness. He did not even try to believe that what was true for them need therefore be true for him. He recognized that just as for all their violence they remained truly the gentle people, so in some way the savagery of war left their innocence unassailed. And even so, for killing as he had killed, consciously and deliberately, there could among the tribes be only one penalty: outcasting.

'Leave us and never return . . . .'

It was almost a relief to recognize it at last.

Kedrinh had never known such a summer as there was that year, when it only rained by night. But it would not rain tonight, thought Nicholas. The night was still and too warm for sleep. He was covered by a single linen sheet, but still he lay wakeful. The curtains of his bed were open, hanging like columns of pale green marble, and through the unshuttered window he could watch the cool stars.

He stretched, yawning, and trod the sheet down from his body. It made no difference. Perhaps I ate too much, he thought, and grinned ruefully, rubbing at his already roughened hair. Looking back over the day that seemed very probable. It was the last day of summer, and a festival among the Harani. The King of Lunieth had come from Kuniuk Emneth to Vanh's castle, and Harion from Kuniuk Bannoth.

Nicholas sighed restlessly and sat up, then rose and walked to the window. Elsewhere in the castle there was still dancing; he could hear strains of the music. And somewhere someone was playing a harp, very softly, almost too faintly to be heard. Nicholas expected every minute to hear the minstrel begin to sing, but he did not. He leaned his head against the chill stones, waiting to be lulled by the delicate wandering melody, but it seemed if anything to have the opposite effect.

Whoever the player was he was a superb musician. Nicholas could not decide from which direction the music came. Sometimes it was quite clear, sometimes dissolved almost entirely into the stillness, so that he must strain his ears for its return; and the more he listened the less like a harp it sounded. He could hear no separate notes, only a single thread of melody drifting like gossamer between heaven and earth.

Nicholas stood enrapt, in a calm deeper than sleep yet intensely wakeful. The faintest of cool breezes stirred the indigo stillness of the night. Arched over the castle the circling stars shone in calm unceasing watch. Within the music had changed to a measure as intricate and majestic as theirs, while between the dance above and the dance below a silver web was woven of the fragile music which faded and swelled in time with the pulsing of the stars.

Then Nicholas's door opened.

Every nerve in his body leapt, and he sprang round from the window with a half-smothered cry. It would not have astonished him to see Hairon there; but it was a young man he had never seen before.

His first impression was that the stranger had just that moment arrested his movement and was caught in a rare instant of repose; then it seemed rather that he had stood there for ever, poised in stillness while the slow ages wheeled about him. The cloak that wrapped him was the blue of the night sky, and in the shadows of the folds it sparkled and glimmered as if stars hid there. He looked on Nicholas almost gravely, but his mouth was closed on laughter, and his blue-black eyes were alive with a fearless youth that need never yield to age. For an eternal instant they stood in silence, then the strange music swelled to a climax and surged past Nicholas into the room—and out of the music the young man spoke.

'This is not a night for sleep,' he said. 'Come, dress yourself as your sister has.'

He had not even noticed Penelope; but she was standing there, hazy with sleep, at the stranger's side. There was something strange in her appearance, but Nicholas scarcely glanced at her before turning away and seizing his clothes. He was lacing his shirt when the stranger said, 'No, no. I said dress yourself as your sister has.'

He looked at Penelope then, and saw what had seemed strange about her. She was oddly dressed, in pale blue trousers of thin cloth, a very thin short white jerkin, and over the jerkin an open shirt of vivid blue. He stared in astonishment, then recognition, then slow realization of the meaning; and looked his question at the young man. And smiled back at him and nodded.

Nicholas swallowed, 'Right now?' he asked, 'Tonight?' He did not know whether he felt excitement or dismay. The stranger left Penelope's side and walked to the window, glancing down into the courtyard. 'Tonight indeed,' he said. 'My horses are waiting.' Then he looked back at them and suddenly laughed, with a joyous sound which made them prickle with delight. 'When else? Is this not a night of music?'

The horses were there, in the courtyard below; three of them, the colour of night, standing motionless before their chariot. They had not been there when Nicholas looked out and he had not heard them come, but he could readily believe that they were only ever to be found when their master looked for them.

They followed their guide out, and to his chariot. The horses pranced and shook their arched necks. There were stars on their brows and stars in their manes, and their eager feet disdained the earth's support. The chariot was dark blue and its wheels were rimmed with silver. Nicholas and Penelope stepped up into it, looking in wonder down over the horses' backs. There were no reins. The stranger left speaking to his horses and came round to mount the platform. Nicholas turned to watch him, and as he did so a door opened and Vanh, In'serinna and Hairon came out.

For a moment they were motionless, looking; then In'serinna gave a cry and started forward, the men following. Penelope turned at the sound and called out in her turn, and she and Nicholas would have sprung to the ground again. But the charioteer leapt to bar their way, calling out sharply and spreading his arms before them, and they stopped startled.

'No one who once steps up into my chariot may step down again before his journey's end!' he warned them. 'What? Shall the world turn backwards?'

Awed, they moved back. He mounted beside them, and putting a hand on the shoulder of each turned to face their friends.

They too had stopped when the stranger had spoken, and now In'serinna alone came forward. She spoke no word and did not look at the children. Her eyes were on the young stranger, who gazed calmly down upon her as she drew nearer, and she stopped and sank down in a curtsey before him. Deep down she bowed, a deeper obeisance then ever she would have made Kiron, until her skirts were spread about her and she bowed her face against them. The onlookers stared unbelieving; then with the same grace she rose again, looking up.

'All hail, Shepherd of Stars,' she said.

'Hail, Lady of Lunieth,' he replied, and his voice was strangely tinged with compassion. Only then did she look at the children, and smiled though there were tears in her eyes. Vanh and Hairon came and stood with her, but no one found anything to say, and their farewells were taken in silence. Only the music still floated in the air, preventing grief and muting their sadness to a deep solemnity. Without a sound and almost without their realising it the chariot began to move forward. The three who remained walked after it while they could keep pace and then when they began to fall behind suddenly Hairon found his voice.

'Good-bye!' he shouted after them, then, cupping his hands at his mouth, 'Be good!'

They laughed a little breathlessly and waved back to them until they were far beyond sight. Then they turned to face forward. Their companion put his arms about their shoulders, and Penny sighed.

'And we won't see them ever again!' she mourned. But the young man laughed aloud.

'Ever!' he said, ' "Ever", is far too big a word for mortals to use!' Then he cried aloud to the horses, and flinging high their manes they leapt forward.

For a moment it seemed that the wind of their speed would claw them from the chariot, but the charioteer's steady hands sustained them. The world reeled away beneath them, the deep night poured past them, the music sang about their heads. With a shudder of awe Nicholas realized that they were mounting far and farther above the earth— speeding, it seemed, swift towards the stars. Light spun back from the wheels, before them the horses' manes tossed against the jewelled sky, netting the constellations in their starred darkness, and their companion's cloak billowed and spread until it arched behind them like the starlit heaven itself. The singing stars rocked and spun before and about them, but motionless ahead flamed Arunuthë the north star, and answering shone the star on the brow of the leading horse. Miles, hours whirled away beneath the flying hooves, until at a call from their lord the horses reared and wheeled. The skies swung giddily around them and they galloped now southward.

The rising of Varathil told that night was near its end before the pace of their wild ride slackened, and a new sound told them that there was firm earth beneath the hooves once more.

The horses cantered lightly down a long slope, into a green bowl between two hills. Grey walls and arches grew up out of the grass—they were among the ruins of a city. Walls or gates it had never had; now it lacked roofs too, and the broad streets were paved with flowers. Yet there was no desolation in the ruin, but a tranquil beauty. Even in destruction Netharun the City of Mysteries retained her loveliness.

They passed among the fallen houses up into what had once been the King's High Hall. Two of the tall walls still rose intact, pierced with windows, and the massive arch of the door still stood alone. The other walls were brought low and a green lawn grew in place of the paved floor, while the hall was roofed with the night sky, and that at least was a lordlier canopy than it had known in its days of glory. Once a stream had flowed past the hall but over the centuries it had forced a way through the wall, and now ran splashing and murmuring from corner to corner.

The horses walked under the arch then halted. The young man sprang lightly down and beckoned to the children, who followed more slowly. Nicholas looked about him uncertainly.

'Are we still in Kedrinh?'

Their guide did not answer for a moment, gazing into the distance; then 'Yes,' he said, 'yes; you are still within the boundaries of Kedrinh. But this is Netharun; and Netharun, like all of the Nine Fair Cities, stands on the Border.' Then he turned away as if to discourage further questions and went up on to the dais.

The warm ground still smelled of summer, but the air was cool and moist. Nicholas and Penelope sat down on fallen stones, Penelope groping for her skirts, forgetting for a moment that they were gone. The Shepherd of Stars stood motionless, gazing down on the court that was departed with a smile on his lips. The music sang low, and silence gathered. A waiting stillness stole on them all.

Then suddenly their guide gave an exultant cry and spun to face the east, holding up his arms. The music spiralled, clear and sweet, and there was a new note mingled with it, faint and golden-mellow, like the sound of a far distant horn. Nicholas and Penelope sprang up, catching at each other's hands, and turned eastwards. The stream ran chuckling at their feet, dark blue streaked with white, reflecting the stars in fragments. Straight before them Varathil burned steadily, but below her a pale light welled into the sky. A breeze arose and flowed serpentine through the air, fanning their faces; and in its moist chill there was unmistakably the tang of autumn.

The Shepherd of Stars leapt down from the dais and came lightfoot over the grass until he faced them across the stream. His eyes quivered with changing colour like still water fanned by wind or trees with ruffled leaves: dark blue shimmering sometimes into silver-grey. He gazed at the children and smiled, and began to sing.

The glory of his voice mingled with the music, shaping it, strengthening it, guiding it; and it lapped Nicholas and Penelope about, filling their ears and head and hearts until they could no longer bear the beauty. The shining laughing eyes called to them irresistibly, and crying out they sprang towards him.

The running water at their feet had drowned the galaxies. The singer's eyes had swallowed the sky. Heaven whirled about them, and the dancing stars. For an instant they saw Varathil beneath them, Tinoithë beyond; then the tide of music swept them away and Kedrinh knew them no more.

Chapter Thirty

The Last Ordeal

The winds of autumn drove the Khentorei southward, shrivelling the grass about them. From all the plain, tribes and herds drew down to where sheltered green valleys wound among low smooth hills whose sides were shrouded in trees, amber and rust and flame. Here the streams flowed all winter long and the grazing rarely quite failed, but knowledge of what was to come lay like shadow on the hills. In the life of the tribes there are three great fears, fire, and epidemic, and winter, and of these ordeals winter is the grimmest.

Autumn is the time of the gathering of the tribes and of the great feasts, and the first and gladdest of them is the Feast of New Men. Waiting among the hills were the boys who had been sent out in the spring to win their horse and their manhood together, and at the Feast of Kem'nanh they were welcomed back into their tribes. Their braids were cut off and they were given spears of bronze and received as equals of their fathers. That year not one of those who had left the Hurnei in the spring failed to return, which was a wonderful thing, for usually two or three are lost.

First and gayest is the Feast of New Men, but last and greatest is the Feast of the Mother. A feast of darkness and mystery and great power, it lasts two days and the night between, and for that time Li'vanh Tuvoi took himself away from the tribe. That year Mneri was among the maidens whose feast of womanhood this was, and after it she was not only a woman but the Priestess of the Hurnei also. She had begged Li'vanh earnestly to break his rule against worshiping with them, and join in the Feast, but he had refused; and she never asked him for anything again. But although he went far up beyond the trees on to the heathery upper slopes of the

245

hills, lying in the evening by his solitary fire he could still hear the drums far below him booming their urgent, ancient rhythm, and even when the drums were silent, the soreness of his heart would not let him sleep.

A day or so after his return Yorn sought him out and said, 'I have a message for you, Tuvoi. Your brother and sister have been taken back.'

It took him several minutes to understand, and even then it did not shake him as he felt it ought. It was like seeing a gong struck afar off, knowing there was a great noise but not hearing it. They were gone, but gone from Vanh and In'serinna, not from his side. He wondered about the manner of their going and whether it had made them unhappy—though Nicholas at least, he thought, was more likely to be glad. The loss to himself was so remote he could hardly feel it.

Nevertheless they were his brother and sister, and they were gone from Vandarei. Their departure was ominous. He looked at Yorn and knew as always that the Priest understood his mind. He asked bluntly, 'Has this a meaning for me?'

Yorn raised his brows and answered calmly, 'You have an ear to hear for yourself, Li'vanh. You do not need my guidance.'

'But I do, Yorn. What must I do? Ought I go to the White City? Ought I go to Kiron?'

He would have been so grateful for a command, but Yorn only shook his head and turned away smiling. 'Your way is for you alone to choose, Tuvoi. You are your own lord.'

Frost set fire to the last of the trees, and the wind from the Plain smelled of snow. Deeper and deeper grew Li'vanh's certainty that he must leave, yet still he did nothing. In truth he hardly knew what to do; but having for the third time resolved to go to Kiron he still delayed, until Kiron took the matter out of his hands by sending another message.

Yorn sent for him, and when he was kneeling opposite him in the darkness of the Priest's tent he asked, 'Have you yet decided what you must do, Li'vanh?'

He sighed, 'I cannot stay.'

'No.' Yorn's calm considering voice gave the final certainty to it and Li'vanh was glad of the darkness to hide his face. 'No, Tuvoi, I do not think you could stay for ever. Though we have all forgotten it, you are still Li'vanh the stranger. But had you thought what to do now?'

'I had—I thought that the best thing to do would be to go to Kiron. Only I never quite found the—the—I never quite went.'

Yorn seemed not to hear the dangerous unsteadiness in his voice. 'A god restrained you, Tuvoi,' he said, and Li'vanh had to laugh a little. He could not have found it hard, he thought. 'It would have been a wasted journey, or one without need at least. Kiron bids me greet you, and to say that he is coming here to see you.'

Li'vanh's head came up, and his eyes were wide with astonishment. Why should the High King make such a journey? But Yorn went on calmly, 'He has told me what brings him and has given me leave to tell you the chief part of what he has to say, if so I wish. He lays no charge upon me, because it is a task he relishes little himself.' Despite the smile in Yorn's voice Li'vanh shivered a little.

'Does it concern my—departure?'

'Closely, Tuvoi, but not as you think.' Then even he paused, to gather his words. 'This is Kiron's message. Li'vanh Tuvoi, the time comes for you to go to your own place, but I have not the power to send you.'

He sat quite still, unable to believe it. 'What did he say?' he asked, faintly puzzled, as if he had not caught the words. Then suddenly he trembled violently and cried out, 'Yorn, *what* did he say?'

If Yorn flinched a little the darkness hid it, and his voice was as even as ever. 'Be still, Li'vanh. Kiron has received a message from Ir'nanh, whom he calls the High Lord Ivanaric, and he has been told "We have no authority over Li'vanh Tuvoi. He must find his own way home." '

Li'vanh had been half rising but he lacked the strength now. Limply he sat back. His own way home. What did they mean? How could he? What could he do?

'Yorn . . .' he said desperately, 'Yorn . . .' But he did not even know what to ask.

'They lay hard tasks on you, Tuvoi.' There was deep compassion in Yorn's voice, and Li'vanh noticed afresh its beauty. 'But so far they have not been beyond your strength.'

'Oh, but Yorn! This is another thing! How will a warrior's skills help me here? Yorn, when I first came you said that Ir'nanh would guide me back, as he had guided me here!'

'I do not doubt he will. There will be a way, Li'vanh, and

it will be revealed. It rests with you only to recognise it, and
to take it. And,' he added, 'when I spoke of your strength, I
did not mean the strength of your hands. That was not what
took you to face Fendarl.'

Li'vanh was silent a moment, then said bleakly, 'I am to
watch and wait, then, is it?'

'Yes,' Yorn paused, wondering how much he might say,
how much Li'vanh would understand. 'And Dur'chai—
Dur'chai is no bad guide.'

After a moment Li'vanh sighed and stood up. 'Then I will
take any guidance Dur'chai offers. And I will wait and watch.
I thank you, Yorn. I mean, a good day to you, Yorn.' He
bowed and left the tent; but there was none of his usual
steady firmness in his step, and Yorn sighed.

'Great Gods,' he thought, 'you lay heavy burdens on the
Young Tiger. And the way is dark that you have prepared
for him. The way is very dark.'

For maybe two days Li'vanh's anger against the High
Lords was hard and bitter. They denied him any life in
Vandarei, yet would not help him leave. He who so desired
to stay must himself find some way to go. They had brought
him here without his consent, and used him for their own
purposes until he was spent, and now they abandoned him to
find his own way home. He grudged nothing that he had
done, but this last was beyond his strength.

Yet his anger passed and even hope began to revive,
faintly. For he remembered how when he faced Fendarl he
thought he had been left weaponless, and had not.

On the night of the white moon's last quarter he had been
watching over the sheep. At the end of the watch one of the
young men who had only that year won his horse came to
relieve him: Li'vanh smiled, but as always the young man
greeted him shortly and without warmth. Among those who
had begun courting Mneri, this young man was the most
persistent. It was a new experience for Li'vanh, and one he
did not enjoy, to be hated by one of the Hurnei.

He sighed as he rode away, then yawned. It had been a
peaceful night, without frost and without disturbance. He
would be glad to sleep.

He did not notice that Dur'chai was veering away from the
camp until they jumped a stream for which he was not

prepared. His spine cracked like a whip, and he came full awake. 'Dur'chai! Where are you going!' With reins and legs he urged the horse to his left, but Dur'chai for the first time would not obey. He only snorted and shook his head free, and cantered faster. He galloped over the spur that marked the end of the Hurnei encampment, across a narrow empty valley and up the hill beyond. The low trees closed around them; a barrier formed of a sapling trunk laid across two white stones loomed before them, and Dur'chai leapt over it, with a backward flick of his heels to show that it was no concern of his. Li'vanh flung himself along the horse's neck to avoid being swept from his seat by the branches. He disliked riding under trees, but Dur'chai slowed to a silent trot, and then to a walk, and stopped at last.

Half annoyed and half puzzled Li'vanh looked around him. The woods at first glance looked the same as those by the camp, but at a second they did not. They were fuller, more inviolate. No one had been gathering firewood under these trees, or felling them for wagons or weapons. No children ever climbed them, or broke the silence with their games. They were secret, eerie, unwelcoming. Li'vanh remembered the gate which Dur'chai had jumped so carelessly, and his skin crawled.

His horse was grazing unconcernedly. He dismounted and walked uncertainly forward. The damp leaves were silent beneath his feet. So soundless was his passage that the woman huddled in the shadows against a tree-trunk did not see him until he was right before her; then she leapt up with a stifled scream.

'Mneri!'

It still seemed strange to him to see her wearing the long woollen khechin and two plaits that were the mark of a woman, instead of the knee-length clothes and loose hair of maidenhood. He had hardly spoken to her since the Autumn Feast, and she had often been absent for days together, for she was the Priestess, the Lady, the Luck of the Tribe. The dark secrets of the Tent of the Mother were hers to guard and often it seemed that she carried some of that secret darkness in her eyes; but now, startled, they were a girl's eyes again.

'Li'vanh! What are you doing here? You should not be here! This is the Holy Hill! Only the Priestesses come here, and to men it is forbidden on pain of death!' A shiver went through him, and she, as if with haste he might escape the curse, began pushing him backwards, urging him down a narrow path, pulling at him—always, always until now, she had avoided touching him. Astonished he fell back before her, until out of the shadows the moonlight fell full on her face and he saw the tear stains on her cheeks.

'Mneri!' He caught and held her wrists so that she could not harry him. Bird-delicate, they were still strong, a horse-girl's wrists. 'Mneri, you have been crying. What is the matter?'

At once she stiffened, all priestess, and turned her face away. 'I have not.'

'But you have. What is the matter?'

'Nothing! Li'vanh, you must go, and now! Why did you come here?'

'Dur'chai brought me. Dur'chai brought me, and he must have had a reason. No, Luck of the Hurnei, I will not go until you answer me.'

She struggled to pull away, but he only held her wrists more firmly. 'Li'vanh, let go! You are hurting me!'

'You are hurting yourself. Tell me what is the matter. I will let go if you promise not to run away. Do you? Very well, there you are. Now, why were you crying? What troubles you?'

She drew herself up, rubbing her arms, trying to be haughty. 'I am not to tell,' she said. 'It is a secret!' But she said it like a scolding child, not as a priestess speaking with power. She longed to share it with someone, and this was Li'vanh, and in some ways he was outside the laws. Her eyes stung again, and she bit her lip. Li'vanh stood silent, waiting.

Then her shoulders shook and she hid her face. 'O Prachoi,' she said, 'It is Vir'Vachal.'

All at once it seemed a new darkness was added to the night, and he shuddered; but his voice was steady. 'What of Vir'Vachal?'

Her voice was heavy with dread. 'Where she comes, Li'vanh, the people and the animals run mad and die. Unless she is under it, the earth will not bear fruit.' She drew another breath. 'And we cannot bind her.'

'Cannot . . .'

'We have been trying, Prachoi, since the feast and before.

We have done—everything. Everything. And nothing has been enough. She is still loose.'

He did not wonder at her fear. His own throat was dry. But Mneri had not done. Twisting her hair around her hand nervously she went on, 'So the Chief Priestess has said there will be a feast in the—the dark of the moon; and it will be a ninth-year feast for us all.' Her voice shook; she cried out in anguish 'And suppose it is Mnorh!'

It made no sense. A feast? What was a ninth-year feast? And what had it all to do with Mnorh?

'I do not understand, Mneri. Why a feast? And what is a ninth-year feast?'

She had not expected that he would not understand; now she swallowed, and explained. 'Every nine years, in the Autumn Feast, each tribe gives a young man to the Dark Mother. In the dark of the moon we must make this offering, though it is not autumn, nor for all of us a ninth year.'

He stood still as stone, holding off understanding. 'A young man? Why? I did not know the Mother had priests. And why now?'

'For the binding of Vir'Vachal, Li'vanh. And—and they are not as priests; they are a sacrifice.'

It was true then. He had not believed it. He felt cold and sick. A blood sacrifice. A human sacrifice.

He told himself that he should have known. He had heard of it before. Had not Kiron spoken of the Khentor's royal sacrifice? Did not the heroes die this death? But he had never believed that it still happened. And this was not Kiron speaking of something remote, nor a story teller telling of a King's glorious end. This was his foster-sister, this was Mneri, her soft voice saying that a young Hurno would die in the dark of the moon. This was the priestess who would offer the victim. Mneri.

His gorge rose, and he broke out in anger. 'Why does the Chief Priestess not offer herself?'

Mneri looked at him wonderingly. 'She will in her time, Li'vanh. But her death would be of no use now. Always it is a young man who dies for the Mother. A boy or young man within two years of his manhood—either before gaining it or after. That is why I fear for Mnorh. Who knows whom the Goddess will choose?'

He was too engrossed by the horror of it to have particular fears. 'Why? Would he offer? I do not think so.'

There was a pause and Mneri bit her lip. When she spoke it was with constraint. 'They—they do not offer, Li'vanh.' she said hesitantly. 'They are chosen.' She swallowed, then said almost defiantly. 'They are taken out from the others in the dance.'

He recoiled. When he could speak again he said in disgust, 'So it *can* get worse! It is not even the offering that matters. It is only the blood!'

'Li'vanh.' She was puzzled and distressed. 'Li'vanh, it is the Goddess! It is not my fault. And this is the earth magic; there is always blood. But still less this way than if Vir'Vachal is not bound. We did not wake her, but we must bind her. What can we do?'

So Fendarl's evil is still working, he thought. And it is true that it is not her fault. He shuddered, and sighed, and shook his head. And I have shown myself a stranger again, not to know of it, or understand it, or accept it.

He sighed again. 'I do not blame you, Luck of the Hurnei. Come, Dur'chai shall bear us both home.'

She assented silently, and rode pillion behind him back to the camp; but she parted from him outside it, and walked the last part alone. He went to his tent but he could not rest.

All that day he could not be at ease. He could not stop thinking what Mneri had said. Every time he met one of the young men he could hardly bear to talk to him. And as for Mnorh, Mneri's fear soon laid hold of him. He had never seen before that Mnorh was good to look on; now that and his vitality, and even his singing seemed all to mark him out. Li'vanh could not eat, he could not be still, and by the time he retired to his tent his mind was in a turmoil.

He had not expected to sleep but he did, almost instantly, and woke about an hour later. It was only then, in the quiet of the night that he realized that Mneri's words had been working in him like yeast; and the thought had come unbidden to him was so terrible that horror froze his heart.

It was that someone had to go, and he could not stay.

This did not come like the other call—it was not so clear or firm. He could not say when the thought first came to him: it stole on him slowly, coiling his mind round like mist so that he hardly realized what he was thinking.

What could be the way home that Ir'nanh was to show him? What part in him did Ir'nanh have—he who was not a warrior's god like Marenkalion, but was called the Dancing Boy, the Doomed and the Destroyer? What did he want of Li'vanh?

Why had the women from the beginning called him Prachoi, the Favoured One? It was a title given in songs to the young men who loved goddesses, and were doomed. How was he favoured? And Tuvoi, the Chosen One—he had thought he understood that. Was there more to it than he had thought?

He sat up trembling. No, he thought, no, this is nonsense. I will think of it no more. And his thoughts drew back obediently, only to return after a while like waves of an incoming tide, mounting higher each time.

He would be his own age, the Hurno who died—at the end of his boyhood or the beginning of his manhood. And he would not be the only one. How many tribes were there? Fifty? But a freely offered sacrifice was stronger. If someone offered, would so many deaths be needed? He tried to bury his head, to think of something else. Why had he to hear of this? Why could he not have come back to his tent to sleep in peaceful ignorance, and not have known that in five nights' time fifty Khentors would be dying in the flush of their youth? Why had he made Mneri tell him—why could he not leave meddling? And why had Dur'chai ever taken him there, to the Holy Hill—the ground that a man might not tread without dying for it?

He shook his head and covered his ears, as if that would help. I cannot! I cannot! I will not! What is it to do with me? I came here to fight Fendarl!

But this was the same battle. This was all Fendarl's work. He had roused Vir'Vachal. Should he not finish what he had begun?

And there was the most frightening memory of all: Vir'-Vachal had seen him. She who saw only the earth and its fruits had seen him, though she had seen neither Kiron nor the Earth Priestess. He remembered the grip of her fierce eyes, how she had drawn him and held him—singled him out—marked him; and he hid his face and writhed. Chosen One. Favoured One. He thought of the Earth Witch's hungry questioning, and how he had feared her, enough to make him lie to Kiron, without knowing why he feared. Now he understood.

'Blood will have blood and life will have death, as always, King Kiron.' His heart hammered with fear. Blood will have blood, he thought, and there is blood on my hands. He looked at Mnorh, sleeping on the other side of the tent. It might not be Mnorh, he pleaded, then answered himself, but it will be someone. And he will be to others what Mnorh is to us.

Blood will have blood. And Vir'Vachal must be bound. Someone must die. 'I do not belong here,' he thought, 'I have no life here before me. Somehow, I must go. Why not this way? At least, I would give one person his life back.'

But 'life' was such a huge word. It meant everything. How could he think calmly about giving it away? Yet he must go. And why not do some good in going?

He knew that he was not being called to this; that even the High Lords did not ask it of him. But it was there to be done by someone. He had not yet failed; had he come after all to the end of his courage? He had done all that was asked of him, true; why not do this last thing unasked? A shiver went through him, and he clenched his hands. I cannot! It is no concern of mine! I do not even worship the Mother!

And he caught at that reason. He did not serve the Goddess: maybe it would even be wrong for him to offer. Hope struggled in his heart, but it was not unmixed with shame, and he knew he could not trust to his own decision.

When he did pray, he called as the Harani did on Kuvorei Naracan, the High God. He did so now, kneeling shivering on his bed. 'Tell me what I should do. Send me a sign. I cannot choose. Show me what I must do.' He shook in every limb—not from cold alone—and waited, tense. There was neither sound nor movement in the darkness; he held his breath for long minutes, but in all the camp it seemed there was no sound but the far-off whinny of a horse. He waited, then pulled the covers up around him and laughed suddenly. He was free of it, he thought, and lay back. Then he sprang up again as the horse whinnied once more, and his heart leapt up to choke him.

Dur'chai. He heard the approaching hooves and scrambled into his clothes. Dur'chai is no bad guide. Something near to a laugh ached in his throat as he pulled back the tentflap.

Dur'chai had been prancing restlessly before the tent, but when Li'vanh came out he stopped and looked at him. Moonlight drained the colour from everything, but not from him. Silver light fell on him and splashed to the ground, and he cast no shadow. Li'vanh gazed, and thought Here is my sign, and oddly the laugh in his throat trembled into life, and he was filled with a strange reckless lightness. He would do it. Whether from defiance, or love of his people, he did not know, but he would do it. He would do more than had been required of him; and spent and weary though he was, somehow that made him the winner.

Chapter Thirty-One

The Dark of the Moon

It was dark in the passage and it smelled of earth. Li'vanh brushed his knuckles along the wall as he walked and kept his eyes on the tiny point of the next lamp. Light was an intruder here; darkness was the rightful element of this place where neither day nor night brought any change. The cold was the deep still chill of a place where winter and summer were both alike unknown, and time did not wear its gaudy trappings of hours and seasons. The roof of the passage was low, less than arms reach above his head, and his bronze shod heels rang loud on the rock beneath. The noise of his booted tread went on before him like a herald proclaiming the approach of a man along the corridors where only soft-shod women ever trod. Deep in their cavern the Priestesses heard it. They looked at one another frowning, and one struck the gong.

The singing roar surged out to meet Li'vanh, so loud and sudden that his whole body clenched with shock. The wave of sound seemed almost solid, and he fell back a pace. Just for a second he nearly fled, but long before the gong-note had died his pride hardened him again. He stood firm and waited.

'Who are you, who dare enter into the secret places of the Great Goddess? Why come you here, none but her servants may enter?' The bodiless voice with its shivering echoes made his scalp draw tight.

'I am Li'vanh of the Hurnei, and I come seeking speech with the Chief Priestess.' His voice rolled deeply along the passage, and a moment of silence followed. Then 'Come forward,' he was told.

He went on. He was nearer than he thought. Two bends in the passage had hidden the light from him. He came quite

suddenly into a round cavern filled with a yellow glow of
lamplight. Eight Priestesses were there, watching the entrance; all their eyes were on him as he entered. None of
them moved or spoke. He went forward into the cavern and
paused, uncertain; then he heard the rattle of a curtain being
drawn back, and looked up.

From the far side of the chamber rose a flight of steps,
and in the arch at the head of them a woman stood. She
glowed in the lamplight against the darkness at her back.
Over her white dress she wore a long wide tabard of saffron
wool and a deep pectoral of copper and ivory. The braids
of her dark hair were coiled over her ears and her head was
crowned with a high diadem clashing with plates of ivory
and discs of copper. A yellow cat wove about her skirt. She
looked down on Li'vanh unmoving, and he gazed back in
silence. He had seen her often before, but never looking like
this, like a great queen of the ancient days. In her majestic
calm was gathered all the passive strength of the abiding
earth, all the mystery and might of the one who needs not to
do, but only to be. In her dark gaze he felt all the weight of
unfathomed ages of growth and decay before which the quick
activity of man seemed a frail and transient thing.

Then the cat mewed softly, and stalked away behind her.
She raised her arm in summons and turning moved away.

Li'vanh walked quickly across the hall and up the steps,
pulling the curtain behind him and hearing the low murmurs
break out at his back. The passage sloped to the right and he
turned along it.

The passage bent and lamplight shone through a swaying
bead curtain. He hesitated an instant, then put the curtain
aside and stepped down into a circular chamber about thirty
paces wide. The lamps burned in niches in the rock walls,
and as their flames flickered half-seen paintings seemed to
move among the wavering shadows. The floor was smooth
yellow stone. A round copper brazier burned on either side
of a raised dais opposite the door. The air in the room smelt
heavy and warm, and the stillness awed him. In a canopied
chair on the dais sat the Chief Priestess, and the sacred cat
sat at her feet.

He stood still in the middle of the room, and the Priestess
raised her eyes to his face, and spoke.

'I greet you, Young Man.' She made the words a title.

'You stand where no man has ever stood until now. What brings you here?'

The words he wanted would not come. 'I was given a sign good lady,' he said at last. She waited, and he took another breath. 'It was told to me that there is to be a great feast made in the dark of the moon.'

'Doubtless the Lady of the Hurnei will learn with time to guard her tongue.' She spoke calmly, but there was an edge of displeasure to her voice, and he bit his lips. 'The secrets of the Goddess should not be spoken of.'

'She is not to blame, good lady. It was meant that I should know.' The Priestess met his eyes consideringly, then inclined her head so that her diadem sounded softly. Li'vanh's reluctant tongue stumbled on. 'I heard also that many will die in this feast. Is it so?'

'There will be a great offering made to the Giver of All Good Gifts. Yes, this is true.'

There was a pause. He felt his heart thudding, and his breath would not come easily. 'It seems a dreadful thing,' he said at last.

'And so it is, Young Man. Where is the power, if there is no dread?'

Now I must speak, he thought, and summoned his courage. His mouth was dry and his lips were stiff.

He said, 'Why are so many deaths needed, when for other offerings there is only one sacrifice?'

She replied without looking at him, 'Because these do not go freely. They are chosen. They do not offer.'

His throat was choking him. Out of its tightness he spoke.

'Would one then suffice, if it were a free offering?'

'Maybe. But it does not happen.'

'But if it did, if someone offered himself, then ...'

'But it never happens.'

'Yet if it should?'

'Not for this rite! No one ever offers freely for this rite!'

'Why?' he asked 'Is it forbidden?' At this idea hope and dread leapt in him, and he did not know which was stronger, and clenched his hands together.

'No! No, it is not forbidden. When the Mother was served aright, in daylight, it was always so. The young men strove for the honour. But now, no one offers of himself.'

He said, 'I am offering.'

His words filled the cavern, and then there was utter silence. He heard them aghast, and terror shook him for an instant. The Priestess rose to her feet and looked at him, but she said no word. He stood upright and alone in the middle of the chamber, and met her eyes unflinching. The fire shifted and the lamp flames wavered.

The priestess said, 'Do you know what you are saying?'

'Yes,' he said automatically, then 'No. No, I suppose I do not. I suppose I cannot truly know what it will mean. But I understand enough.'

She gazed at him searchingly. 'And you are willing to do this?'

'Yes.' His voice would not serve him for a longer sentence. The room was so silent, he could hear his leather clothes creaking faintly as he breathed. Then slowly another sound grew on the air, a soft uneven roughness: the sacred cat was purring. Stronger and stronger grew her voice, reverberating around the cavern, and the priestess came slowly down from the dais. Forward she came until she stood before Li'vanh, and looked intently into his eyes that were as grey as rain.

'Let your mind be at rest,' she said. 'What need of many, when there is such a one? Li'vanh Prachoi, the Goddess has ever demanded the best that we have; but surely she has never received an offering greater than this.'

There were five days before the dark of the moon. Five days, during which Li'vanh could only wait, and realize fully what he had promised, and make his farewells.

Much to his own surprise he never for an instant regretted what he had done. He found that he was astonishingly calm and, after so many weeks of being restlessly miserable, even strangely happy. It was a great relief to be finally committed and to see his way clear before him. There was no turning back now, and his heart lightened within him. He had wanted to live and die a plainsman, and he could even laugh at the thought that half of his desire had been granted, and he would at least die a Hurno.

It was long too since he had felt so much one with the tribe. The distance between them and him which had for a while seemed so great was shrunk again to nothing, and for those four brief days life for Li'vanh was as near perfect as it can be. Even the weather was flawless.

Then on the fifth morning he was woken by the dawn drum as always, and lying listening to the salute he thought, 'I will never hear this again.'

His blood chilled. He looked across at Mnorh and thought too that when he woke next morning, he himself would be gone. He had in these four charmed days held back his fear, whenever it stirred, by thinking 'It is not yet'. Now he could do so no longer. Now the length of his life could be measured by the brief course of a winter sun.

He had told no one of what he intended. He had a vague idea that it was not permitted, but even if it had been otherwise he could never have found the words. It had been plain from Mneri's smile and lightened eyes that she knew there was to be no ninth-year feast, but no more. Well she at least would know, he thought, and Yorn surely would. But it hurt him to think he could take no farewells of Mnorh and Silinoi.

He rose and dressed slowly, and went out of the tent. The dawn was still glowing in the east, and he stood before his door and watched until the last of the glory was gone. Then he went in and woke Mnorh.

All that day was a leave-taking, and a counting of all that belonged to the past: sleep and waking, dawn, bathing in the river, grooming Dur'chai, weapon-practice, the evening fire. He knew he was tormenting himself needlessly, yet could not stop. He went through that day in a strange doomed trance, dizzy with fear, yet outwardly calm. When others spoke of plans for the days ahead he answered without a tremor, but his hungry eyes followed the steady turning of the shadows and the curving leap of the sun as if by watching he could slow them down.

Then the time came when sunset was near and Mnorh said, 'Shall we go to the river?' and Li'vanh answered him lightly, 'I must go first to the tent. Do not wait for me.'

'As you will,' said Mnorh cheerfully, and turned away. And Li'vanh stood and watched him out of sight. Then he rode to his tent.

Once there he changed swiftly into his best clothes. He unsaddled Dur'chai and spread out his harness and horse-ornaments by Mnorh's bed. He put his spears in the rack, laid his knife and horn with his clothes, and his sword in a place apart. He wore none of his jewels save his silver medal,

and when it seemed that he was ready stood looking around
the tent, fastening his cloak with trembling fingers. Then, No,
he thought, I will not wear it. And he swung it off his
shoulders. As the folds swung he caught for an instant what
he had never noticed before, the smell of it. It smelled of
horses and dung and grass, wind and milk and bitter smoke;
it smelled of the plain, and the bitterest pang of all smote
him as he put it aside, for that seemed truly his farewell.

He heard Dur'chai's soft whinny, and Yorn came into the
tent. Li'vanh turned and they faced one another in silence.
At length Yorn spoke.

'Kiron is near at hand, Tuvoi. He will be here tomorrow.'

'My sorrow that I will not see him, Yorn.' His voice was
only a little roughened. 'Greet him from me, and give him
my farewell. Tell him that I have found my own way home,
and follow it of my own choosing.'

There was a brief pause. Then, 'Is it so, Li'vanh?'

'It is so, Yorn.'

There was no sound but the beat of his heart. Yorn looked
at him and shook his head with only half a smile. 'For once it
seems I have no words.'

'No. Nor I, Yorn. I—I have not been able to take my
leave of anyone. Say everything to them for me that I would
say if I could. I have no need to tell you. And—and thank
you, Yorn. And—farewell.' His voice choked, and he shook
his head. Without looking up again he stepped hurriedly past
the Priest and out of the tent, and sprang to Dur'chai's back.

Up on the hill he stopped to watch the sun set for the last
time beyond the tents, and saw the glow of the kindled fire.
Then he turned his back on the Hurnei and rode swiftly to
the Holy Hill.

He did not seek to guide Dur'chai. Where the horse
stopped he slid from his back, and turned. He hid his face in
the horse's mane, stroking his satin neck and running his
hand over his flanks. He caressed his nose, and Dur'chai
sighed and lowered his head against Li'vanh's chest so that
his horn laid over his shoulder, while he rubbed his soft ears.
A moment he stood thus; then arched his neck and looked at
Li'vanh with his strange eyes glinting. Li'vanh gazed at him.
'Remember me, my brother,' he whispered, 'when you drink
at the Dancer's Fountain, and graze with your brethren
among the stars; remember.' Dur'chai snuffed his hair one

last time, then reared and neighed, loud in the quiet night. Then he wheeled, and tossing his fiery mane galloped into the darkness. Li'vanh strained his eyes after him until he was far beyond sight, then turned away to follow the priestesses' path up the hill.

The darkness under the trees closed him round, and the secret whispering night watched him pass, and he was alone with his terror. He knew now that he had not really feared death when he had faced Fendarl. Now the certainty was close before him, and he was sick with dread. There was a cleft in the Cave of the Offering, the Chief Priestess had said, a cleft that reached to the deep places of the earth. That way he must go. His heart was turned to water and he stumbled as he walked, catching at the trees. Once he stopped, fear enveloping him, and thought No! I will not go! Then the bitter thought came to him that he need not, he could turn back if he chose. No one was compelling him to do this. He could go back, and let the others die. The choice was his. The irony almost made him laugh, and he went on up the hill.

At last he stood among the bushes and trees, looking towards the low mouth of the cave. He could see the light. It was only yards away. He had only a few more steps to take. And he could not move.

He turned his back on the low opening and looked about him, printing the shape of trees and bushes on his mind. He drank deep of the raw night air and looked up at the sky. Between the branches of the trees the stars shone, but the moons he would not see again. North to the distant plain he looked, and stood a moment still on the edge of the wood, then turning on his heel walked swiftly to the cave entrance. And as he stepped into the light a long low wail of greeting and of grief rose up to meet him.

Thereafter he moved in a strange haze. There was low pitched singing and a throbbing that was not quite music. Women with covered faces swayed and wove in strange complex dances, their shadows looming distorted in the pale light. They were robed in yellow, like the Chief Priestess. He saw the altar at the back of the cave, with the strange squat image of the Dark Mother, ugly and holy. On the floor before it burned a round earthenware pot of fire, a thin plait of smoke rising from its hole, and before that a circle was drawn on the ground. He smelt the scented sweetness of the air, he saw the Goddess's cat watching from the shadows by the altar. But more than all he saw the streak of darkness, looking like a furrow from the front of the cave but widening as he approached into an abyss.

The rite was long. He could not follow it and did not try. The language of the ritual was strange to him. They came and went about him; they washed him and anointed him, and the Chief Priestess marked his face with a greasy paint. The dance wove about him and moved back from him; the shadows clustered beyond reach of the firelight. They put a garland about his neck of green leaves bound with saffron wool, cool and pungent, an odd contrast to the heavy heat of the cave; and veiled priestesses bowed before him. The Chief Priestess moved from place to place and spoke long prayers, or long hymns. The chanting rose and fell, now exultant, now grieving, but always hypnotic. The fires flared and crackled when more herbs were thrown on to them and Li'vanh watched the cleft as in a trance.

They brought him milk thickened with honey and he drank it; then another priestess brought him a bowl of milk that smelled heavy, and it came to him that it was drugged, and he put it back into her hands untouched. Only then did he recall that Mneri was somewhere among these shrouded women, but it was impossible to guess where, and it did not seem important. Nothing seemed important, by comparison with the black gulf between him and the altar. The music quickened, and the song rose and fell more urgently. The dance wreathed closer and closer about him, until it took him, and he too was a part of it, stamping and leaping in the midst of the saffron skein of dancers, all the while drawing nearer to the chasm. The shadows clustered thicker, the air grew heavier, even the light was mixed with darkness. The song from the priestesses swaying against the wall was a wild and fierce lament; then the diademed Priestess gave a sudden loud cry and held out both her hands, and silence fell. And Li'vanh, facing the back of the cave, stood rooted by awe, sweating and shuddering like a tethered horse where the leopard prowls.

For there was a glow in the rock at the back of the cave, and a heavy sound growing on the air, a pounding double beat like the throbbing of a mighty heart. And the glow moved and deepened and seemed to approach, and the beating grew stronger. It was as if the rock were a thin curtain behind which a fire burned, and the light grew closer and took on form, and was brown and crimson as well as golden; and the pulsing sound thudded to the rhythm of their blood, filling the cavern with its double boom until it seemed that the very walls were beating. And the rock thinned before her like an insubstantial mist, and Vir'Vachal was there.

A vast sigh sounded, and every woman sank to her knees, bowing before the Eldest Daughter of the Goddesss. But she gave them not a glance. She stopped on the other side of the cleft, and her eyes were on Li'vanh.

A clear path lay before him, ending on a slab at the brink of the abyss. With fear and will both drowned in the pounding heartbeat, he walked slowly forward. She watched him come, and he looked at her, and was not afraid. With the gulf at his feet he stopped, and hot air rising from the deeps smote on his face. Less than twice his height parted from Vir'Vachal; yet this time she did not rob him of his strength. He was strong, strong as she herself, and he would bind her. Gazing back at her he stepped up on to the slab. The dark depths at his feet called to him, the eyes of Vir'Vachal drew him. He drew a deep breath and raised his arms. Then savouring the sweet terror of doing just as he desired, he laughed and sprang out from the edge.

For an instant he seemed to hover above the gulf, then he plunged into the darkness. Fast and faster he fell, while the air roared in his ears and light burst behind his eyelids. The heat smothered him, his blood thundered, and the darkness closed above him, filled him, enveloped and overpowered him, devoured him and destroyed him, and Li'vanh Tuvoi was no more. Vir'Vachal flung up her head and sank from the sight of mortals for ever; and in the cave the women beat their breasts and cried Rahai! Rahai!

Epilogue

The Dancer's Fountain

It seemed to Oliver that he had been lying on his back for some time. His mind was full of the memory of falling, yet his body did not feel bruised. He lay turning the thought in his mind, and breathing deeply of the fresh air. There was cool pricking grass under his hands, and light beyond his eyelids. He put up his arm to shield his eyes as he opened them, and was puzzled to see it clothed in vivid scarlet wool. He sat up staring at that and at the coarse blue cloth of his trousers, then rose to his feet and looked about.

The land about him was deep green, and the sky above bright silver. There was neither sun nor moon nor any stars, and the trees danced against the still heavens. Faint pipe-music threaded the air. Oliver gazed in wonder, and slowly turned.

Behind him stood some trees and some rocks, and a spring welled up and made a pool among the rocks. And beside the pool sat a boy, naked but for the kilt of a dancer, before whom the boldest warrior would have bowed in terror. He lowered the pipe from his lips, and came with quick grace to Oliver.

'Welcome!' he said, and his voice was the original of all music. 'Your battles are over, Young Tiger. It is time to be the Crowned Victor again.'

His beauty was more than mortal. He was lithe and tanned, poised alert for movement on his strong dancer's feet. His dark hair seemed to curl, with such energy did it spring from his head. His eyes were alive with changing colour, now green, now gold, now the deep indigo of his kilt, and they brimmed with laughter, and with the delight of life.

'Lord,' said Oliver, bewildered, 'how came I here?'

265

'By the only way open to mortals,' the boy replied. 'Have no fear. Your trials have been stern but they are behind you. Now will we show that we too can be generous. All that you have lost shall be restored, and all that you have gained remain untouched.'

Then Oliver met his eyes steadfastly, and said 'Young Lord, your words are gracious. But I have gained knowledge that will not leave me, and I know that you speak your truths too easily. There is something I have lost which you cannot restore, and that is innocence.'

There was an appreciative leap of laughter in the young one's eyes, but he answered gravely, 'And have men sunk so far, that the best they can hope for is innocence? Do they no longer strive for virtue? For virtue lies not in ignorance of evil, but in resistance to it.'

Oliver bowed his head. 'And what have I gained?' he asked.

'What does silver gain in the fire, and iron in the forging?' He laughed suddenly, and drew Oliver to the spring, and said 'Come, drink.'

And Oliver stooped to the water and drank. Clear and cold was the water, and as he drank all weariness and fear and grief fell from him. Strength flowed into him, and he rose refreshed. Once more he felt his youth in his blood, and he laughed aloud; for a feeling he had almost forgotten, the sheer joy of living, surged through him. And looking again at his strange companion, he said, 'Lord, who are you?'

'I am the Keeper of the Fountain,' he replied. 'Tremble, mortal, for you have drunk of the Dancer's Fountain, the Spring of the Immortals.' Oliver's eyes widened, and the boy shook his head. 'No. It will not give you the life eternal. It will need more than water to do that, and a power far beyond mine. But it will give you new life, and heart to enjoy it.' Suddenly he flung up his head, and proclaimed 'This is the pool of Life and Death! Those who drink bidden, drink blest, and drink life: but those who drink unbidden, drink death!'

A wave of awe and wonder shook Oliver. 'Who are you?' he said again. 'Young God, who are you?'

'Do you not know me?' He laughed exultantly, springing to a rock, and flinging out his arms. 'I am the Lord of Wood and Water, I am the Leader of the Great Dance. I am the guide. I am the messenger, I am the interpreter and loosener of tongues. Music is mine and song is mine, and I am the wielder of the lightning. I am the Doomed One, I am the Reborn, I am the Young King, the Spring and the Summer. I am the Dancing Boy, Iranani, the Lord of Life and Laughter!' He leapt to the ground, and swept his arm. 'Follow me!'

He sprang away, and Oliver followed. Whether he was running or dancing he hardly knew; he sang, but he knew not what. He was filled with delight and wonder at this strange new form of Godhead, a divinity undreamed of, a god without gravity, a god of might without majesty, a god of harmony without law, with such gladness, such vitality. He raced and leapt at his heels, exulting in his own youth and strength. Time could not hold them, and distance they spurned beneath their flying feet. Oliver stretched his legs and strove to catch his companion; but the boy looked back and laughed, and danced faster. However fast Oliver moved, and he ran until the still air thundered in his ears, the Dancer was just ahead of him, never hurrying, but not to be caught.

They stopped at last by a dark trunked tree, and Iranani turned with a graver face to Oliver. A goblet stood at the foot of the tree and he took it in his hand.

'This one last thing,' he said. 'This drink will cloud your memory of what is past and save you pain, if you desire it.' He placed it in his hands. Oliver raised it to his lips—then paused.

He saw again the fire in the evening, the leaping dance, Yorn's tiger-lily hair. He remembered Derna's growl, and the silver voice of Mnorh raised in song, Silinoi's face, Mneri's eyes. He thought of H'ara Tunij, and Kiron. He remembered Dur'chai. All things have their price.

He held out the goblet. 'I thank you,' he said, 'but I will not drink.'

Iranani nodded and stepped back. His eyes were the colour of his kilt. 'Then here lies your way. Go with gladness, and may Kuvorei Naracan, the God who is above the gods, have you in his care.'

Then Oliver walked as he directed, around the trunk of the tree.

The sharp spring air blew on him as he came running up the field. Nicholas and Penelope crashed to the ground together, and struggled up as he reached them. 'Penny, you fool! What did you do that for? Have you hurt yourself?'

'I've only grazed my arm. It was the compass . . .'

They were caught suddenly into silence, looking at each other uncertainly. What had happened? The world swung, out of focus. Where were they?

'Oliver,' said Penelope, 'your hair. Your moustache. It's gone.'

'Only the moustache.' Nicholas looked at his brother seriously, nursing his arm. 'I didn't think you would get back at the same time as us, Oliver. I think I've sprained my wrist.'

'Oliver—was it all true?'

He did not answer her at once. A shaft of loss smote him, and he turned quickly, stepping forward, as if he would find it all there. But he knew he would not. There was no return. He had come through a door which only opened one way.

'Yes,' he said softly. 'Oh yes, Penny. All of it.' He looked back at them, with a sudden awkward smile. "Bad luck, Nick. You always seem to do something. I'll lift your bike over. We had better get home.'

Penelope scrambled over the gate. Nicholas paused astride the top bar and smiled a slow smile. 'And they'll say to us, "You didn't go far". Oliver, you've got something on your head.'

'Something on my head? What on earth—I can't feel anything. . . .' He put up his hand, then stopped, arrested. 'So I have,' he said in an altered voice. 'I've got this.'

Between his hands he stretched a leather browband, embroidered with the mark of the Hurnei.